Diamond Dust

Diamond Dust

K.F. Breene

ALSO BY K.F. BREENE

Demigods of San Francisco

Sin & Chocolate

Sin & Magic

Sin & Salvation

Sin & Spirit

Sin & Lightning

Sin & Surrender

Leveling Up

Magical Midlife Madness

Magical Midlife Dating

Magical Midlife Invasion

Magical Midlife Love

Magical Midlife Meeting

Magical Midlife Challenge

Magical Midlife Alliance

Magical Midlife Flowers

Magical Midlife Battle

Magical Midlife Awakening

Finding Paradise

Fate of Perfection

Fate of Devotion

Deliciously Dark Fairytales

A Ruin of Roses

A Throne of Ruin

A Kingdom of Ruin

A Queen of Ruin

A Cage of Crimson

A Cage of Kingdoms

Demon Days,
Vampire Nights

Born in Fire

Raised in Fire

Fused in Fire

Natural Witch

Natural Mage

Natural Dual-Mage

Warrior Fae Trapped

Warrior Fae Princess

Revealed in Fire

Mentored in Fire

Battle with Fire

FAERIE

◎ CASTLES
◆ ORACLE

THE FRINGE

DIAMOND
KINGDOM

RUBY
KINGDOM

EMERALD
KINGDOM

OPAL
KINGDOM

SEA OF
STARS

SAPPHIRE
KINGDOM

TOPAZ
KINGDOM

AMETHYST
KINGDOM

OBSIDIAN
KINGDOM

For the women who love dancing in the flames.

Chapter One

DAISY

Tarian turned, Daisy's hand still tucked into his. The animals waited within the barn-shanty, and Tarian's *Fallen* were over picking through the wreckage from the darkrend. They'd had to stall while Daisy and Tarian hashed out their deal.

The creatures waited placidly, their great maws grinding dried grasses. Each stood about six feet high at the shoulder, with powerful legs ending in three hooked claws at the front and one toward the back. Thick horns ran along their heads and out to the sides, with big manes of coarse hair and something like a beard off their chins. Their wings were tucked into their sides, furry along the ridges but feathery on the actual wing part. Their tails were a combination of fur and feathers as well, most of them swishing periodically.

1

"What are they?" Daisy asked as Tarian gently tugged her around the first, giving it a wide berth.

"They are stormbacks. They inhabit the mountain regions and don't have much time for my kind. They often find us too dimwitted." He laughed. "At least, that's what they'll tell you."

"That's what...they'll *tell* you?"

He pulled her to the largest of them at the back, its shaggy mane streaked with gray and black. The fur on its body was a fuzzy gray-white. The creature was as scary as it was beautiful. She wanted to pet it as much as she wanted to avoid it.

"Yes. They can communicate mentally. They don't often use words. They are more inclined to use imagery and feelings. When they lower themselves to communicate with fae, that is. They can understand words just fine, though, so let's keep the running dialogue to a minimum. What you've thought is great, but if you insult them, they won't allow you to ride."

The great beast let out a deep huff before stamping its foot. *We are not so prickly as that, child.*

"Beg to differ." Tarian let go of her hand and put his arm in front of her. "Stratow, this is the human I spoke of. She's a captive who doesn't know how to shield her thoughts. She has a right to be surly and needs our forgiveness for her horrible bluntness."

Daisy tried desperately to keep from saying a sarcastic remark. She was fine pissing off Tarian and his *Fallen*, but this was one beast she was inclined to mind her manners around.

The creature huffed again. *She has more sense than you ever did.*

Tarian grinned and winked at Daisy. "These creatures don't enjoy fae, and enjoy giving rides like common mules even less. I was such a pest, though, that we ended up making a deal. After he tried to kill me, of course. I fulfilled my end of the deal, he did his, and then...well, what can I say? I'm likable."

"About as likable as sand in your ass crack, yeah," she grumbled. "A constant nuisance and really hard to get rid of."

The creature made a sound like a low growl, and Daisy stepped back and threw up her hands.

"Hey, look, to each their own," she said quickly. "I'm sure his personality...rubs off on you eventually. You know, in a non-abrasive sort of way."

The beast's growling continued, and Daisy started to sweat. She licked her lips and glanced back. The other beasts pushed in closer, blocking an easy exit. The claws on their feet glistened. Daisy felt her knife pulse within her shirt.

"That's the sound of his amusement, not a growl," Tarian said, grabbing her hand and tugging her around him. At the back of the shanty, there were two large doors. He dropped her hand to open them. "I figured I'd let you sweat because of those comments." He gave her a smirk. "You like my *personality* just fine."

He motioned her toward him as the *Fallen* came around the corner. Their appearances were uniform—the lower part of their heads were shaved with long hair on top, half done in a knot or bun. They all wore pocketed skirts, almost like kilts, outlined with fur. Leather bracers encircled their wrists, and the females wore tight, fur-lined tops in a strip across their breasts. The males only had various leather straps crossing their bare torsos, with a lot of ink on display. They all looked fierce, as well as sexy, male and female alike.

"*Thank* you!" Niall put up his fists in victory. "She called me sexy. Goodbye, ugliness, hello, sex god."

"She thinks our *outfits* are sexy, dummy," a female said. She had hard gray eyes and a button nose, with wheat-colored hair and knockout curves. The lady was a stunner.

"Let him have that one," said Lennox, the one who looked like a Viking of old, with his flowing, wavy hair, reddish beard tied under his chin with leather and tassels, and his thick frame. "It's about as good as she's going to give him."

Half of them burst out laughing as the stormbacks walked out of the barn, their heads bobbing with each step. Stratow glanced over the gathered fae, snorting through his nostrils as he passed.

They detest the flatlands, Tarian told her, the thought something like a faint murmur. *They also get annoyed this close to the fringe. They have a keen sense of the purity of magic and are having a hard time tolerating how out of balance things have become.*

Purity? she asked.

He turned to her, his large hand coming around to brace along the curve of her hip. He splayed his fingers, gently squeezing in something akin to possession, as though he couldn't help himself.

Warmth emanated from his presence and touch, sizzling along her body. She was thankful his gaze was directed behind her, affording her the space to breathe in his delicious proximity, bathe in his sensual heat, and bask in the buzz between them that licked along her nerve endings. It had to be her ability to heighten his magic, though it felt so horribly divine.

He looked down at her, his eyelids hooded. *I have to pour magic into the crystal chalice to activate its—your properties. It's complicated and taxing, and trust me, I'm not doing it right now. This buzz isn't magic. It's chemistry, little dove. Our chemistry.*

Call it whatever you want, but the gods created it.

Maybe. His gaze traveled over her face. *Or maybe you're so fucking beautiful that I can't help my attraction to you. And vice versa.*

She crinkled her nose at him, but she couldn't deny that she agreed about his incredible appearance, from his breathtakingly handsome face, to his spectacular physique, to his confidence and swagger. She liked what she saw and loved watching him move. Still, she'd seen handsome men before, and she'd never felt this way. She'd never been mesmerized by their touch and delighted by their witty banter. She'd never felt this desperation—this *ache*—for someone. If it wasn't magic, she was utterly fucked, because their story couldn't end any other way besides tragically.

His chuckle was a ripple of black satin. *Suit yourself.*

Regardless, I'm not trying to distract you in that way right now, though it is working admirably. Despite what Stratow said, stormbacks are prickly creatures. They don't like being talked about unless they can hear what is said. They find it incredibly rude not to have their say, and rudeness is never tolerated. He might decide not to do me this huge favor, and that would add days to our journey. Days we can't waste.

I assume they are far enough away not to hear my broadcasted comments.

His smile was faint. *Yes. And so we're going to pretend to drink in each other's proximity while we wait for them to be ready. And maybe we're going to...*

He leaned down and touched his lips to hers. An explosion of pleasure lit up her world. She clutched him, her eyes drifting closed, her mouth opening. His tongue darted in, swiping through, filling her with his taste. Her fingers tightened, but she forced them open again, leaning away. Considered slapping him. More than considered slapping herself.

He smiled deviously. *Go ahead. If the former, let's see if you can land it. If the latter...that's something I'd like to see. I'm sure the others would get a kick out of it, too.*

She narrowed her eyes at him but said nothing.

Purity of magic meaning...the rightness of it, I guess, he said, staying close but allowing some space. *Fae magic isn't like human magic. It is not isolated to the person who wields it. We derive our magic from Faerie itself. Magic here is circular. We are all part of it—we feed from it, and it from us. So if the wylds get twisted, for example—*

corrupted—or the Obsidian royals or various creatures get twisted, that feeds back into Faerie. It disrupts the magical system and creates a ripple effect. If a fae or creature gets too bad, like that darkrend, it cannot be redeemed. It must be destroyed so that Faerie—the magic of Faerie—can heal itself and everything can return to perfect harmony. Balance. The dawn brings the light so that it may shine. The light must give way to dusk so that the dark may have its reign. And so on. Dark and light, with dawn and dusk to balance them out. If things are too light or too dark, it pulls everything out of balance. The magic tries to compensate, and twisted magic is fed into the minds of all who draw upon it. It twists the very fabric of Faerie. Does that make sense?

The Celestial colors... Sunrise and sunset, the colors so remarkably similar but reversed in order of appearance.

He nodded.

So the stormbacks can feel the imbalance?

Yes. Even when it is subtle. They are gravely worried about Faerie, which is probably why they are lowering themselves to acting as transport. They're doing their part. I think the wylds helping you was the same. The heart of Faerie wants to right itself, but it needs help. Our help, as I explained. He ran his thumb along the edge of her jaw. *Look over my shoulder and see if the stormbacks are nearly ready. They detest being rushed.*

She couldn't look over his shoulder without rising onto her tiptoes. Instead, she angled him a bit, leaning against him and glancing at his *Fallen.* They waited idly, chatting amongst themselves like they had all the time in the world. She let her gaze swing toward the stormbacks, but she couldn't help but think about the appearance of the hard chest against her. Or the perfection of his back and the amazing design covering it.

Do your tattoos mean anything or are they for appearances? she asked as the breeze caught and flung her hair.

He grabbed a strand and curled it around his fingers. *The stormbacks?*

Oh. She leaned away so her hair would pull out of his fingers. *They're getting into a half-circle formation, facing the north.*

He sighed, looking off at the trees. *I really shouldn't be impatient. They are saving us a lot of time. It's just...*

Tattoos?

He glanced down at her again. Something indecipherable lurked in his eyes, his true emotions hidden behind his carefully cultivated humor. *They mean something.* He took a small step back. His arms flexed as he unbuttoned his shirt, revealing each delectable inch of skin as he went. *Since you enjoy looking at my nudity so much...*

She pressed her lips together at the taunting tone but couldn't deny it.

He pulled the shirt away and paused, giving her a chance to once again marvel at his incredible physique. He reached for her hand and brought it up, using her finger to trace the design across his chest that looked like a thick necklace curving against the edge of his pecs and then wrapping around his neck. Her nail scraped his flesh, raising goosebumps.

This was a necklace that was burned into my skin by Equilas when she helped trap me in the Obsidian kingdom. It's a marker of station. Not with the Obsidian kingdom but—

As a High Sovereign. I haven't forgotten. Or...I guess... the memory hasn't been taken from me yet.

He stilled, his brows pinching together in confusion. She didn't miss the flash of hope lighting his gorgeous green eyes.

Every time someone looks upon this necklace, he said, not commenting on her retained memory, *they get a flash of recognition. Every time, I wonder if they'll know who I am. If I'll regain some piece of my former life within their knowledge of me. And every time, their eyes dull after a moment. Well, dull or turn to disdain. I'm not well loved within the Obsidian Court. I'm feared, so I'm given a wide berth, but at best I'm tolerated. I do not fit in there.*

Like she didn't belong in the magical zone. She remembered his sentiment in the hotel room those many months ago. She remembered feeling connected with him. This was why.

She nodded, taking in his pain and bearing witness to his struggle. This time, she didn't move away when he wrapped a lock of her hair around his fingertips.

These—he lifted an elbow to indicate the tattoos on his arm—*are my rings of ascension. They denote the various trials I have mastered through training and perseverance.*

What kind of trials?

Magic, weaponry, battle planning...various things. The trials are open to all of Faerie—to anyone who wishes to ascend. With each mastery, a title is granted and added to our name. The title increases status. The marker on the arm is proof of ascension. The royals of the Diamond Throne are pushed to collect as many as they can. It looks good for the Sovereign if you have at least ten. Most are able to do this.

She frowned as she rubbed her thumb across one of the lines. *How is this proof? Someone could just make the tattoo themselves.*

He broke out in goosebumps again as her thumb traced his skin. *What you see is not...how they should look. It's further mockery of my situation. If Equilas sought to make me harder than any fae has a right to be, she chose the correct tortures. If she sought to make me cruel, more cunning, more willing to destroy...she chose correctly there, too.*

Her gaze flicked back and forth between his eyes, seeing the darkness lurking there. The wicked deviousness. This fae had suffered, and it had crushed him into something she could identify with. Something dark and twisted, maybe not magically, but certainly morally.

"Is he telling you he didn't really earn all those rings yet?" Niall called over, the others all watching. A couple of them snickered.

Tarian shifted uncomfortably. "I...had an advantage."

"Bullshit," a female with bright red hair down to her waist said, a braid running down each side of her face. A splash of freckles stretched across her nose. "The amount of power a person possesses only helps in *one* of those trials. You mastered the others because of natural talent and staunch determination. We were with you—we saw the many hours you put into training."

Daisy looked at their arms, not seeing the same lines. "Did they not want to participate?"

The *Fallen* looked between them, many flaring their elbows. "When Equilas stripped our wings," the redhead said, "she also stripped away the proof of what we are. Except for the scars. Those you can still see if you look hard enough."

"Or, in Gorlan's case, if he constantly shoves his arm in your face so you can't help but count all fifteen of his rings," Niall said, pushing a darker-skinned male with thick black lashes.

"Well?" Gorlan replied. "Besides Tarian, I got more than all but one of the royal family, whom I tied. That's kind of fucking awesome. You'd shove it in everyone's face, too."

"Besides the king, too," said Darryn, Niall's similar-looking brother. "He has sixteen."

"He doesn't count. It was easier back when he took the trials. He made them harder so no one could match him."

"Joke was on him." Niall smirked.

Daisy looked at Tarian's arm, counting the rings. Ten down to his elbow on his right arm, ten on his left. "How many trials are there?"

"Twenty," one of the *Fallen* said. "No one alive, save

for Tarian, has mastered them all. Any others are recorded in ancient scrolls. They might as well be myth."

The others puffed up in pride at Tarian's achievements, except for Tarian himself. He ran his fingers through his unruly hair.

"What is your advantage?" she asked him.

His gaze hardened. "My advantage turned into a curse, and the trials helped solidify the Diamond Court's wariness about the possibility of my taking the throne forcefully."

"And your family's wariness that when the king passed on the throne," Lennox said in a slow, deep drawl, "he'd pass it to the most qualified of his heirs. They all knew it would be you—not because of your magic, but because of all you'd done within your few short years—"

"Enough!" Tarian barked, his command crisp and effective. Everyone fell silent. "It doesn't matter now. My so-called advantages landed me—and all of you—in this position. It ruined our lives. All of us, including this innocent human who has to suffer because of the gods' ill humor. Who has to fight a battle she has no part in. There's no point in discussing it further. It won't do any good. That advantage can't help me now. Equilas made sure of that."

Daisy wanted to ask again what the advantage was. She wanted to judge for herself if it helped or didn't. The *Fallen* didn't seem to think so, but it was clear they thought the sun shone out of his ass. She wondered if she'd be so generous.

His pain kept her from prying, though. The raw

misery she could see before her tightened her chest in sympathy. She pushed aside the empathy threatening to overwhelm her and tucked away the gnawing curiosity. She'd delve another day when he might be more inclined to share.

We are ready. Stratow's mental voice was like a boom of thunder.

"I thought you said he was too far away to hear," she whispered as quietly as she could.

They are. They have the ability to push out their mental voices to be heard a long way away. It's necessary as a flier.

So you can do it, too?

He took her hand and pulled her with him. *Once. I'm not a flier anymore. That magic is lost to me.*

Forever? She hadn't meant for that question to sound so crestfallen. Before finding out what he was, she couldn't imagine a way for him to be more attractive. Those beautiful wings, though, and that beautiful, well-cut outfit that Celestial had worn would really round him out.

He gave her a strange look. *That remains to be seen. Come on, we've stalled long enough.*

It wasn't really an answer, but then, what did it matter? If he was to be believed, and she had a sinking feeling he was, she wouldn't be around long enough to enjoy it anyway.

"What's a champion of the court?" she asked, tugged along to the great beasts.

Lennox shot her a guarded look as he also started forward. The others wouldn't look at her at all.

"A great distraction for the court," Tarian said gruffly, "and the way I will explain your presence. The way I will hide your importance."

"I do love me a good riddle," she replied. "But what *is* it?"

The stormbacks waited in a half-circle, now facing northeast. Stratow stood in the middle, at the top of the arc. His mane ruffled around his face as the wind picked up speed, blowing in the direction they were all facing.

Tarian stopped beside Stratow with her hand still in his. "The royals call it games. The gentry call it entertainment. It's actually a blood sport. Each member of the court puts forth their champion of choice to participate in these bloody games. The entrants might be servants, some are pets, and many are slaves bought or abducted specifically for the games. In addition, the throne puts forward a collection of captured fae and prisoners to attempt to win their freedom. The goal is—"

"To survive. Yeah, I get it." She looked up at the stormback, its wings pulled in, blocking any easy way of climbing onto its back. Not that getting up that high would be easy. It wasn't a fence she was scaling. The odds of her looking graceful were slim to none.

"No. That would imply these games are set up for the contenders. They're not. The games are political, like everything else. The contenders are just pawns. Some players set up their champions to fail, thereby sucking up to royalty or making another of the gentry look stronger, tightening their alliance. You never know why a player chooses a champion and what their end game is. There is a lot of maneuvering amid the show. Maneuvering I won't bother with. No one in their right mind would form an alliance with me. I need only to buy time to get set up without the king becoming too impatient."

"I assume using a human in these games will further your image as the butt of the court's joke? Your champion doing well, therefore, will be a slap in the face of those same people. If I don't die immediately, I will be a target to dispose of gruesomely and for an audience, something like they did to your girlfriend?"

He studied her for a long time as the other *Fallen* jumped and climbed and scrambled onto the backs of the other stormbacks, there being no stirrups to help, and no saddles or reins to hold once up there.

"I won't have to do much schooling in the political side of things, I see," he said. "I'm impressed. Essentially, yes. We'll have an uphill battle from here on out."

"I have next to zero magic except this mythical chalice situation that doesn't help me in the least, and you're going to pit me against powerful, bloodthirsty fae? Super. Sounds like a real fun time followed by a wonderfully peaceful grave."

"As I said...an uphill battle."

She shook her head. "My life has been filled with terrible luck, and you might be the worst of it."

Chapter Two

ALEXIS

Bria was already waiting when Alexis showed up at the Magical San Francisco Government Building, right next to one of two spots labeled "Demigod." The other was occupied by a cherry-red Ferrari, an older vehicle with all sorts of sentimentality. It was the car Kieran had nearly (and purposely!) run over Lexi with, resulting in the first time she and Kieran had met. Good times.

He'd obviously been thinking about the past when he chose it to drive today. Thinking about how Daisy had resisted his integration into their lives and her tight family unit. Had secretly stolen money from him at every turn to create an "out" should he become power hungry and abusive like his Demigod father before him. Daisy had been thinking of the future and preparing should she need to rip them away from this life. At fifteen years old, she'd been trying to protect her family. *Fifteen!*

She didn't feel more secure now, Lexi knew. Daisy had become an ace at investing—*just in case*—in both magical and non-magical markets. Had contacts every-where. Had safe houses, secret offshore bank accounts, and friends in *very* low places. She was ready for the Demigod apocalypse, even though Lexi was now a Demigod herself. There was nothing Daisy wouldn't do to help her family. Nothing. She was hard, but she was sweet, in her own way. Ravaged by life, but saw the joy in it, too. Above all, she relished in the love of her family.

And that piece-of-shit fairy fucker had stolen her from the only happiness she'd ever known. He'd pay for this. The Celestials, too. What the fuck were they doing? Besides *not* doing their jobs. They needed a hard lesson in work ethic, that's what they needed.

Lexi planned to give it to them.

She flung open the door of the beat-up old Bronco and stepped out in clothes she'd picked herself. Let the magazines and gossip columns talk shit—for once, she didn't care. Daisy wasn't there to pick out her clothes and style her. Now the columnists would know Lexi hadn't grown a sense of fashion; it was still all thanks to her "filthy" Chester ward who "didn't belong" in the magical zone.

Fuck those people.

"Well, hello," Bria said, her platinum-blond hair falling straight to her shoulders. She wore a light blue Nirvana T-shirt, acid-wash jeans, and a spiked dog collar around her neck. She had never cared about the fashion columns. "Love those pants. Are we preparing for a flood?"

Lexi left her handbag in the Bronco and the doors unlocked. She half hoped someone was stupid enough to steal it. It would really help her mood if she could get some of this pent-up pain-turned-aggression out of her system.

"Oh! And we're free-boobin' it, too?" Bria cracked a grin and stepped out of the way. "Nice! I'm diggin' it. How's the mental health?"

"How do you think?"

"I think you keep jabbing me in the spirit box by accident, and it is not so pleasurable."

A spirit box was the casing of a person's soul, and as a Spirit Walker (not so affectionately called a Soul Stealer), Lexi had the power to crack that thing open and rip the spirit right out. She could kill with a flick of her power. Then, if she wanted, she could stuff that spirit back in, tether it to the dead body, and reanimate it, creating the walking dead. She had a rare type of magic that was generally regarded as horribly terrifying. It was a "glad she's on our side" situation in magical San Francisco.

"Sorry," she told Bria, pulling back and tamping down her power. "I'm not doing great. It's been two days since Daisy was taken right under our noses. We were in the fucking car, Bria! Our whole team was with her, and we couldn't keep those...*things* from grabbing her unconscious body."

Her stomach filled with lead at the memory of those

disgusting, shadowy fae things swooping in and scooping up Daisy's limp form. Lexi had felt the bright effervescence of her soul, so she knew her ward was still alive, but the image still haunted her and racked her with guilt. She was supposed to be protecting Daisy, not offering her up to the enemy. To the creatures—fae— they'd *known* about but hadn't done anything to fortify against.

They'd failed her, and they all knew it.

"Self-loathing doesn't get the job done," Lexi mumbled dutifully, quoting Zorn. He'd said that to her a lot over the last couple days. To himself, probably, too.

"No, but it does help us make terrible decisions, like buying every tub of ice cream in the store and eating until you throw up. The good news is, I've found a couple new favorite flavors. Bad news...well, last night didn't end well. It'll be okay. You'll see, Lexi. That little gremlin is adept at staying alive, Kieran is amaze-*bouche* at complex planning, and our team is excellent in the trenches. With Zorn's lifelong collection of notes on all things Faerie, we'll get her back and hopefully kill a great many fae as we do."

Their inner crew, what they'd all come to think of as their family, stood around the oval table in the conference room. Kieran glanced up when she entered the room, his blue eyes fierce and his hair mussed from running his fingers through it. The others continued to look at the documents rolled out across the large table.

"What've we got?" she asked as Jack scooted over to

make room. He wore a tan suit that barely fit around his huge arms.

It was Amber who spoke. "I've checked three well-known portals to the fae realm. All are open and operational. None are guarded by fae—not on this side or the other. If the fae mean to set a trap, it isn't around the portal." She paused for a beat. "But the people who service the portals say there has been a lot of activity in the last few years. More and more each year."

"Do we know why?" Lexi asked.

"The attendant who asked the fae, a year back, was killed for the question." Zorn straightened. "No one else has dared. But given the other information we've been able to collect from various fae entering this realm—creatures as well, however they are getting through—we can assume the Celestials aren't doing what they are supposed to do. I can believe there is one very clever, very powerful fae, but bands of them?" He shook his head. "This problem goes beyond Daisy. We've seen more death and violence recently, as well. The fae coming over are not trying as hard to fit in. The longer they are ignored, or the more that are let through, the bigger the problem we'll face until their magic takes root. In which case..."

Disaster.

If that magic rooted and grew, it would change the face of their world. They were seeing the beginning stages. If they allowed this problem to linger, it would turn nasty in a hurry.

She nodded, waiting for more.

"We think we have a lead on her, but..." He put his fists on the table. "The fae that took her into the portal seemed to be from the Sapphire kingdom, given their skin was greenish. They smelled like...sea salt and kelp. The fae we saw on our cameras, when the body was dropped off on the lawn, didn't match that description. We have multiple factions of fae interested in Daisy. We don't know where she was taken." He paused, and she could see his struggle to keep his emotions at bay. "We don't know where to go to look for her."

Lexi bit her lip. This was her piece of the puzzle. She could slip into spirit, leaving her body behind, and track a soul. Once she found it, she could figure out where the person was in the world. Time was of the essence, though. Leave the body behind for too long and it would die without its soul. It wouldn't allow the soul to re-dock. Have someone else find her body without her soul in it, and they could kill her as easily as a sleeping person. Maybe more so, since she'd have to travel back to re-inhabit, and a sleeping person would just wake up. For those reasons, extra precautions were always required.

She wouldn't have given a shit about those precautions the night Daisy was taken except for being in a moving vehicle. She'd never chased her body while in spirit. She didn't want to try and fail—and die—when Daisy needed her. By the time she'd gotten home and safeguarded herself, Lexi couldn't find Daisy's soul. She could feel it, but it was a strange...echo, almost. Neither in existence nor gone. She hadn't known what to make of it. Then the next day, the soul was gone entirely. Vanished.

Based on the time frame, they were guessing the echo must've been when Daisy had crossed the portal. In this world but...not. She wasn't in the underworld—Lexi had checked. No one could hide a soul from her, save for Hades himself, and she knew the undertaker personally. Hades didn't know what was going on.

Then, when her soul vanished, Lexi could only guess —dearly hope—that Daisy had crossed into Faerie, a place ruled by other gods. Older gods with a different spirit plane. One Daisy was hopefully not in. Lexi had to believe her kid was still alive. She *had* to believe she could still get Daisy back.

To do that, they had to go after her. Lexi desperately hoped she could track Daisy once in the other realm. They didn't have time to blindly check several kingdoms. Daisy's life was dependent upon Lexi's being able to use her magic across the portal.

Chapter Three

DAISY

Tarian climbed up onto the large beast after her. He scooted forward as far as he could, fitting into a groove between Stratow's ribs and the start of his back. He then put his hand against her lower back and shoved, sliding her until she was basically bowing around Stratow's head, with her legs curved around his thick neck and applying a lot of extra weight.

You weigh nothing, the beast countered within her mind.

"Grab his mane tightly," Tarian said. "Really tight. If you feel like you're going to fall off, think it as loudly as you can. Takeoff is dangerous for us on his back, and there aren't usually two riders. The storms are the most dangerous of all, though he'll afford us some protection through those, as will I."

"Storms?" Daisy tried to look back at him as muscles bunched and moved beneath her. "What do you mean, *storms*?"

Images flashed through her mind of blistering lightning, turbulent skies, freezing cold, and rushing winds.

"Yes, I know what a storm is," she said as Stratow huffed and clawed at the ground. "Why are we going to fly through one?"

"They are stormbacks. They create the storms. Now hold on tightly and squeeze with your legs. He has assured me that he won't let you fall, but...do what you can to help."

"Why is he assuring you? Why isn't he assuring *me*?"

"He is. You're just not understanding him."

No images flashed through her mind. No emotions. If he was communicating, she had no idea how.

Stratow tensed and bowed, his front legs bending and his head coming down. She gripped his mane tightly as he sprang forward.

She screamed, thrown backward by the force of his sudden gallop. Her cheeks flapped in the wind rushing against her face, and her body jolted with each step. A sports bra would've gone a long way in this situation. The ground blurred around her, the trees whipping by so fast they lost their shape.

Her butt slid backward as her mind flashed to the knife in her loose and horribly out-of-shape bra. She squeezed with her legs and loosened one of her hands to clutch it, ensuring it didn't fall.

Don't you fucking dare, Tarian yelled in her mind. *It's going to get dicier in just a—*

Stratow launched into the sky, the power of the move so intense it felt like her teeth were trying to find the back of her throat. Her eyes watered. Her hands slipped on the silky mane.

Hang on, dove, Tarian said with a rough edge to his voice. *I'm right behind you. If you slip, push back to me. Slide into my body and I'll hold us on.*

She couldn't focus enough to ask how *he* was holding on. The creature was climbing at an insane angle, the massive wings reaching out much farther than she had anticipated they could. Each flap propelled them at a force that tore at her grip. That made her butt continue to slide.

Almost there, Tarian said encouragingly. *Just a little more.*

Was walking really such a terrible idea?

Too late now, he said, and she could hear the strain in his mental voice.

Wings pumping, Stratow started to level off. Her hands stopped sliding and her legs found their purchase. The wind still tore at her cheeks, and if she opened her mouth, they'd flap, but the fear of sliding off reduced.

You made it, Tarian said, his hand on her lower back. *That's the worst of the climb. Stormbacks typically take off by gliding. It's why mountains are the best places for them. Taking off from flat land means they need the winds to be right, space to get speed, and it requires a lot of exertion.*

His mental touch changed slightly, and she realized he was no longer talking to her. *Thank you for the effort, friend.*

A feeling of humble gratitude swept over her, and she knew Tarian felt it, too. That must've been Stratow's response.

She ducked a bit as they continued to climb in elevation, the air starting to thin and cool. In no time, she was shivering and gasping for breath.

It's okay. Here, lean back into me. She felt Tarian's hands on her upper arms, coaxing her to lean back.

Had he lost his fucking mind? The wind threatened to rip her right off this creature's back and fling her into the great, wide abyss. She wasn't afraid of heights, but usually, when she encountered them, she had something to hold on to or a metal enclosure around her.

Concern radiated through her as she gasped harder. It wasn't her emotion, though. It came from Stratow. He leveled out, and she felt a hard grip on the back of her shirt. Tarian yanked, ripping fabric and forcing her to slide back.

She screamed again and wasn't embarrassed about it. She tried to clutch on to the mane as her fingers slipped, but the yank was too hard and unexpected, and suddenly, she was sliding. Falling back. Her legs kicked at nothing as air washed around her.

Tarian's strong arm wrapped around her middle. His hand splayed against her ribs, and even through her clothes, she could feel the heat of his touch. The hard planes of his chest pushed against her back as he leaned over her, enveloping her in a warmth that couldn't just be from his body. The wind stopped rushing her face, and the atmosphere gained density, offering more oxygen.

She took a deep breath, somehow inhaling his delicious scent despite the wind. Her body shook, not from cold, but from fear. *You could've put that bubble around me while I was still clinging to the mane.*

I'm sorry, he whispered in her mind, his face brushing against hers and nestling into her hair. *I panicked. I didn't realize humans couldn't tolerate the change in air pressure and temperature from flight. I have you now. You'll be okay.*

His legs gripped the stormback, and his hand fit in a deep groove at the back of the stormback's wing. For all intents and purposes, he'd had a handle to hold and purchase for his legs while she'd been up at the neck sitting. She'd gotten the shit end of the stick on that one.

His arm squeezed her tighter, and his thumb moved, stroking against her, the tip barely sliding along the underside of her breast. This time the shiver wasn't from cold or fear. *The force is greater back here, and I worried you wouldn't have the grip strength to hold on. If you'd slipped from the neck, you would've slid into me. I could've held us both.*

It would've been nice if he'd done that in the beginning with his oh-so-mighty grip strength, the weasel. It would've kept her from thoughts of certain death.

A vibration under her legs and a rolling sea of mirth

indicated Stratow thought all this was humorous. She didn't see the joke.

That's because you're the punch line, Tarian said, and she glanced to the side, wondering how much effort it would take to push him off. The rumbling continued.

Other stormbacks flew in close, the *Fallen* atop them looking at ease and windswept, but with concerned expressions. They really needed to focus on hanging on better. A little turbulence and those fuckers would be headed for the ground.

The rumbling intensified.

Honestly, what is so funny? she thought in exasperation.

A clusterfuck of emotions ran through her. They were complete gibberish. She wasn't good at stormback communication.

She thought about looking over the side to see how high up they were but couldn't bring herself to do it. Not with only Mr. Grip Strength to keep her on this beast. Their angle had changed again, back to climbing. Her stomach was getting queasy, and now would be the worst time to figure out she actually *was* afraid of heights.

He says you are not like any fae he's ever met, Tarian said.

He does know I'm human, right? And why doesn't he speak in words anymore? She closed her eyes, swallowing thickly. It would be embarrassing to throw up. It would be more embarrassing if she had to use the restroom.

He probably couldn't be bothered. That, or he's trying to force you to communicate with him properly.

She shook her head, not wasting effort on answering. She didn't have many cordial things to say, anyway. The fear was getting to her. She'd probably blurt out the wrong thing, he'd roll to the side, and bye-bye, dumb human.

How are you now? Tarian asked, his strength surrounding her. She had to own that it helped. The warmth certainly did.

She thought about looking over the side again. When her bowels started to roll, she decided she'd better not.

I'm okay, she thought, focusing on breathing. *I thought I had beaten fear. Occasionally, I feel it when I'm going up against a magical person I'm not ready for, but otherwise, I thought I was pretty tough. That I could stare death in the face without blinking. That I could stay logical in the worst situation. I've trained for it, you know? But fuck, bro, this is throwing me for a loop. And that darkrend—that thing scared the crap out of me. I might not be any good to you, Tarian. I mean, besides the lack of magic, I might not have the courage for any of this. I'm having some...second thoughts.*

Still clutching her tightly, Tarian held out a thumbs-up for the others. He didn't comment for a moment as he watched them pull away. It felt like he was giving her some privacy, the moment turning intimate, allowing her to work through these thoughts.

The leap in her heart at the possibility was unexpected and even a touch unsettling. The warmth within her that he should care, that he might try to comfort her, help her, was even more so.

Fuck, this is a terrible situation. A really terrible, awful situation. For the first time in a long time, emotion welled up, and tears filled her eyes. Homesickness. Desperation. She didn't want to die. She didn't want to fly to her doom. She wanted to go home and see Lexi and Mordecai again. She wanted to chat with Bria, play games with Amber, and crack jokes with the guys. She shouldn't be here. She couldn't *do* this.

Shh, shh, shh, Tarian cooed softly, huddling around her. Soothing emotions also came from Stratow. *I know this is hard. It's a lot, all of this. You're in an entirely different realm with strange and dangerous new creatures. All without preparing. That darkrend scared me, too. It scared us all. Flying like this, when your kind is not used to it—not even naturally capable of it—has got to be terrifying. But you are tough, Daisy. You're the toughest, most courageous human I've met. You're smart and you're fierce and you do not say die. That darkrend scared you, but it did not get the better of you like it did the rest of us. I know you will do whatever is necessary to reach the end of this. You'll protect your family. You'll kill a bunch of fae even though the odds are against you. You, above anyone, will survive. You were built for it. There is a way. We simply need to find it.*

He hugged her tightly, his other arm coming around to join the first. A tear overflowed, and she had to clench her jaw to keep the sobs at bay, surprised by his speech. Surprised by how much hearing those words meant to her. Surprised by how much she wanted to fall apart in his arms.

She struggled to pull it all back in. To regain some of her former strength.

Right now, you don't need to be tough, he murmured. *Right now, you can give in and let go. Purge. We have a few hours. Lean against me. I won't let you fall.*

With that, she completely fell apart. She allowed herself to drop her guard and give in to it. Give in to this moment, to the fear and the uncertainty. With him holding her, she closed her eyes and gave herself over to his safekeeping.

The tears came, fat and painful. The memories of her life with her family played through her mind bitter-sweetly. She hoped they had stayed in the human realm —stayed safe. She hoped they'd lead long lives filled with love and laughter and adventure.

Thinking of them, she was reminded of why she had agreed to this in the first place. It was there she found renewed strength. Because even if she would never see them again, they would live on. They'd be sad to lose her, but they'd have each other. They'd laugh at family dinners and relax with a glass of wine in the living room together. Someone would take over guarding Mordecai's back, probably Bria, and everyone would make sure to check in with Dylan periodically to ensure he was doing okay. They'd handle this. Their light and love would continue, and she would continue through their memories.

Her crying reduced to sniffles, and she stared out at nothing for a while, the crisp air sweeping by them, nothing but a light breeze within Tarian's magical bubble.

The air smelled fresh and rich, a balm for all that ailed her. The sky sparkled overhead, like someone had sneezed glitter all over it.

I thought fae were supposed to be vicious and awful, she mused idly, watching the other stormbacks and their riders soar around them. *Not comforting and supportive and uplifting.*

Surprisingly, it wasn't Tarian who answered her.

Fae are mirrors of Faerie, Stratow murmured, using words this time. *As a whole, they are the light and the dark and the in-between. They are, in themselves, a balance. Some are effervescent and pure, too sweet for the senses, and some are the reapers of death and destruction. But most are both. They are vile and vicious and willing to slit a throat for their own gain, but in a society that lives forever, that is necessary for population control. They also practice moderation and goodwill. That is how the kingdoms thrive. It is how the society grows. Most fae pretend at constant cruelty, and members of the court are unpardonably egotistical and priggish, but most fae will surprise you when you most need to be surprised.*

She nodded, turning her head so the side of her face rested against Tarian's neck. His palm gently cradled her face, his thumb wiping away a tear. He didn't speak, and the air around them was subdued, as if he were fascinated by her turn of emotions. As if he *had* to wipe away her tears, used to seeing her so strong, so determined, and doubting they were real. In awe of her allowing him to see her walls crack and break away. His nose traced a line on her cheek before his lips softly pressed against her temple. His actions soothed her frayed edges. She could feel him all around her. His strength. His comforting touch.

She understood what Stratow had said. It was how the human world worked, after all. Good people and bad, with the mostly insufferable Demigods to rule over it all. On the magical side, at least. She didn't really know how the Chester side worked other than in theory.

The same, Tarian said. *I've had dealings with both. They are not so very different creatures, magical and non-magical humans. The issue is power. Chesters view magic as power, and they fear it. They work hard to defend them-selves against it. They create borders and bombs and weapons. They do not realize that, in their innovation, they have become equally powerful. Their weapons could create so much more destruction—from a distance—than a Demigod and their army. But of course, one on one, it is another story. Very at odds, that realm. It's fascinating to learn about. I greatly enjoy my time there.*

No one else enjoys your time there, she grumbled without thinking.

The rumbling started again. Stratow liked it when she picked on Tarian.

Yes, he does, Tarian said dryly.

They fell into silence for a while, the wind drying Daisy's eyes as she contemplated what was to come. She needed to prepare. She needed more information. And so, she requested from Tarian all he knew. He complied by filling her head to bursting with images and anecdotes and names and appearances, political maneuvering and how he'd been playing the game. There was so much complex information that she shut her eyes again, focusing solely on that and forgetting everything else around them.

That was...until the storms came.

Chapter Four

Daisy

"What's..." Daisy's face went slack as dark clouds churned and boiled nearby. Light flared from within before jagged forks of lightning crackled between them. The wind picked up, whipping her hair even from within Tarian's protective magical cocoon. Thunder rumbled with a bone-rattling growl, so similar in pitch and cadence to Stratow's growling laugh.

"Are we under attack?" she asked hopefully, probably barely heard above the howling wind.

Kieran could do this. He could create weather like this. Dylan could supply the lightning so precisely that he could kill Tarian without harming her. He could knock them all down from the sky. Before she hit the ground, Donovan could catch her with his magic.

Together, they had the skill to save her. They had the ability. Their power, as a group, was great enough.

No, but that is very interesting to know about the might of your crew, Tarian said. *It's always been believed that the Celestials are much more powerful than the Demigods of your world, but after meeting one of them, I always wondered if that was actually the case.*

He'd met Lydia, a Demigod of Hades who had tried a power play by making a deal with the fae. She hadn't fulfilled her end of the bargain, whatever it was, and had lost her life for it. She was the reason Tarian had needed a distraction at the Demigod Summit. A distraction that had nearly killed Daisy and her family.

Lydia was a fool and not the best of her class, Daisy said, ignoring the anger from the past. That was behind her. If she needed a reason to kill this fae, she had plenty.

Gotcha. But once again, no, this is not an attack. You can't bring a stormback down with lightning or winds or anything to do with storms. They create the storms that invigorate Faerie. The rain nurtures plant growth and fills the streams. The lightning's destruction clears out old growth and leaves room for rebirth. The thunder...well, that's just scary, I guess.

Thunder is the sound created by the fast expansion of air around a lightning bolt. The lightning creates a shock wave that manifests as a sound wave.

The more you know, hmm?

She wasn't sure if he knew he was reciting a tagline from some old Chester show.

I do now, he thought.

Rain fell in heavy sheets, slashing through his magical bubble. The air electrified around them, and the temperature dropped further. Lightning flickered ever closer as the clouds continued to close in.

"What are we doing?" she asked softly, her voice quivering. "Why are we riding a creature that literally creates dangerous storms?"

It'll be okay. Tarian gave her a squeeze. *Stratow will shield us a great deal, and I will take care of the rest. It'll be uncomfortable, but it won't be incredibly painful.*

She licked her lips, not wanting to speak in her mind. Needing to have the words spoken physically for reasons she couldn't understand.

"Is this like the time *very recently* when you didn't realize humans couldn't tolerate high altitudes?"

No. I am well aware humans can't handle a lightning strike.

A bolt zipped down beside them with such force that the crack made her scream. Her corresponding jump nearly launched her off Stratow's back.

I've got you, Tarian said, and she heard the humor in his voice. She was forever the butt of the joke in this realm. He'd pay for that one day.

Add it to the list, he said, and he'd pay for that, too.

Another bolt crashed down, striking the stormback Kayla was riding. She leaned back marginally, not at all alarmed that the lightning had struck a foot from her.

"Oh my god," Daisy said, pushing into Tarian. That

bolt had landed right between the stormback's wings, where she was currently sitting.

It's going to be okay—

"Stop saying that! This is *not* okay. This is very much..." An ominous cloud rushed toward them as though it had a vendetta. Her scalp tingled before her hair started to stand. "Oh fuck, oh god. Oh god, oh fuck. Fucking—"

The bolt nearly blinded her with its brilliance. The air cracked with an ear-splitting boom before a flare of heat washed over her body. The bolt landed right between her legs in the center of Stratow's back. Stratow, though, was not affected. His hair-fur didn't blacken, nor did the skin show red or black underneath.

"Why?" she asked herself. "Why do they get struck by lightning? I understand the water and the natural order of things, but why do they get hit by their own magic?"

That's...just the way it is, Tarian said haltingly, and it was clear he had never asked. Nor did Stratow offer any explanation, not that she could feel or understand. *They can somewhat control where the lightning hits their bodies. Usually, they like it in the center of their backs, between their wings, where it is striking the others. But Stratow is redirecting it so you are safe. I am minimizing the electrical discharge and the corresponding heat.*

The human world had its oddities, but Faerie was a weird fucking place.

The human world definitely has its oddities. So many

and so strange that I began keeping a journal to remember them in years to come when I am closed out of that realm. Obviously, that was before I realized I'd have to die to set right the fissure I created. I find the human world so much more interesting than this place.

She shook her head, closing her eyes as another bolt struck. This one hit another of the stormbacks. The winds persisted, shoving at her from one way, then another.

How did your birth create the fissure? Just because you have—had, I guess—more power than most?

You still remember? he asked quietly.

Your being a Celestial? Yes. Hopefully I will forget this journey when we're through, though. I'm concerned I'll definitely be afraid of heights at the end of this horror show. And I haven't even looked down!

His cheek brushed against hers. *You're a stranger and you're not from my past, but it is nice to know your memories won't be stolen. That I can tell you of my past, of the good times, and you will keep them—for now.* He took her hand, turned it over, and placed a kiss on her palm. He curled her fingers to trap the sentiment inside. *By the end, you will almost certainly hate me. Remember, I have no choice but to play my part in all of this. My cruelty, and my indifference, will be necessary, and it will be brutal. This is the light...and it will balance the incredible darkness I must become.*

She pushed aside his warnings. His regrets. They meant nothing to her. She'd chosen this path; she'd weather what came. Literally, it seemed. She wasn't afraid of his darkness and thought it was sweet that he kept trying to prepare her for his personality change.

She put her hands on his thighs to comfort him. She didn't know what it must be like to essentially be a ghost. She was displaced from her family, but she knew they'd remember her. She knew they'd lament her passing. She didn't know how she'd find comfort in all of this if she didn't have them to think back on.

Continue with the court info, please, she murmured.

They didn't get there until after dark. Nervous adrenaline had started the second Tarian mentioned a descent into the kingdom. She hadn't opened her eyes the whole time, and not because of the slow downward flight and surprisingly soft landing. It was because she was full of uncertainty about what was to come. She knew what everything looked like, thanks to Tarian's shared images, and given his perceptions seemed dark and twisted and ominous, she knew seeing it through her human eyes would be downright nightmarish. It was best she didn't create terror before there was a cause.

"Thank you, Stratow." Tarian put his hand on his heart as he faced the large creature. "You've saved us much time and effort that we greatly needed."

Rain pelted down from the stormy skies, obscuring their limited vision within the darkness. They all stood in a field at the back of what was presumably a large castle. Only a sliver of a moon lit the sky, and very little light came from strange globes glimmering in the distance. What seemed like vast and enormous steeples rose out of the murky darkness way above them.

Daisy stood off to the side on shaky legs.

I enjoyed our time together, little human, Stratow told her with mental words. *It was a wonderful surprise. I'd like to know more of your kind, I think. So free with your words and thoughts and emotions. I look forward to seeing you again someday under much brighter circumstances. Watch yourself in there. You are our unlikely hero. In you, great things will manifest. I feel it in the winds.*

What a lovely, positive outlook. She could get used to sentiments like that when faced with a shitstorm.

Her teeth started to chatter from the cold. "Th-thanks for the ride. Sorry about screaming so much when you were changing course."

His deep, growling hum signaled his laughter. *Thank you for the entertainment. Fae like Tarian need a reminder that they are not as great as they think they are. They are merely fae, nothing more.*

Tarian's brows pulled together.

The others said their goodbyes and thanks, and then they turned away, presumably to allow the stormbacks privacy as they organized their return to the skies.

The ground was flat and somewhat sandy, with nothing in the way to impede her feet. She followed behind the others, in a loose cluster with tense bodies and tight shoulders. They were not happy to be home.

This is not our home, Niall said, glancing back at her.

She couldn't make out his expression, but his mental voice was rough. *This is our battlefield. Don't forget that.*

Of all of us, she's the last person who will be able to, one of the others replied.

Not of all of us. Tarian's voice was hard.

A creature to the right somewhere let out a long, mournful moan. Another answered with a whistle. They weren't like any animals Daisy had heard. Something thumped repeatedly against wood away to the left, masked in darkness even though the light should've reached that far.

Do not look around, Darryn hissed, Niall's brother with small braids lined with ribbons. He grabbed her arm and yanked her closer. *Do not seek out what awaits in the darkness. Never venture into the shadows by yourself. Do you understand?*

Y-yes, she said with a nervous flutter.

The shadows here are not merely the absence of light, Lennox said. *Many of them are sentient. They are spies or assassins. Creatures or pitfalls into a trap.*

Nothing here is as it seems, Niall intoned. *Nothing. This place is twisted. The rancid magic has affected much of the court and the creatures on the grounds. Danger is everywhere. You have grown to trust Tarian, and us through him. We are the* only *ones you can trust. Do you understand? Eat only that which you have prepared yourself or what we have given you. Starve before you rely on this court for food. Die of thirst before you take their water, for it will be a less torturous death.*

Kill before you are killed, Gorlan said. *Always.*

The nervous flutters turned into body tremors as the gravity of her situation once again sank in. This time, Daisy wouldn't have Tarian holding her to make it better. She wouldn't have anyone to guard her. The danger was solely on her shoulders. She had to remember that. She had to remain vigilant. Back to reality.

Scout every room you enter for a weapon you might use. Kayla looked back at her, and a plethora of images scattered within Daisy's mind—various rooms reduced into examples, from a hot fire poker, to cutlery, to a blunt object. *Constantly reassess which one will be best given your exact location. Don't let the enemy know you are doing it. Do not touch it until you need it.*

Try not to touch anything unless you have to, another female said, speaking to Daisy for the first time. *The magic of the chalice is alluring. It lingers. The more powerful fae might be able to trace its flavor. Make it as hard as possible.*

Will baths help? asked a male, another she hadn't spoken to.

I don't know, Tarian responded, not looking back. He rolled his shoulders, his posture tenser than she'd ever seen. *The texts mentioned something to this effect, but it didn't sound remotely as potent. I need to spend some time researching how to mask it.*

At least your claim distracts from the chalice's magic, Kayla said. *Small miracles.*

I've laid my claim once before, Tarian replied, guilt lacing his voice. *If the royals remember that, they will realize Daisy's flavor is different.*

That was before the magic became so badly twisted, though, Darryn replied. *Their memory of that time likely was twisted with it. Distorted, at least. Plus, she is a human, not a fae. We can say it is different for her. How would they know that is a lie?*

No one responded as they passed through a stone canopy that looked like the darkness was physically moving across it. They entered a tunnel with echoing walls of midnight. Orbs faintly glowed at a point in the ceiling, the light diffusing and not reaching as far down as Daisy. She stumbled and reached out to clutch Kayla's arm.

I can't see, she thought.

Shh, Niall replied, as though she had control over how loudly she thought things.

Whisper in my mind. Kayla grabbed her and patted her arm. *Act like you are trying not to let Tarian hear your words.*

She tried to do as Kayla said. The result was her hunching strangely with the effort and kinda stutter-stepping like an old man who'd just found a golden ticket in a bar of chocolate. She didn't have much control of her body when she was trying to hamper her thoughts. *I can't see.*

Someone up ahead wheezed and another cough-spat. Kayla's hand shook on Daisy's arm as she sucked in an audible breath through her nose.

I've never had a harder time not laughing in my entire life, Niall said through obvious strain.

What in the blight was that, human? Gorlan asked in a flat voice.

Three people spat out laughter and quickly muffled themselves afterward. The wheezing from earlier turned into a strangled laugh.

Turn the mirth into cruelty, Tarian said, no humor in his voice.

I'd really rather not devolve into something that fits in this disgusting court, Kayla told Daisy quietly. *Just stop thinking until you know how to shield your thoughts.*

She couldn't stop thinking. She didn't know how. Hers was the sort of mind that never shut up, twirling with thoughts and memories and often a random song in the background. Instead, she started thinking of things that might be on the walls, terrifying stuff made of nightmares. If someone was reading her thoughts, they'd expect her to be scared—of her captors, this strange place, the horrible creatures. She went in cycles like a frantic mind would, envisioning the worst of everything, worrying about her fate.

I shoulda thought of that, Gorlan said, barely more than a leak of a thought in her mind.

You're more the brawny type, not the brainy type, Niall told him in the same soft mental tone.

Like you can talk. You didn't think of it.

I never claimed to be smarter than her just because she's a human.

It's not because she's a human. It's because she's a female.

45

Kayla huffed beside them, and Daisy could feel the smile in her voice. *Cute,* she thought sarcastically.

She is smart, though. I'll give her that, the male she didn't know thought, his mind more muffled than the rest. Either he was better at shielding his thoughts or was compensating somehow for being worse. If the latter, she needed to learn that trick.

She is ingenious, and I have a feeling she will shine, Tarian said stoically. *Her training makes it seem as though she were preparing for this fight. It was a stroke of luck that she and I came to regard each other as...*

He paused, and she felt a weird fluttering in her chest.

...allies, he finally went on. *If we hadn't, she'd be calm and logical and analytical, trying to outsmart us instead of playing a part and using us to outsmart the court.* He took a deep breath. *This will be hard for you,* Fallen, *given she is new here and a human, but trust her instincts. They are...infallible. I tested her in the human realm, as I told you, and she's battled at my side here. She's earned that trust. Give her the information she seeks and the help she requires.*

They reached the end of the corridor as pride welled up within her, mixing with that increased fluttering in her chest. He stopped under one of the glowing orbs, this one showering light on his hard face, horribly devoid of any emotion. His eyes didn't sparkle with teasing or soften when he looked at her, something she hadn't realized they'd done lately until right this moment. He looked at her like she was a stranger.

"Take her to the dungeons. I'll send for her when I have a craving for her flesh," he said with haughty command and disgusting arrogance.

Something withered inside her, even though she knew he had to play his part as well. Her personality rushed to the surface with unstoppable force. "Go fuck yourself," she blurted, then went with it, spitting at him and accidentally hitting Gorlan instead.

Gorlan barely flinched, then tensed, stopping himself from recoiling. She would've thought that funny if not for the cold indifference in Tarian's eyes. Kayla and the beautiful, curvy woman grabbed her upper arms, holding her tightly between them. Tarian studied her like he might a finger painting done by someone else's child. No humor moved behind his eyes. No kindness.

"Do that again, and I will whip you unconscious before I toss you into the dungeon to rot. Do I make myself clear? You are nothing here, human. Less than dirt. Remember that."

Cold crept through her insides. Steel entered her gaze. Her bearing. A smile pulled at her lips, and she let it. Then she coaxed it into full-fledged laughter.

"Whatever you say, boss," slipped from her mouth, flippant and willful and challenging without completely crossing the line.

He was acting like one of the court members here, and they were probably real assholes. Let the record show that she was calling his bluff. *Your move, Highness.*

His eyebrow twitched up slightly. A tiny crease formed at the corner of his eyes, though she couldn't tell which emotion that might be. Then he was giving directions to his *Fallen*. Before he left, his voice slithered into her mind.

Stay alive, little dove. Kill first, ask questions after you hide the body.

The feeling of lips ghosted across hers. Phantom hands held her tightly. Then he walked into the darkness with all but two of his *Fallen*, taking his protection with him. She was on her own.

Chapter Five

Kieran

"Just don't..." Bria held up her hand to Lexi as the crew stepped out of the vehicles at the portal site. "Don't fly off the handle. Let Kieran handle it."

The portal waited just up ahead, and the surrounding area was certainly something. It was like a superstore for realm crossers. Horses swished their tails or ran around their large enclosures. Goats and sheep roamed. Wagons were in neat rows off to the side, and three huge barns spread out on the other side, with tackle and other supplies. People in actual uniforms waited near a saloon. Across from the wagons, he could just see a counter within a rectangular building, someone ringing up a purchase.

This wasn't just attendants helping; this was a business. The Chesters, who were often wary of or outright hated magical people, and who tried to separate themselves from magic, were opening their arms to fae. To a race ten times more dangerous than a magical human ever would be, at least now that this world had the Accords and the many drawn-up truces between magical and non-magical societies.

Fucking idiots.

"Don't fly off the handle?" Lexi mumbled, her fists clenched so tightly that her knuckles were white.

"We need supplies—"

"Oh, we'll get the supplies. Don't you worry about that." She walked beside the pen for the goats, looking in. "Why the fuck does anyone need a goat? What, do they want fresh goat's milk to go with their breakfast as they journey to their lands?"

"At least they give milk—why the sheep?" Jack asked, following closely behind Lexi. His anger at the setup was palpable. Everyone's was. "The journey is supposed to take a day at a moderate pace—are they planning on knitting a sweater in that time?"

Zorn cut right to Kieran, falling into step. "What's the plan?"

What he was really asking: *Should we let Lexi kill any fae she comes across?*

If she didn't, Kieran damn well would. It was time to ensure the fae knew they were *not* welcome here. As far as Kieran was concerned, it was time they figured out a way to not just monitor the portals but destroy them altogether.

"Leave the humans alive, but make it *very* clear that if

they speak one word about our crossing, we'll make them sorry. I'll want information from them when we get back."

Zorn nodded and peeled off to the side, motioning for Henry and Amber to accompany him. They were the best at shutting people up in a very short amount of time.

"Hey there." An attendant sauntered toward Kieran as another headed to greet Lexi, their eyes scanning Kieran and Lexi's people.

Kieran had only brought their inner crew, nearly a dozen people. Even that might be too many. They needed to get through the Faegate and then through Faerie without drawing too much attention. No one would've stayed home, though. Not even Mordecai. He'd threatened to come on his own if they didn't take him.

It was for the best. This team, as it was, had a staggering diversity in magic and a gut punch of power. At the Demigod Summit every year, when they fought the crews of other Demigods, Kieran and Lexi's team dominated. They were masters at their various magical strengths, and they worked together better than anyone else in the magical world. Individual Celestials might have more power, but they weren't family. Not like Kieran and his team. They wouldn't be as effective. Kieran wholeheartedly believed that. They all did.

Soon they'd be proving it.

"You folks magical?" the attendant asked, bracing his hands on his hips and squinting against the glare of the sun.

"Babe," Kieran called to Lexi. "This man has a question for you." Kieran stepped around him and headed for the wagons. Lexi's magic was ten times scarier than Kieran's. She'd get the point across way more effectively.

"Yes, we're magical," Lexi said, anger blistering through the magical bond she and Kieran shared, forged in intimacy and strengthened over and over with love.

"Oh well, I'm sorry to say, you can't pass through here. This portal is for—"

He let out a high-pitched scream as Lexi's magic whipped out. Kieran knew she was slicing through his middle, raking against the very foundation of his being. It was a terrifying and painful feeling, a primal fear that no one could be prepared for. Even training against it didn't fully chase away the complete and utter vulnerability it caused.

"We can't pass through here?" She stopped in front of him and stood over his cowering form. "You let *fae* pass through here—"

He continued on. Donovan, the sun highlighting his blond hair, led two horses toward the wagons. Dylan and Boman led two more. None of the horses wanted Mordecai near them. That was the problem with being a wolf shape-shifter.

"We definitely need to shut all this down." Thane met Kieran near the wagons. "We shouldn't have been blind to this."

"No, we shouldn't have. Nor should we have been complacent about the portals on the magical side."

Hindsight.

With the others readying the supplies, Kieran filled

the doorway of the cashier station and found a female attendant shaking on the ground behind the counter. She could hear the screaming from the attendants Lexi was using to make an impression. A man huddled against the wall, in the middle of purchasing supplies. Various items and tags lay strewn about the counter.

"Rounded ears," Thane said, looking around Kieran. "Human. Non-magical, too, or else they wouldn't be serving him."

Kieran stepped in and grabbed the man by the shirt. He hoisted the man up the wall, holding all his weight with one hand. A Demigod's excess strength sometimes scared Chesters more than magic.

"Why are you here?" Kieran asked in a growl.

"I—I...I...I..." The man was reduced to sobs. "My h-house. I want m-my house b-back." He heaved, retching into the air. "D-d-deal. M-make a d-deal. I-I got passage. I-I-I got p-passage."

"To where?"

"R-Ruby kingdom. *Rubў!* Please. P-please, don't hurt me."

Kieran lowered him an inch, looking back at Thane. Kieran knew the names of all seven kingdoms—eight, including the overarching Diamond kingdom—and their affinities for the natural elements of Faerie, having studied with Zorn the moment he'd heard they might have a fae problem. This was the first he'd heard of fae infiltrators from the Ruby kingdom, their element aligned with fire.

He wasn't sure what they'd wanted with Daisy, only

knowing it had something to do with those magical stone and crystal items, but other factions of fae were working their way into the human realm for different reasons. This guy had gotten passage, and that had to be granted by royalty. Fae were looking for desperate humans with which to barter. The gods only knew what they wanted.

Shivers washed over Kieran at that thought. Whatever it was, it couldn't be good for the human realm.

"Only a fool barters with fae," Kieran told him, dropping him to the ground. "You might get your house back, only to realize you unknowingly granted them to stay, as well. Or something much, *much* worse. Dealing with their kind never ends well. Now get out of here. This portal is closed."

Kieran stood back. When the man didn't move, Kieran gave him a light kick in the thigh. The man started, scrambled up, then went running.

"What could fae want with a magic-less human?" Thane asked as Kieran stepped out again. He didn't bother sparing a word for the cashier. Either the other attendants would fill her in, or Zorn would be in shortly to handle it. Lexi had done the heavy lifting.

"Same thing as Daisy?"

"Right, but what did they want with Daisy? We all handled those chalices or whatever they were. Why her specifically?"

"The easiest way to get information on us?"

Thane shook his head as Kieran followed one of the wagons around to the back. "None of the fae have had any interest in our territory or our faction. Can't be that.

When they worked with Demigod Lydia, they dealt with her directly. They made a deal, she forfeited, and they rummaged through her memories before they killed her. They don't have much fear of Demigods, so why choose a magic-less Chester who didn't work in our office and didn't have access to all our secrets?"

Kieran was at a loss. "I really have no idea. None. The fae in this world don't make any sense, other than if it's to collect magical items. That, at least, has some logic to it—an end game. Dealing with that Chester in there? What's the point?"

Thane scrubbed his hand through his unruly hair as they heard a voice from off to the side. Mordecai, staying quiet and out of the way. Suffering from his grief for his sister. He'd stay reserved until needed, and then he would dominate. That was his way.

"A toy," Mordecai murmured. "Non-magical humans make great toys. They can't fight back. They aren't as dangerous as magical people."

He was quiet for a beat as Lexi passed, arguing with three ghosts from home. They wanted to come along.

When she was again out of earshot, Mordecai continued.

"They made a mistake with Daisy, though." He pushed off the side of the cashier building. "Daisy isn't less dangerous than magical people. Because of her upbringing and constantly having to assess the danger around her and find a way to kill it before it kills her, she's ten times *more* dangerous than magical people. Than you, Demigod Kieran. Than even Lexi. She's at home in the shadows, has no moral hang-ups where survival is concerned, and knows how to manipulate people, spy, and play games. She won't ever break. Not ever. She won't give them the satisfaction. If there is one human in all the world they *shouldn't* bring into Faerie, it is my sister. She'll burn that place to the ground and wonder why we took so long to show up and join her in dancing around the flames."

Chapter Six

Daisy

"Come on, you stupid human," said Curvy Woman.

I'm Revana, she murmured, pulling Daisy roughly down the dark tunnel on the left. *Gorlan said to tell you how gross that spit was, and he does not appreciate it.*

"I can't see, you fucking idiots. How am I supposed to walk?" Daisy gritted out, resuming looking at the walls and thinking of the horrors that might await there. Then thinking of her captors and how hard it was to stop herself from falling to the ground and sobbing.

Kayla and Revana hoisted her up, carrying her. It was not at all comfortable, so Daisy grunted and squirmed until they had her in a better hold that didn't yank at her shoulders so much.

Don't take it personally, Kayla said. *About Tarian. He*

disappears into the creature he needs to be to survive this court. He has to battle harder than we do to keep the twisted magic from infiltrating his mind. It's not an easy feat when you feel it as often as he does. The royals—the princess, especially—plague him.

We are sitting down to a game of chess, Daisy thought in that way Kayla had described. Her body twisted weirdly, and it looked like she was trying to moonwalk in the air, her legs dangling as the females carried her. Why the hell couldn't she think quietly like (apparently) a normal person? *I would expect him to play his part correctly, so that I might play mine.*

You can think more freely now, Revana thought. *Anyone powerful enough to possess the mindgazer magic won't be in these tunnels. And if they are, they are easily spotted. Tarian said you have a distinct eye for human fashion—*

He sounded very impressed by that, Kayla murmured. *He loves human fashion.*

If that is true, Revana went on, *you should be able to notice the finer attire here. Those who wear it have gold and status. They will be more powerful, more prestigious, and crueler. Try not to gain their notice.*

Only the more powerful half of the court has the mindgazer magic, Kayla said.

Yes. If you see someone with less quality attire, you may be safe in assuming they cannot hear your thoughts. Soon, hopefully, you'll learn to block your thoughts. Tarian thinks the chalice magic should make you powerful enough to do so, even against the royals.

And your crew? Daisy asked.

Are an exception, Kayla said. *An exception the true nature of which no one knows. To them, we are the Thornborn, a rough and hardy group of kin that exists on the outskirts of fae society. They live in the wylds on the borders of this kingdom and the mountain ranges of the Topaz kingdom. We found some of them working here, as hired muscle, mostly. They took us in when the gods stripped us of all that we are.*

A pale blue glow interrupted the darkness, and a putrid smell hit Daisy like a wall. Her stomach churned. It was a combination of damp stone and mold, stale body, and decay and rot. She shut down her senses as the glow grew into a dim magical light that washed over a cramped space filled with strange contraptions. They appeared to be intended for physical suffering, and she wanted to inspect each one, curious to see what they did. How creative fae got with torture.

Beyond, the area opened into a narrow hall two stories high. Cells existed on each side, and darkness waited through the rusted bars. At the top were more cells, and one had long, spindly fingers curving around the bars.

"Lovely," Daisy murmured. Her stomach fluttered. She'd never been kept in a genuine dungeon before. Zorn had tossed her into a jail cell or two and left her there for a couple days to sleep on the floor and use a bucket for waste, but that hadn't held a candle to this. It hadn't had the smell, the splatter of dried and cracking blood, the pockets of midnight with strange species wasting away inside. It hadn't had an utter lack of safety like this. Zorn had trained her, but he'd never hurt her. The new Tarian and the dungeon masters of this place presented a different situation.

She let out a very slow breath as fear threatened to overwhelm her.

There is no point wasting one's last moments to fear, she said to herself.

But these weren't her last moments. Not by far. She'd need to endure this. If things went bad, death wouldn't quickly embrace her; first would be pain. Incredible, horrible pain.

She pulled in a deep breath and let it out again. Her goal was not to break. No matter what happened, she couldn't break. Survival meant keeping an intact mind. Pain was merely a device to alert a person that they were still alive. If it came to it, she'd have to remember that pain was living. Living was protecting her family. She could do this.

A stooped figure with wispy white hair falling down to its mid-chest waited along the wall. Wrinkles sagged along the arms and overlapped at the neck. Its face was lost to shadow, even though the rest of its body was visible in the dim lighting. That shadow had to be magically created.

"Prisoner," Kayla told the creature in a rough voice.

The creature shook, as though it were being electrocuted, before raising a bone-thin arm and pointing down the tunnel into the blackness beyond.

"No!" Revana barked. "This is a human. They require a window or they will wither. His Highness Tari-anthiel Drystan Windryker's orders. He needs it alive for the court games."

The creature started to shake again. Its voice came out like a wave of insects skittering over a dusty stone floor. "But if it lives, it will kill us all."

"Even if that weren't preposterous," Kayla replied fiercely, "if you don't do what His Highness asks, you'll be dead long before a human can bring down an entire court."

The creature stalled for a long moment, and then the shaking elicited a new finger point, this one aiming higher. Somewhere above, a loud click preceded the whine of hinges.

The females didn't react. They turned Daisy, still carrying her, and headed for a set of narrow, curving steps.

That has to be the chalice magic, Revana said, her mental voice uneasy. *That creature has been lost to the blight for some time. It senses Daisy's danger. The chalice's danger.*

Kayla's fingers tightened on Daisy's arms with unease. *We need to let Tarian know. He hasn't prepared for that.*

Do fae not know much about humans, then? Daisy asked, collecting each scrap of information she could.

Most fae know almost nothing, Revana said, looking to the right as they reached the top of the stairwell. They took her left, though, to an opened cell door down the way. *They'll think you are weak and useless and, because of that, that you can die easily. We'll use that for as long as we can. Once you start killing fae in the games, we'll need to pivot.*

If she started killing fae in the games. There was that small issue of magic. They had some. She did not. And while in the human world she could get around some of it, she had no idea about fae magic. She didn't know any of the nuances or how to combat it. She was flying blind when up against life and death. It was far from the best-case scenario.

They walked her into the dank cell. A barred window at the top of the high ceiling let in a sliver of bluish moonlight. A flat stone slab lay at an angle with manacles attached to chains. The females walked her to it before turning her and pushing her against it. They fastened the manacles and pushed the stone so she was essentially lying down.

Toilets? she asked with very little hope.

Kayla shook her head, lips pinched. She didn't elaborate.

Food? Daisy tried. *Water?*

One of us will deliver it when it is safe, Revana replied. *Remember, do not eat what they give you. They won't push. You'll be hungry and thirsty until we can get you out of here. We just need to get some things ready. We can't release you to the main floor until we can hide your thoughts.*

Kayla reached into Daisy's shirt with a regretful look before pulling out her knife. *If we leave this with you, they'll take it. We'll keep it until it's safe for you to carry it.*

Daisy let her gaze drift away from the two females as they finished up. She closed her eyes when the heavy metal cell door clanged shut. Silence replaced their retreating footsteps. They hadn't said goodbye.

Fear and panic fuzzed the edges of her mind, but she focused on her breathing. She let her mind drift elsewhere. She sank into the homesickness for her family so that she had at least something familiar to think about. Then she tried to sleep.

Babbling brought her quickly to consciousness. The screaming on the lower level didn't trouble her anymore. It had started an hour into her stay and persisted. They were busy with someone down there, but it wasn't her. While part of her recoiled at the thought of what was going on, the need to survive won out. She let it drift through and away from her mind. Now that clawing sound was no more than a hoarse groan, the voice gone but the poor bastard not yet dead.

The metal latch on her cell opened. Two creatures came through, humanoid but lopsided, and they mostly hobbled toward her. Their faces were lost to the shadow, like the creature down below. Definitely some sort of magical phenomenon. Weak light filtered in through the window above, highlighting parts of her cell she wished might stay hidden. Violence had been done in here.

The first creature reached her. Dirt and grime smeared its arm and something dull and black glistened in patches on its skin. Obsidian?

It yanked the stone slab to mostly vertical. She slid down to her feet.

"What's this?" it asked the other, its voice creaky, like an old, forgotten rocking chair pushed by the wind.

"Ah. The human. They brought one in last night," the other said, its voice similar. They both wore dirty, holey frocks in flat black.

The first grunted. "Him Highness wants something different, them says. This is something different. It looks good. Him wants a female. This is female."

"Yeah, but..." The second scratched its head with long, broken nails. "This belongs to Him Highness Tarianthiel. Can't you see the magic mark? I can see the mark."

"Him Highness, the king, don't care about Tarianthiel mark. That curse magic don't work on royals. Them can take what them want. Tarianthiel can't hurt they. Magic stop him. This one will work."

"What about it being intact?" the second said. "Him Highness wants one intact, them says."

The other froze. "I'll check. Maybe Tarianthiel didn't get there yet. That why he put it in here, maybe? To keep it from the guards."

The first grunted as the second moved in front of Daisy. It reached for the button on her pants, and she knew a moment of blind terror. A conversation she'd had with Tarian flashed through her memory.

"Otherwise you'd be used by the royals and then their guards. A pretty human, such as yourself, won't go unnoticed. I'd end up having to kill half the palace when coming to your aid."

"I wouldn't live long enough," she'd ground out, her whole body burning in anger. *"The first person to touch me would die, and they'd surely have me executed shortly thereafter."*

Daisy bent her wrists to grab the chains of her shackles. She'd tested them last night. They'd be long enough to yank forward and wrap around this thing's neck.

Her logic trickled back in slowly. These things wouldn't be the ones indulging. They were trying to recruit her for their king, and *intact female* surely meant virginal. She didn't fit the criteria, thank fuck. They wouldn't be taking her. If she killed one right now, it would very likely result in a worse situation than ignoring them checking her out. It wasn't pretty, but neither were gynecology appointments.

She gritted her teeth as her pants were tugged down. Her brain filled with murderous rage. She yanked against the shackles as the creature prodded. It took everything in her power not to reach forward and wrap the metal around the thing's neck. Instead, she waited, surviving the violation so she would live to fight another day. Someday soon.

It muttered, "Filthy humans."

Like it could fucking talk. *How about a bath, bub? Maybe a comb and laundry service.*

The creature backed away, leaving her clothing as it was.

"No," it grunted, turning for the cell door. "It's busted."

She nearly blurted out a laugh at that.

"There might be some fresh ones—" Its voice was drowned out by the clang of her cell door.

Daisy refused to let shivers of disgust envelop her. She'd dodged a bullet. If anyone ever tried to slut-shame her, she'd recall this instance right here. Sexual awakening for the win.

The vigor of Mr. Screamer below had renewed. Or maybe that was someone else. Regardless, she pushed her hunger away and let her head loll, closing her eyes again. She used this time to go over, in minute detail, all Tarian had relayed to her about this place. Everything she knew about the fae and the wylds. Everything she knew about fae, period. She might not be great at shielding her mind, but she was excellent at distracting herself with a whirlwind of thoughts.

Because of that, it seemed like no time had passed when she heard her cell door open again. More light trickled in through the window, but she couldn't judge what time of day that might mean. Lennox was the first to walk through, his hair cascading down the shaved sides of his head in a glorious, loose wave. His beard was tied with a fresh toggle, this one showing a sun design. He'd had time for a shower. And probably food. And water. Fuck, she was thirsty.

He halted, his gaze on her pants. Well, that was embarrassing. Her stripteases were usually voluntary.

He was shoved forward but hardly budged. Kayla came out from behind him, and her eyes lit with fire. Her step didn't hitch, though. If anything, she got slinkier as she walked, like a predator sighting its prey.

Chapter Seven

DAISY

Are you okay? she asked Daisy, stopping right in front of her. Her eyes jogged back and forth between Daisy's. She must've been reading the memory of what had happened and known the relief mixed with blind rage Daisy was feeling. Daisy had escaped, but some other poor female probably had not. She waited, though, for Daisy to answer. She was allowing Daisy to have a voice about the situation.

Warmth filled Daisy's middle at the care and attention. She was not treating Daisy like a prisoner, but as an equal female. It was...endearing. It thawed Daisy's built-in mistrust of strangers a little.

Yeah, she said, nodding to accentuate her answer. *They weren't looking for me.*

Kayla nodded as well before lifting her hands to the manacles. *Lennox has turned around. Go ahead and fix your clothes, and then we'll go.*

The manacles popped open without a lock, Kayla's magic releasing them. Daisy pushed forward to stand on her own before adjusting everything. When she was done, Kayla split the flat black, robe-like cloth she wore to reveal crisscrossing straps and weapons across a slick black leotard. She pulled out Daisy's knife and handed it over.

Hide it, she said. *Quickly.*

Daisy didn't waste any time, and Kayla stepped away before grabbing Daisy's upper arm. She yanked Daisy toward Lennox, who glanced over and reached out to take the other.

Just one arm, Daisy said, pulling away from Lennox. *It'll make me look like less of a threat.*

Kayla glanced at Lennox, who paused before stepping away.

Sorry about...you know, Lennox said as they started walking. *Staring, I mean. I wasn't...looking. I was dumbfounded by the level of rage that hit me. I froze. It was a shitty reaction. I'm sorry about that.*

Kayla shook her head and spat to the side. *This court is diseased from the top down. We're running out of time to make a difference. At this rate, we'll have to kill the entire court to keep the twisted magic from bringing down Faerie.*

Daisy kept from looking around, her gaze directed

straight or a little elevated. She didn't want to put a face to Mr. Screamer or know what else went on in that dungeon. She didn't want to know what she'd possibly face.

They didn't go back the way they'd come, nor did she see any dungeon personnel. The tunnels opened up, and the smell receded. The dim blue lighting turned into orbs of various colors, contained in beautiful sconces bolted to the walls or dropping from arching ceilings. Bright sunlight streamed through rows of windows.

Farther still and the ceiling continued to rise. Stone was now painted or wallpapered, adorned with weaving black designs or shiny obsidian. Fae dressed in a similar garb as Kayla and Lennox hurried on their way, heads down and hands often full with chamber pots or water pitchers or something else indicating they were at work.

Kayla jerked Daisy this way and that as they walked, as if annoyed with her. She fell into the treatment, a mask of fearful fretting on her face and an occasional tear rolling down her cheek. All the while she took in every detail, every servant rushing by.

Up a flight of stairs and they stopped in front of double doors in a stone frame. Lennox opened the door and Kayla shoved Daisy inside.

Your mind is safe in here, she said, following.

Three cots lay spaced out within the room. Couches and cushions lined one wall and a rack of various instruments lined the other. A short bookcase made of metal scrollwork leaned against the back wall.

A fae with a deeply lined face and wearing a black

apron advanced from the side wall. His hair was cut short except in the front, which fell across his forehead. His dark eyes surveyed Daisy before he looked at the others.

"What have we here?" he said in a light, playful voice.

"His Highness Tarianthiel requests the mind *shiv* be applied to his slave," Lennox said haughtily.

Shiv? Daisy asked. *That means shank in the human lands. Is that what it means here?*

Kayla wandered a couple steps away and turned, sparing a quick and confused glance at Daisy's face before going back to acting like she was bored. *What's a* shank? *Never mind, it doesn't matter. This male will apply a barrier over your mind so that your thoughts will stay within. Your wandering thoughts, I mean. You can think—we can explain later. This will protect your mind.*

"Does he now?" Bangs said, pursing his lips as he looked Daisy over again. "What is it, a human? Why would he want to spend his gold on a human? Surely her mind will be cracked open by someone powerful, anyway. This is a waste of time."

Lennox stepped closer to the male, his size dwarfing the other. "Whether it is or it isn't doesn't matter. He wants it done. Do you intend to resist?"

Bangs quailed, shrinking. "No, of course not. I just wondered what secrets a human might know that he'd want to protect, that's all. It seems outlandish. No matter. I'll do it. Let me get prepared." He gestured at the first cot. "Place her there and strap her down."

Daisy couldn't help a nervous glance at Lennox as

Kayla grabbed her upper arm again. She yanked Daisy forward, shoving her toward the cot.

"Lie down, human. We haven't got all day."

This is going to hurt like hell, Kayla said with no remorse. *It's necessary. Stay strong. Pain sharpens the senses.*

Lennox pushed down on the center of Daisy's back, her stomach on the cot. Kayla began strapping her in.

This is a temporary fix, Lennox said. *It'll buy you time, nothing more. Once it is solidified in your mind, you will need to train in earnest to protect your thoughts. Tarian has a device to help. He's confident it won't take you long. If it does, we'll need to reapply this magic. The more you do it, the more it negatively impacts your mind. Once is really the most you'll want to contaminate yourself.*

"What the fuck?" she muttered, thrashing against the newly buckled straps. Part of that was for show. Only part. *Just give me time with the device. I'm sure I can do it quicker than he thinks I can. I don't want to contaminate even a bit of my mind. I need it. It's all I have.*

You'll be okay, Kayla said. *Once almost never messes anyone up.*

And my inability to fly really high without magical help was a surprise, too. Let's not do this.

They tensed, not having thought this through, but then Bangs was leaning over her. She couldn't see the contraption in his hands, but she felt it when he put it on the back of her neck. Her whole body jolted from the pressure. Pain seeped into her, winding through her blood and wrapping around her bones. It traveled to the very edges of her limbs and back before crawling up the back of her throat and forcing a scream. Her hair follicles tingled and the back of her neck was on fire. It burned like actual flame, and she could imagine it blackening her skin and shriveling it away. Next her brain started to sizzle, inch by inch, until the agony nearly made her black out.

She didn't know how long it went on or if she screamed the whole time. Eventually, it ended. The pressure eased and the pain with it. Her body still convulsed against the straps, but numbness had thankfully started to spread. Or maybe that was just the absence of pain.

"What..." Bangs still leaned over her but had put the contraption onto the ground beside the cot. He pushed her hair away from the back of her neck. "What is this?"

She breathed heavily as Lennox and Kayla approached the cot.

A finger brushed against the back of her neck, right near her hairline. Surprisingly, it didn't hurt, as though what he'd done wasn't surface level. It meant her skin hadn't burned away after all. That was good news.

Shit! Kayla exclaimed. *Fuck, Lennox, what do we do?*

What is it? Daisy asked.

A nail scratched at her neck, light at first, then harder.

Lennox bent to undo the straps.

"But...this can't be..." Bangs said hesitantly.

"It's a trick of the light," Lennox said as Kayla blurted, "It'll settle into black. It's because she's human."

Bangs leaned back as Lennox finished. His eyes narrowed. "Well, which is it? A trick of the light, or because she is human?" He tsked. "I think it is something else. What is His Groveling *Highness* really up to here? This isn't just a human, is it? Where did you get this creature? The wylds? Is it twisted and therefore a more effective human? It's no secret that simpering fool wants to kill the royalty and take their place but can't because of the magic locking him in his station. The whole court laughs about it. Is this his solution?"

Kill him, Lennox thought forcefully. *Quickly—*

Daisy popped up, the loosened straps falling away. She was on Bangs before his eyes widened. Had her hands in the right places before he could start. Delighted in the vicious *crack* before anyone had made a move to stop or help or shriek in surprise.

Bangs's lifeless body slid to the ground.

Kayla and Lennox looked on with rounded mouths and raised eyebrows. Both had also frozen, Kayla with her hands held out.

Daisy panted, shakily sitting down on the cot. Her body was still jittery and her brain felt fuzzy from the treatment.

"What was that about?" she asked, her voice hoarse from screaming. She wiped sweat from her forehead.

"The gods smite me, human." A crooked smile worked at Kayla's lips. "You're quick to kill, huh?"

Daisy frowned at the fae. "Isn't that what you

wanted? Lennox said *quickly*. I assumed that meant quickly. As in fast. As in *get it done*. What's the problem? I'm hoping it isn't that my thoughts will stay fuzzy for the rest of my life. That'll fuck us all in this venture."

Lennox huffed out a laugh and bent over to grab Bangs. "Tarian said she was vicious for a human. I didn't think that meant she was on par with a fae. That'll be useful."

"Bloody right it will." Kayla donned a full-fledged smile before it withered. Her expression took on a perplexed look. "We'd planned to mark you for Tarian, but...that can't happen now. You'll have to make a show in the court to get the point across."

"Why? What's going on?"

Kayla stepped behind her and brushed her hair out of the way. She pushed Daisy's head forward.

"The procedure we did tends to leave marks at the base of the hairline, at the back of the neck. That's how you can tell it has worked and for how long it will work. If the marks start to fade, that means the magic protecting your thoughts is fading. Given it is applied by someone with unseelie, obsidian magic, the markings show up black. Like our markings and Tarian's. But your markings..."

"Aren't ink," Lennox finished. "They look like... diamond dust. Not even the Celestials have markings like that. Theirs are golden. I've..." He swallowed thickly. "I've never heard of this. We need to consult Tarian."

"Oh super," Daisy said dryly. "One more way I'll stand out in this place."

Kayla nodded. "I'll get rid of the body. You get her some food and water and then take her back to the dungeon. The magic won't fully solidify for a sun's turn. Threaten those fucking guards while you're there, Lennox. If she is taken to the king, we're all fucked."

Chapter Eight

Daisy

The day waned. Her mind had cleared somewhat, but a huge, throbbing headache persisted. Her head felt like it was glued onto her neck poorly. When she moved it, it felt creaky and like it was about to fall off. Her belly was full, at least. Before Lennox took her back, he'd given her a heavenly loaf of bread covered in the finest cheese she'd ever tasted, drizzled with something that tasted somewhat like honey. With it, he'd set out hunks of meat so tender she could pull it from the bone and suck the juices from her fingers. None of it tasted exactly like what she was used to in the human world and was presumably various types of fae animals, but it didn't matter. It was rich and filling and delicious.

Lennox had tilted the stone slab until it was almost

flat, but she hadn't been able to sleep much. Each time someone walked by her cell, they'd rake something metal across the bars. The racket gave her no peace, even if she was successful in ignoring the latest screamer.

Now, as the light slowly disappeared from her cell, she was startled out of a fitful doze. Her cell door whined as it opened. Her heart kicked up its pace, and she rolled her head to the side to see who was coming. Deep shadow obscured her view, like a solid black haze covering whoever walked within it.

Beyond it, in the hallway just outside her cell, a broken and grotesque body had a hook shoved down its throat and protruding from its ribcage. The skin was torn away to show the metal, and the insides of the ruined stomach dripped onto the floor. Limbs were snapped and dangled strangely. An arm was severed, and fingers littered the ground. The sign around its neck read, *I touched Tarianthiel's property.*

It was the guard who had "checked" her for the king. Its face was no longer obscured and almost seemed like a wax sculpture after too much heat.

She licked her lips, bending her wrists to capture the chains. It was the only weapon she had for whatever was entering her cell—the other's friend seeking vengeance, perhaps.

Easy, little dove. The familiar voice was like a gentle lick in her mind.

At once, her whole body relaxed. The nervous breath gushed out of her.

The black haze peeled away from that handsome face and regal, stoic bearing. He was refined brutality.

Tarian drew up beside her, his hand reaching out for the top of the slab. He pulled, straightening her until her feet hit the ground. Then he stepped in front of her, and the black haze filled the cell around them, once only obscuring him from view and now obscuring them both. No gold shimmered within. The dawn-light colors were totally absent, his magic cloaked in midnight.

His brilliant green eyes shone brightly, even in the gloom. The gold within had bled away to jet black, increasing the size of his pupils. None of his Celestial magic was present, giving way to pure unseelie magic.

In response to her observations, he said, *I am forced to use their obsidian magic and dance with the corrosion forever tugging at me. It tries to steal all sense of goodness and toss me up to the court to relish in their torment. My thoughts are dark when in this court. Carnal. You are an allure I can barely withstand. That I wish to twist and corrupt, to fuck and ruin. I have never wanted anything so badly in my life.*

His eyes roamed her face, and part of her wondered why she wasn't terrified of this change in him. Of this new creature that visited her in the dungeon and was pushing ever closer in his want.

But the other part knew why—she'd always been terrified of him...and not. Afraid of his kind but not really of him. This creature before her seemed dark and depraved, volatile and wicked, but she had the same depravity lurking within her. It was what Zorn had always seen, it matching his. She realized that with Tarian, she was comfortable dancing in the flames. Let him show her his worst, and she'd laugh as she matched his stride.

His smile was slow, and his breath fell across her lips, so close his heat chased away all the gaps between them. A punch of magic made her eyes water, the smell acidic, not like when he'd used it before. Her damp and dirty clothing from a moment ago was gone, replaced by a servant's attire, fresh and clean and dull black. She breathed out gratefully. Things had gotten pretty gross, but as far as she could tell, her body was just as clean as her clothes. She didn't understand this magic, but she was grateful for it.

His hands curled around the chains securing her. He lifted, raising her hands up above her head before using a thick black band of magic to secure them there.

"You look good enough to eat," he said, his fingers drifting down her arms. *I remember your taste, sweet and tangy.*

She closed her eyes as he leaned closer, not sure if anyone could hear them. Not sure how much she should give in.

Yes, they can hear us, he murmured, his lips drawing near her cheek. *And they are listening hard to glean any scrap of information they can to take back to the king and his minions. They do so love to damn me for my follies.*

He pulled back, his gaze washing across her face. Gold now fought the black in his eyes, turning and twisting around the pupil and flaring into the iris. Two magics at war. Two sides of him equally so.

And desiring a human to this magnitude, he went on, *is an enormous folly, one they must not uncover lest you become a target long before you've earned it.*

"If you touch me, I'll kill you," she said in as hard a voice as she could muster.

His laugh was rich and dark. "Hmm. That sounds like consent...with strings. I imagine you'll wait until after you orgasm, yes? But remember, little human—you are mine. My toy. To do with as I please. To break at my leisure."

His lips tracked across the side of her neck, and her eyes fluttered. She yanked at the manacles, shaking the chains as though trying to get free to push him away.

"Tell me, my treasure," he said. "Do you feel vulnerable? Or do you succumb to my allure like the fragile-minded human you are and feel only lust?"

His hand ran over her breast, his thumb swiping across the peak. She moaned despite herself—despite the game she was supposed to be playing in this twisted, fucked-up scenario. Then again, maybe that was perfect. Let them think she was lost to this fae's touch. That he controlled her mind. And maybe he did. Maybe he always had.

"That's right," he whispered, his lips grazing hers. "Give in to your tormenter. Soak in your depravity like a good little human."

His lips pressed down, and the taste of him swept her away. She pulled against the chains, wanting to free her hands and grab him. To yank him closer. She opened her mouth, and he filled it. His hand glided up her shirt, against her skin. His hard length rocked against her.

Her groan was tortured.

"Tell me, little human. Would you be disgusted if I fucked you in a prison cell?" He continued to rock against her. Her eyes fluttered as he did.

Her rebuttal was sultry and wanton. "If you try, you won't make it to sunrise."

"Hmm, delicious threats. Should we see if tonight will be my last?" He hiked her legs up to his hips to increase the friction.

The pleasure sizzled within her core. "Only someone deranged would consider fucking her jailor."

"Yes, and that is why you are so very fun, don't you see? You can't help but want me, your superior in every way. Your better. Try as you might, but you are unable to resist me. Now be a good pet and unravel for your jailor."

He rubbed against her harder. His fingers lightly pinched her nipple the way she liked, and his magic delved into her. All at once, the sensations were over-whelming. Incredible. She blasted apart, shuddering against him, loud in her climax. Supposed to hate him but unable to resist him, she would absolutely look weak and pitiful for this. The result was perfect, and thank the gods, because she didn't have much of a choice. Not with him. Not ever.

Same, he murmured, shaking against her, his breathing fractured. He'd been consumed by the game.

Now, quickly—mutter curses at me so I can check the mark on your neck.

She did as he said, leaning forward and twisting. He pushed her hair away, paused for a moment, and thought, *Fuck!*

When he leaned back, his eyes were searching hers. The image flashed into her mind: four pretty, intertwining symbols at the top of her neck that shimmered like a sea of tiny diamonds. They caught and threw the light into a gorgeous halo. A very noticeable halo. This was the wrong time to think of all the outfits it would work best with.

Fuck, he said again, his gaze filling with regret and remorse. He let go a breath. *I might have no choice but to fully claim you in front of the court. I had hoped a mark would make a big enough statement, but diamond dust speaks of prophecy. What prophecy? I don't know. I doubt anyone does. They have somewhat insane myths in this court based mostly on doom and destruction. Diamond dust is just one of many.*

He shook his head and stepped back, his physical words taunting and drifting into the background, because his mental words were something entirely different. Something that sounded distinctly like him and not the creature produced by this court.

I don't have time to figure it out, and it doesn't matter anyway, he ground out. *I didn't foresee this. I apologize. I'll... We'll...* He shook his head, flustered. *I am sorry for what happened to you here, dove. I have placed watchers to alert me if anything else should transpire. Endure this*

*place for a little longer. After that, we can move you. I just
need that mind-shield magic to take hold. Never, ever lift
up your hair. Not ever. Your safety depends on it.*

He swore again as he pushed her back to flat.

Fully claim her? In front of an audience? Didn't that
mean...

Blackness rushed in and stole her consciousness.

Chapter Nine

ALEXIS

"Frank, seriously, for the *last* time, you cannot come." Lexi faced him as the last of their new gear was being organized. His wispy hair arched over his mostly bald head, and lines creased his face. He'd known Lexi's mom way back in the day before she died...and he'd died. Now he hung around, occasionally helpful, usually not. "None of you can." She looked at John and Mia, two very useful spirits. "I can't reach spirit on the other side of that portal, and I have no idea what Faerie will be like. I have power in this world because of my magic here. Hades, lord of the underworld, grants that magic. He's not a god in Faerie. His domain ends here. My magic might, too."

"They have the Amethyst kingdom in Faerie," Mia murmured, picking at the big wooden button on her sweater from yesteryear. It was the one she'd died in, and she'd never decided to change her ghostly image. "Their affinity is for spirit."

Lexi frowned at her.

"I've been listening in on your and Kieran's planning and studies. I can't understand time anymore, but I can retain new information."

"Right..." Lexi hadn't noticed that Mia had been taking an active interest in all of this.

"If they have an affinity for spirit," said John, usually the commander of their undead army when they needed one, "they will have a setup for the afterlife. Hades was banished to the underworld here. He didn't create it, or so the legends say. You can traverse it because of *your* affinity with spirit. If we have fae in our underworld, they'll have humans in theirs. And if humans are admitted, you can traverse the spirit. It's only logical."

She lifted her eyebrows. That was, indeed, quite logical.

"Yeah," Frank said, not one of the real thinkers in this group.

"When did you all come up with this?" she asked.

"It's been somewhat peaceful for years now," John said. "We're bored."

They'd continually refused to go across the veil and find peace in the afterlife because of their devotion to Lexi and Kieran and their team. They could only speak to her and Kieran, but they were as much a part of the family as anyone. The others just didn't know it.

She sighed. "I can't guarantee your safety. The fae are

wicked and their gods are vicious and awful. Even in death, things might be...difficult for you. I can protect spirits here, but I don't know if I'll have that power there."

John chuckled, but it was Mia who spoke. "You didn't know Valens. He was as ruthless as those Faerie gods sound, and just as cunning. He wasn't even a god. He didn't have any compassion. Not like they must have to keep their world working. He was evil all the way through...and he had friends. Close friends. Those friends are quiet now that you've been blessed by Hades, but they aren't gone. I remember hearing all about them when I eavesdropped. The Demigods of old weren't as reined in as they are today. They didn't do truces or give quarter—"

"Your dad killed all his kids except you," John told Lexi.

Mia nodded earnestly. "I don't think we'll be any worse off over there. If we are, you'll fix it. You always do."

Lexi shook her head. "No, you don't understand—"

"I'll take my chances," John said forcefully. "Dying has to be more of a shock than changing locations while already dead."

"As a man who has changed many locations, I can attest." Frank nodded, his hands on his hips. He didn't seem to have a handle on the crux of the conversation.

Lexi bowed in resignation. "Fine. Do not blame me if this goes tits up."

"Oh, it will absolutely go tits up." John grinned.

"That's what's fun about working for you. You're very inventive when you're under pressure."

Most people didn't understand why she was every bit as protective of spirits—of ghosts—as she was of people. That was because they didn't understand her magic. Her duty to the spirit world.

She wondered if the fae had anyone like her. They had a whole kingdom with an affinity for spirit, like Mia had said, but was it the same thing? Protectors? Guardians of souls? She'd never voice her curiosity. That she wanted to visit and speak with them, just to see.

"Right, let's get cracking." She clapped once and headed away from the structures selling animals and merchandise. A hundred feet away, off on its own, a collection of weathered boards encircled a large area big enough for a horse-drawn carriage to fit. The air within it was waving lines of purplish haze, billowing like smoke that disappeared ten feet up. The portal, obviously.

Kieran met her there, all business until she was beside him. Then he turned to her and his hands fell around her face. His eyes delved into hers, and she could feel the concern through their bond.

"How are you?" he asked softly.

She steeled herself, willing her lip to stop trembling. "Hanging in there. If I could just feel her through spirit and know she's okay..." She leaned against him. He was always so confident and strong. So sure of himself and the situation. "I feel responsible. I should've—"

"We all do," he cut in, not letting her devolve into the self-loathing and despair that had plagued her since

Daisy's abduction. He held her close. "Every single one of us is responsible for this, me most of all. I have a duty to protect my family, and I failed. But baby, I promise, we *will* get her back. All she has to do is stay alive. If she can just stay alive, we'll get her back. The fae think their twisted magic is all-powerful, but that's because Demigods have always had a history of steering clear of them—those of us smart enough not to get shackled with a deal. There are two of us and a team of level five magical workers. They won't know what hit them. We'll get her back, and we'll close these portals forever."

She nodded into his chest.

"Now..." He pulled back to look into her eyes. "It's time for war. Are you ready?"

She took a deep breath. Daisy needed her strength. "Yes."

Kieran and Thane led the group into the portal. If something was waiting on the other side, they'd encounter a Demigod and a level five Berserker capable of laying waste to anyone and everyone in his path. Lexi's huge cats bounded up to her. Each about as big as a Great Dane, they had magical powers of the Hades line, a special gift created in a somewhat gross way. They'd been kept in the cars until the last minute so as not to spook the horses.

Given there wasn't a threat in the portal area, Lexi, the spirits, and the cats went next, grimacing as the magic raked through her body and across her skin. Winds tore at her and the pressure nearly snapped her spine...

Then she was walking into a similar place. Stables

waited off to the sides with horses tied to wooden posts. A sheep *baa*'ed somewhere behind a building that looked like a house. An attendant in the same uniform as the one on the other side had stopped, holding a horse by the lead and staring at Kieran with wide eyes.

"Made it this far," John murmured as he, Mia, and a stark-faced Frank staggered out of the portal. "We could only make it through while clinging to you, Lexi. Remember that within the next phase."

"What..." Lexi looked around in confusion. She'd expected a wasteland with barren ground and dirt for miles. Instead, it was a somewhat cultivated area with dried grasses, trees, wildflowers in the distance, and a garden harboring a pop of colorful flowers. This didn't seem like a halfway human area at all. Were they already in the fae lands? But no, they couldn't be, because it was a very obviously scared human cowering under Kieran's questioning.

Mordecai and Dylan came through next.

"This is it?" Dylan asked in surprise.

"Come on," Kieran said, motioning for Lexi to get moving. "Let's get out of the way for the others."

"What is this place?" Lexi asked as they followed his lead.

"Human lands but not. Whatever that means. This doesn't look like what the texts suggest, and the attendant says this is normal." He looked back at the portal. "We need to leave him here. There are a couple groups of fae in front of us. Apparently, at the other end near the Faegate, there is another portal through which to send the animals back here. At night, when things are usually quiet, the attendants send the livestock and supplies to the place we just came from. It's...quite a system."

"It's some bullshit," Thane said. "Some real fucking bullshit."

Lexi couldn't agree more.

"Huh," Bria said after she came through, the last of them. She pulled a cart of bodies behind her. "This is pleasant."

"The portal wasn't that pleasant," Jerry said, able to move anything to do with rock. Two of them rolled beside him, as part of his arsenal.

"Meh." Bria shrugged, hitching her cart to the back of a wagon. "Try burying yourself alive. *That* isn't pleasant."

"Why..." Jerry cocked his head with an alarmed expression. "Why would you...? How did you...?"

She waved him away. "I wanted to see what it was like. The pipe didn't give me as much oxygen as I would've liked that far down, but it's fine. It all worked out. Okay then, we have"—she checked her empty wrist and looked at the sky—"some amount of hours until sundown. We best get a move on."

Lexi rode on the wagon's driver's box with Kieran, at the front of their caravan. They followed a large dirt path through the trees, the terrified attendant telling them to follow it all the way to the Faegate, not veer off, or they might never find their way back. So he'd heard, anyway.

It could just be a fae tactic to keep him put, not that he needed any convincing.

The sun sank toward the horizon as the vegetation grew sparse, and then sparser still. It might become a wasteland yet. That wasn't what interested Lexi, though. The Line pulsed beside her. Along the path, within the trees, wandering aimlessly, were a plethora of spirits. Animals, fae, and human, they were all mixed together in this strange way station between the living worlds. It had been created without thought of the dead. No one had set up a place for spirits to go. The veil didn't lead anywhere, empty save for Frank, Mia, and John riding within it. Once a living being died here...here they stayed. Trapped.

"Now, *this* is the life," Frank said as they floated along, looking out with a pleasant smile. "We're not being dragged, or yanked, or pushed, or flung—no, no, we're riding in style. I feel like royalty." He preened.

Lexi glared at him as John rolled his eyes.

"This is horrible," Lexi said.

"It reminds me of the house Valens trapped us in," John said, his eyes haunted. "I take it back. I'm not so inclined to take my chances."

"Too late now," Kieran murmured, his eyes flitting from spirit to spirit. Someone stood in the middle of the path, stooped over and bending to the side, watching them bear down on him. A creature walked along the side of the wagon, drool running over its long fangs, watching Lexi as though it were still alive and hunting them like prey.

"What's that?" Bria popped her head out through the opening at the back of the wagon, between Kieran and Lexi.

Lexi scooted over and explained what she was seeing.

"Okay, hear me out." Bria tried to crawl out farther. Someone grumbled within the wagon. "Well, if you weren't sitting so close, *Jerry*, I wouldn't accidentally kick you." She resumed speaking to Lexi. "What if we throw a couple of those fae into a body or two and see what damage they're capable of? I bet we could figure out their magic, and then we'd know a little of what we're getting into in the fae lands."

Lexi started to shake her head. She didn't like forcing spirits to do things they didn't want to, like inhabit a rotting body.

But Kieran said, "It isn't a bad idea, Lexi. It's not like they'd be any worse off than they are now. And you could try to march the spirit-filled cadavers into Faerie and release them there if you wanted. Let them go to their afterlife, whatever that might be."

The creature at the side of the wagon lunged for the nearest horse, twice its size. Lexi flinched. The horse's ears flattened as the creature sailed through it. In life, it would've landed perfectly to rip out the jugular. In death...it hit the dirt, rolled, shook itself off, and watched the progression go by. She wouldn't mind one of those bodies to control in the human world. That would scare the living hell out of people.

"Yeah, sure," she finally said. "We can do it when we stop for the night."

. . .

The flare of sunset lit the sky in a beautiful array of pink and violet and gold. Lexi sat next to a cold firepit, the remains of the fire fresh and a scuffle around it evident. A petite body had lain just...there, so close to where Lexi was now.

Footprints matching Daisy's size and the tread of her shoe the night she was taken were just over...there. Disturbed by much larger prints in some places. The echo of her soul wasn't here. Her spirit was not in this plain. Whatever had happened, she had lived long enough to get out. She'd moved on, presumably to Faerie.

Lexi's crew was active behind her—half getting ready for the night, the other half pulling Bria's cadavers off the cart and positioning them close to Lexi.

She pivoted her gaze to a blue-green fae with hair sporting branches and twigs, something like scales adorning his chest and shoulders, and an important-looking head-dress perched on his cranium. He held himself straight and tall, with shoulders that were too broad and muscles too big for his frame. He'd thought more of himself in life than he actually was, and the echo of that showed in death.

Others of his kind hung around, their postures stooped and their eyes lifeless. They knew they were dead and weren't handling the transition as well as their leader. Their passing had happened recently, even though no bodies surrounded the area. Signs of a scuffle, yes. Zorn had gone through the footprints stamped in the dirt indicating sword work, strangely not disturbed by anyone else who might want to use this campsite. Whatever had happened, the evidence of bloodshed was gone. Except for these guys. Spirits all.

Most of them watched her crew—the leader with a frustrated expression—as the bodies were lined up. Two of them stared at her. She chose one, the less forlorn of the two, and stared back.

He looked behind him and saw nobody standing there. Back to her. His hairless brow lowered...and he looked behind him again.

"Yes, I can see you," she said. It was how communication with new spirits usually started. Had since before she'd known what kind of magic she had and thought she was a Ghost Whisperer, like a Medium.

The other spirit that had been watching her started... and looked behind his friend. These guys weren't very bright. If they were the ones that had taken Daisy, it was obvious why they were dead. She would've made quick work of them.

"You..." He put his hand to his chest. "You can see me?"

"Yes. Who's your leader?"

He looked behind him yet again.

"Great god of the underworld, man, I can see you," she barked. "And you just made me use Hades's name for a curse. Do you know how delighted that makes him? He doesn't need a bigger ego. Who's your leader?"

Bria hastened over and sat beside Lexi, leaning

forward. "I'm ready." She paused. "I can barely feel these ones, though. They aren't very powerful."

"I don't care. Unless there are a bunch of ugly blue fuckers coming and going, these are the guys who snatched my kid. I have questions."

"Totally. While you do that, though, I'll grab some of the other spirits in the area and stuff them into cadavers, yes? They're all over the place around here. Easy snatching. Call me when you got something."

She was right—there were. Lexi would have to do something about the spirits trapped in this area. Maybe find a way to punch a hole into the underworld, or maybe just yank them with her when she crossed through the portal. *Something.* No matter their sins in life, she couldn't leave them to this wayward fate. It wasn't in her.

Later, though. After Daisy was safe. She had to help the living first. The dead were used to waiting.

"How can you see us?" Finally, the leader realized what was going on. "You are a useless human. What power is this?"

"A real good one. What happened here?"

"How did you come by it? Do you have fae blood?"

"No, thank the heavens. I'm giving you a chance to answer my questions on your own. If you don't, I'll make you answer them. I have the ability. Now, what happened here?"

It turned out he wanted to do things the hard way. No problem.

After she'd heard all she needed to and a few things Kieran wanted to know, she cut out their voices as she disintegrated their forms. There was no afterlife for them to retire into, no veil for them to slip behind, but this place had spirit woven into its fabric, like in her lands. Hopefully like in Faerie. It was what allowed a soul to exist. Now they would be part of it, no longer existing as themselves. Fuckers.

"Interesting," Kieran said when she'd finished. "The courts are not harmonious. The Sapphire Throne seems to want the power for themselves even though they'd need the Obsidian Throne to help them make the bridge." He thought for a moment. "They probably wanted Daisy to give themselves the upper hand. Hold her, hold the power."

"I still don't get what kind of power she has. She has no magic other than what I gave her. And that's just standard blood magic. That barely shows up on the testing units without power of her own."

He shook his head as Bria's third cadaver shakily rose from the ground. Lightning streaked across the sky and a saddle went floating by, Dylan and Donovan testing their magic in this place, ensuring it worked like normal. So far it did, Lexi's included.

"It sounds like she sets off the power, somehow," John said, having listened to everything. "He said she made it come to life, thereby increasing his power. Remember in the sergeant's barn? You were standing around for a while, but it was after she got in there that they started to buzz and vibrate. That can't be a coincidence."

Lexi squinted at Kieran, knowing John was right but

still not understanding. "What kind of magic is that? I've never heard of such a thing."

"Something the fae want," Kieran said with a look around them. "Something the dark fae know how to use. Something they'll kill for."

Bottom line, they didn't need to understand it. They just needed to get to Daisy before the dark fae created that bridge. Once she was no longer useful, they'd kill her. Given the fae had a head start and those chalices, it didn't give them much time.

She stood. "Bria, we need to find a few fae who have been back and forth through the Faegate. I want to know what to expect. Tomorrow, we confront the Celestials."

Chapter Ten

DAISY

The slap rang out before the pain across her cheek registered.

"Wake up, you vile human."

The stone slab had been straightened, and she hung from the chains, her feet dragging against the ground. A male fae stood in front of her, and another stood back by the door of her opened cell. Deep night had fallen, only a silvery slice of light coming from her window. It was just barely enough to make out the fae within her space.

They each wore a sturdy tunic of forest green, belted at the waist with two sheaths each for long knives. Embroidery ran across their breasts and down the sides, leaving the stomach area mostly bare. Their sleeves flowed with a material similar to silk, showing more embroidery, which matched what circled the bottom of the tunic. Something like tights covered their legs in deep black, ending in supple leather boots. The fabric was cut simply and looked of moderately good quality, but nothing at all like the Celestial she'd seen in the human world. Unless she was mistaken, their attire and presence here suggested they were a middling sort of servant. Not someone with mindgazer magic. Not that it mattered if they planned to drag her to the king or some other noble. Or take her for themselves.

Her stomach fluttered as she remembered what Tarian had said. She hoped someone had alerted him and he could get here in time if anything should happen. Otherwise, she'd kill whom she could and hope for the best.

A mask of shadow did not cover their faces, but strange black lines crept from their eyes and over their cheekbones. More spiderwebbed up from the high collars on their necks and along the edge of their jaws. She didn't know if that was ink or something else. Their skin looked sallow, but that might have been a trick of the light.

"Get her. Hurry up," the one at the cell door said. "This place stinks."

She didn't notice the key until the fae in front of her had lifted his hands to the manacles. Metal clinked before it released, and he stepped around her hanging frame to do the other. She dropped fully to the ground, hitting her knees against the stone floor before rubbing at her wrists. She glanced up in time to see that leather boot, freshly polished but nearly worn through, swing toward her. She rolled as quickly as she could, but the blow connected with her side, knocking the wind out of her.

"Get up!" he barked.

Fucking fae. These didn't have any more patience than the blue ones that had abducted her.

She treated the situation similarly, doing as they wanted but letting out sounds of panic and fear as she did.

The one near the door walked through, his eyes tight after seeing the mangled corpse still on display. A rickety wooden ladder waited near it, but either they hadn't gotten around to freeing the body, or Tarian had magically made it so they couldn't.

Two creatures that were this castle's version of prison guards waited in the shadows. Darkness obscured their faces, but they were watching the situation.

"Your betters will be hearing of this," the fae who held Daisy hissed at them. "This is *your* job, not ours. We should not have to come all the way in here to get the human. You'll be destroyed for this, mark my words."

The fae who held Daisy tensed as he yanked her out of the cell, his face long as he looked at Tarian's display. It seemed the prison guards had taken the warning to heart. They didn't want to end up like their comrade, regardless of who was giving the orders.

The prison guards didn't respond, and the fae kept grumbling, pulling a handkerchief out of a pocket Daisy hadn't noticed and placing it to his nose. He led the way toward the tunnel Lennox and Kayla had taken her through earlier. Or was it yesterday?

They each breathed a sigh of relief once they were far enough out, taking in lungfuls of air. The one in the lead ran his fingers through short-cropped hair. They didn't spend much time, if any, in those dungeons.

Around a couple corners and they headed a different direction than Daisy had been before. The interior of the halls looked similar, but the walls were starting to spread wider apart. The ceiling began to climb. Paintings hung along the walls, bloody affairs with crimson splatter and broken weapons. Servants increased in number, their clothing equally fine as those who were escorting Daisy and sometimes more so, with more embroidery and occasionally pearls or other shiny objects sewn into the fabric.

Daisy's stomach churned as they turned another two corners, the finery of the halls becoming obvious and ornate golden and onyx chandeliers dripping from the ceiling. They were taking her to someone important. Her gut said it wasn't Tarian. That it was someone who wanted to have fun with a strange new addition to their cages. Based on what the guards had said, it was likely the king.

She kept her hands from tightening into fists. They hadn't restrained her. That was a stroke of luck. She could do great damage very quickly when in a tight spot.

Zorn's voice rolled through her head. *If you can save yourself, don't wait. Being on the run gives you better odds than being locked in a box.*

Her gaze flicked down to the knife sticking out of her captor's sheath, ripe for the plucking. Her own knife had been taken again when she was put back into the dungeon. She could snatch this one before they locked her in a room and use it before they knew it was gone. The king's magic wouldn't save him as he died from a quick-acting fatal wound. If it *was* the king—hopefully, it was someone with less status and power. Less danger.

Adrenaline seeped into her blood, carefully contained. She ensured her movements stayed consistent and hoped to fucking hell the magic meant to contain her thoughts had started working.

She felt a prickling sensation at the back of her neck, a heightened awareness pulling at her. Pressure throbbed around her, someone's focus tracking her. Someone's gaze bearing down. She'd gotten very familiar with this sensation in the magical world, needing to know when someone planned to take out or "give a lesson to" the Chester who didn't belong.

A male of medium height and build walked down the side of the hall toward them. He held ancient-looking scrolls with tattered edges, rolled up and shielded protectively within his arms. His jacket was a fine thing, with gold embroidery on deep green fabric layered in places with red edging. Loose pants in fine silk flowed down his legs, ending in pointed slippers of velvet. She couldn't tell if any of these materials were the same as in the human realm, but they were something similar.

A gold chain hung around his neck, an oval locket resting on his breast. Eight gold earrings pierced each lobe of very large, pointed ears that stuck far out from his head. Eyes so pale they almost looked white surveyed her. He continued to slow in his walk until he stopped altogether, noticing her shoes and then her clothes, her hair and then her face, studying her like she was a fascinating book. Or scroll, in his case.

The fae escorting her passed him without so much as a glance. Nor did they put their heads down in respect. He could've been a ghost despite his obvious wealth. His gaze stuck to her, though. Her eyes. He'd finished looking her over and was imploring her to glance in his direction.

She had no idea if he was a mindgazer, or if the magic supposedly employed to protect her thoughts was working. Just in case, she started mentally singing her favorite song, imagining the musical instruments and focusing on the lyrics. She finally met his eyes, ready to drop her gaze if he took offense. Almost immediately, she felt a strange tickle in her mind, like a feather stroking the surface. Yeah, definitely a mindgazer.

She thought of her favorite bird as he watched her, his gaze delving into hers. His pale peepers, a very pretty color when up close, with dark blue speckles and a hazel ring around the pupils, glimmered with knowledge. With a question.

She had no answers. Not for him, or any of them. But goodness, weren't the feathers of a flamingo so lovely and pink? They got that coloring from their food. And the ostriches, with their plume of— Actually, llamas were cool, weren't they? Some could be very surly, though—

Her mental babble was cut short when the fae who held her arm jerked in surprise. She whipped her head around to see Tarian stopped at the mouth of the hallway, his body pointed to the right but his head turned her way.

It looked as though he'd been passing by when he glanced this way, then stopped.

The image of him took her breath away.

His clothing was made of material as fine as the male with the scrolls, but the cut was so much more interesting. A high collar on his tunic jutted close to his jaw and cinched in at the base of his neck. Silver designs entwined within, sparkling and shining in the hallway lighting. Another collar nearer his shoulder looked like hardened leather, or rubber, even, sitting atop a flat piece that curved slightly at the edge of his shoulders. Another piece of the same material covered his upper arm, all of this swirled in golden braids, lines, and accents. It made his already broad shoulders seem that much bigger and looked like armor. Sleek, gorgeous armor.

The material hugged him down his front and around his waist, the design just as extraordinary and interesting. His sleeves were loose fabric that flowed under bracers fashioned after the shoulder plates. The same material covered his shins, the rest of his leg in something like leggings. The ensemble called for the velvet shoes Mr. Scrolls wore, but instead, Tarian sported leather boots polished to a high gloss.

His loose curls hung around his face, and it was the only part of him that wasn't pristinely tailored. On anyone else, it wouldn't have fit. It would've distracted from the overall *look*, but for him, it seemed purposeful, like a rebellion against authority. It made him that much hotter. Her heart sped up.

"Keep going," the fae in front murmured furiously, a nervous waver in his voice.

The fae who held her stutter-stepped, jerking her to a stop one moment and lurching forward the next. His hand tightened in an unconscious reaction. Nerves, probably. Whoever had sent them to fetch her didn't stop them from worrying what would happen when Tarian found out.

A strange excitement simmered in her middle, as though she were headed toward battle.

Tarian turned toward them slowly, purposefully, his eyes feral. Darkness saturated the space around him, boosting his dangerous energy. It was impossible to know which side he inhabited, good or evil. Angel or devil. He probably didn't even know himself. Right now, it was both. Her savior, and her captors' damnation.

His gaze fell over her, making her body tingle all over. He started forward. Toward her.

The fae that held her slowed dramatically, as though fighting to keep walking through a windstorm. The other wasn't much better, both of his fists clenched at his sides as he trudged farther.

"What are you doing with that slave?" Tarian asked as he neared, his voice like dark satin, his approach terrifyingly beautiful.

The two fae stopped. The leader lifted his chin in defiance, but he couldn't hide his full-body tremors.

"The king has requested the human female for his amusement," the leader said, and cold washed down Daisy's spine.

"Don't be absurd." Tarian now only had eyes for the leader. His magic billowed around him, stuffing the hall with bone-crushing pressure. "He detests taking another's seconds. She has been spoiled. By me. He'll have to be amused by his queen for the evening. Or perhaps one of his many mistresses. The human is mine."

"But sire—"

Suddenly, Tarian was right in front of the leader, vicious brawn and robust strength. His height topped the other male by a foot, and he made it a point to lean down into the servant as he spoke.

"Did you not see the warning I left in the prison? The last of the king's insufferable minions to touch what is mine met his demise. I made him suffer greatly. I can bless you with the same treatment, like I will bless your friend."

The fae holding Daisy started to scream, ripping his hand away from her and throwing himself back. He stumbled as blackness sliced across his body. Blood soaked into his clothes in the groin and stomach. It gurgled up through his throat until he was choking on it, thrashing and then crashing into the wall. The light in the hall flickered, dimming and flaring, casting manic shadows across Tarian's unflinching face. He hadn't looked away from the leader, his gaze promising vengeance while otherwise handsomely unimpressed about the carnage he was creating.

The fae who had touched her fell. He slumped, quieting. Blood pooled around him. He wouldn't be getting up again.

She stood breathless, eyes wide, as she watched Tarian's ruthless side in all its menacing glory, making a show of protecting her. His strength and power and ferocity fascinated her, but also unnerved her—intimidated her now that she knew what would happen if his callous side drowned out the Tarian she'd grown to know, turning him into something dark and disturbingly wicked.

"Is that what you would like?" Tarian asked the guard teasingly.

The leader visibly swallowed, edging away from him. "No, sire. It must've been a misunderstanding."

"Yes, I should think so. You can tell your king that I will be entering the court games for the first time this year. I found a delightful creature in the human realm whom I mean to put forward as my great champion. I know how much he likes my jests. I also know that, as a courtesy, he does not *dabble* with our champions until after the games have terminated. You can see why I had to stop you. Had he handled my toy, the other court members would have become concerned about him breaking long-standing promises. *More* concerned, I should say. They are already chattering about other... infractions. The situation would result in trust grievances and overall court instability." He tsked, cocking his head. "Given the current turmoil, I cannot imagine the king would welcome such fractures."

He gestured to Daisy like he was summoning an obedient dog. She bent, as though cowed, before going to his side.

His tone lightened as he continued to look at the fae.

108

"I consider this matter closed. Since you did not actually touch her, you may keep your hands." He waved the male away before glancing down the hall in the direction he'd come. "Scamper along. Your presence is tiring."

"Yes, sire," the fae said, bowing deeply. "As you wish, sire." He turned and half ran down the hall.

Tarian held up his hand like he was holding something. A dark black line ran from his fist downward, and then into an arc and back up before looping around Daisy's neck. There it cinched, flattening her hair to the back of her neck and leaving no room to get her fingers in between her skin and the magical material.

"Well?" Tarian didn't look at her. "Walk. I do not like to be kept waiting."

The rest of the hall was entirely empty, the servants having found somewhere else to be. That, or scared they'd end up like the fae on the ground.

Except for one.

"Master Tarian, sire," someone called, the voice old and scratchy.

She took a few hesitant steps but stalled when Tarian looked back.

"Might I have a word?"

Tarian's gaze flicked to her for the briefest moment before he turned to Mr. Scrolls. Daisy didn't mistake the fear in his eyes.

Chapter Eleven

DAISY

Arrogance dripped from each syllable. "Master Eldric, how may I assist you?"

"Yes." Eldric continued to clutch his scrolls as he neared, no longer studying Daisy. "First, welcome back from the human realm. I trust the Celestials were no more troublesome than usual?"

Daisy nearly missed it, but she noticed Tarian's shoulders tense. "Not much, no."

"Fantastic. I was able to look over the items you brought back. Most of them are the standard low-capacity items, but a few will do nicely. There is just one item I have not seen yet, of course." Eldric paused. "The most important item, I think. I'd love to go over that in some detail. Perhaps in the morning, when I am refreshed."

"That chalice is in the king's possession," Tarian said in a bored voice. "For safekeeping."

"Yes, of course. Of course. Something that powerful—that valuable—should be kept safe."

"Exactly. We can set up the configuration without it. He will supply it when it is needed to create the bridge."

"Ah. Yes. Except..." Those pale blue eyes flashed to Daisy for a moment, so quickly that she would've missed it had she not been staring straight at him.

I can help you, he said into her mind at the same time as he spoke to Tarian. She barely contained her startled surprise. "I must test the amount of magic that runs through it. It does more than you think, Tarian. Your studies aren't quite—"

He is a fool for entering you in the court games. A magic-less human has no place there, even with a mind shield. Even the meagerly magical would outclass you, but now the king knows a human is present in his court. He finds great joy in tormenting your kind. You have no hope. He will alter the games to get the most sport out of you.

What delightful news, she thought sarcastically. *Thanks for the vote of confidence. But I don't have much choice, do I?*

Nor much confidence. She could hear the truth in his voice. The utter conviction. It matched the growing uncertainty in her gut.

I can help you, Chalice, he repeated while speaking with Tarian physically. That ability was beyond her. *Tarian does not know all you can do. Purposely. My order protects the sacred scrolls and all that lie within. We merely guide. We only reveal as much as the gods will. The fae would use you for their own designs, but you were always meant to have a choice: to increase and expand power to unbelievable heights...or to wither it away entirely. Balance. That is why the crystal chalice was always meant to be a thinking, rational, logical being—or as close as a human can get. A being not of Faerie, not raised in Faerie, and without the pitfalls of life here. You are the balance, Chalice, and you are needed now more than ever, the gods willing.*

Wither it away entirely? she asked him, knowing he had heard her directed mental voice a moment ago but wondering if he could also hear her thoughts. Wondering if the magical mental shield was working, because if not, Tarian could just shoplift this information from her mind anyway. Telling her like this made very little sense.

My kind are not hindered by magical mental shields, he replied. *The gods will it so. No information is kept from us. No information can be hidden, except what we will. He cannot access this conversation unless you verbally reveal it. It is locked in your mind, safe, unless you* choose *to impart it.*

Then why would he want to keep this from Tarian if he knew Tarian's real plans?

Because fae cannot be trusted, especially in this court where the magic is so horribly twisted. This ability, this burden, falls at your feet. You alone must choose which is a worthy cause, and which is not. He paused. *If he truly wishes to enter you into the court games, then you must make your way to me quickly. Your life is at stake.*

Cold slithered down her spine at the thought of going up against fae whose magic made no sense to her. At the reality she was facing but had been damn slow to notice. She'd always figured she'd find a way to protect herself. She always had in the human world.

But in the human world, she had backup. She had Zorn standing guard, she had excellent preplanning, and she'd never really been on her own. She'd *never* battled face to face without the element of surprise. If this character could be believed, she wouldn't have that luxury here. The games—and the king—would make sure she was exposed. She wouldn't stand a fucking chance, or even have the knowledge to evade. She was battling blind in a land of dangerous creatures. What had Tarian been thinking?

Eldric made a frustrated gesture at Tarian, crinkled his scrolls, and turned away. He walked swiftly down the hall.

"Come now, little pet." The magical leash on her neck yanked her into motion. "We must not dally. I have matters that need my attention."

You are very stuffy when you're speaking like a member of the court, she mentally murmured.

She felt his magic move over her body deliciously, followed by the press of phantom lips on hers. *I'm not in the human world. I can't use the slang I've picked up there or I'll be ridiculed.*

Her body heated, but her mind drifted. Wither away magic? That meant null it, right? She could essentially render a magical person...not magical?

113

Butterflies swarmed her belly as she vaguely noticed the halls around them. Unlike with the *Fallen*, or with the fae a moment ago, servants didn't just look down and hurry past when Tarian was in their vicinity. No, they pushed to the wall and tried to slink by. Some stopped completely and faced the wall so they couldn't make eye contact. One male shrank into a crouch, head down, making himself as small as possible. Tarian might be the butt of jokes in the court, but his power, and his viciousness, made him a terror.

Her mind returned to the matter at hand. Each facet of this chalice magic essentially had to do with another entity. Either she boosted their magic (you're welcome), or she took it away entirely. And while one wasn't all that exciting because it was making someone else that much better, the other...

She blinked rapidly, suppressing a smile. Hiding the excitement bubbling in her gut.

The other would level her playing field. It would, for the first time, make her an equal to magical people. She could step up to a fight knowing it was skill that would win the day, and skill alone. Her training...against theirs.

Could that scroll-carrying fae be believed? He knew what she was, so he had more knowledge than the blue fae that had abducted her, but he could want to use her for himself. He might lure her with promises of withering magic, only to cage her and use her against Tarian. To strengthen his king's throne.

If there was one thing she knew already, it was that she would never, *ever* choose to strengthen that fucker's anything. She'd been here a day or so and already his antics turned her stomach.

Her thoughts ground to a halt when a door opened down the way and billowing silks stepped out of the opening. The mauve dress flowed around pink-slippered feet—the first mistake—followed by an enormous shawl that looked like a parachute in a plain and yawn-worthy jet black. Mistakes two and three.

Actually, that shawl was so gods-awful that it was its own bad decision. It crawled onto the neckline with strange orange twigs and berries, or some horrible equiva-lent, and made way for a surprisingly intricate bodice with beads and pearls and some nicely textured patterns. But here was the kicker: the bodice was in bright orange to match the fucked-up berries.

Did a trapped human describe a circus tent before they died as fashion vengeance or something? There was no way that outfit was made from an experienced hand.

Please stop, Tarian said with a tight mental voice. *You're starting to break my court façade, and I can't be seen laughing at such a prominent lady. Not until you best her champion.*

That dress alone should break your court façade, as ridiculous as it is.

Seriously, please, *you've got to stop.*

Why are you hearing my thoughts, anyway? Is the magical shield not working?

He didn't get to answer, because Ms. Prominent Lady and her bad fashion choices sauntered into his path like the hallway had been put there just for her. He veered to the side, making way even though he was supposedly royalty. He bent his head slightly, showing deference, and Daisy's insides started to boil as a smug expression crossed the female's face.

Then Daisy had to control her widening eyes.

This female's skin was a grayish hue that looked off-putting and unnatural. Lines of black formed an almost solid mass across her forehead and around one deep blue eye. Streaks of black formed under the other eye as though she had permanently running mascara, and more lines ran around her mouth and down onto her neck. They weren't wrinkles, those hardly having formed, and they gave the impression of sickness. The sight of them made her nauseated, and as the lady neared, an acidic wave crawled through her insides. Something about this female was badly wrong.

"My, my, look who it is..." The female's hips swung from side to side in an exaggerated sweep. "If it isn't the king's mongrel come back from the human world. I wondered when you would show your face after what the princess did to you."

"Lady Nyvarie." Tarian offered her a shallow bow.

Avert your eyes, he told Daisy. *Look at the ground and try not to be noticed.*

She did as he said, making no sudden movements and pulling all her energy into her body. It was what always worked best in the human magical world. If people didn't notice her, they didn't pick on her.

"I have no choice but to return." His voice was light, and she wondered if he was smiling. If so, that smile would be a death threat. "This is my home, after all. Princess Elamorna has a peculiar humor, that's all. I came to no harm."

The female's laugh was pitched high and dripping with disdain. "If court jesters can have homes, hmm? Because that is the humor we all have, or didn't you know?"

He offered another bow, and Daisy marveled at the loose and easy confidence with which he did it.

"Hmm." Something snapped. It sounded like a paper or silk fan hitting a palm, and then mauve skirts and the wrong slippers moved and swished as the female started walking again.

Take two steps forward in a straight line, he told Daisy, and she glided, careful to only move her feet. A glimpse out the side of her eye said he was putting his body between the lady and her. *One more.*

He turned with a release of breath. The leash disappeared, and he took long strides.

She kept up, veering closer to the wall and making herself as small as she dared, much like a servant that scurried to and fro in these halls.

Miraculous, he murmured as they rounded a corner and he picked up more speed. She was nearly jogging beside him. *You stood right there...and she didn't notice you. You walked up with me, stood* right beside me, *and she didn't notice your presence.*

I've had a lot of practice blending into the background. She probably tracked me as a servant. Those types don't lower themselves to look at the staff.

Too true. He glanced at her, looking amazed and grateful. *The fates chose well. But what about the chalice magic? The Celestials swarmed. The darkrend focused on you. How did she not see it?*

Daisy had no idea. Maybe these people were prone to blindness, secure in their court and not noticing the magic of others.

That is not usually the case, Tarian said thoughtfully. *I'll need to ask Eldric about that. There has to be a reason.*

She thought again about what that fae had said: *We merely guide. We only reveal as much as the gods will.*

She needed a *lot* more guidance.

But first, she needed to know the state of things. *You didn't answer me—did that shield not work?*

It must've, thank the gods. Lady Nyvarie is one of the most powerful mindgazers in this court. Not noticing your presence is one thing, but she is always, always *listening into thoughts where she can.*

Yours?

She's not strong enough. The obsidian discs temper my power and my magic, but they don't touch my mind. My thoughts are secure as long as I have the strength to fortify them.

Yet you can still read my thoughts.

His head cocked to the side as he angled right, his hand coming out and touching eggshell-white double doors with round bronze handles. Metal clicked, and he opened one of the doors, stepping aside so she could enter. He followed right behind her, the delicious buzz of his proximity setting her aflame. It wasn't great timing.

She hurried to give herself space before turning to survey him. Light glowed from various places within the chambers, softly washing across his face and revealing the dark circles under his eyes. The beautiful green of his irises had dulled, and a crease seemed permanently etched into his brow.

His body sagged as he closed the door and locked it. A black sheen fitted over the door. A ward, probably.

"Yes," he said, and his voice sounded drawn, like he hadn't slept for a year. "The twisted magic is pulling at me. It's always this way." He pushed off the door and passed her into a large room with all the furniture and placement of an apartment, minus a kitchen. "As I said, yes, I can still read your thoughts. That should only happen if you are actively thinking them at me. Like talking to me. I expected I'd have to teach you how to do so. This saves time. Unfortunately for you, it also prevents you from hiding anything from me."

"Fortunately for you," she said, "you don't have to trust that I am telling the truth. Since I can't lie in my thoughts, I mean."

"*Unfortunately* for me, I have to hear all your commentary about the fae you meet. It is...distracting."

She shrugged, perusing the large table in the dining room and exiting into a solarium with glass walls and windows that had to be magic because it was in the center of the chambers.

"It is," he said, and fabric rustled.

She paused within it, looking at the night sky dotted with millions of stars twinkling brightly. The moon rose over lush green grasses and beautiful trees, with flowers and nightlife nestled within. The colors were something he might see, much more vibrant and radiant than her dulled vision.

His bathroom was essentially that—a place for a bath. There didn't seem to be any running water, but a bucket system at the side ran up into the ceiling on a chain with another coming through the floor. Odd. She wanted to see how that worked. There had to be an easier way, not that she knew much about plumbing solutions.

There was another room for the toilet, a throne-like seat over a chamber pot. Before yesterday, she might've thought someone cleaning that after she'd used it was embarrassing. After...well, it would be nice not to wear her bodily fluids.

She found him in a new jacket that was just as stylish as the other except for the buttons, which were much too large and did not go at all.

He looked down at himself.

"Oops, sorry. I didn't think I was in range," she said. Still...

He shook his head, paused, and then shrugged out of the jacket and returned to the room on the other side.

"No, it's fine. They aren't that bad. Compared to Circus Tent Martha, they are downright amazing. Seriously—" She cut off at the next selection, not really understanding the gold chain draping down the side like he were some eighties pop singer, but the diamond-crusted bling would go a long way toward helping people forget the hitch in fashion.

"Are you kidding?" He fingered the chain and huffed, leaning heavily in irritation. "Which, then? This or the other. I don't want to have to change my *trews*."

She didn't know what trews were but laughed at his antics. The clothes were so different, but the dedication to fashion spoke to her. Made her feel like there was a piece of her life, her home, with them right then.

"That one," she said. "We can figure out the buttons on the other one another time."

He nodded and headed into a room to the side. On closer inspection, it was an enormous closet.

"Dressing chambers," he supplied, as if there was some great difference.

"So..." Two things were on the tip of her tongue, and one she wanted to think about in much more detail, so she voiced the second. "What did the princess do to you last time you were here?"

He jerked as though struck, facing an ornate mirror. His arms stopped moving where he was fiddling with something on his jacket. His back expanded with a deep breath before releasing.

"Something that happens more often than anyone at this court knows. I'd rather not speak about it. It's enough that I have to endure it. Given the sort of...actions I will need you to do in order to goad her, though, I suppose I have to." He turned, his eyes haunted. "But not right now. When I got word you were being taken from the dungeons, I was in the middle of some important business. I need to return to it."

Her heart quickened. She hadn't had time to think

about it right then, but part of her had wondered if his meeting them had been a coincidence or a safety precaution. She was happy to know it was the latter. It made her feel much less alone in this strange place.

He came to stand in front of her, his eyes deep, delving into hers. "No, you are not alone, my treasure. But remember, Daisy, I cannot always come for you. If you had been admitted into the king's chambers, I wouldn't have been able to save you. Nor if the other royals took you. You need to watch out for yourself. It is the nature of this court. Neither of us have any alternative."

Something the guards had said flashed through her memory: Tarianthiel couldn't hurt them. Magic stopped him.

Of course he wouldn't be able to kill the royalty and blast his way out of this place. If he were trapped, the first thing they'd do was prevent him from taking down his jailors and freeing himself. That was just logic.

You grant your own salvation, Zorn always said. *Do not wait to be saved. Save yourself.*

Suddenly she didn't know if she'd thought of that because of her own predicament...or because of Tarian's.

"Someday, I'd like to meet this Zorn," Tarian said, interrupting her whirling thoughts. His gaze drifted down to her lips. "I must go."

He spared a moment to kiss her softly. As he pulled away, she had an insane desire to clutch on to him and keep him put. To coax those lips open and feel what was beneath the fine clothing.

His lips pulled into a teasing smile. "Clearly, I should've fucked you in the dungeon." Fire raced through her core, and he winked. "I'll return as quickly as I can. You'll be staying here now. Given my...status and role within this court, I have a lesser noble's quarters. I don't have a lot of space, and certainly not a spare room for you."

This was paradise compared to the house she and Mordecai had originally shared with Lexi. He'd lose his shit if he ever saw that. Except for the plumbing situation, of course. She'd trade it all for good plumbing.

"You are welcome to my bed," he finished.

"Where will you sleep?"

"On the side you don't choose. You are also welcome to have the floor." A smirk twisted his lips. "I *might* even try to find you a blanket."

She huffed. "So chivalrous."

"As always. I do not have traditional servants. I have only my *Fallen*. One or two of them will be here to attend to you shortly. They will let themselves in. They are the only ones who can. *Do not* open the door. Not for any reason. Not for anyone. You are in Faerie, now, little pet. Fae are tricky. Some can take on the voices of trusted allies. Others might take on their shape. Always look at the eyes. The eyes do not lie. If you can't see the eyes, do not trust the voice. Okay? Rest. Test the mind shield on the *Fallen* and see if it works. I'm interested to see if they can hear your thoughts as easily as I can." He kissed her forehead. "Protect your mind so that I may protect you."

And he was gone.

She stared after him for a long moment, then refocused to look solely at the door. Specifically, the handle. She shouldn't open the door...but she *could*. If she wanted, she could go to Eldric. She could do it and be back before Tarian ever knew she'd gone...

Chapter Twelve

DAISY

Magic held him in place. Black spikes speared into his sides and bands wrapped around his arms and torso. He stood in front of the king's dais—in front of the whole court. The nobles snickered behind their hands or fans, laughed and guffawed while in their plush seats. They were eagerly watching the show.

"Let's see this physique you have worked so hard on, shall we?" Princess Elamorna looked up at him with lustful, cruel eyes. The black ring of obsidian royalty ran like a river around her pupils.

He didn't fight the bonds of magic. Didn't give her the satisfaction of showing his embarrassment. His shame.

She sliced through his tunic. Yanked at the shoulders and cut down the back. After baring his torso, she moved on to his pants, creating long strips of torn fabric to give the court a peep show.

"Hmm, such fine stock. Yes, court?" She turned to her audience, who whooped and hollered, their usual demure mannerisms long lost to the twisted nature of the magic running through this place. She looked up at him again and whispered, "So many accolades with the highest court in the land, and just *look* at what you've become. Nothing but a whore."

She ripped the fabric away, revealing all of him, and stepped aside so the court could see his nudity. She laughed as she stroked his body and rubbed up his legs.

"Who would like a sample?" she called to the court. "Or should I alone have my fill?"

Several females stood, laughing uproariously. They staggered as they came up, drunk or high or out of their minds with magic. They knelt before him one by one, using their hands and their mouths...but they had no effect. There was not an ounce of lust within Tarian. In fact, the sensations disgusted him. Shriveled what the gods gave him.

A few males tried as well, a contest to make him erect. But in all the years he'd been here—been subjected to this treatment—only one had held that mantle. Only one had coaxed lust from him. And they'd killed her.

Princess Elamorna laughed, waving them away. She thought she'd finally be able to master him. With whatever magic she'd concocted this time, she thought she'd *finally* be able to reduce him to her groveling little pet.

Her eyes shone with confidence as she prowled

around him, her long nails, like claws, raking across his skin. Gashes opened up in their wake, but he didn't feel the sting. Magic curled around him, a black haze soaking into his pores. Pleasure coursed deep, tingling his balls, willing him to give in to her ministrations. She took him in hand and knelt in front of him, and he looked down at her as he struggled against the magic holding him. As he struggled against the obsidian burned into his back, locking him in this hell. As he raged against the god who had damned him to this fate.

He would not give in to this. He would not allow the magic to take hold. He *would not* become twisted within this court—a stranger to this realm. He loved Faerie too much to forsake it.

So he resisted that magic. He resisted *her*.

Her face was a mask of fury when next she looked up at him. Saliva coated the corner of her mouth.

He forced a condescending smirk.

"If you weren't so hideous, maybe you'd have some effect, hmm?" he said flippantly, as though none of this bothered him.

He barely felt the whips afterward, the blades parting his flesh. He barely noticed the pain as they made pulp of his body and dumped him into his chambers for his *Fallen* to attend. He'd won. He'd beaten her yet again.

He would beat her still.

Daisy sucked in a breath as she jerked awake in Tarian's large bed. She clutched her chest where the pain had felt so fresh, grasped her cloth nightgown to ensure it was still draped around her body. The images from the moment swam before her eyes, haunting her. Breaking her heart and seeping down through her middle. They faded, having felt so real. Seemed real, like she'd been there. She felt like she'd been him.

The emotions of the moment took longer to dissipate.

Soft light filtered in through fake windows at the back wall, the magic mimicking the time of day, like the solarium. Apparently, lesser nobles didn't get rooms with real windows and fresh air. If they didn't have the magic to create it themselves, they felt their station.

Tarian lay on his side, his head propped up on his hand. The covers pooled at his waist, and a sad smile crossed his handsome face.

"Didn't decide to run, huh?" he said, the teasing tone not reaching his solemn eyes.

She'd thought about leaving for a split second...and that had been stupidly long enough. She wasn't a complete idiot.

Instead, she'd used the makeshift toilet, shed her clothes, dressed in a huge robe Tarian had in the bathroom, and stared at the water contraption until Kayla and a female called Faelynn had come in to help. Faelynn was their healer, incredibly powerful and insightful in all things medicinal, and incredibly introverted. She hardly made eye contact the whole time she'd been there.

Daisy didn't answer Tarian's question. She'd thought a lot about things last night—about whom she might trust, why, and all the reasons behind those answers. She'd gone over all the details she knew, all the ways this venture could unravel, and thought about the choices at her disposal if Eldric was correct. She'd thought about the ways this new information, if true, would change her mind.

"I didn't wake when you came in last night," she started.

"No." His gaze didn't waver. "I magically made sure of that. I needed some attention from Faelynn. My... meeting didn't go as smoothly as planned."

"Why didn't you want me awake for that?"

He hesitated. "Because you needed your rest. And it...wasn't pretty."

She felt like smiling...and like cursing. He didn't want her to worry. How cute. But it wasn't his fucking choice to make.

Smoothing down her anger, she said, "Please stop deciding when I should and should not sleep. If I want to sleep and can't, I'll ask for help. If I want to be awake when you stumble in bloody and crying, you need to let me." She shrugged. "If only so I can make fun of you for not being able to defend yourself."

He watched her, his eyes starting to sparkle from the last comment. "Fair enough," he murmured.

Now it was she who was watching him, noticing the tension in his body that he was trying to hide. The embarrassment...and the shame from the treatment he'd had no control over. That this court and those horrible creatures had forced upon him. That they, and the gods with them, needed to answer for.

Anger unfurled in her. She kept a tight rein on it, though. Anger wasn't needed from her right now. Anger would come later.

Because of Dylan, she had a lot of experience in this role. She'd been the third leg of his tripod for many rough nights as his memories of the past had resurfaced. He'd occasionally needed someone to help him out of the darkness, and he trusted her.

Sometimes all she'd done was listen, sometimes she'd raged, but she'd always made it clear she was there for him. No matter what he needed to share or what he chose not to, she took it in stride and returned unconditional love and support. And she would—if she ever saw him again—for as long as she lived. That was what it meant to be family.

Tarian wasn't her family—far from it—but she wouldn't turn away a wounded soul. She wouldn't pass up the opportunity to help him claim vengeance. Fuck this court. Fuck those royals. Fuck those terrible gods who shit on their children instead of helping them.

She took a deep breath. Not giving in to the rage was easily the hardest part of this role. She constantly struggled with it.

"That dream...was your memory," she surmised in an even tone. "The one Circus Tent Martha was talking about."

He barely nodded. "You need to know why I will ask for various things from you. Why I need to make a show of my reaction to you."

She shook her head slowly. "I don't need to know

why. I trust you, remember? What I need is to believe your reasoning is valid. And I do. I need to know your past in order to stand witness. I need to understand your pain so I know how to support you when you need help shouldering it. When it overwhelms you, I will stand in and be your strength. And so help me gods-that-actu- ally-give-a-shit, if she tries to do that in my presence, I will—"

She clenched her jaw. *Easily* the hardest part of this role.

He grabbed her as though he couldn't help himself, cupping her cheeks, his fingers diving into her hair. He kissed her passionately, his tongue delving into her mouth and tangling with hers. He held her in place, kissing her with everything he was, like it was a compulsion. A deep, desperate *need*. She felt it with every fiber of her being, swept away with his taste. His touch.

They were both breathing hard when they separated. His eyes sparkled harder now despite the pain she saw there.

"So adorable," he whispered, his tone gravelly and deep. "Your fury is refreshing, actually. I have always loved your viciousness. The *Fallen* are supportive and sympathetic. They are mad, but I think the years here have worn us all down. That was the most public display she's ever done, but she has wanted to claim my desire since the very first time I set foot in this court. A big part of me thinks that's why they killed Sansy the way they did."

Sansy must've been his first love, whom he'd trapped

with affection and they'd tortured to death in front of him.

"Well, as long as my anger is refreshing... We're not going to die until *after* we burn this motherfucker to the ground. How's that? We will restore balance and all that, but we're claiming vengeance on this bitch. I'll fuck you on the floor in the middle of the court if that rubs salt into the wound. I don't give two shits. Fuck that bitch. She'll pay for what she's done. They all will. I'll make sure of it. You're not family, but you're all I've got. No one fucks with all I've got and gets away with it."

"You'd be trapped, Daisy."

She laughed. "I'm in Faerie. I'm *already* trapped. I'm absolutely fucked, actually, and since I'm sentenced to die, I might as well get a little pleasure out of it, huh? Want to knock this out right now? I'm game. I could use some pounding to work off some steam."

A smile peeked through his solemn demeanor. Gold warred with midnight around his pupil. She could turn him on with only words when this court couldn't do that with magic, hands, or mouths.

"Not words...just you," he said softly, his eyes open and honest.

She leaned toward him and gently ran her thumb under his eye. "Why do some fae have that ring around their irises and some don't?" she asked, remembering Eldric and the princess. "Your memory said royalty, but Eldric didn't seem royal."

He trailed his fingertips along her arm. "It denotes an elevated station in Faerie," he replied. "Royalty in the various kingdoms have it, the color matching their throne. Here, it is obsidian. The Diamond Throne's is gold."

"Not...diamond?" She dropped her hand and he caught it, stopping it on his heart and keeping it braced there. She could feel the slow, rhythmic pulse under his smooth, warm skin.

"No. I asked Eldric once why that is. He never answered me." He shrugged. "He chooses which of my questions to answer and which not to. So he says. I think he simply doesn't know and never thought to look it up. For me, after I was...stationed here, obsidian replaced the gold in my eyes until...you. I have no idea why."

Until the crystal chalice situation. Though that didn't explain the very first time they'd met.

"And Eldric?" she asked. "Is he royalty, then?"

Tarian shook his head. "He's in the order of scribes. It's a subsection of fae who devote their lives to knowledge. If they rise high enough in the order, magic burns their irises." He paused. "Daisy, listen, there's something about...our next steps that you should know."

Her eyebrows lifted. "How many secrets do you have?"

"A great many."

In fairness, she was sitting on a big one as well.

"You go first," he whispered.

She wanted to move closer. Hell, she wanted to cuddle up next to him, her skin flush with his. But this needed to be hashed out. They needed to make plans.

She pulled her hand back and threaded her fingers

together to focus. The sheet was still at his waist, his defined and tattooed torso on full display, distracting her.

He moved a pillow behind his head, sitting up to rest against the headboard. Getting comfortable for their talk. She watched the play of muscle as he did so before swallowing, her mouth suddenly dry. It was almost painful how much she wanted him. To taste him. To take him deeply into her body until neither of them could focus on anything but the other.

She inhaled and tried to get her head in the game. "Eldric had a side conversation with me in the hallway while he was talking to you." She told him essentially what had been said, and ended with her potential for a choice. Her potential for a power that was useful to *her*, not just to someone else.

"I heard that conversation, yes. I also heard your thoughts about it," he said when she'd finished.

Her eyes widened. "He said it would be safe in my head. That his kind know all, but don't share all."

"Yes, that is usually the way of it. 'As the gods will it,' he always says. Well, it seems the gods are giving him the same fucked-up treatment they are *willing* on us. Usually, mindgazer magic won't work on his kind—"

"And a scribe is actually different from a fae?" They looked the same.

Images, emotions, and, most of all, information flashed through her head. Eldric the Timeworn, he was called. All of Faerie produced such beings, no matter the kingdom or station in life—someone with more capacity for mental information storage, a better grasp on difficult concepts, a master of many dialects, cultures, and languages, and someone who could endure a mental transformation that turned them into a different kind of fae. No one knew what that transformation entailed unless they'd been through it, because to fail was to die.

They thought of themselves as *apart* from fae. They were the protectors of information that in turn protected the realm, as the gods willed.

They sounded like genius, scroll-hoarding zealots, but whatever.

Tarian spat out a laugh. "They are, in many respects. I am warning you, they are very literal creatures. Your humor will not register."

"Half the time you laugh at things I say that aren't jokes, so maybe that'll be refreshing," she drawled. "So you knew all of that? You heard him say I should see him as soon as possible, without your knowing—that I'd have a choice to help or not—all of that, and you left me to my own devices in here?"

One of his shapely eyebrows lifted. "Do you assume I have any control over you? I recall one instance in particular where you stabbed me with my own knife. I knew instinctively, early on, that you'd need to choose your path. I tried to force you where I could, and it always backfired. It was when I offered you a choice, and you chose to help, that we were most effective. That we lived through obstacles that would've killed most. You'll remember that I let you talk yourself out of running after I arrived at the camp. I didn't restrain you when you could've run through the portal. You are smart enough to stay alive. I figured last night would be no different."

"You had your people—fae, whatever—watching, though, right? Just in case?"

"Obviously. I'm not a fool. Your unpredictability is endearing...until it is a pain in my ass."

She huffed out a laugh. Then she licked her lips, unsure, studying his face. "And so you already knew the other half of the chalice magic has the ability to nullify magic?"

"No. I only knew there was something more to the magic. The texts have vague references to an additional element of the power. When I asked about it, Eldric verbally did what scribes always do when they don't want to answer a question—spout enlightened nonsense until I was so bored I gave up. They think they are so very intelligent, but study with enough of them and you learn their tricks. His mind would then usually clue me in, but in those instances, I couldn't hear his swirling thoughts over the din of his verbal nonsense. I couldn't make out what the additional magic was. I assumed it had something to do with the setup of the chalices. But I could never find the answer."

"Until he outright told me. You were *allowed* to hear it that time."

"Yes, and it was for the best. I'm not sure how I would've handled things if I'd known you could cut out my magic and stab me in my sleep. I would've been a lot more...strict with you. I realize now it would've backfired. There is no way you would've softened to me if I had remained hard with you. We wouldn't be in this situation we're in now, where you are consenting to trap yourself to me because of vengeance and plain bad decision-making."

"Let's get one thing clear—it's also because you're hot and incredibly desirable. But yes, there has been a lot of bad decision-making when it comes to you."

"So..." He studied her again. "When you figure out how to nullify magic, what will you choose? Are my days numbered?"

He was surely joking. She'd seen his sword work.

"First, I don't know if he is telling the truth," she said.

"He is. He doesn't lie about information such as this. Cannot, I don't think. Nor is he lying about being uncertain of my motives. He knows my plans. His kind is dedicated to the prosperity of Faerie, even if they mostly read about its past. He has done everything in his power to help me. His entire faction has, including by keeping my secrets. But he also knows I am in this court, with its degradation and twisted magic. He sees me lose more of my grip with each passing thrush."

"Thrush?"

His eyelids fluttered. "Sorry, *year* is your equivalent, though a thrush is significantly longer. The thrush happens one time each year across Faerie. It's a time for reflection and repentance as the thrush falls from the stars. It's a sort of..." His gaze drifted away as he thought of something similar in the human realm.

"Never mind, it doesn't matter," she said. "Here's what I will choose: to destroy this fucking court. Then I'll be a hero and balance Faerie, however that might happen, and save the human world. If I can work in a way to punish your gods, I'll slide that in there as well. If you're going to aim, aim high, right? I just need a cape." A crooked smile worked up his handsome face. "Now, what's this thing you have to tell me?"

His smile slipped, replaced by a red hue in his cheeks. "I haven't... I've never..." He cleared his throat. "I'm...intact, we'll say."

Her brow pinched in confusion. "I know you don't mean you still have balls, because I've felt them. That's no secret. So intact...like...they checked me for? Like..."

"A virgin," he said. "I've never had sex. You would be my first and very likely my last. You'd be my only."

Chapter Thirteen

DAISY

Now it was Daisy who had a crooked grin, stunned into silence. Finally, she said, "I can't tell if you're joking."

"Joking right now would be lying, and I have repeatedly told you I can't lie to you anymore."

"Okay, but..." She sat up and faced him fully. "I thought you trapped that female—Sansy, you said her name was. I thought you trapped her with sex?"

"With a kiss. Just a kiss, like you. We were young. She hadn't been ready to fully engage. By the time she was...she wanted another. But because of the magic, she couldn't place her lips on anyone—anywhere on them—without triggering my need to kill them. She couldn't take another lover unless all they did was have sex. Only that. She couldn't even accidentally brush her lips against a shoulder passionately. I owned her intimately, and she grew to hate me for it. I doomed her with nothing but an innocent kiss I didn't fully understand. I told you, I never wanted to subject another to that. I still don't. I just don't know that we'll have any other choice."

Daisy's heart dropped for him. He was a virgin...and was routinely subjected to the disgusting treatment of this court. Princess Elamorna wanted him sexually, and only the royals could "enjoy" him without being trapped in the pleasure, so she tried to force the issue. What an absolute troll.

Well, Princess Elamorna had set herself up to get mindfucked. Daisy specialized in that type of warfare. She had to—it was often the only non-weapon arsenal she had at her disposal. She'd gotten very good at it.

She wasn't sure what to say to Tarian, though. She was utterly, completely at a loss about this. She had no experience in this situation, and she was woefully shallow emotionally. Her life had never allowed that part of her to flower. So she just got down to the details.

"Why don't we have a choice?"

His crooked smile was back. Lord knew what he found hilarious this time. Her deficiency in normal human emotion, perhaps? Her somewhat robotic social skills?

He started chuckling silently. "Because Princess Elamorna will have someone verify whether you're beholden to me. If you aren't, she'll taunt me by having the lowest of guards take you in front of me..." He shook his head, and she was glad he didn't go on. She got the picture, and she had a feeling he knew all this from experience. From Sansy.

"And you thought a tattoo would be enough to throw her off my scent?" Daisy asked incredulously. She laughed, shaking her head. "That never would've been enough. Cool. Fine. You've done *some* sexual things, though, right? Because the night when the darkrend was attacking, you were exceptional."

He sat up fully, his eyes on fire. He crossed his legs in front of him, mirroring her. The sheet fell away from his large, pierced erection and butterflies filled her stomach. He might be the virgin, but she was suddenly more nervous than her actual first time.

"I've done everything a mouth can do. And most of the things fingers can do. And I cheat." His eyes flashed. "Your thoughts direct me. You make it easy to please you."

"You have my permission to keep cheating." She looked into his eyes quietly for a long moment. The space between them shrank. His magnetism pulled at her until she was inching closer. The air filled with energy and electricity, sizzling like lightning.

"Now?" he whispered.

She licked her bottom lip, drawing his eyes.

"Now," she responded quietly, inching closer still. Going slow because for *her* first time, she had wanted it slow. Slow and thoughtful. She'd needed to be built up high to counteract the pain that would come.

"Except I won't have pain," he murmured, watching her advance. "I have wanted your kiss from the first moment I saw you, when you looked right at my glamor, at me, and frowned. When I was on that ledge, though, a new craving took over. A carnal craving. I've salivated over you ever since. Dreamt of you. Wondered what it would be like—if I would ever receive the gift of the gods and touch you."

"Fuck your gods. You're getting a gift from *me*." Her knees brushed his, and he swallowed thickly. She knew how he felt. This seemed...more important than a first, somehow. More consuming. Uncharted waters.

"I'll probably be shit at this," he admitted.

She laughed. "I think you'll figure it out pretty quickly. Dry-humping me has gone very well. What about pregnancy? I know our kinds can reproduce together. Diseases? Not that the latter matters much, since our time is limited."

"Fae have to see the oracle before we can procreate. That happens when a male is at least twenty, but often it is much, *much* later. I've never been concerned about it. We don't have sexual diseases."

"And you are how old? Eight hundred? Two thousand?" She lifted up before climbing into his lap. She had the short nightdress on and the fae rendition of underwear, which was something like briefs, but she figured he'd want to unwrap her, like a present.

His eyes were hooded, the gold winning the war against the black around his pupil. "I'm a mere thirty. An adolescent in fae years. Not often taken seriously."

Her family hadn't treated her that way, since she'd

grown up fast and early, but everyone else did, given she was young for humans. She knew how he felt.

She slid her hand around to the back of his neck and gently coaxed him closer. Her knees hit the mattress beside his hips, and she tucked her shins under his crossed legs. Chest nearly to chest, she started to lower herself onto him.

He stopped her, grabbing the edges of the nightdress and lifting it. She raised her arms so he could pull it over her head. He tossed it away before one hand landed on her back and the other slid up her stomach. His gaze stuck to hers as he leaned over, until the last moment, when his tongue flicked her taut nipple.

She breathed out, letting her head fall back as his hot mouth enveloped her. He sucked and played as his other hand kneaded the opposite breast. He switched, and she pulsed her hips, feeling it deep in her core.

He pulled back, his eyes on hers again, and slowly lowered her. His thumb found her apex as his hard length settled against her underwear-clad core. He moved his thumb as his lips found hers, groaning when she gyrated on top of him.

"Wait..." She pulled back but he kept going. She drank in the sensations. "You were sleeping naked next to me? Is this what you were planning all along?"

He smiled, capturing her lips again. "I passed out in the other room, actually," he murmured against them. "They must've brought me in here. I woke up not long before you did. That's why I played the memory for you. I figured that was the least embarrassing way."

"For you."

"Obviously. What, you thought *you'd* be embarrassed by the princess making a show of how much I didn't want to fuck her?"

She deepened the kiss, reaching down between them and capturing his length. He sucked in a breath as she stroked. He hooked his thumbs into her underwear.

"Equilas, help me. I want this so badly," he breathed, pushing her back until she lay on the bed. He pulled the underwear away before kissing up the insides of her thighs.

She nearly told him not to use that god's name but refrained for the sake of the moment.

"Let's try to quiet that mind of yours, shall we?"

She could feel the smile on his lips...and hear the jingle of the lock on the door in the outer room.

He paused, then kept sliding his lips up and up until he licked right where it counted. Her eyes rolled into the back of her head, and she spread wider. He sucked as his fingers became active...and someone appeared in the bedroom doorway.

"Oh shit," Niall blurted before peeling away. "No, no," he said in a frantic whisper. "Don't go—"

Someone else filled the doorway as Tarian pulsed his suction and two of his fingers filled her just right.

"Oh shit," Lennox murmured, exiting quickly. She should've died from embarrassment, but...it felt too good. She'd count this as practice for what was almost certain to come.

"What did I *just* say?" Niall demanded. "No, not you too!"

"Why? What is he— Oh, hell yeah!" Kayla snickered before she left again. "See? Please the female. We are much more manageable when we've been properly seen to."

"I guess you've never been *properly seen to*, then, huh?" Niall asked her.

"Just like all the females you've been with, yeah," she responded.

Daisy started to chuckle helplessly, her focus fractured.

Tarian pushed up to his elbows. "I can make them go, but time has gotten away from me. I have important matters to see to this sun. Either we do this another time or we hurry. I vote hurry." He paused for an answer, and she couldn't bring herself to say *another time*. "Yes?" Tarian lifted his eyebrows. He nodded. "Yes."

He ducked back down between her thighs.

"No. Damn it!" She grabbed him by his hair and dragged him up her body.

"I'm getting mixed signals here, dove." He crawled up with a smile, sliding his big body between her knees.

She half laughed, half moaned as his hard length settled against her wetness. She dragged his head down and captured his lips. The feel of him against her felt so right. So comfortable. Easy, as though this was how intimacy was *supposed* to be. Safe...when he was the most dangerous person she'd ever met in her life.

"We shouldn't do this now." She swore to herself as

her core pounded. "Your first time shouldn't be rushed. I don't want *my* first time with you to be rushed."

"Ah, so this is really all about you, is it?"

"I mean...yeah." She smiled at him. "But seriously, I want us to take our time. You need to be properly laid for your first time. A quickie only scratches an itch. It's not enough. I want us to try all the things."

"All the things..." His eyebrows started to climb as something she couldn't read flashed through his eyes. "Like...in the butt?"

She sputtered, pushing at his shoulders. "Fucking men. You haven't even put it in the first place and you're thinking about what other areas you can stick it in."

His unabashed smirk was cute. "I'm not a man. I'm fae..."

"In this, there is *zero* difference. Come on. I want to see about that magic. How are we going to get me there without some fucker trying to accost me and drag me to the king?"

Chapter Fourteen

ZORN

The colossal structure of the Faegate loomed before them. Feelings of inadequacy, fear, and depression pressed on him. Bria, behind him, moaned out her displeasure. Someone growled in frustration—Thane, it sounded like. The fringe would affect them all differently, intending to warn them away from crossing.

"See?" Lexi's voice was totally unruffled. Whatever she felt did not affect her, not when her kid needed her. She was the strongest of them all in times like this. She would see them through if anyone could. "They have *all* this set up, and we have a few humans in uniforms trying to make a buck. Something is a *little* off on our side of the line."

"I feel a little off right now," Jerry grumbled. A few people nodded their agreement. "I won't be of any help,

Lexi. There's no rock. Desert for miles—my magic is no good here."

"You see desert?" Jack glanced back at him as they led the horses toward the hazy purple areas dotting the way. They'd send all their traveling supplies back. Zorn had to admit that despite it being a terrible idea to help the fae, it was a smooth system. "I see a huge mountain of...like...briars or something. I feel like I'm going to shit myself, though. Fuck, this isn't ideal when going into a fight."

"It's all part of the illusion," Demigod Kieran said, only a tensed jaw belying his discomfort. Zorn could feel it through their blood link, though. He was fighting it the same as they all were. "Once we cross the border, this feeling will wither and we'll need to fight off the Celestials."

One of the spirits housed in a cadaver took the lead from Kieran and proceeded to walk jerkily toward the first haze of purple. He veered, moving around it, so that the animals would follow. At the last moment, he threw the lead into the air, over the invisible doorway, and the animals walked through and vanished.

He was one of ten fae spirits Lexi had convinced to help them across the fringe. She hadn't had to threaten or force them—she'd simply offered to set them loose on the other side, allowing them to find peace in their afterlife.

So she'd said, anyway. What would likely happen was they'd fall in love with her style of leadership and want to see this through. They'd sign on to their team like so many had before them. She had a *way* about her.

Those spirits had given them a rundown on how crossing the fringe worked. If another group of fae stepped out of this strange portal haze, it was kill or be killed. Fight or run, depending on magical power. After that, it was a mad dash to the Faegate. And, very importantly, they were supposed to keep from killing the Celestials. If they did, the Celestials would hold a grudge against the killer's kin.

The Celestials could go fuck themselves.

"All right, let's get to it." Kieran stepped to a line that their head spirit guide, the most powerful of those they'd found, pointed out. "Beyond this misty area we will run and fight. We are aiming for the third hole on the left. Stick together. Try not to kill a Celestial. We don't need them following us across the fringe."

Zorn gritted his teeth. His adrenaline pumped, ready.

The small cluster of undead spread out to the sides, a haphazard crew in comparison to what they usually worked with. Lexi stepped up next to Kieran, her face hard and her hands fisting and relaxing, over and over. Two Demigods stealing across the fringe was probably a first. Zorn was incredibly curious about the power dynamic.

"Now!" Kieran burst forward, Lexi at his side. The rest of their team followed.

Winged fae hovered close, much closer than it had appeared a moment ago. They were swooping and diving at a band of fae ahead of them. The ground bucked and split as the fae ran, half dodging the Celestials, half raising their long staffs toward them.

Zorn couldn't tell what brand of magic came from those staffs, but the ground acting the way it did hinted at the Emerald kingdom, which had an affinity for seeding and growth and all things natural. That kingdom was supposed to be nestled deep in the wylds, hard to find unless one knew where to look. It was yet another kingdom that was dabbling in the human lands. Zorn wondered if any of them *weren't.*

More Celestials descended from the sky, their delicate wings catching the noon sun and sparkling with gold and pink and purple. Gale-force winds swept up around them from Demigod Kieran, blowing the would-be attackers away to the right.

Their wings curled and their limbs flailed, faces shocked. They hadn't expected that level of power and magic.

In a moment, their team was running down the fae in front of them.

A staff went wide as a Celestial plunged with some sparkly bullshit magic. Zorn didn't much care about the specifics. He puffed into his gaseous form. The fae in front of them likely couldn't see him or track him now. The Celestials probably still could. He was a couple generations removed from anything fae, and human blood greatly watered down fae blood. They'd be able to pick him out. He'd revert as soon as the fae in front of them were dealt with.

Kieran's magic slammed into the fliers in front of them, only three trying to block a group of six fae. Paltry numbers. Heavy fog poured in, clouding the sky over-head and cutting down their visibility.

Before they could even reach the group of fae, one and all fell bonelessly to the ground. Lexi really did make things boring for the rest of them when she just ripped out souls like that. Then, one by one, the bodies started to shake. They slowly got to their feet, confused, looking at their hands. Lexi had stuffed their souls back in and was controlling them like a Necromancer would.

A spear shot down toward them. Donovan, a Tele-kinetic, flicked his hand. His magic batted it away. Light-ning spiderwebbed through the heavy fog, and someone screamed above them. A body came twirling down, unconscious, wings fluttering uselessly behind.

"Catch it," Kieran told Donovan.

Sparkly magic speared Zorn, blistering within his middle. It was just pain, though. It wouldn't kill him, and it had nothing on the sort of feeling Lexi could adminis-ter. He ignored it.

She didn't.

"Really?" Lexi looked up into the sky. "That's the game you want to play?"

Her jaw clenched, and screaming sounded within the heavy fog. The Celestials were hidden from the naked eye, but Lexi could feel their souls.

Another spear sliced through the air. Donovan set down the body he'd caught to bat that one away. Arrows met the same fate. Donovan could do this all day. Had, on occasion, when they'd had to battle a team of Ares-type magic.

"Shit." Lexi knelt by the limp Celestial, a gorgeous male whose hair was starting to curl within the moisture. They clearly straightened their hair for the aesthetic.

"Should I shield us from sight?" Boman, a Light Bender, asked.

"Yes," Lexi said, bending over the Celestial. "Do these things heal at advanced rates?"

Wind spun around them and up into the sky. The fog pulled back for a bit, exposing five Celestials readying weapons and looking down. They didn't plan to get that close and certainly didn't plan to land. No wonder fae were coming and going. With a barrier like this, everyone was wasting time.

"I believe so," Zorn said, visible and waiting near Lexi with his weapon ready. He was useless until they got closer.

Rocks blasted into the air. Jerry had found some boulders. The first went so high and fast that the Celestial couldn't dodge in time. The boulder slammed into its arm and chest, knocking it through the air and nearly hitting another of its kind. She grabbed her arm as she cried out, lifting higher into the air to put distance between herself and Jerry. That hit would've broken bones. The next boulder was anticipated, and the Celestial darted away in time.

"I can dock his soul. It's fine," Lexi said, wiping her brow. "He's trying to live. He just needs a moment for his body to heal. I've got it."

"Sorry," Dylan said. "I didn't account for the moisture in the fog. I made the lightning too strong."

Let him die, Zorn thought, looking skyward. The Celestials fought against Kieran's wind. One flung out her hand. A hail of magic sliced into their crew, the feeling like a whip. Zorn knew from experience.

He ignored that, too. Pain was nothing more than a reminder that you were alive.

Henry, a Reflector, threw up his hands in retaliation. He had the power to assume the magic thrown at him and use it on the attacker. It wouldn't be as strong, though. Still, it would help.

"How much longer?" Kieran yelled at Lexi, constantly changing the airflow and messing with the fog, keeping them guessing.

"Just two more prongs," Lexi said. "The soul will stay in the body if he can keep just two more prongs from deteriorating."

Kieran labored as more magic crashed down upon them.

"I sure would like to help out," Bria ground out, knives in hand. "If they'd come closer, I wouldn't feel like such a freeloader."

"Ditto," Jack said.

Another Celestial swooped and two more came in after her. There were about eight in the sky, half of them staying too high to engage in the fight. Watching, it seemed. Magic rained down from the four, and a deep pounding of pain and agony felt like it was twisting Zorn's bones.

"Do you want me to let him die?" Lexi roared, looking up from where she knelt over the Celestial's body. She put her hands wide for showmanship, not needing them for her soul magic. They wouldn't know that. "He's barely holding on. If I leave, he'll die, and we'll make it through the gate anyway. You must know you can't stop us. Is that what you want?"

Lightning again spiderwebbed across the sky, just barely missing everyone in it. Dylan's control was incredible, and his warning was plain. He could fry them. Rocks tore from the ground and through the rifts in the ground that the fae before them had created. They blasted into the sky, more warning. Kieran stilled the air and pulled back the fog.

"What are you?" a Celestial called out.

Lexi went back to looking at the male on the ground. "A Demigod Spirit Walker. A Soul Stealer, when I need to be. Right now, I'm trying to keep this guy's soul in place while his body rejuvenates. He's almost there. He'll be right as rain...except for maybe a little PTSD."

"Humans shouldn't be this powerful, Demigod or no," the Celestial said.

Lexi laughed. "I have news for you..." She spread her hands again. "I might be a smidge more so because of my bond with another Demigod"—she hooked a thumb at Kieran—"but ultimately, yeah, humans have about the same level of power as you. Good thing for us the books were wrong about your power, huh?"

The Celestial lowered in the air, hesitantly getting closer. "What do you want with these lands?"

"At least she didn't just assume we wanted a deal," Donovan murmured.

"Good looking out—no one make any deals," Bria said.

"Our ward was taken from the human lands," Kieran said, his voice deep and full of confidence. "She is in Faerie against her will. We seek to reclaim her."

"We have *zero* desire to be here. Trust me," Lexi said. She pushed to standing and pointed down at the Celestial. "He's got a wing that's all fucked up. He might need a hand back to...wherever, but he'll live. I think his heart stopped for a bit, but he should be good now."

She took a deep breath and stepped back.

"Listen," she continued, "I hear you people—creatures, whatever—can read minds. You're welcome to come and get the answers you seek. I've got nothing to hide. I want my ward, and then I never want to see one of your kind again. If you were doing your jobs, I wouldn't be here in the first place."

"That's one direction to take things," Bria mumbled.

The Celestial on the ground sucked in a breath and started coughing.

The Celestial in the sky lowered slowly, several others hurrying to join her. They'd descend in a group. More gathered above, staying high. They didn't plan to get involved. Or maybe they were waiting for someone else to cross the fringe.

The Celestial at Lexi's feet groaned and patted himself, trying to hold himself in a few different places. He might've healed enough to live, but it still hurt. The others landed, their gazes going to him quickly and lingering. They cared about his wellbeing.

Seeing that he was doing okay, the female neared cautiously. Her eyes flicked between Kieran and Lexi, the others right behind her.

"We're going to take the wounded," she told Lexi.

Lexi took a step back and Kieran went with her, giving them plenty of space. The three Celestials behind rushed forward and helped the wounded stand. He was barely able to, needing more time to heal. Two of them grabbed him and pushed off into the sky, their wings making a humming sound as they went.

The female locked eyes with Lexi for a long moment. Silence fell around them. Zorn watched the body language but neither gave anything away.

"I just want her back," Lexi said. "I don't need your help, and I don't want to make a deal. I'll either force my way through the fringe and Faerie beyond, or I will walk a red carpet, but I *will* get through."

"A red"—the Celestial cocked her head—"carpet? What is..."

"Never mind." Lexi waved it away.

"Several humans have crossed the fringe." The Celestial's voice took on a hard edge. "More now than ever." Her muscles tensed. She didn't approve of that fact. One wondered why she didn't do anything about it. "I don't recall one that was carried or forced. Several have not had magic, female and male. You believe this tale, and so you may pass to do as you wish. We will not darken your path. However, given you were not invited by a royal, you will need to brave the wylds as any human would. You—"

Her head jerked left. A group of three fae had run

through the border line, appearing from nowhere. A body could see the fringe from a ways off, but on this side, they could only see a white haze.

"I got it!" Bria shouted. "I need something to do."

She took off toward the coming fae before the Celestials above could descend.

"Wait for me!" Jack took off after her, Thane after him, followed by a few of the undead. Those were probably the human spirits they'd brought with them. The others were hunching and uncomfortable in the presence of the Celestials.

"What strange creatures you are," the Celestial said, watching the others confront the incoming fae. "It is not your battle, but you would still defend the fringe?"

"No." Lexi's eyes were hard. "They realize you lot are mostly ineffective and want to stop your kind from coming and going. Killing them will do the trick."

The Celestial's light eyes, a beautiful shade of blue, bored into Lexi.

Lexi huffed, the Celestial having said something directly into her mind.

"If this is the best of your ability," she said, "then it's the task *asked of you* that is the problem. That implies a leadership that doesn't want Guardians to actually guard, no?" She paused. "Sure, sure. It's complicated, yeah."

Lexi turned and strode toward an enormous gate that appeared within a massive wall.

"I'll take my chances," she told the Celestial. "Keep your deal for the next fool that comes along."

With smirks and sparkling eyes, the others followed

after Lexi. There wasn't a creature in this whole land who would speak to Celestials like that and get away with it. Lexi definitely had a way about her, and it didn't matter if she was sweet or spicy, she made herself heard.

Zorn stayed where he was, looking at the female. Glancing at those flying above. Waiting for Bria and the others to rejoin him.

The female's eyes slid to his. They narrowed.

Your quarrel is not with me, she said into his mind.

We shall see, he thought back, peeling away as an out-of-breath Bria caught up with them.

"Zero power or know-how," she said without sparing the Celestial a glance. "Guarding the fringe has to be child's play. It's a wonder they need so many people..."

No, it was a wonder their leadership didn't want them to do a better job...

He pondered that as he neared the large, arching doors leading into Faerie, clearly the main entrance that held no peril. A trick, a trap, or a pass, they would soon see.

As he moved to pass through, something above caught his eye. He glanced up.

A massive being rested its forearms along the top of the walls, hundreds of feet in the air. The face smiled down at him, with hair as dark as the night and spotted through with what looked like stars. She, for it seemed female, covered her mouth with her hand as though to hide a laugh.

What fun, he thought he heard, the voice strange and echoing, far away but in his head at the same time. The form pulled her hand back to bite a nail. Her violet eyes flashed as she looked down at him, her skin fleshlike one moment, then wispy and nearly see-through the next. *The humans have come to play in my games. One of the human god's favorites, no less. Maybe I will invite him for the show. This will be a grand treat...*

Her laugh was horrible and beautiful at the same time, and then she was gone. Vanished like the darkness within the new day.

Cold washed through him. It didn't seem like this would be as simple as going after Daisy. This seemed a lot bigger than any of them could ever possibly know.

Chapter Fifteen

Daisy

Slightly too-big servants' attire draped down her frame, hiding the weapons stashed or strapped on her body. The cloth was old, her slippers worn, and ash from the fireplace marred her face. No one seemed to notice her passing through the halls behind Niall and Lennox.

They stopped beside a set of nondescript double doors. Niall pushed his way inside and Lennox paused so Daisy could go in the middle. The room opened up into a lovely domed affair with stained glass, couches, maps, and scrolls everywhere. Literally everywhere. On chairs, the floor, stuffed in bookcases, overflowing from two different desks, from all the tables... It was madness. Mayhem.

"Nah." She stopped in her tracks. "This looks like a conspiracy theorist's lair."

"A what?" Lennox grabbed her shoulders to keep her walking.

"A person who has lost the thread of reality and—"

"Oh." Eldric stepped out from an alcove. He had a feather quill in one hand, ink on his face, and a sleeveless shirt showing pasty-white, heavily wrinkled arms that would fry immediately if they ever saw the sun. Which they probably wouldn't. "I thought I heard someone. What is—"

He sighted Daisy and lowered his quill. His pale gaze took in Lennox and Niall, and his lips pressed together.

"I choose Tarian," Daisy said without preamble. "I told him everything. I will help him help Faerie, and in turn, he will help my family. I'm okay with that. I'm okay with what will happen to me should I fulfill this plan. Also...we made a deal about it. I'm pretty sure I have to at this point, anyway."

"Yes, I see." He hadn't moved. "My gentle fae, would you excuse us, please? You may wait outside, or in the room just...there."

He indicated another alcove blocked with something that looked like a metal door with a thick bolt locking it from the outside.

"Holy hell," Daisy muttered.

Neither of the guys moved.

"Tarian is not here to make this call, and we don't know you," Lennox said with a vicious note in his voice that Daisy had never heard. She shivered.

"Ah." Eldric brought his hands closer to his chest.

The quill seeped blue ink into his shirt. "Protective of her...or of what she is?"

They didn't answer, so Daisy said, "Does it matter? They're protective. They want assurance you aren't going to kill me. Or, like, magically bug me in some way."

"Magically...what?" Eldric said.

"Track me or mess with whatever I am or hinder what I can do," she elaborated.

"He wouldn't do that," Niall said. "It's against his order's rules."

"Neither would I—or *could* I—kill the crystal chalice." Eldric frowned at them. "But if it pleases you..."

It took them ten minutes to make a deal. If Eldric tried to do anything but help her, they would be summoned.

"Now, then." Eldric studied her after the others had stepped outside. They'd wisely chosen not to be locked in what was apparently an iron chamber. A smile ghosted his lips. "I am eternal, yet...I never thought I would see one of you. Come in, come in."

He motioned her farther into the chaos. She wasn't usually a stickler for cleanliness, and didn't need to be terribly organized to get things done, but the mess made her skin crawl. Mostly because she worried something might creep out from under some of the dusty piles and literally crawl on her.

"It is nearly impossible to find one of you, you understand?" He zigzagged through the space, somehow not stepping on a single scroll.

Paper crinkled under her foot.

"Oops. Sorry—" Stepping away led to more crinkling.

"Your lifespans are so short. A blink, really. And that is if you aren't killed off earlier than normal, which many are for one reason or another. When Tarianthiel—I will call him Tarian, since you and he, and he and I, are so familiar with one another—set out to find you, I thought he was wasting his time. Without a sanctioned pass from the Celestials, who would never grant one for this in the current turmoil, he only had moments at a time. He had a whole world to search, over several billion humans, with nothing but stolen moments. Never, I thought. Yet in only four thrushes—three?" He paused. "Six?" He put a finger to his chin while shaking his head. "I've lost track of time. Anyway, he was able to manage it. I knew he was special. Not just because of his power, mind you. He is a favorite of the gods."

"They have a funny way of showing it."

He stopped at the largest desk of all, way in the back of the chaotic room. This one, miraculously, was spotless. Only a single scroll lay on the polished surface. The two chairs in front of it, however, were covered.

He affixed half-moon spectacles atop his nose as he looked at her. "We must never be quick to judge the gods, young *elara*. Oftentimes, their plans are dense and complicated, but they always serve a purpose. The hardest trials reap the greatest enlightenment."

She couldn't contain her look of skepticism. "Cool."

He studied her. "A nonbeliever. I do so love those. I hope I shall be there for your revelation. Assuming, of course, you have the mind power to grasp it."

Was he calling her stupid?

"How did you know what I was?" she asked.

"Human? Because the chalice has to be human—"

"No, the chalice. You saw me before Tarian found me in that hallway."

"Oh." He gave her a pronounced frown. "Once the crystal chalice is formed, the magic shines."

"But no one else here can see it."

"Oh," he said again, waving her away. "My order can see magic the wielder is trying to hide."

"But I'm...not trying to hide it. I mean, I don't know how."

"You clearly do, since you clearly are."

"You don't seem to have the mind power to grasp what I am telling you," she said, and his frown became a scowl. She barely stopped herself from smiling. "I don't know that I am hiding it. I must be doing it unconsciously. How can I learn to do it consciously?"

He busied himself with the scrolls at the side of his desk. "Let us see. Now, how much do you know about the crystal chalice magic?"

She paused beside one of the piles on a chair.

"Oops, let me clear that away for you." He scooped up the scrolls and dumped them on the floor behind the chair.

"Great," she drawled before explaining all she knew. It didn't take long, given she knew very little.

"And you made a binding deal?" he asked.

"Is there another kind?"

He narrowed his eyes in thought. "No." He tapped

the feather portion of the quill to his lips. "You have a very succinct explanation of what you are. Expected, with a human's limited range of thought. Let me elaborate and hope it sinks in."

It was her turn to scowl. He didn't think much of humans in general.

It soon became apparent that it wouldn't be the court games that tucked her into her final resting place. It wouldn't be facing the Obsidian kingdom's royals or the gods or godlike power. It would be sheer boredom. When he was done, she wondered if he'd magically kept her awake. There could be no other explanation.

"So, you see, you are so much more than a conduit for magic. You are an actual vessel, my dear. You can store magic for up to...oh...five turns, I should think. Even magic as robust as Tarian used to possess. But—and here is the danger—you do not, yourself, create magic. You steal it."

She blinked, coming out of her drooling stupor. "What?"

His eyes startled to sparkle. "Ah, yes, now we are doing more than just absorbing. We are *listening*! Yes, you can steal magic. You steal from the magic wielder and house it in your vessel to be used at a later time. When you take it, you deplete their magic. Say you steal just a fraction—they will only become a fraction weaker. Steal it all, and they will die of magiclessness. Do you see?"

She turned that over in her head. "Not about the last part. If a fae loses all their magic, they die?"

"Magic here exists within the fae—"

"I thought it came from Faerie?"

He beamed. "Yes! My goodness, you are a credit to your kind. It comes from Faerie, and Faerie is in us all. We are the very fabric of Faerie, living and breathing. Eating and pooping. We draw on Faerie for our magic, and it draws on us for survival. We are connected. All of us. Everything. If you were to siphon away all the magic of a fae or creature, it would take the fabric of the being with it. It would take their life's breath, and the empty shell would fall."

Her heart leapt at the possibility. At the thought that maybe she'd have more of an arsenal than a fae. "So...I can kill fae with this magic."

He paused. "Is that any different from what you can do with your knives?"

She frowned at him. "Easier, I imagine, right?"

He held up a finger. "Maybe."

"Oh good. I was worried I wouldn't get straight answers when I came here."

He walked to the bookcase on his left. The fourth shelf held nothing but scrolls, some rolled, many not. He reached into them.

"It is not as easy as simply taking magic. You have to be sly, like an actual thief. If they sense you depleting them, they will react like all creatures you are trying to kill—they will defend themselves urgently and ardently. They will usually react violently. You can then wither their magic, but they will still possess it, and—"

"Wither means nullify, right?"

"—therefore still have—yes, keep up, please—still have their magic. Then they can overpower you. In a regular fight, like with fists or knives, they might be content to wound you and walk away. If you are caught depleting their magic, however, their instinct will be to kill or be killed. Getting caught will almost always become a fight to the death. Yours...or theirs."

She barked out a laugh. "So just a normal day in the life of a Chester, huh?"

He paused in rummaging through the scrolls. "A... chezzure?"

"Never mind. What happens when my vessel's capacity is full?"

A section of the scrolls toppled over on top of him, cascading to the ground. He froze, then looked down at his feet. "What a mess."

Her eyes widened as she looked around at everything else. That was a mess, but the rest wasn't?

He continued his search, knowing what he sought wasn't in the dropped items.

"You hold it for as long as you can," he answered. "And then..."

Her nerves started to dance. This was the part where the terrible news made the magic more of a curse than a boon. The part where this entire meeting became a waste because she was no better off.

"And then?" she asked.

Chapter Sixteen

Daisy

"Ah! Here we go." He pulled a rolled scroll from deep in the back of the bookcase before stepping back. Despite the mess around his feet, he could still keep from stepping on anything. He glanced at her as he made his way back. "Uhm..." He pushed his glasses up before pulling his chair closer to the desk. "Oh, well, it goes back into the fabric of Faerie, obviously. Now..."

He started to unwrap the scroll.

"Wait..." She pulled her chair closer and grimaced when a scroll tore under one of the wooden legs. Pale eyes drifted upward to look at her over the spectacles. "Sorry," she said. The eyes moved back down. "So I steal the magic, try not to die if they find out, and after some amount of time—"

"Five turns."

"Fine. After five turns"—she'd ask about it later—"it just...goes away? From me, I mean. I don't explode or deflate or lose a limb or some other horrible thing if I don't use it?"

His gray brows pinched together and his eyes drifted back up. "Humans have a very warped and twisted way of viewing magic. It is not out to get you, my dear."

Speaking of deflating, her released breath sounded like a balloon losing all its air. "O-kay. So...what do I do with the stored magic?"

"Save it for someone to use. I swear, it is like talking to a rock. You are a vessel. That is the nature of a vessel. You store things until they are needed, and then you release them." His expression was one of exasperation. "Humans find the simplest things so very complicated."

She ignored that last comment. "I'm essentially an item for someone to use."

"Well..." He leaned on his elbow, peeling off his spectacles as he looked at her. "That is not a nice way of looking at it." He put his glasses back on. "But yes, essentially. You are the chalice."

She leaned back. "And to boost magic, I am not stealing magic. I am..."

"You are a conduit. It is really such an interesting magic, isn't it? A vessel, a conduit, and a stagnant."

"A stagnant?"

"The nulling part."

"Right. For the vessel and the st-stagnant, I actively have a role. I choose when and how much to steal, or I can nullify them if I want to."

"Yes."

"And you'll teach me how to do that?"

"No."

"Great. Excellent. This trip has been worth my time. And the conduit, that is something Tarian initiates?"

"You have to allow him. No one can use you without your permission." He held the scroll open on the desk, looking up with a rare smile. "Isn't that the greatest caveat to this unlimited, godlike power? The vessel must agree with its use. It is why the crystal chalice was always meant to be—"

"A thinking, logical being. I got that. If I allow him, can I stop him before it means my death?"

Eldric's smile didn't wither because of bad news, but because he was thinking. "Yes, you certainly could. But if you do, he won't be able to achieve godly power, and his plans won't work. Faerie won't see its balance, the fringe won't be granted its protection, and fae will still trickle into the human realm until someone stops them, which is unlikely in the current state of turmoil. The human world would be destroyed and your family with it."

"Fuck, man. Don't break it to me gently or anything."

He looked at her. "Yes, this must be complicated for a hu*man*. I am not a *man*. Man implies your type of being—"

She ignored him and looked at the ceiling. Well, at least she'd get that nulling magic. That was huge, assuming she could figure it out in time for those court games. And she could siphon magic to store for Tarian in case the princess came for him. Again, assuming she could figure it out in time. It was something. Hell, it was more than she had dreamt of. Her fate was still sealed, but she had a few more tools to help her reach the finish line.

"Okay, then—"

She jumped with the *thunk* on the desk.

Eldric rested his hand on a triangular device with gold and silver running around it and pink glowing at the top. "This will help you learn to shield your mind. It's the fastest way to achieve results. Tarian said you wouldn't mind a little pain if it protected your thoughts."

"Tarian said that, did he?"

"Yes." He walked away.

She looked at the device, wondering what kind of pain it would entail. In a moment, Eldric was back with a similar device, but this one was a circle with a purple glowing bit at the top and green at the side.

"This is to learn how to wither magic, which is fairly straightforward, I'm given to understand, and how to steal it, which is quite a bit harder. There is a steep penalty for failing in thievery, but you'll be well used to it with the shielding training, so you should be fine." He held out a finger. "Some advice—go ahead and scream. Sometimes, it helps."

She closed the door behind her, and Lennox and Niall straightened up from their crouches. Her head hurt, her chest hurt, and her mood was very sour.

How'd it go? Lennox asked as she walked toward

Tarian's chambers. She wanted to see if she remembered the way.

In addition to being a magical vessel, I am also a vessel for information. I store it easily and my recall is excellent. Eldric decided that as he was teaching me to use the very horrible and painful contraptions. He expressed too much surprise that I'd make a prime candidate for a life of information, contemplation, and godly worship. Have no fear, though. I can't become a scribe. Females are fine—he didn't get my joke—but humans really are the worst. They are so often dumb as rocks that if the order lets one in, they might have to let in more, and then the gates will be overrun. She turned to give them a glower. *I shit you fucking not.* She turned back around. *I also do not appreciate your smirks.*

Sorry, Niall said. *Tarian always leaves in a similar mood. What'd he say about the other forms of magic?*

She rubbed at her chest and made sure to keep her head down as she gave them a summary of what Eldric had said.

I tried out the apparatuses he gave me. The mind-shield trainer feels like a punch in the head when I don't get it right, and the other feels like shock treatment to the chest. They are not pleasant, but they should work if I prove less idiotic than the average human. She shook her head. *He's never even met a human besides me, but boy does he have* thoughts *about them. He wasn't even trying to be mean about it. He was mostly cordial and conversational about the shortcomings of my kind.*

Yeah, you got lucky with Tarian, Lennox said. *He likes*

the human world. He's a lot more open-minded about them.

Well. Daisy sent back another glower. *Not all that lucky, right? He found me, manipulated the situation, and brought me here to my death.*

Lennox grimaced. *Fair.*

When they got closer to Tarian's chambers, more fancy people filled the corridors. Females and males wearing swishing dresses or gold-laden jackets sauntered down the middle of the space as though they were the most important creatures in all the world. Some had mostly clear faces with soft skin, but others had that strange sallow appearance, grayish, with the black lines and circles under their eyes.

She meant to ask about it, but before she could, one of the males caught sight of her. His eyes flared with interest, and he veered, putting himself in Daisy's path.

Try to go around, Niall said with a hint of caution.

Obviously she was going to try to go around, but she didn't have high hopes.

Sure enough, the male stopped in front of her and put out his hands to detain her. Gold chains dripped down his design-laden jacket, and everything about his posture and poise suggested he was likely gentry or close. He had power. His rich brown skin was devoid of black lines or that gray hue. He didn't seem affected by the twisted magic, assuming that was what caused the effect. His belly protruded—he was a little portly—and he was taller than Daisy, though not as tall as Lennox or Niall.

"I haven't seen you before," he purred. "Such a beautiful little thing. Whom do you belong to?"

Pressure ripped through her head as though someone were using their nails to pry it open and look inside. She winced, and the back of her neck heated from the pressure.

"She belongs to—"

"I didn't ask *you*," the male cut off Niall, not sparing him a glance. His eyes gleamed as he looked Daisy over. "I'm asking this clever little *tricklet*. Someone has taken great pains to hide their secrets. Would that someone be Tarian?"

The pressure in Daisy's head increased until she struggled to keep her knees from buckling. She reached to get her knife, hidden between her breasts, but her arms wouldn't move. Magic twisted through her body, riddling her with pain to make her compliant. Behind her, Niall and Lennox staggered, Lennox reaching for the wall to stay upright. They were getting the same treatment.

"My goodness," the male murmured, stepping closer to Daisy. "Your mind is strong for someone who looks so weak. Not strong enough, I think. What is he doing for the royalty whom he hates? They have plans they are not sharing with the court, but they are, for some reason, putting their faith in him. What are they?"

Black spots pulsed behind her eyes. Her vision grew hazy. Still the pressure pounded, an agonizing throb. A sharp stab of pain speared her temples. She clamped down, having only gotten a couple lessons with that shield device but trying to practice now. Trying to stay upright. Trying to save her life by protecting what was in her head.

"Why does he visit the human world?" The male was almost whispering, but his words pinged around the inside of Daisy's skull. Magic, obviously, trying to find purchase. He crept closer, his movements sinister, and leaned over her. She couldn't even recoil, all her strength going into standing upright, unable to push his prying mind away. "What errand is he running for—"

A shock wave of magic blasted through the corridor. The light dimmed—it was as though someone had leeched away the glow. Swirls of liquid night curled through the air and slunk between Daisy and the male. The pressure in her mind cut off, and she sucked in a sweet lungful of air.

"Glimrey," a thankfully familiar voice said. Tarian walked up, handsomely unimpressed, but the dangerous energy around him was palpable. "What *are* you doing speaking with my new toy?"

The male—Glimrey—straightened before taking a step back. He affected an air of pompous disinterest, but he couldn't hide the wariness in his eyes.

"Ah, Tarianthiel. Back from your journey, I see."

Tarian spread his hands as he stopped beside Daisy. She scurried behind him, badly wanting to rub her aching temples.

"I am. Was it just me, or were you asking questions about matters that do not pertain to you?" He cocked his head, tsking at the other male. "Why could you possibly need to know about royal business? Unless you've made new friends outside of this court..."

Glimrey tensed. "Not at all," he said, slipping a hand into his pocket casually. "I just wonder why the royals allow someone such as you to come and go as they please."

"Hmm. Maybe that is a question for the king...and not my property."

Glimrey lifted his eyebrows, affecting Tarian's unimpressed stance. "Speaking of your property..." He took a few steps toward the wall, inviting Tarian for a more intimate chat. His voice lowered until Daisy could barely hear it. "Outsiders know how you are treated in this court. I know your power alone granted you your title. Wouldn't you rather find a court more interested in your...talents? One that treats you like an official member instead of a kick-box? I have friends of a certain status, Tarian. They are interested. I can work out a trade."

"What kind of trade do you think might entice me?"

"Oh, you know, the usual. Status, placement, the most eligible gentry as a possible mate. Sire a powerful heir and you will be set for years to come."

"And for you?"

Glimrey shrugged, looking around in pseudo-boredom. "A few nights with your property, for starters. A pleasure loan."

"A *pleasure* loan? That only? Because it seemed like you were trying to access her thoughts. Surely a few nights would give you plenty of time to break my favorite toy."

"Break? Nah. That isn't the kind of pleasure I seek from my nighttime activities."

"Well." A black haze once again dimmed the light in the hall. It curled around Glimrey, thick and dark and forbidding. Tarian's voice turned rough. Wariness once again leaked into Glimrey's features. "While I would greatly enjoy the ramifications of your touching my plaything, I happen to know the king does not want you dead. Not yet. So I will simply inform you that I do not share. I do not loan."

He leaned in aggressively. His magic coiled, then spun. Daisy felt a painful yank from her middle and knew Tarian was boosting his magic through the crystal chalice. Now would've been a fantastic time to have stolen magic stored, because *fuck* that hurt like Hades had kicked her right in the twat.

Gold glittered within the black, and an earthy scent mingled with the acidic smell of the obsidian magic. His power pulsed, hard and hot and heavy, so enormous it felt like it had chased all the air out of the corridor. Glimrey's eyes rounded in fear.

"If you *ever* attempt to push past my blocks and ransack my pet's memories, I will defy my king and turn your body into a mangled mass of tissue and bone. A *living* mass that will beg me to end its suffering. But I won't. Instead, I will put you on display as the spy you are and let the king fuck your eye sockets in front of the whole court. Do you understand me? She is *mine*. Touch her again, even with magic, even from afar, and I will make good on my claim."

He stared the other fae down, his magic pulsing, solid black but with a gorgeous sheen of gold. Then he turned away, not sparing Daisy a glance before he was walking down the corridor, back the way he'd come.

And we're walking, Niall said quickly, plucking her sleeve to get going. *Don't look back.*

That was fucking close, Lennox said, shaken. *Glimrey was putting all his power behind cracking my shields.*

Yeah. Niall hurried them along, getting glances and not caring. *If there hadn't been three of us to split his focus, he might've gotten through. He's desperate to know what the king is planning.*

Do fae not usually do that? Daisy asked as they turned a corner. They didn't slow down.

No, Lennox said. *Oh, they'll read a mind that is open for the taking, but to get past shields, they're usually sneaky. Drugs, pixie wine—something to loosen up the victim or knock them out entirely. They'd need the victim to be too far gone to remember what happened, because the practice itself is an act of hostility in a court. It is essentially sneaking into someone's chambers and rifling through their possessions. Glimrey really ought to know better. He is gentry with one of the highest statuses in this court.*

He thinks Tarian is a puppet, Niall said. *A fool. They all do, even though they fear him. They think the king can keep him on a leash. That trade offer was nothing but smoke. Calling attention to Tarian not being of royal birth, as far as Glimrey knows, was a slight. He knows Tarian is trapped here by some sort of deal. They all know that. He knows very well that Tarian can't leave, or he would've done it by now. Glimrey wants the information regarding that bridge. Everyone must know that Tarian brought back the crystal chalice, which they think is the item in the throne room. With the Celestial unrest growing and magic starting to twist, everyone wants out. They want to escape to lands where they can rule themselves with unlimited power.*

They reached Tarian's chambers. Niall worked his hands, using magic to tear down the ward, before opening the door and ushering her inside.

"Think he believed that Tarian was capable of following through on that threat?" Lennox fell onto the couch with a sigh. He massaged his head.

"Wouldn't he be worried that Tarian knows he's a spy?" Daisy asked, sinking into a chair. She massaged her head as well. That had been rough.

"The king knows Glimrey is a spy." Lennox let his head fall back. "He says he is loyal to the Obsidian Throne but that he needs to trade information sometimes."

"And the twisted king believes him." Niall huffed and shook his head, finally taking a seat.

"He has no reason not to," Lennox replied. "Not yet, at any rate. So far, Glimrey has given the king everything he wants, and Tarian hasn't mentioned the times Glimrey was selling more than he was gaining. Tarian has it in hand...though..."

"He'll have to make good on that threat to keep it in hand," Niall surmised. "And I bet Glimrey doesn't believe Tarian would do it, not when he'd have to defy the royalty."

"They don't think that," Daisy murmured softly, remembering the look in Glimrey's eyes. Remembering the guards who had relinquished her to Tarian, the prison wards, the servants who had hustled away... "This court is scared shitless of Tarian. He's wild. He's dangerous. He's trapped, but he's not tamed. They all know it." She sucked on her bottom lip, going over everything she knew and the possible allure of the crystal chalice. "But Tarian's threats don't matter if they get what they want before he finds out. They can leave...and they know he can't."

"They don't know how to use the crystal chalice, though," Niall said. "Even if they grabbed it, they wouldn't get what they wanted."

Daisy shook her head. "They want what's in our heads. You heard him. He thinks I know the details about all of this, and he thinks he can break into my mind. Honestly...he might be able to if I don't fortify myself better. That was an iffy situation back there."

"Besides the royals, he's the most powerful person in this court," Lennox said gravely.

She believed it.

"If I don't figure out how to null magic, I'll have my head cracked open, and then they'll take me and try to use me. I have to get to work."

Chapter Seventeen

Daisy

The cooling water lapped at Daisy's neck, and her hair hung down the sides of her face. The rest of her body was submerged.

The contraptions from Eldric had shown up in Tarian's chambers shortly after Daisy and the guys had sat down. Lennox said Tarian must've visited Eldric right after he'd pried Glimrey out of their minds. Only he could magically send things across the ward to his private quarters. Daisy had wasted no time working with the apparatuses.

Twenty minutes in—or that was what it felt like; Tarian's clock was a bunch of symbols she didn't understand—and Niall had sent for Faelynn. Those contraptions gave no quarter. If she didn't get it perfectly right, she got a shock or a head slam. Partial learning was not an option.

When she couldn't take any more, she'd skulked off to the bath to twitch in peace. The shocking system had been slow to dissipate.

As the water cooled further and time trickled by, she thought about getting out. She should go back to training. Everything counted on her mastering the chalice magic. It was the only thing that would keep her alive in this court. She felt it. Hell, just today, she'd been given proof of it.

Before she'd fully decided, the soft light from the magical orbs positioned around the room dimmed as a figure loomed in the doorway. She sucked in a breath when she saw Tarian's appearance.

Shadows pooled under his eyes, and his face was drawn with weariness. His wild hair had frizzed, a bit of it matted at the side of his head with blood. Blood splatter decorated his neck and had dripped down. His tunic lay open, and the white undershirt was stained crimson all down his front. It didn't look like the blood had come from him. His pants were ripped, and his boots were gone. He leaned heavily against the doorframe.

"Hello, darling," she teased. "Busy day at the office?"

His answering smile was slight, and he leaned his head against the frame as well. "I had a few meetings that didn't go as planned. Then I had to track down that nutsack who nearly killed me last night and gruesomely claim my vengeance. The last required a lot of effort, and

I wasn't really in the mood, but I had to send a message, so..." He shrugged.

"You got it done?"

He held out his hands, indicating the blood.

"I would've rather gruesomely killed someone than what I was up to," she murmured, then swished the water. "Want in, or do you have another life to expend by narrowly escaping an assassination attempt?"

"Another...life?"

"Yeah, like a cat. Nine lives?" She paused. "Do you have cats here?"

"Oh." He pushed off the frame. "No, we don't. We have something like it, but they feed on entrails. They aren't as moody, but much more violent." He looked down at himself and then at the water. "I should rinse off before I get in or I'll get the water all gross."

"We should drain it and put in more, anyway. It's gotten cold."

He shook his head as he ventured closer, his steps unsteady. He grabbed the edge of the copper tub, and slowly it began to heat, then faster. In a handful of moments, she had to hold up a hand and say, "Whoa, okay. That's getting hot."

He nodded quietly and began to strip as she called up the various magics in the human world that might be able to do something like that. There were fire elementals, of course. They could heat a body of water like this. Or just set her on fire, if they wanted to. A couple Ares magics could...

She let her thoughts drift as she noticed Tarian staring down at her, his bloodied shirt halfway off.

"What?" she asked.

"You look exhausted, you sound exhausted, yet your mind is forever whirring. How do you do it?"

"Oh. Well." She dunked her head in the newly warm water. "I have a mind for information. If I wasn't human, Eldric would recruit me for the scribe order."

"You'd never pass." He shrugged out of his pants and left them in a pile on the floor. "Your humor is too dry. You'd tell sarcastic jokes, and they'd think you were saying facts. You'd get accused of lying and eventually killed, since you can't quit once you're admitted. In the meantime, the whole place would be in disarray."

"The whole place—have you *seen* Eldric's mess of a library? There's shit *everywhere*. He kept giving me *looks* when I stepped on discarded scrolls, but the floor was littered with them. It's madness. I'm not super tidy, but that would drive me insane."

"Yeah, he's somewhat chaotic. It works for him, though. He's one of the best. It's why he moved into this kingdom."

"The gods willed it."

"Yes, they did."

"To help you."

"It seems so."

She grunted. She had some things to say about that help, those gods, and this whole shitshow, but it was nothing new, and she was tired. There was no point in the anger.

"That's about where I'm at, too," he said at the basin in the corner. He filled it with water and started washing away the evidence of his day. "Just stay alive, get it done, and walk away."

"Walk away? I thought you were going to offer your life for the betterment of the realm."

"Yes. But *walk away* sounds much nicer."

She had to agree there. Maybe she'd adopt the lingo.

He had a few gashes across his back and what looked like a stitched-up wound. A couple of those fights looked like they'd gotten too serious for comfort.

"The underbelly of this court doesn't fight fair." Red water ran down his toned muscles and taut skin. "They like to bring all their friends and attack in numbers. I'm wise to their antics, though." He gave her a low-energy thumbs-up.

"Are you constantly battling when you're here?" she asked as he finished up, leaving water all over the floor. She frowned at it, but it wasn't her bathroom, so she didn't say anything.

"It'll dry," he said, answering her anyway. "I couldn't be bothered to sop it up. Lean forward. I'll get in behind you."

A wave of heat and butterflies rolled through her body, but the feeling subsided as her body twitched with a dart of lightning.

"What's wrong with you?" he asked as he slid his long legs on either side of her in the large bathtub. "Fuck, this is hot."

She didn't bother answering with words, but instead

185

mentally replayed her afternoon and into the early evening.

"Hmm." He sighed and leaned back, pulling her in tighter against him. "Seems like it hurts."

"Yes, thank you. It does. Nice choice in contraptions to train me."

"You'll get it. The learning curve is only steep if you're a dum-dum, and Eldric doesn't think you are. High praise coming from someone who thinks humans spend most of their time drooling because they forget to shut their mouths."

She shook with silent laughter. He laughed as well.

"No, I don't spend all my time here fighting. Usually, it is more politics and an occasional assassination. And hiding from Princess Elamorna. This time is different. The king is trying to settle things in preparation for going over the fringe, and I'm having to pry information out of certain individuals who won't be missed. I need to know what the king is planning without his knowing that I know. He will try to use me and then destroy me, I've learned, which I've always suspected. I need to do the opposite. Things are progressing quickly, and I'm running out of time. Hence the long, blood-soaked days. Not to mention this court is badly twisted. Worse, even, than when I left. I've never seen a group of fae so badly off. It's dangerous to all of Faerie. The Celestials have a lot to answer for."

"I thought it was the gods."

He pulled her hair from around her neck and bent forward to kiss her jaw. "My brother didn't have the power to kill me on his own. He made a deal with King Valanor—the king of this court—that the Celestials would turn a blind eye to what was going on here if the king helped set a trap for me. The king went for it, and my brother delivered the deadly strike. If not for the gods, I would've died. The rest, you know."

"Then the king was cool with your just taking up residence in his court even though he helped trap and nearly kill you?"

"Why wouldn't he? He has the Ancestral Sevens Celestial at his beck and call. He has a Celestial trapped in his court and forced to use his style of magic. He knows how much that rankles one of my kind. We represent the balance. The turning points of light and dark. To be forced to use, solely, his shadowy power..."

She was glad he couldn't see her crooked grin. The Celestials had their fair share of arrogance, she'd say that much.

"Maybe try harder on that mind-shield device," he said grumpily.

She laughed as he leaned back again, his head *thunking* against the edge of the tub.

"Regardless," Tarian went on, "a god offered me to him. You don't turn down a god's favor."

"That god is fucking him over, though."

"Only if I can get my shit together, and let's be honest, the verdict is still out on that."

She traced her fingers over his knees. "What's the ancestral magic of sevens?"

He rested his hands on her tummy, stroking softly,

then took a deep breath and let it out slowly. "The result of bad decision-making and a troubled past."

"Sounds like what I'm doing with you."

He leaned forward to kiss her bare shoulder. "My father is a seventh son. I am his seventh son."

"What's the significance of that?"

"It is said that a seventh son of a seventh son, or a sixth daughter of a sixth daughter, will double in power. They had many more sons than daughters, so when they got close to seven sons, my father pushed my mother to keep going. He wanted to be the first Celestial king to create the Ancestral Magic of Sevens. But my mother's body was starting to fail. By the time she had my brother, the sixth boy, she'd had nine children and lost two. She pleaded to give up. Technically, fae live forever, and one would think they could procreate forever, but babies are hard on a female's body, as you probably know. It was becoming dangerous for her. The healers advised against trying for more. He would not be deterred. So she agreed to have one more, come what may. If she produced a daughter instead of a son, she granted him to try with another, something that must've killed her to say. It is said she loved him greatly. She did not share. She did have one more son, though. Me. But it was her last. She died in childbirth, and I nearly went with her. I got the Sevens Magic and then some. Some healers think she imparted her dying breath unto me—a boost to my already boosted power."

"So you were mighty."

"I was. And naturally gifted in my physical abilities,

as well. I set hard to training, at first because the kingdom was watching. I wanted to earn my place in the family—the place my mother had died to give me. Then the court started to grow wary of my constantly growing power. They started to mistrust me. So I trained to keep busy. I spent all my time training—hiding, really. I made myself more than just my magic and stayed out of the court's eyes while I did it."

He twisted to grab a washcloth and a chunk of soap from the stand. His arms came around her, and he rubbed the cloth against the soap before sweeping it over the dips and curves of her body.

She closed her eyes as he washed her, letting her head fall back to rest on his collarbone, feeling his touch as it moved along her skin. "In turn, you scared the court more because of it."

He soaked the cloth in the water, washing it of soap, before dripping it over her skin. "Yeah. I learned that too late."

"Don't we always?" she whispered, angling her head to the side so he could run his lips across her shoulder and up her neck. "Did your father blame you for your mother?"

"No. He blamed himself. That's why the court is failing. He is wallowing in misery. He has lost control, and the vultures are circling."

She lay harder against him, reaching back to loop her arms around his neck. She thought about all he'd said. What a tragic past. He'd caused a rift just by being born, through no fault of his own. Because yes, with that level of power, physically and magically, it was no wonder they wanted to get rid of him, especially with the throne in jeopardy. He was powerful beyond compare, decorated, tight friends with soldiers, and a natural heir. He would be the number one contender to take over for his father. No surprise that he'd ended up here.

"It would've been helpful if I'd known you then so you could've filled me in *before* I ended up in this situation," he murmured, tracing endless loops across her pebbled skin, where the warm water ended and the cool air of the bathroom began.

She breathed out, falling into the feel of his touch tightening her core.

"I've learned all this in the last handful of years, like you," she said. His fingers moved up and down her arms and across her stomach, as though he were memorizing every inch of her skin. "In your situation, I likely would've ended up in the same place. Well...I kinda did, didn't I? With godly magic that will get me killed. A perfect pair."

His hands drifted up her stomach. The mood deepened, their movements slowing.

"Yes, a perfect pair," he said, and she could hear the conviction in his voice. The truth. He wasn't lying. He wasn't being sarcastic. He actually thought they were perfect together.

Strangely, surprisingly...she agreed.

She lowered her arms, letting her hands fall. They landed on his, and she directed them farther upward. His palms moved over her breasts.

He breathed out heavily. His thumbs stroked across her budded nipples. He kissed her cheek, then waited while she turned so he could kiss her lips.

"All I thought about today was getting back to you," he admitted, his tone deep and filled with reverence. "I was finishing what had to be done so I could see your beautiful face again. So I could taste your perfect lips. I haven't known much of heaven in my life, but lying here with you, feeling the closeness of your flesh, it was worth the deal I made. It is worth all the hardships I've endured. If I only know this moment, it will have all been worth it."

She deepened the kiss, desperate for him. Needing to feel him deeper. "Make love to me, Tarian."

He reached lower with one hand, down over her stomach and on between her thighs. She sucked in a breath as his fingers explored.

"I nearly lost my mind when Glimrey suggested I loan you to him." He leaned forward and nipped at her neck. "I wanted to kill him on the spot. It took all of my control to stop at a threat."

His finger moved in a tight circle. She pushed her knees wider and drank in the sensations.

"I want to mark you so badly," he murmured.

"Won't you be embarrassed that I'm human?"

He breathed out a laugh, stroking down and in, the heel of his hand grinding, hitting everywhere at once. His other hand kneaded her breast. She arched, his fingers plunging, her body tightening up.

"Fuck 'em."

She lost her breath as he worked faster, stroking her higher. She rolled her hips as the pleasure pounded, as she braced at the edge, and then she was flying, hitting her crescendo and coming apart.

She breathed deeply as she came back down. He kept exploring, lighter now, firing aftershocks through her. She twitched with the aftermath of that damn contraption.

"The mark is the tattoo, right?" she asked as she angled her head back.

He leaned in to capture her lips. "Yes. A tattoo that marks you as permanently mine. I thought the magic would be enough, but others think that is something for pets. That I might still share, as some do. A mark means I won't. I assume. This court is so fucked up. Who knows anymore?"

Shivers coated her body as she realized she liked that. She liked that he wouldn't even think of sharing, despite the customs. Despite the status difference. Not that she'd allow herself to be shared.

Still, being with him felt strangely natural. It felt like what intimacy was supposed to be, something she'd never thought would come naturally to her. Or at all, honestly. Her version of intimacy was usually just physical. She didn't share her thoughts, didn't have much in the way of emotion, and figured her life had stunted her for the type of closeness most people took for granted.

With him, though, she hadn't had a choice. And now it felt comfortable. She liked that he could read her inner-most thoughts, her secrets. He'd opened her up, allowing her to be blasé about sharing her vulnerabilities with him.

In turn, he'd shared pieces of himself. His own vulnerabilities. They were on equal footing where their true selves were concerned, and she'd never had that. She'd never allowed it. Without his mindgazer ability, she knew she never would have. She was glad for it now. Happy for this with him, as short as their time together would be.

"You can't mark me because it might turn to diamond dust, right?" she asked in an almost quivering voice.

"Yes."

"Even though that would be really pretty."

Humor entered his voice. "Even though. You are a rare and special treasure, little dove. You don't shy away from the creature I have become in this court. The creature you met in the dungeon—the dark side of me that rages and kills without remorse. The part of me that is distinctly, unequivocally fae. That part makes Eldric very nervous. He doesn't trust me. He hopes I'll do as I've said, and he can read in my mind that I mean to, but he worries that the second these obsidian shackles fall from my shoulders and my power swells to its natural heights, I will claim your magic for myself. That I will be unstoppable, and my desires will turn from healing to destruction. Ruling rather than disappearing. That my time here has twisted me the way it has twisted so many others." He huffed. "My own family didn't trust me. One nearly killed me. I think that is why Equilas put me here, to test me. To see if my darker side would boil over and consume everything around me. I've spent thru—years wondering the same thing."

"I trust you."

"I wonder if you should."

She shrugged. "I'm not a gullible person, nor am I prone to allow feelings to blind me to reality. I think we can agree on that."

"Yes. It gives me assurance."

"Then I'd think my having the final say on whether you can use my chalice powers to restore balance would assure you *and* Eldric that the right thing will be done. I will trudge to the end of the worlds to protect my family. He seemed to get that. I know you do. I'll see this to the end, as is my duty as the chalice. I ultimately have control, and I'll use it."

"Wait..." Tarian tensed. "What's this now?"

"I thought Eldric would've told you—" She went through the memories from earlier, showing their conversation about what would happen if she pulled back before the magic killed her.

"No," Tarian drew out. "He didn't mention it, and it wasn't in his head from the meeting."

"Well, now you know I hold the power. Suck it."

He huffed out a laugh. She could feel his body move as he shook his head. "The gods are tricky, I'll give them that. So yes, the power is in your hands, after all."

"I mean...kinda."

"You can stop me."

"Yes."

"You can nullify me if you don't want to go through with this."

"Assuming I could ignore being repeatedly shocked and learn how, yes. In theory. It would be your sword against mine. And I'm not so sure I could take you, to be honest."

"Don't be absurd. I'd be dying before I realized you meant to kill me. I'd already be dead if my knife had allowed it."

She preened, angling so he could see her smile.

His eyes were deep and soft. He brought a hand up to trace a thumb against the edge of her lips. "You're so fucking beautiful, little dove. The pleasure of looking upon you is so sharp it pains me. We've always been worried about your breaking, but I think it will be me who suffers the most."

"I don't know about that," she replied, sitting up and turning around. She pushed his legs in a bit so she could crawl over them and sit on his lap. His hardness rested against her, and she closed her eyes to savor how good that felt. "Little by little, you've peeled me apart. Shy away from the creature you are? I've been living with that creature all my life. I *am* that creature. My trainer recognized like for like, because *he* is that creature. You're just another of the same. You don't scare me, Tarian. You excite me."

He wrapped his hand around the back of her neck and pulled her toward him. Their lips smashed together, hard and bruising and needy. Desperate for each other.

Chapter Eighteen

Daisy

An urgency she couldn't understand took her over. She stood in the bathtub, slipped, and nearly fell. He was up a moment later, his lips locking with hers, the two of them climbing from the tub together.

"Where's the perfect place?" she asked, running her hands up his wet chest, feeling his incredible body. "Hurry. Where's the perfect place for your first time?"

"What the fuck are you talking about? The tub would've been perfect. The bathroom floor, the wall—I don't give a shit where we do this, as long as I can fulfill this unquenchable thirst for you."

Boy was he going to be annoyed when he realized that thirst was never going away. For either of them. This was more than a lay, and they both knew it.

"I'm right here, Daisy," he said dryly as she

grabbed his hand and pulled him from the bathroom. "I can hear you. Maybe work on that shielding."

She snickered, remembering all that teasing in the human lands.

Her hand tightened, and she was essentially dragging him behind her. Emotion bubbled up out of nowhere, memories of their meetings, of working together, of how she'd felt each time she'd kissed him. How she'd felt when they'd huddled together in the wylds, clinging to each other, depending upon each other for survival. How she felt right now.

The thought of falling in love whispered across her mind before she shut it down lest he hear it. Could there be a worse fate? Falling for a fae who planned to kill her with their combined magic?

Where did you go? he asked, and she had no idea what that meant. Nor could she concentrate on abstract questions. Lust blazed through her.

A few of the *Fallen* looked up from the couches, their eyebrows high.

"Get the fuck out," Tarian barked.

They didn't waste any time, a couple snickering as they left. Tarian didn't wait for the door to click shut before he spun her around and dumped her on the couch. He was on her a moment later, pushing wide her knees and dipping in between her thighs.

She put her fingers through his hair as he licked up her center and sucked. He threaded one finger into her, then two, working in time with the suction on his mouth.

She arched as the sensations quickly built. He worked her faster. Harder.

She groaned with her release, clutching his hair before dragging him up.

"Thank fuck it doesn't hurt guys on their first time, because I don't have a lot of control right now," she said, pushing him up to sitting and dropping to the ground between his legs. She looked up at him in supplication. He studied her feverishly, desire and devotion plain in his beautiful green eyes.

She took his hard length into her small hand, swirling her thumb around the tip before she lowered her head. Her tongue flitted against the slit and around the tip, playful. Teasing. Tasting him and savoring, drawing this out for him as well as for herself.

"You're perfection," he said, breath heavy.

She sucked him in greedily. He groaned as his body tensed and relaxed at the same time. He threaded his fingers into her hair. She used her hand and mouth at the same time, and he applied pressure, directing her at a fast pace. She sucked down as much as she could, not used to working with something so large.

He grunted, and his torso tensed. His head fell back, and his hand tightened before he looked back down at her, the gold nearly taking over the black as the river ran around his pupils. His breathing turned rapid, and his magic washed over her body pleasurably. He gave a long, low moan as he shuddered.

She prepared for the onslaught and gave a confused look at his cock when nothing happened.

"Do I...keep going...or...?" She looked up at him from around it.

He didn't release her hair, still looking at her, still erect.

"That is a beautiful sight," he said, and she gave him a few more moments to take it all in, momentarily distracted by his handsome face. It was a guy's delight, for some reason. She'd never understood why (and this was the only one she'd allowed to have a good long look after she'd serviced him).

His eyebrows lowered. "What...just happened?"

She tried to push up, but he held her firm. "You watched me over your dick. I am pretty sure we are all on the same page there."

"No." He leaned down to look into her eyes. "You never understood why guys like that...then your mind went dark. The same thing happened on the way out here. I thought I was preoccupied, but it happened again."

She swatted his hand away, thinking back. Ah yeah, allowing Tarian to have a look when usually she wouldn't (because she wasn't ready to admit special treatment, since that would lead to *feelings*).

He grabbed her chin, peering deeply into her eyes. Her skin tingled, and pain flared in her temples.

She froze. "What are you doing?"

"You did it again. You're blocking your thoughts from me, and right now, I can't retrieve them. I see the absence of them, but not them. That's not normal. I should feel a block, but yours are gone. I can't see a way to pry into them." He leaned back against the couch, releasing her. "Are you doing something from your training?" He shook his head. "I can't think about that now. I can't focus. Come here. I need you."

She crawled up onto him, her expectations rising. Her knees indented the couch beside his thighs. She lifted up, her hands on his cheeks. She captured his lips as she swung her hips forward. His tip dragged against her wetness, and he drew in a shaky breath. She reached between them and took hold of his length, running the tip more firmly against her. He groaned, gripping her upper arms tightly.

The world paused, and then she sat down slowly.

"*Daisy...*" slipped from his lips, a whisper of unwavering devotion.

She stopped and came back up, rolled her hips, and worked down a little more. His girth was nothing to sneeze at, and she had to take it in slowly to grow accustomed to it. She wrapped her arms around his large shoulders as she continued to kiss him, their tongues wrestling, his body sliding more deeply into hers.

"Oh gods—*fuck*," he breathed, his hands starting to shake where they held her. He squeezed her tightly as she took him deeper still. "Fuck, this feels..."

She gyrated her hips and took him all the way in, sitting down on him with a pleasurable sigh. *Fuck* he felt good. So fucking good. She couldn't remember anything ever feeling this fucking good.

"*So* fucking good," he whispered, and his deep, raw voice gave her shivers.

He ran his hands down her back as he groaned. He leaned back and dragged her with him. His eyes drifted shut.

"I want more of you," he rasped in a tortured voice. "I want all of you."

He braced his hands on her hips and his feet against the floor. He held her firmly and started to drive up into her. Her downward slide met his upward thrust, and all the air left her lungs with a moan. Suddenly, she couldn't get him deep enough. Hard enough.

"Yes, Daisy," he said, his lips against hers. The way he said it, his tone, sent butterflies through her middle, made increased emotion bubble up. "*More.*"

She rolled to the side, and he followed her eagerly, fitting between her thighs and striving harder. She wrapped her legs around him. Her nails raked across his back.

"Fuck, *dewdrop*, this is—" He drove with punishing strokes, and her slippery control fled entirely. Their bodies fit together perfectly, and the feelings transcended the moment.

She called his name, squeezing her eyes shut and chasing her climax. He was right there with her, gripping her, his lips never far from hers. The feeling of him consumed her. Took her to a place that had no name. Everything in her body tightened up, relishing in his strength bearing down on her. In her.

"I'm going to...*I'm going to*—" She cried out as she blasted apart.

He groaned as he shuddered against her, getting in the last strokes of his release.

Their breathing was harried as they continued to clutch each other tightly. He held himself firmly in her, not pulling away, and she closed her eyes as she drank in his proximity.

That was better than she'd expected. Better than she ever could've expected. Fuck that was good. The best, actually.

An aftershock made her shiver, and he lifted. She expected him to pull away, but instead, he grabbed her body and lifted her with him. He returned to sitting with her lying across his chest.

"It's a really good thing we waited to do that," he murmured, his palms flat against her back.

"Why?"

"Because we've just finished and I want it again. The craving hasn't gone away at all. It's gotten worse. If I'd done that before now, I would've never gotten anything done."

"What about now that you have?"

He slid his hands down her back and gripped her butt. "Your ass?"

She yanked away from him in incredulous mock fury. He laughed, and she noticed his eyes. The desire had faded with his orgasm, for now, but the little line around his pupils didn't return to black. It remained gold, like in the human lands.

His laughter died, and his eyes jogged back and forth

between hers, probably dipping into her head and looking through her eyes.

"Your eyes were normal when I first met you," she murmured. "Like this. Before I became the crystal chalice. Why is that?"

His look was puzzled. "They were? Are you sure?"

"Positive. I thought of you after those first meetings. Dreamt of you. I remember your eyes vividly. They always had that burnished gold strip around the irises. The first time they were black was in this court."

He studied her for a moment. "I have no idea. They shouldn't have been, though I do have more magical freedom outside of this kingdom. Here, the obsidian burned into my back has a tighter hold on me. The king has a tighter hold on me, actually. Outside of the court, his leash loosens. He affords me more freedom so I can see about the chalices. Maybe it was a usual occurrence in the human realm and I hadn't known about it. I didn't stop to look—"

He choked, as though the words he was about to say literally got stuck. He put a hand to his throat and gasped, his eyes tightening.

"What?" she asked in sudden alarm. "What is it?"

He coughed as a smile worked at his lips. "I was about to say I didn't stop to look in many mirrors in the human world, and it wouldn't come out. It's a lie. I looked in quite a few mirrors. I never noticed anything different about my eyes, which means they must not have been gold. Always black. Always what I expected."

She laughed. "You're so vain." The song encompassing those lyrics started to play in her mind.

"With a face and body like this, can you blame me?" He laughed with her. "I do so love human fashion. I know you can't blame me. I definitely took a few detours into the human shops when I had a chance." He shrugged. "You need the mirror to know how it looks."

She laughed again before settling. "So why do I have any effect on the gold?"

He shook his head. "I have no idea. The obsidian is still there. I feel it, like an ever-present sickness. Maybe Eldric will know."

"Also, I *really* don't understand why the Diamond Throne has gold instead of...I don't know...white. Or something more strongly representing the color of diamonds."

"The gold is slightly metallic. If white were slightly metallic, it would look like silver, which isn't worth as much as gold, here or in the human lands. Gold signifies wealth."

She leaned back to look at him with raised eyebrows, then started to laugh, falling into him again. "Oh my god, Celestials are so fucking arrogant. I can't handle it."

"*Well?* Logic."

"Sure, yeah. Logic." She kissed his neck before resting her cheek on his collarbone. "I'd really prefer not to go back to Eldric again. I'd be fine not knowing the answers."

"We'll see. He's a necessary boredom."

She didn't feel his release dripping down and remembered the blow job. "Do you not ejaculate?"

"Not until after the oracle has blessed a male with the ability to procreate."

"Huh." She kissed him along his neck. His hands lightly traced her back. "That's pretty great."

"Why is that?"

"Less messy."

He tugged on her hair to get her to pull back so he could kiss her. "Move with me, dove. I need more."

She did. She let all the troubles they had ahead of them slip from her mind as she lost herself in him. She'd get a few days to practice her shielding and her magic, and get ready for the court games, and then she would have to pull her weight.

Until then, though, she would revel in these new feelings. In his body. In his kiss. Until then, she'd try to forget she was a dead human walking.

Chapter Nineteen

KIERAN

The sun was starting to sink low on the horizon, casting long shadows across the dusty path. A circle of dwellings lay up ahead, a larger spread than the first structure Daisy had spent the night in.

No one could figure out what was going on with her situation. Zorn had picked up her tracks outside of the Faegate and followed her throughout her journey. She'd helped that fae. There was no denying it. Possibly risked her life for him, given the tracks they'd found by a stream. There had been one skirmish when others had joined her and that fae, but otherwise, she'd seemed placid. Maybe helpful.

When the fuck was Daisy ever placid or helpful to a captor?

Zorn was at a complete loss. None of this made sense.

Daisy was hard. Harder than any of them, save for himself. She didn't bend unless she had an ulterior motive, and she didn't break. Something else had to be going on. This had to be her plan, somehow.

Lexi looked out to the side, her body tense, but didn't say anything. She was monitoring souls. She'd felt creatures along their way, lurking. Watching. None of them had made a move. Once, she'd felt a soul in a tree. Or... the tree had come alive. It was still too early to tell. Kieran did not look forward to when the path started to close down around them and the wylds crawled in closer.

"Oh shit..." Jack stopped at the edge of a circular grouping of dwellings with one larger structure farther removed. "What happened here?"

The crew hastened toward a building in the middle that looked to have been crushed.

"Aren't those the tracks that we saw by that stream?" Boman pointed at the huge prints next to the destroyed area.

"Lexi, check for signs of life," Kieran barked.

She jogged toward the other dwellings.

"I smell her," Mordecai said from the edge of the destruction. He looked off at Lexi with a question in his expression.

"Her spirit is not here," Lexi called, trying the door to a dwelling. "As of last night, her spirit wasn't in their version of an afterlife, so we have to assume she didn't die in that...situation."

They had to hope, at any rate.

207

"These are clear," Lexi said, pushing into one. "Only a few are open, though."

"This one won't budge!" Jack called, ramming the door of a dwelling.

"Probably a ward," Zorn murmured.

"She was in here," Mordecai called from the dwelling at the far end, covering ground quickly. He was an incredibly efficient shifter. He had the best scent of any of them.

The door and some of the structure had been damaged. Except for the destruction of the one in the middle, the other dwellings appeared untouched.

"That's...strange," Lexi said, looking around. "Maybe it was going after the fae? Maybe he...tried to...catch its attention to distract it from his people? Or fae, whatever —you know what I mean."

"This place housed...animals of some kind," Thane called from the more removed structure. "No blood. No signs of struggle. Seems recent."

Kieran turned to look at Zorn, whose face let through the confusion they were all feeling. What sort of creature would destroy a structure, go after a couple of people, and leave livestock unmolested?

"Same tracks as by that creek," Zorn confirmed. "Maybe this creature holds a grudge."

Kieran did not want to think about this place propagating creatures smart enough to hold grudges.

Mordecai traced the room and ended up at the bed, the only one in this dwelling. It was still mussed and had obviously been shared.

Mordecai's eyes were uncomfortable and wary. "Heightened bodily scents," he said in a growl.

"What does that mean?" Lexi asked as Mordecai bent and looked under the bed.

"She spent time hiding under there." He straightened and gave Lexi a long look, then looked at Kieran. The kid would rather not say.

"Forced or consensual?" Kieran asked, his stomach tightening. "Can you tell?"

"Consensual," Mordecai replied. "She got where she was going. I don't scent the same for him."

The breath left Lexi in a gush. "Oh."

"Stockholm syndrome?" Kieran asked.

"In only a couple days?" Lexi replied.

"No." Zorn stood in the doorway, looking over the room. "She's resistant to Stockholm syndrome. It would take a lot longer for her to break, and in that time, there would be a lot of bloodshed."

"How do you know?" Lexi asked.

He looked her dead on as he said, "I've never taken her on a cruise. I used that excuse for training you wouldn't be fond of."

Her fingers tightened into fists, and Kieran lifted his eyebrows. He hadn't known. Zorn had kept it to himself so Kieran wouldn't be in an awkward position between him and Lexi, for which Kieran was thankful.

"You...did...*what*?" Lexi dragged out.

"I challenged her," Zorn said, "and I should've stepped in more quickly, because she ended up slitting her abductor's throat. An abductor I had hired and paid and should've looked out for better. It took me a second to find and recover her." He motioned at the cramped space. "If she chose this path with the fae, there is a reason. A seduction or a closeness we don't have all the facts to understand. The main thing is that she is alive—or was when she was here—and her captor seems to be fond of her. If that's the case, he won't want to kill her. Let's take that as the gift it is."

Zorn had a point.

"She won't break," Mordecai said, heading for the door. "My sister will not break. She'll hang on long enough for us to get to her. I know she will."

Kieran could hear the desperation in his voice. The desperation they all felt.

Hang in there, Daisy, he thought, heading out to continue scouting with the others. *Hang in there.*

Chapter Twenty

Daisy

That is a very handsome jacket you have there, Lennox, she thought with a smile. (*For someone with no taste.*)

Niall spat out laughter, sitting next to Lennox on the couch with blankets draped over it. In three days, Tarian and Daisy had graced every available surface with their lovemaking. The *Fallen*, upon learning this by walking in on them, hadn't taken the news well. They'd been down-right disgusted, actually. Now they wanted something between their butts and the "ruined" surfaces.

Lennox narrowed his eyes at Daisy. She'd thought the first at him and Niall, and the second only at Niall. Helped by the *Fallen* and the contraptions, she could split her thoughts much better now. She could also hide most of her thoughts in the void. It was a place that didn't register to a mindgazer. The thoughts weren't behind walls or shields or tucked away in a forgotten corner. Not that Tarian could find at any rate. Not even that Eldric could find. They were just...not there.

This was not welcome knowledge to Eldric, who'd never heard of such a thing. He was hard at work within his chaotic library, researching what was going on and why he was excluded from her mind. The rest of the *Fallen* thought it was a human side effect.

It wasn't. It was because of the nulling magic. She was positive. The moment she swirled even a whiff of that magic, delighting in the earthy scent and feeling the hum in her body, her thoughts drifted away from prying minds. They weren't stored at the edge of her brain for someone to pluck out. They existed for her and her alone.

"What'd she say?" Lennox asked as Daisy tugged at his magic, siphoning it delicately. So very delicately. Any faster and he'd notice and attack her. Then the rest of the *Fallen* would have to jump in his way as Daisy took off.

The trigger in a fae was immediate and intense. She had to be *very* careful with that magic, which wasn't great because, while she'd developed an instinctual use of it, she'd only been at it for three days. She was a fast learner, but she wasn't a genius, as Eldric loved to point out.

"She probably said your beard tassel is ridiculous," Revana said, adjusting her top bun as she passed behind the couch.

"Nah." Kayla grinned. "It was that your braids are all crooked. Why are you still so bad at those?"

"I think she noticed that you're too soft to be a Thornborn," Gorlan murmured, standing by the door.

Lennox put up his hands. "Really? We're all taking shots?"

"I mean, when it's so easy," Kayla replied.

Daisy stood for a distraction and fixed her hair, siphoning a little more. She passed by Lennox, giving him a slap on the shoulder as she went. Proximity boosted her magic's strength. Physical contact distracted them from what was happening magically.

Lennox jerked his hand up as though to grab her but stalled. He looked at his hand in confusion, then at nothing. His eyes tightened.

Fuck. He was cluing in.

It was a somewhat scary thing when Lennox charged. That male might seem like an even-tempered, chill fae, but when he was roused, he was fast and powerful and determined. Give him an axe and he'd cut down a door to get to an enemy.

She'd been on the other side of the door when she learned that.

She slowed the siphon to a trickle. In a moment, she stopped it altogether. The siphon had to be started and stopped slowly. Sudden movements triggered the crazy.

"Daisy." Tarian stepped into the doorway of the dressing room, his face a hard mask. He'd be taking her into the lion's den this evening. The Court Hall.

She met him there dutifully and tried her damnedest not to run a hand down his chest, or over a shoulder, and definitely not over his groin. It turned out he didn't have much control when it came to sex. He wanted it as often as possible, and he wouldn't be rushed, not even when he was late for a meeting. Or a trap he'd set.

She wasn't any better. She couldn't stop thinking about him. Keeping her hands off was a lesson in control she so often failed. He just felt so damn good. She'd never experienced sex that gave her such huge highs. And she had never dreamt of the closeness and intimacy they experienced in the quiet aftermath, when his fingers glided across her skin and they talked of trivial nothings. His was a presence and proximity that had hooked her, and she didn't want it to let go.

He held out a dress.

Her focus snapped to attention.

"What is this?" She took it by the bodice and lifted it up for inspection.

"As of today, you are officially a toy. I dress my toys how I wish to view them," Tarian said, readying to go into court and speaking and standing (and acting stuffy) accordingly.

He frowned at her. "And what accordingly?"

"None of your business." (Usually, she allowed him in her head because it was comfortable, but sometimes, she naturally omitted things without realizing it until he wanted to know what shit she was talking about him.)

He leaned forward for a kiss and let it linger, his arms coming around her and holding her tightly.

"Stop." She pushed away. "If you show too much affection, they'll kill me for sport. You yourself told me this. Let's keep our heads in the game."

His hungry eyes watched her, but he let her increase the distance.

The dress had warm brown tones with hints of dusty rose. A subtle sheen overlaid a pattern that resembled delicate lace. The bodice had a sweetheart neckline with intricate black lace detailing that cascaded down the sides and center. It was formfitting, would allow for cleavage while hiding her knife, and was absolutely beautiful. She'd wear this in the human lands, no problem. Some thick-soled boots would be best for daytime wear, a delicate heel for nighttime, and who knew what he had available here?

"Jewelry?" She slipped off her servant's dress.

He blew out a breath and turned around. "Warn me when you're going to do that."

He couldn't handle her nakedness any better than her touch.

She smiled to herself as she looked over the underwear options. She wouldn't use anything for her bottom half in case he wanted to make a show, but she needed something in which to store her knife. For that, she grabbed something similar to a strapless bra in the human world. He must've had that made up specially for her and the knife.

The dress had a shoestring contraption in the back that was a decoy. Along the side was sewn a zipper that blended in seamlessly.

"Is this the fashion, or does the dress have human embellishments?"

"The zipper is from the human lands. I figured you wouldn't want to be strapped into a dress in case you needed to fight."

"Ladies here don't fight?"

"Not when they are dressed for court. They have bodyguards, servants, and eyes on them. They don't leave anything to chance. Neither do the males."

"Yet they still die."

"Not at court. Not in front of witnesses."

Ah. It was leaving court or showing up to court that was treacherous. The corridors and hallways, the gardens and promenades, posed the danger. They had rules here.

She'd need to exploit those rules.

"Jewelry?" she asked again.

"No. Jewelry is stitched on the clothes of nobles— we use the general term of *nobles* for anyone of noble birth or higher. When speaking about gentry, though, which is the highest layer of wealth and privilege, we only say *gentry*. Royalty is in a tier of their own." He paused to make sure she had it, then went on. "Male nobles have the jewelry stitched in, as I said, and the females can also wear it about their person, like humans. Anyone lesser than a noble is plain, as befits their station."

"Champions are plain?"

"Yes, unless they are of noble birth and trying to rise above their defined station."

She cocked her head, thinking that through. "I'm a human. I should be different. Not as a toy, maybe, but as a champion. If I try to blend in, I'll look ridiculous.

Besides, you told the king I was a joke. Dress me as a joke."

He turned to study her. "Of course. You should have human fashion."

"That would be ideal, but do you have female human garments lying around?"

He put his hands on his hips, and his eyes went distant. He stepped out of the dressing room. "Does anyone still have any of the human clothes I brought back as gifts? Female human clothes."

"*Ohh*, busted!" one of the guys shouted.

"I do!" one of the ladies said. "I think. I don't usually throw gifts away. You never know when it might be useful."

"I...may," someone else said uncertainly. "I do love presents, but...you know...where would I wear it?"

Turned out that a couple dresses hadn't been thrown away or used as rags. They'd been tossed in trunks and were horribly wrinkled, all of them from a couple years and many fashion seasons ago, but they were salvageable. The court would think they were as weird as the *Fallen* had. Only Tarian and Daisy knew his impeccable taste.

When she was choosing between them, she tsked and shook her head. "I don't have time for the alterations these need. We'll have to sew them smaller, and I'll pass off the length as purposeful."

Tarian pulled a small trunk from a high shelf and set it on a round table. He flicked two clasps and lifted the lid. Jewelry glittered in the glowing orbs of the dressing room, diamonds and rubies and big-ticket items.

"When searching for the chalices, I grabbed anything of value that was easy to carry," he said by way of explanation. "I stored them in case I ever got out of here. If my family doesn't take me back, any wealth I possess will be stolen. It's not pretty, but—"

Her poignant look and small smile stopped his flow of words. She reached out to take his hand. This moment reminded her of that hotel room, what felt like so long ago, when he had shown he understood her.

Now, it was she who showed she understood him. More than understood, maybe. Was the same. Had to live the same way. They were alike in ways few other people could be.

"I've built quite a fortune myself," she said, her smile growing. "Most of it stolen one way or the other. I get it, Tarian. Trust me. Been there, always do that. I could give you some pointers." His smile matched hers. "Okay, give me a moment and I'll put something together."

It was a little more than a moment, but she was still on time, so she called that a win. The fit of the dress was a clusterfuck, but she'd altered it so her bra peeked out, gathered it in some places, let it flow in others, and found a pair of slippers that nearly fit and set it off perfectly. She'd stitched jewels into the tops of those slippers, had jewels cascading down her chest, bangles on her arms, and looked a little ridiculous, but she absolutely stood out. That was the goal. She was the frail, gaudy, misplaced human. The fae of this court would think they were the predators. They wouldn't know they were being hunted.

Her hair was next, and she was mindful of the diamond dust that sparkled and glimmered on the back of her neck just as much as it always had. She hoped it stayed forever. Or for the couple weeks or whatever she had left in this miserable realm. Her hair parted way to the side, swished over her head and dropped down, often covering one of her eyes.

Her makeup was a bit harder. This place had a bunch of powders and dyes. Thank god her skin was still doing well, because no foundation existed. She'd made the best of it with a smoky (kinda blotchy) eye and a nude lip. She didn't bother with blush.

"Okay." She stepped out to the waiting *Fallen*. Only a couple of them were allowed to go, but they all wore the plain servant's outfit in case they were needed.

They looked up as she stopped in the sitting room where they waited.

"Okay is right." Revana stood from the couch, looking Daisy over. "If I had known this was how to wear the clothes, I would've used them instead of smooshing them into a nearly forgotten trunk."

Daisy barely glanced down at herself. "This? No, this isn't how you wear these clothes. I don't have near enough curves for this outfit. Tarian was right to get it for you. You'd rock this thing. But the furs and things you wear outside of here are hot, too, so I'm not sure you could go wrong."

"I'm inclined to look and see if I do have any of those

clothes he brought back," Kayla murmured. "I wondered why he had bothered, but..."

She nodded appreciatively as Tarian stepped out of his bedchambers. He stopped just outside of the doorway, noticing her and freezing. His whole body tensed.

She held up a hand. "I know it's gaudy. But it—"

"It's like the stars shone down and deposited a miracle just for me," he said in a release of breath, coming forward again. His beautiful green eyes swam with gold, sparkling like the stars he'd just mentioned. "You are absolutely beautiful, little dove. You are perfection. I see now what you were saying."

"Yeah, she nailed it," one of the females murmured.

Tarian's eyes connected with Daisy's, and he lightly kissed the back of her hand. She melted right there in front of everyone, fluttering her lashes and offering him a simpering smile she couldn't quite help. His other hand slipped around her waist, drawing her closer. He placed a soft kiss on her forehead.

"I wish we could just stay here tonight," he murmured, moving side to side in a silent dance. "I wish we could've found each other under different circumstances. A different life."

"We're fae and human." She closed her eyes, her heart aching. "Despite our feelings to the contrary, we never would've worked."

"We could've figured out a way. To feel like this, to have you, I would've figured out a way."

"Maybe you can put your attractive heads together

and *still* figure out a way," Niall said. His brother, Darryn, nodded silently.

Tarian stepped back, his eyes full of regret. "Maybe so."

(And maybe not, because she wouldn't save herself and sacrifice her family. That wasn't how family worked.)

His brow pinched in that way it did when he realized she was keeping something from him, but he stepped away without asking. The hard mask of court settled over his features. His posture changed to venerable playboy mass murderer, sexy and vicious and violent. It made her a questionable person, but fuck she found that so hot.

He entered the corridor first and waited for her to walk out in front of him. Now was her chance to pull her weight. So far in this court, all she'd done was get picked on, get saved, and learn. Now it was time to use her training. Because she *had* trained for this.

Every little bubble of society operated differently. Even in one city, for example, the people just trying to get by were vastly different from the wealthy people making the rules. Criminals were different still. And that was all in the same geographical location. Fae would have their own social bubbles, different from humans, but they would have rules, like not killing people in court. Those rules could be learned, worked within, and exploited.

The one thing that would help had also given her the most trouble to understand. The magic here all came from the same place. There weren't different types, like in the human world. There were different creatures using it. Each fae decided how to work within the magic offered to everyone according to their power level and, most importantly, themselves. Figure out the fae, figure out the magic. Play the player, not the hand.

It was time to meet that shitty princess and her disgusting father.

Chapter Twenty-One

Daisy

The corridor filled up quickly with swishing dresses, sewn-on jewels, and fierce-gazed "servants" following too closely. Bodyguards, obviously, amid actual servants who gave the powerful elite a lot more space.

As they moved, gazes found Daisy. They had barely turned a corner when the whole corridor worth of nobles eyed her.

I assume the crystal chalice magic is on full display? Daisy surmised. She still controlled that part unconsciously. The contraptions weren't helping her figure it out.

Yes, Tarian said. *You want to be noticed, and you're letting your magic shine. As you should.*

She wasn't sure about that last part.

Careful not to look anyone in the eye or seem to

notice them at all, she took in every garment. Every jewel and its possible worth, its placement. Every shoe.

Okay, well, noticing the shoes was because she was just not getting the fashion here. The footwear never seemed to match the clothing and accessories.

It was when she noticed skin that she started to feel uncomfortable.

The black lines on these fae's skin are because of magic, right? she asked as a male stopped along the wall of the somewhat busy corridor to watch everyone pass. He was up to no good—his shifty eyes gave him away. He had lines curving around his cheekbones, running under his eyes and over his forehead—he had so many black lines on his skin that they almost ran together. Between them was the unnatural gray, obviously caused from the same affliction.

The result of twisted magic, yes. Remember when my magic was healing the poison from the Celestial weapon? That's what these fae's magic is trying to do. They are trying to heal the wrongness *in their system. But their magic is twisted, so they are making things worse. They are pushing the magic more out of balance, and it will then seep into those around them. It is black because it is unseelie magic. Celestial lines would be gold. Those of the Ruby kingdom would be deep crimson, etcetera.*

They don't look in a mirror and get nervous that their magic is very clearly fucked up?

They can't see it, he said, slowing as the way before them grew more crowded. *Twisted magic doesn't want to*

224

be rooted out. It's a disease. It wants to infect. They see themselves as completely normal.

And no one is like, "Hey, you've got the twisted plague, bud. Maybe get that checked out."

In this court? No, because the royals are worse. To call it out is to call them out, and no one would dare. Usually, the Celestials, on a routine visit, would see what was happening and step in, but because of the deal concerning me, there are no routine visits, at the peril of the realm and the destruction of this kingdom. And so everyone here fights with that magic every day. They fight the toxicity that tries to seep into their bodies. Into their very beings.

Fuck, this place was awful.

Yes, it is, Tarian murmured.

But... Daisy paused as a lesser noble female, with hardly any jewels and no arrogance at all, stepped in Tarian's way. She was all smiles and flashing eyes, her gaze gliding over his body and sizzling at his physique.

Daisy looked away as a flash of jealous rage blind-sided her. Suddenly, she was siphoning off the female's magic without knowing she'd started, ready to bleed her dry and leave her as a pile of bones and sinew on the floor.

Hmm, I like that you are possessive of me, little dove, Tarian purred. Magic swirled across Daisy's body pleasurably, making her gasp at the sensations.

"Stars above," the female said in shock, looking at Tarian's eyes. She beamed, slinking down into a sexy pose and using her fan to cool her heated face. "I would brave the curse for you, Tarianthiel. I would—"

His look of disgust could've wilted flowers. "I have no use for someone such as you. Be gone, despicable varmint."

"But...but your eyes—"

"Have nothing to do with you." He walked past her, a hardcore rejection despite his using "varmint."

She was one of the females kneeling at my feet, forcibly trying to get me hard, he spat. *She can rot in hell.*

Fair enough.

Also... He sighed as the way remained crowded. *What is taking so fucking long?* He angled his body away from a pair of females who also had their fans active, their lips curled in a snarl at Tarian, but their eyes appreciating his appearance. They might hate him, but they couldn't help admiring his beauty. *Varmint is a grave insult here. I think humans are better at insults all around. We don't have quite the same punch.*

Daisy continued to siphon magic from the varmint. The female didn't seem to notice, and Tarian needed vengeance—the female would soon die of questionable causes.

Will they know it was you? he asked, moving himself and Daisy more toward the other side of the corridor.

The siphon started to wane, allowing her to increase the power. The result would be the same.

Only if they know what I am, and Eldric assures me that only you, the Fallen, and he have that information. Speaking of which, what are you going to do if Eldric tries to betray you?

Kill him and seek restitution with the order. I have him monitored, and he doesn't seem to know it.

As the gods will it.

Tarian started chuckling before wiping his fingers over his mouth to hide his response.

That would never do. She was a toy—her purpose was to amuse. She was also here to mindfuck these fae. They wanted Tarian...and she had him. Time to make them squirm.

She slunk closer and ran her hands up his chest. She grabbed his lapels and angled her face up, wanting a kiss.

His eyes tightened warily. He wanted to pull away. She saw it. He wanted to follow the script he knew from years of trial and error, presenting himself as an angry, though aloof, murderous fae.

He trusted her, though. They'd made a pact, and even though she didn't know this place, she knew how to properly interact with people to get what she or her family needed. She had an affinity for it.

He ran his hands across her hips, bending toward her and lightly pressing his lips to hers. She opened her mouth, and he complied there, too, swiping his tongue through. She ran her hands against his chest, the tides of desire pulling at her. Struggling for control, she looped her arms around his neck, but jolted when he reached around her and grabbed her butt. He pulled her in, rubbing his hardness against her.

She groaned as she thought, *Are you in control?*

Nope, and it feels fucking amazing.

He'd always liked the free fall. Even in the beginning,

even when they were fighting for their lives, he had wanted to get lost in her. Jump into the abyss with her.

He was doing so now.

He rubbed against her as he deepened the kiss, consuming her. Pulling her with him. Fae stared, clustered in groups and starting to chatter. In a moment, it all faded away. All she knew was his body pressed against hers, his kiss, his hands.

You gotta get moving, someone said in their heads, one of the *Fallen,* but she was too distracted to know which one.

Tarian complied, but not in the way they'd wanted.

He ground against her harder before reaching up her dress.

"Holy fu—" She clutched him.

"Hmm, you're so wet for me, *dewdrop,*" he murmured against her lips, sliding two fingers in. "Touch me."

She pulled one arm from around his neck and reached between them, finding his length through the fabric and rubbing.

"That's right," he growled, his thumb touching down and sending her reeling into pleasure. "Pull out my cock and show everyone what you do to me. Prove how much I lust for you."

She angled herself so she could get at his pants. His buttons fell away, and she reached inside, not finding underwear. He'd had the same thought as her. She freed him and, with the other hand, pushed his shirt higher to expose him.

"Good." He worked her harder. "Stroke me slowly. I

want you to come before you drop to your knees and suck my cock."

Desire tightened her at his words. At their display.

She did as he said while he worked faster. His thumb circled, and his fingers plunged. His kiss was passionate and deep.

She rocked against his fingers. Her body wound tighter.

"Come for me, *dove*," he commanded her, and she peaked, curling her toes. Her eyes fluttered shut as she groaned. Stroking him was forgotten while she reveled in bliss.

Her movements were slinky in the aftermath, and she didn't need his next command. She opened her eyes and captured his gaze while she dropped down. He took over holding his shirt as she took him in hand again. She stroked once, twice, while giving him a seductive smile. Everyone saw his state of arousal. They all stood by, transfixed.

She'd never done something like this in front of an audience, but somehow, it heightened her pleasure. She liked knowing so many watchers were rapt, seeing what she could do to Tarian. Seeing how eagerly he responded to her when he wouldn't respond to any of them. It made her feel exposed, but sexier. Taboo but powerful.

Thoughts of love once again whispered across her mind as she licked the tip sensuously, a bit dramatically, then sucked him in deep. Deep as she could and then a little more for good measure. Her eyes started to water, and she let them. Let the makeup run. She backed off and sucked in again, working her hand in tandem. He reached down and grabbed her hair as she bobbed on his length, looking up at him the whole time.

His eyes were on fire as he watched her. As everyone watched her. His body started to tense. His breathing became ragged.

It's really too bad you can't come all over my face, she thought, and he shuddered in climax, throwing his head back and groaning for all to hear.

She finished up as he jerked, sensitive now. When he was done, she rose gracefully and tucked him back in.

He looked down at her, wobbly-kneed and with a grin. "Perfection," he cooed before straightening his clothes and tucking her under his arm. *That is what I was talking about in the fringe.* He tilted her chin up with his fingers before running his lips across hers. *The rush. It was as perfect as I'd imagined, and in the perfect place. The princess has been watching us. Shall we go meet her?*

Daisy barely stopped herself from looking around.

Sure, she replied. *By the way, do you need some magic?* She smiled ruefully as a body hit the floor up the way. *I happen to have some from that vengeance I claimed on your behalf a moment ago. You're welcome.*

Fantastic. I'll use it to vanish the royal black from around my irises when I meet the princess. She'll be thrilled.

He took her hand amid cries of worry and outrage, gasps and startled looks. A bodyguard knelt beside the noble female, and the servants had scattered to the wall.

The other nobles in the area pushed well away, bumping into each other.

Questions flew within the murmuring crowd.

"Who killed her?"

"How'd she die?"

"Was it an alliance gone wrong?"

"Did she wrong someone?"

"Tarianthiel," someone whispered, near Daisy's ear. "Tarianthiel...naughty, naughty. I know it was you."

A female waited in the center of the open doors leading into the Court Hall. Black lines so thick they looked like pasted-on hair covered half of her face, drifting down over an eye and ending at the top of her jaw. It almost matched Daisy's hairstyle, except her hazel eye peeked through with a reddish hue taking over the white. Another smear of black crawled in from her hair-line on the other side, over her cheekbone and almost to her mouth. The gray of her skin nearly looked like paint. Every other inch of her was covered in a billowing black dress with a shining black design woven through, easily lost amid the staggering number of jewels.

Daisy couldn't decide if she was putting her enormous wealth on display or using it as a cover-up for what she knew was a problem. Even though Tarian said they didn't see the effects of the twisted magic, the fae most affected were the ones with the most cover. That couldn't be a coincidence.

The female's bodyguards stretched to the sides amid the columns. Their eyes constantly surveyed the crowd, all stopped and waiting for the princess to get out of the way and let them through. But she was waiting for Tarian.

Tarian's shoulders tightened, the only indication of her unwanted attention. He strolled toward her confidently, Daisy's hand in his.

The princess's eyes were locked on him. Her smile twisted into a disturbing, cruel thing.

Then her gaze swung to Daisy, and pain flared in Daisy's body. She hadn't even been introduced and she was already under attack.

Chapter Twenty-Two

Daisy

They're pushing us back, Gorlan said in alarm, one of only two *Fallen* allowed to join Tarian inside. *They're trying to separate us from you two. They've never done this before.*

We're at the end of the line, Tarian said in an internal, monotone voice. *I've found their chalice. I'm drawing up instructions. The moment they don't need me, they won't have any reason to keep me alive.*

What about the gods? Daisy asked, feeling a chill roll down her back as she internalized the pain before letting it flow away again.

This court forsook the gods a long time ago. Besides, they agreed to take me in. They didn't specify how long they'd keep me.

The chill turned into a whole-body tremble.

Stick to the plan, Tarian murmured, his gaze locked on the princess's while she stared at Daisy. *I know what he intends. I know the timelines, give or take. I have not been idle. Stick to the plan and we'll play them at their own game.*

That was all well and good, but Daisy didn't *know* the fucking plan. She loved chess, and she'd hoped to play with Tarian, but now she was on the outside looking in while supposedly a big player.

Your piece is surviving, he said, very unhelpfully. *You've done amazingly so far. Keep it up.*

Help him, Faelynn said to just Daisy from somewhere behind. *Maintain your courage. He cannot take on this court alone.*

She was walking up with him, wasn't she?

He threaded his fingers between hers tightly as they kept going, and Daisy looked away to the side, still not making eye contact with anyone, but not deferring to the princess. Apparently, her entire existence would focus around *winging it.*

"Stupid human," she heard from those watching them pass. Over and over they muttered it, or something like it. And she smiled at the name. Not a Chester, but a human in general. Magical people would have been so annoyed to be lumped in with the likes of her.

"What is this?" the princess hissed. Her words sounded like a thousand snakes singing a chorus. Dark, forbidding magic slithered over Daisy's body to match the sound. A horribly acidic smell like sulfur wafted up.

It used to be an earthy smell, Tarian thought. *Even the smell gives away the rotting nature of this magic.*

Everything in Daisy recoiled. It definitely didn't feel natural, that magic. Her hair stood up on her arms and prickled on her scalp. Still, she kept from looking at the royal figure, instead pulling up her free hand and checking out her nails. She popped one into her mouth, chewing on the end as she scanned a pair of weird fucking shoes that really shouldn't exist. The shoemaker needed to be dragged over to a well and tossed in until he could come up with better ideas.

Tarian laughed, not covering it this time. The sound was light and carefree, like he'd been freed of this terrible place.

I have, he murmured. *Through you.*

That was a stretch because they were marching toward the undertaker, and if they made it through her, they'd be greeted by the prison-robbing rapist next. What a fucking family.

"Princess Elamorna, hello." He tugged on Daisy's hand, and she finally dragged her attention in that direction.

She didn't look at the princess, though. Oh no. She was a stupid human, after all. She had to play her part.

She looked up at Tarian to see what he wanted. The gold in his eyes had settled but still moved around the pupils, no black to be found. The black hadn't returned since they'd first made love.

...made love...

The words echoed in her mind, and she knew Tarian was echoing them back to her, teasing her.

I'm just being tasteful, she groused.

His smile was sweet and intimate. He winked at her, making the princess wait.

The princess didn't take it well.

The hiss reverberated throughout the corridor and off the ceiling. Needles dug into Daisy's flesh, and slick fingers pried at her head, burrowing deep into her mind.

Daisy winced and pulled herself in tight, hiding her thoughts from everyone in case the princess was stronger than Daisy's diamond dust or her amateur mental shield. She thought about nulling the onslaught, but if the royals were readying to get rid of Tarian, they might have more knowledge than he suspected. One hint and she might run the risk of revealing herself as the true chalice.

A surge of magic welled up. Daisy felt the tingle of Tarian grabbing some of the power she'd accrued, and then it was whisked away, his training ten times smoother with that contraption than hers had ever been. He clearly had plenty of experience.

Black magic sparkling with gold sliced through the air. It danced and played around Daisy, burning away whatever the princess had done. She took a deep inhale as the pain cleared.

"As I was saying before the princess rudely interrupted us," Tarian said to Daisy, not having looked away, "we must look at the princess when she is greeting us, little toy."

When he finally turned to the princess, her eyes had

grown wide with disbelief and worry. She wasn't used to his having that much power.

"You must excuse her," he told her lightly. "Such stupid creatures, these humans, but so incredibly pleasing. I never thought I'd desire anyone again, let alone be pleasured. It seems I just needed someone outside of this court, especially after you and your minions tried, and failed, to produce those results, hmm?"

The princess lifted her chin defiantly, but it was clear he'd shaken her. "Why did you bring it here? We have no need for those *things* in my court."

He tsked at her. "But it isn't *your* court. It is your father's court, and he has no desire to pass it to you. As to why I brought her here—didn't you hear? This is my champion. Isn't she the most delightful little human you've ever seen? I found her on my travels and, after charming her as only our kind can, brought her back for sport. I figure by the time I tire of her, one of the other champions will have killed her."

He draped his arm around Daisy's shoulders, and she practically purred as she nestled into his side, playing along. She angled up her face and pouted when he didn't give her a kiss.

"Now, now." He booped her on the nose. "This isn't the time, remember? Not until I give you the command to pleasure me." He looked back at the princess, and his voice dropped an octave in warning. "If you handle my toy again, either with magic or physical touch, I will mutilate one of *your* favorite toys. I cannot kill you, but I can kill everyone you hold dear. Remember that."

A moment later, the princess subtly jerked, as though another message had been delivered privately.

Her throat bobbed as she swallowed, and she stepped to the side like she didn't have a choice. Tarian straightened his broad shoulders, his arm still looped around Daisy, and walked forward. It looked like he owned this court and everyone in it. The Celestial prince had come out to play.

Siphon magic whenever you can, he told her as they walked through the double doors and into a huge and lavish room. *Keep yourself full of it. There's no telling when I or the* Fallen *will need it. Hide your thoughts whenever you are outside of my chambers without me. Do not go near the shadows—any shadows—and do not go anywhere alone. The predators are salivating, snapping their jaws at our necks. There's no telling what is in store for us.*

Time passed incredibly quickly. After they sat down, nobles started pouring into the space. It was clear the princess had been waiting to make a display with her trophy. When it didn't go as planned, she'd probably retired to lick her wounds and plot how to kill Tarian and torture Daisy.

The dimly lit area had a dark, gothic-looking interior that would normally greatly appeal to her. It had vaulted ceilings with various arches along the sides, decorated with ornately carved stonework housing seats and couches within. A large, circular window existed at the back above an empty stone dais shimmering with blue-silver light. A grand chandelier hung as a centerpiece above the open area in the very middle, where court members walked in twos and threes, each holding a crystal glass of liquid.

Unfortunately, all the beauty and finery were ruined by the unsettling feeling that slithered in the atmosphere. Reddish light mingled with the blue in the rest of the room, and deep black shadows crouched in the corners, occasionally rippling as something within shifted position. Fae or beast, she couldn't tell.

Suddenly, voices hushed. Fans started waving quickly, covering excited or expectant faces. The lighting on the large stone dais changed color, turning blood red. A shock of acidic magic curled throughout the room, and a large throne appeared in the center.

Daisy leaned forward from her place beside Tarian on the couch in his appointed location. From there, she could see the whole of the dais and most of the high-profile gentry beside it.

A dramatic and striking array of obsidian crystals jutted from what looked like sculpted obsidian. The crystals differed in size, looking like a crown but creating the back of the throne. The base seemed to be one piece, a wide chair supporting finely carved obsidian arms on either side. Beside it, a gray fog lightly curled into the air.

He moves it from the throne room to here and back again, Tarian murmured. As well he should. That thing was a work of art, perfectly setting the tone of power and authority. A king needed his symbols.

What about the queen? she asked as a blue spotlight shone down from a spot ten feet above. There didn't appear to be a source from which the lighting originated.

She mated into royalty; she wasn't born to it. She's a figurehead, mostly.

A fae walked onto the dais from the side, cloaked in shadow. The court reduced to a few whispers, and then nothing at all except for the rustling of fabric. As the figure entered the circle of the spotlight, the shadow fell away to reveal the creature within.

Daisy's breath hitched, and she froze. Her instinct was to lean back, but her logic told her that movement caught the eye of predators. She did not want that...*thing* noticing her.

The king's face was a mess of wrinkles in what appeared to be leathery skin, but on closer inspection, it was covered in the toxic magical rot plaguing this kingdom. His lips looked like they were made from a prune, and his eyes were completely blood red except for the ring of black, no white to be found. A gorgeous crown sat atop his grotesque head, with an elegant, open framework of obsidian that arched to a central point. Jewels lined the base intricately, giving it a majestic appearance.

He ruffled his robes of black lined with sparkling silver accents, fairly plain compared to the princess's. His hands looked like they had been dipped in liquid obsidian, no gray to be found. He looked out over the court, and Daisy itched to lean back, hunting for shadows within which to hide herself. But this creature would find her there, she knew. He'd probably feel her drifting in and amongst them.

The creature's head turned slowly. Deliberately. He scanned the crowd until his gaze stopped on her.

Hello, human.

The voice was raspy and old and felt like it was covered in slime.

Her survival instinct went into overdrive. Every necessary memory or thought about self-defense, her role here, or Tarian's plans pulled so far into her that they were lost to the void, even from her. Underneath her shield lay items he would already know, like her toy status, her human nature, and her hatred of him and fae. He'd expect that. On the surface of her mind were rambling thoughts that jumbled together, the picture of Eldric's interpretation of a drooling human.

It was not wise for Tarianthiel to bring you here.

She didn't respond, allowing her very real fear to color the crust of her mind and hiding her courage to face it way down deep. So deep she wondered if she'd be able to call it up again. It wasn't just the hideousness of the creature who had sighted in on her, or its power, but its unnaturalness. Its imbalance, as the fae might say—its twisted, seething, magical-decomposing nature. She could feel, almost *see*, the vile magic that poured from him and drifted into the atmosphere around him, searching as though for a host. As though for someone else to infect. When this creature was in the room, more than any other, it felt like dark slime threatened to dig into her pores and twist the fabric of her being.

Power pulsed from inside of her. Pulsed and grew, like a white-hot ball of light. It pushed at her confines, wanting to break free. Wanting to douse this whole room in scalding, cleansing magic.

It was then she noticed what was in the king's hand, mostly hidden within the billowing robes. The diamond chalice.

It pulsed again, calling to her. Begging her to save it from the filthy touch of one so obviously corroded.

Can we leave? she asked Tarian as silently as she could. This time, there were no strange body movements, save for her pulse fluttering under her skin like a trapped animal.

He is too young to know what great sport your kind proves to be, the king continued, and his eyes gleamed. A tear of blood dripped from the corner of one. *You scream and scream and are always so hopeful of being saved. But no one ever comes to your rescue. My favorite is when the hope runs out...right before the mind breaks.*

No, Tarian said, his voice strained. *We're here for the duration. It's okay, I never dance. I never chat. I chase anyone away who ventures near. They know this about me. The only trouble we might have is from the royalty, as you've seen.*

As she was seeing right now, yeah.

Tarian jolted as though struck. His head jerked, just a fraction, like he was stopping himself from looking over at her.

Ignore me, she said as the king's words made her defiance rise up. She might scream, but she would not break.

242

For that thing up there on the dais, she would *never* break. She'd stay alive long enough to kill him, even if she went down with him.

That white-hot beat pulsed inside her again and again, like a drumbeat begging her to act. To stand up and use what the gods had given her. To null the king's magic while siphoning it, feeding it to Tarian, and taking the king down as a team.

...as a team...

The king's disgusting voice sounded in her head. *You've avoided my chambers twice now. When the time is right, there will not be a third.*

(And that will mean your death, you leather-faced varmint. It'll be the start of the fire.)

A Billy Joel song started to play on the surface of her brain, and for a fraction of a second, the king cocked his head in confusion. Then he was looking out over his court as he finally sat down.

The chalice is a team sport, she told Tarian, sighing in relief to be out of the king's gaze. *Both parties working together. A unit. Not you using me, or me nulling and acting alone, but two halves of a whole. I need you to magically get things done, and you need me to carry it out. A partnership.*

Yes, I know that. You are making it very hard to ignore you, though. I can see your strain. What happened? Can I touch you?

Daisy leaned back, watching the king, making sure he didn't look her way again.

Tarian pulled her against him, wrapping his arm

around her defiantly. It was welcomed and comforting and a terrible idea. They didn't want to provoke that bastard just yet.

It hadn't clicked for me. We are a team, yes, but we have *to be for the chalice's magic to be most effective. We were always meant to be. I need to be on board with your decisions. You need to earn my trust. Given I can null you and kill you when you're not looking, you need to trust me, as well.* She looked over at him, drinking him in, feeling her heart move deep within her. *We formed this bond before we knew everything the chalice could do. Before I knew I was the chalice. We were always meant to do this together, Tarian. We were always meant to find each other, both hardened by our lives, unused to giving up, willing to do anything to protect that which we hold most dear. This makes us the most unlucky fuckers I've ever heard of, because this is really fucking awful, and I have a distinct feeling it is going to get a whole lot worse.*

Chapter Twenty-Three

Daisy

The rest of the royal family soon entered, but they didn't get to use the dais. That, alone, held the king, which was very telling about how the family operated. The king called the shots, had a big fucking ego, and didn't give up much control. He was the head of his operation. Cut off the head and the rest would fall.

So many thoughts dumped into her mind that she had a hard time choosing one to notice. That was the problem with learning to split conversations and focus on multiple threads of people's thoughts at once—it opened her up to more avenues of information gathering and things got jumbled. She'd need to sit down and sort it all out later.

The queen was first to walk in, coming from the right and draped in another of the billowing dresses so many of the infected females wore. She didn't have as much magical rot etching her face, with her cheekbones lined, her eyes circled, and her pinched face outlined. Her throne, significantly smaller than her mate's, sat at the side of the dais on the right. The daughter came in next, her gaze never drifting as far as Tarian. Daisy couldn't tell if that was good or bad.

"Bad," Tarian murmured, his words only for her ears. "It means she is incredibly angry and plotting her revenge. I've traveled this road a great many times."

At least she was predictable.

From the other side walked two males, one nearly as covered in the black lines as his father and the other not terribly affected at all. Somehow, he had escaped the worst of the twist overloading his family.

"He's the baby of the family," Tarian said, sitting back and crossing an ankle over his knee. He turned Daisy so she was heavily resting against his side and slung his free arm across the back of the couch, getting comfortable. "He's never been ambitious, doesn't partake in the family dynamics very much, and is gentler than the average fae."

"Which means his father thinks he's weak."

"Exactly. It might save his life. If the magic is cleansed soon, he should be able to come back from it."

"But his family is..."

"Utterly fucked. They are too far gone."

She wouldn't even have to feel bad when she burned this place to the ground.

He laughed softly. "As if you would anyway."

Instruments in an unseen corner came to life, the first

notes floating up and hanging in the air before more joined them. A collection of fae took to the dance floor in odd groupings, each dance organized but changed a little depending on the number of people they had. She watched in fascination, quite liking the look of their flow and movement.

"I can teach you," Tarian said, looking down at her with a smile. "I'm sure you'd pick it up quickly."

"Learning and practicing the magic is much more important." Which was a real shame, because she would've loved the opportunity to dance with him, her hand in his, his body close, his focus solely on her.

"One day, then."

Sure, why not?

Those not dancing sought out food and drink, holding obsidian plates rimmed with gold and decadent glasses sparkling with a ruby elixir.

"Pixie wine," he murmured, voice very low so no one could hear their conversation. She wondered why he spoke instead of using mindgazer magic.

He glanced around in obvious boredom. *To let them know I talk to you. I share things with you. Things I am not allowing anyone else to hear. That'll make them more suspicious of me, which will make them try to seek out the things I say. These royals—the court as a whole—are extremely paranoid, and I have more knowledge about the fringe than they do. It might buy me time, which should, in turn, buy you time.*

"It is extremely potent," he continued. "More than anything I've tried in the human world."

"Have you tried moonshine?"

"Moon...shine? No. That sounds like something inspired by Faerie."

"I think it's more inspired by getting a kick while saving a buck, but sure. How about absinthe?"

"No..." he drew out.

She nodded. She'd tried those things and knew how her body reacted to them. It could help her gauge pixie wine if she ended up in a situation where it was served to her.

"It would've been nice to have a guide in the human world," Tarian mused. Deep night rolled over the shining marble floor along the back wall. A few nobles gave it furtive glances and subtly shifted away. "I learned a great deal from the memories of humans, but that is nothing like experiencing it for oneself or getting the surprise of a new sensation."

His eyes focused, looking straight ahead. Across from them, the shadow stretched across the floor, blanketing the ground. It reached under tables and caressed the feet and legs of various fae it passed. It seemed to engage with those who were the most twisted.

Tarianthiel, a voice said, winding between him and Daisy. *Handsome Tarianthiel...*

Blackness crowded around their feet. Licked at their legs.

What is it? dark and dank voices whispered. They were like that of the wylds, but...wrong. Nightmarish.

"Twisted magic taking root in the castle," Tarian said, unperturbed. "Ignore it."

It does not belong here... The darkness at their feet clutched Daisy's legs and started to crawl up. The dank cold seeped into her bones. Her skin felt like it was changing, like mold was growing. *It does not belong here!*

Her heart picked up speed. She grabbed Tarian's pant leg, barely stopping herself from curling her feet under her on the couch cushions.

"Be easy." Tarian pulled his arm from the back of the couch and ran his fingers under her chin. He applied pressure to bring her face up, looking down into her eyes. "It won't hurt you if you don't let it seep in."

"But it *has* seeped in—"

He shook his head before dropping his lips to hers. "That is the feeling of its touch, but it is just extremities." His volume was normal. He was allowing people to see her uneasiness. Her *differentness* as a human. "Don't open yourself up to it, and that is as far as it will go."

"How do I stop myself from opening up to it?"

"By ignoring it." He traced her lips with his thumb. "When you lean into its siren song, when you allow yourself to be hypnotized by its allure, it will seek to embed itself within you. That's how it will twist your magic. Distract yourself." His eyes sparked fire, and gold ran a river around his pupils. "Pleasure me, little human."

She glanced at the ground, wondering how in the world that stuff could feel alluring.

"Maybe it doesn't affect humans the same way," Tarian said, his brow pinching as he looked at her. Reading her, more likely.

Or maybe it's because of the chalice magic? she thought.

He didn't answer, his gaze sharp despite his obvious desire. He didn't know.

She ran her hand along his hard length through his trousers, certainly distracted, but not by him. The voices kept slithering around her like the shadow swirling around her legs.

It does not belong here. Kill it!

"That can't be good," she murmured, looking around the other seating arrangements, little groupings for the fae of high status and shared circular tables for those lesser. The shadow crawled across the floor there, too, pooling around ankles and reaching as far as waists on the more affected fae. "Why would anyone want to come to court and constantly have this annoying them?"

She freed him from the confines of his pants, and he breathed heavily as she ran her palm against him.

"Suck it," he murmured, his lids hooded. He didn't seem to notice the shadows at all. Indeed, a strange light sparked in his eyes, a little off balance, like when he'd come into the prison. Or when he walked the halls. "Suck it down deep, human."

His fingers curled into the back of her hair before he dragged her closer, forcing a kiss. She opened her mouth to accept it, delighting in the strength and power of his dominance. Needing it to rip her attention away from those horrible shadows, now chanting, *Kill it-kill it-kill it!*

His other hand wrapped around her neck in a choking hold, pulling her higher onto the couch. She had to pull her legs up to accommodate, getting her knees under her and thankfully out of the shadows. The voices died away and, with them, her uneasiness. Still, she knew they were there. Could feel their presence slinking along the floor under them.

Tarian let go of her neck and forced her down to him. She captured the base of his cock and ran the tip along her lips. She swirled her tongue around it, and he sucked in a breath.

"That's right." His voice was louder, commanding. Passing fae would definitely hear him, and likely the clusters seated around them, too. "Good."

He pushed her down harder, and she acted like she wasn't sure, bracing against his thighs and resisting. His fingers tightened, and he worked her up and down his shaft, pushing into her throat and growling with need. Her fingers tightened on his thighs. She sucked rhythmically, swirling her tongue at the tip before being shoved down again. She felt her own desire start to climb, enjoying pleasuring him despite the posture of her body. Delighting in his taste and feel despite her tenseness and the act she was putting on for the court.

"That's it," he groaned. "Nice and deep. Take it all the way in, human."

She did, her wetness leaking down her thighs.

He pulled the hem of her dress up over her rear, exposing her. She jolted, but he cooed in her mind.

Focus on me, little dove. Focus on how good it feels. I'll keep you safe. They will see you—see us—but they will never touch you. I will make sure of it.

With the chalice magic, she felt for the closest person, her vessel not full and wanting to rectify that. That fae had too much power, though. Those were always the prickliest. The most prone to notice when she was trying to take some—or so it seemed with the *Fallen*.

She hunted for another and another as Tarian's fingers ran down her center. He groaned as she repeatedly took him in, and he dipped two fingers into her, stroking just right.

"Hmm," she purred, liquifying against him. The act of restraint was over. It was too hard to pretend.

"Yes, that's right." She took him all the way in, wanting to do this for him in a way she'd never cared to for anyone else. "Please me, human, and I will give you a present."

She'd hold him to that.

He chuckled within her mind as his fingers worked. She redoubled her efforts against him, wanting him to control her harder. To be rougher.

He did so immediately, tensing, his fingers going faster. She strove, tightened—

"Come for me," he said, and she had no choice. She shuddered with him deep in her throat, groaning around his cock. "That's right." He pulled her off him by her hair. Drool dripped from her lips. "Now, you will fuck me."

As though by magic, she felt drawn to obey. To crawl up and over his lap, leaving ample time for the court to glimpse his continued hardness. If they'd missed it in the hall, this was another opportunity.

He helped her guide a knee over his hip before collecting her dress and bunching it at her waist. Everyone in view, and a lot of them had stopped to gawk in obvious surprise, would be able to see him enter her. He was leaving nothing to the imagination. No fuel for the naysayers. They couldn't excite him, but this weak little human slave could hold him in rapture. He would be magically compelled to kill everyone who touched her.

She clasped his face with her hands and found his lips, prideful of the effect she had on this magnificent and beautiful fae. His breath was uneven with desire. He lowered her, lining himself up and then pausing. Slowly, purposefully, he pulled her down the rest of the way.

She groaned from how good it felt, wrapping her arms around his neck and leaning harder against him. His heat radiated around her, and she began to move, rolling her hips and feeling all the delicious friction.

"That's right, *dewdrop*," he cooed, the fae term of endearment that made her heart catch. It was so much more beautiful than "baby." So unique to him, to fae.

He kept one hand on her waist, holding up her dress, but the other tangled in her hair. His lips devoured hers. His body inside of hers consumed her, washing away the strangeness of doing this for spectators. Of being intimate in a fae court.

She moved faster against him, unraveling, losing herself to him. The princess could have been standing right behind her and Daisy wouldn't have known. She dropped her hand between them, working herself as she gyrated.

"You're the only thing that makes this court bearable," he murmured against her lips. "The only beauty this court has to offer."

She clutched his shoulder. Her body tightened. His tensed, and they shuddered with the rush of climaxing together. He dropped her dress and wrapped his arms around her, crushing her into him and hugging her tightly. She held him as well, breathing heavily, the tingle of her high spreading through her.

I apologize, he said.

For what—

He abruptly nudged her off him. She rolled away, a mess of wetness from her assertions. He put his arm against the back of the couch for her to lean into.

I'll make it up to you, he said.

It better be in addition to that present you promised me.

She felt his elation—apparently he thought that was a joke.

She sighed, picking at a gold chain on his jacket.

Now what? she asked.

Now...we wait for the fallout.

It didn't take long to come.

Chapter Twenty-Four

DAISY

The moment Daisy dropped her feet from the couch, the shadows were there. The voices resumed, and the darkness swirled. A new feeling emerged, though—a strange, oily, acidic feeling that curdled her stomach.

"I find these things so dull," Tarian said, his pants still open and his erection finally starting to fall. He was showing himself off to the masses. When he proved a point, he really went for it. "The music is always the same. The dancers never mix it up. The food is hardly varied. It is like watching the same TV show in the human world over, and over, and over again."

"Was the other court like this one?" she asked as the shadows at her feet slithered across her skin and bit down with sharp teeth. She jerked and then focused harder on ignoring them. "The one you came from?"

He twirled a lock of her hair absently. Pleasant shivers coated her body from his magic. His eyes never stopped moving, similar to hers.

"I didn't used to think so, but then I took part in it. I danced. I sang—"

"You sing?"

He glanced down at her. "Of course. All fae sing. Some just do it better than others."

"And you?"

"The best."

"Obviously," she said sarcastically. The princess hadn't looked at them once.

He laughed, pulling her hair back to tilt her face up. He placed a kiss on her lips.

"I'm not the best, actually," he admitted as the acidic feeling grew. The bites dug deeper, going from a mild pain to a dull ache. "I'm not bad—I can entertain a court just fine—but two of my sisters and one of my brothers are much better. They were the first called on to perform. Always."

"Do you miss them?"

He was quiet for a long time. Her skin started to burn. The chant changed from "it" to "her."

Kill her-kill her-killer—

The way the words ran together, it almost sounded like "killer" instead of "kill her." Like a warning to the rest of the court.

"I do. Even the brother who betrayed me. I miss so much of that life, but it feels like a distant memory. I've changed a lot, I think. Grown cruel. Despicable. I doubt they would even know me." He paused. "Or maybe I've become what they feared all along."

"Or maybe you're giving yourself a hard time for the guy you had to become to survive."

He slipped his hand under her hair and stroked his thumb down the back of her neck. "It feels wrong to let myself off the hook so easily."

"It shouldn't."

The shadow sliced across her ankle. She jerked, stopping herself from looking down to see if it had drawn blood. Was she supposed to pretend it didn't hurt? Was that part of ignoring it?

"What..." Tarian stopped stroking, looking down at her in confusion.

Another slice, this one then drilling in. She sucked in a pained breath, unable to help it. Nor could she help looking down. Blood poured out of the fresh wound and seeped from the other. A black claw ran across her other calf, and the feeling of bugs across her chest dug in like flesh-eating beetles.

"Fuck—" She slapped at her chest, but there was nothing there. The pain intensified, magic spearing into her. Through her. It felt like white-hot spikes—*real* spikes.

Tarian quickly did up his pants before bending forward, reaching down to her leg. His fingers came away with a smear of blood. Rage and worry blazed in his eyes. This couldn't have been the magical allure; she was being attacked. He didn't know by whom.

She cried out with another sharp jab. Power pulsed in

her middle—the diamond chalice calling to her. Another slice, this one across her ACL. She bent over, and her breath dried up. She couldn't breathe!

She tried to enact her nulling magic, but it wouldn't work on the shadows at her feet. She needed a fae to target. She needed a body or her magic was no good.

"Gods, Daisy—" Black so deep it was solid flowed over her body. Gold shimmered across her skin. The spikes of magic were dragged out one by one, only the last allowing her to breathe again. The tingles suggested that Tarian was using the magic she had stored. It wouldn't be enough. The attacking magic aimed for her stomach now while redoubling its efforts on her legs.

"Fuck!" Tarian scooped her up into his arms, turning frantically. "Faelynn!" he shouted.

A dozen court members snickered, more hiding grins or smiles. She'd remember each and every one of those fuckers.

Daisy grabbed for the closest fae's magic, someone too strong to steal from this quickly, but black spots danced behind her eyes. Her head felt light as blood soaked her dress around her stomach. She sucked that magic to her and heard a feral cry.

"Use this magic," she said, and coughed. Blood frothed at her lips.

Tarian swore again as a male with his teeth bared and his eyes screwed up in rage came at them. He launched himself, not sure who was doing this to him and beyond logic to care. Tarian dropped Daisy without ceremony, no time to put her down gently.

Take all that you can, he told her.

She hit the ground and groaned, curling up with pain. She siphoned magic from the fae male as fast as she possibly could, without subtlety. It flowed into her, and Tarian took it out just as quickly, combating the magical attack on her.

He drew his knife from a jacket pocket. It increased in size as Tarian spun. He yanked the fae past him in a beautifully graceful move and stuck his knife into the center of the fae's back directly after.

Daisy continued to suck at that power. The fae roared wildly, turning for Tarian with hands curved into claws. He reached for Tarian's face, his thumbs aimed at Tarian's eyes.

That fae's bodyguards showed up behind him, swords whirling. Tarian's were hurrying toward them.

Get her the fuck out of here! Tarian yelled. *The princess is attacking her with everything she has, and someone is helping her do it.*

Faelynn knelt for Daisy, hands out to heal.

No! Daisy shouted, pulling at that magic, offering it up to Tarian. Gorlan filled in the space, staff whirling, iron decorated with runes. *Don't show me attention. They'll question why you would save me over him. That'll raise questions. I'm alive. Help him!*

Faelynn hesitated. Then she quickly stood and brandished a knife, as though she'd gotten it out of an ankle harness. It was a terrible cover, but hopefully in all the excitement no one would notice she'd initially knelt to Daisy. Gorlan stuck his staff into the chest of a bodyguard. Faelynn got behind and dug her blade into the back of the fae's neck. He went down fast.

Tarian's wylds-made blade whirled in a beautiful array of light. He stepped and struck, then ducked and struck again. The fae was bleeding all over, and his limbs didn't want to hold him, but he wouldn't go down. He was fueled by the panic-stricken need to kill the thing stealing his magic. Her. He'd instinctively figured out who it was.

Tarian must've realized it, because he stepped into the fae's way each time and acted as though the blows were meant *for* him and not to get *by* him.

She pulled in the last of the magic as another bodyguard was felled by Gorlan's and Faelynn's blades. Tarian sliced across the fae's neck even as he was wilting. The death would look like Tarian had done it.

The head slammed down onto the floor in a swirl of nightmare black. Its sightless eyes looked her way accusingly. She wished he could see her returned look of *You got what was coming to you.*

The shadowy magic stabbed her, surrounding her. With Tarian's efforts, it peeled away slowly...and then in a rush. Gorgeous golden hues and rose and chartreuse danced within the black. Tarian's magic cut through the attack until she could suck in another lungful of air.

She spasmed in a fit of coughing, still holding her stomach. Faelynn dropped down beside her.

"Let me see," she murmured, pulling at Daisy's dress. Blood still seeped from her wounds, her Demigod's gift working as fast as it could to stitch her up, but she was losing a lot of blood. "It's okay. This'll be okay. I've got you."

Faelynn's hands pushed against her skin, and Daisy stopped herself from crying out in pain.

Take from the well of magic she has stored up, Tarian directed her. He grabbed the collar of the fallen fae's shirt and the waist of his pants. He yanked the fae into the air like he weighed nothing and threw the body out into the middle of the dance floor.

Nobility screamed or shouted in surprise, having stopped their dancing to watch. They scattered out of the way as the bloodied body slid across the marble floor, leaving a glistening red trail in its wake. Flesh screeched as the body lost momentum and stopped fifteen feet from the princess's slightly elevated chair. From the floor, though, Daisy couldn't see the expression on the princess's face.

"Elamorna, you dare attack my champion?" Tarian hollered. His foot twisted as his focus switched. "What sort of court are you presiding over here, *Highness*? Have *all* your rules stopped counting for anything? Is there no order to be had anymore?"

The princess's voice was mocking. "But she is not your champion, is she, Tarian? She is your taboo little toy. You didn't want an equal in your bed. You wanted a sniveling little creature to dominate. You wanted a creature that made you feel godly—"

"Enough," the king said, and the court fell into uneasy silence.

There we are, Faelynn said, closing the wounds, chasing away the pain.

Leave the pain. Daisy winced. *I need to know what is still hurting and how much. You can chase it away when we're safe again.*

"You do not understand, Elamorna," the king said, sounding amused. "That is because you've never been with a human. They are so easily broken that they, in themselves, are a game. How hard can you ride them before you kill them? How can you twist them just right that their spasms of pain milk your pleasure? How can you prolong their death until you are well and truly ready to break them? It's an art, keeping a human alive. Tarian is learning that art. He is starting to crave it. He will join us yet."

He paused and fabric swished, the princess frustrated but unwilling to defy her father.

He spoke again, this time to Tarian. "I do uphold the rules of the court, my dear lad. Of course I do. The fae that attacked you within the court, for example, would have been sentenced to death. Given you had no choice but to take care of that, in defense, I will kill his mate. As for your human, she is not fae, and therefore she is not subject to our rules. She is below them. But I will guarantee her protection in court and in the games...for now. I wouldn't deny myself the pleasure of a human, after all. It's been so long since I've had one. Now, you may go and see to her, if you wish. I know what a sad thing it is for someone else to break your toy before you are done playing with it."

Faelynn sat Daisy up gradually, and pain radiated from deep within Daisy's body. Her dress didn't have any holes in it, but it felt like her skin still did.

"Yes, sire," Tarian said tightly.

He turned on his heel, and Daisy expected him to stalk out of the court, leaving her to his *Fallen* like in times past. Instead, he bent and scooped her up, cradling her gently to his chest.

"Careful," Faelynn murmured, her hand flowing over Daisy's legs.

I'm okay, she told them as Tarian walked toward the dais and around a seat grouping. *Humans aren't that breakable. Not when they have the Demigod's blood magic.*

Thank fuck for that, Gorlan murmured.

Tarian stared directly at Princess Elamorna. *I warned you,* he said in a deathly quiet mental voice. *I warned you what would happen if you touched my property. Now you will know true sorrow.*

He walked across the marble court with Daisy in his arms. The nobility parted ahead of him, wariness or outright fear on their faces. The doors opened when he reached them, and fae servants on either side hurried to clear the way. The doors closed crisply after they'd passed through.

Are you okay? Tarian asked Daisy. Faelynn hurried beside them, her hands on Daisy's ankles, helping Daisy's body repair the damage.

Yeah. I'll heal. My ACL is just about good. I'll be fine

to walk in a moment. Almost there. It wasn't a deep cut, thank god.

The other damage?

Before Daisy could answer, Faelynn dumped a plethora of images and feelings into their heads, detailing the magical maladies and what was healed and what was left to go.

Who was helping her? Tarian mused to himself. *She doesn't usually team up with anyone. She doesn't keep anyone that powerful close enough in case they try to sabotage her.*

Is teaming up with someone a vulnerable thing or something? Daisy asked as they turned a corner.

Yes. Very. It requires great trust. You are linked for a time, and in that time, your power can be used against you. It's the perfect opportunity for a fae to betray another, so very few do it.

Daisy lifted her eyebrows. *She must really want you. This level of obsession is extreme.*

She always has, yes.

Tarian is the ultimate prize in this court, Faelynn said. *The realm, really. The most handsome, the best pedigree, the promise of the most powerful offspring—she wants him like she wants to breathe. And she recognizes that he found in you what she has always wanted him to find in her.*

Let's hope she's the only one who recognizes that, Gorlan murmured, his eyes continually scanning. *Or else—*

The lighting in the hall cut out.

They are trying my patience, Tarian said, setting Daisy down in the middle of the hallway. *Stay there. Don't move. Let us handle this.*

(Like hell she would.)

Daisy. Tarian waved his hand, and diffused light peeked through the black along the top corners of the ceiling. *I don't need your hidden thoughts to alert me to your stubbornness. Stay there.*

Your internal wounds are healed enough for you to defend yourself, Faelynn whispered in Daisy's head as she pulled a dagger out of a sheath. *Be prepared in case something gets through us. Tarian has called the* Fallen. *They are hurrying. We just need to hang on. Don't let anything affect your heart. These types of creatures always go for the heart.*

Great. She didn't have one of those. She was all set.

Chapter Twenty-Five

Daisy

Darkness moved all around them, coalescing into shapes and figures. Creatures grew from the ground, the same sort Tarian had pushed on her outside of the charity auction hotel. Even then, he'd been preparing her for something like this.

Faelynn sliced her palm as the creatures filled the hallway. Blood welled up, and she ran it over her blade. It started to glitter gold in the low light, her magic coating the sharp edge. Gorlan did the same, the three of them forming a protective circle around Daisy, knees bent, postures battle-ready. Tarian's glowing weapon had turned into his favorite, the staff with a blade on either end.

Daisy rose, pulling out her own blade. Her ankle hurt, and her stomach pinched, but she was good enough.

She wasn't the type to stay idle. If Tarian had met Lexi, they could've bitched about that fact for hours.

The creatures jostled each other as they closed the distance between themselves and Daisy's crew.

No, Daisy specifically. All "eyes," hollowed-out holes filled with flickering fire, were on her. The soulless orbs gave her a chill to look into.

At once, they started running, slowly at first, then faster. Claws elongated into disproportionate lengths on the ends of spindly arms. They clacked against the ground on tripod-style legs. The first one reached Tarian. He dodged a swipe gracefully, stepped, and plunged his staff through the chest, then pivoted, yanked his blade, and swung for the next. His movements were effortless and beautiful, someone who'd taken great pains to learn and master the forms of fighting.

Gorlan was next, followed quickly by Faelynn, both of them also showing a mastery of their blades. Gorlan hacked off a limb as Faelynn twirled and sliced her blade across a creature's neck. She stepped as she pulled free and plunged the blade into another. Gorlan did the same, hacking and slicing and stabbing. Their skill was far beyond that of the nightmare creatures advancing, but their number was too few. Way too few. They'd be overrun in no time.

Normally, Daisy would've stepped into the space between Faelynn and Gorlan, hiding her involvement from the person—fae—who had told her to stay out of the fight, but she didn't know them. She hadn't fought with them. She did know Tarian, and so she filled the space between him and Faelynn. He'd just have to get over it.

She sliced through a reaching arm, hacking it at the elbow before sticking her dagger into the creature's chest. The magical blade cut right through. Unlike the first time she'd battled such creatures, these didn't scream. Daisy and crew would be treated to a lovely, quiet fight. That wasn't so bad. Less annoyance.

"She's even entertaining when she's fighting," Gorlan called over the wet sounds of blades finding purchase.

"You fuckers need to get out more," Daisy said, and Gorlan snickered. She plunged with her knife. Searing pain raced across her stomach. It felt like she'd torn something.

She ignored it. The pain wasn't bad enough to suggest she'd done something terminal.

She jerked the blade out and went on to the next, her mind settling into a comfortable haze. Her muscle memory took over, hindered by her wounds but not thrown off track. Her middle tingled as Tarian reached for magic.

Magic.

What the fuck was she doing? Besides *not* trying to use magic. She had some now but was acting like she didn't. *Idiot.*

She cut and slashed, stepped and parried. Tarian moved around her like they were dancing, so much more interesting than on a ballroom floor.

That's because you've never danced with me on a ball-room floor, he murmured, his voice strained.

That was true, she supposed.

The teachings from that contraption filtered through her mind. She sighted in on one of the creatures, then switched to another when Tarian killed the first. She tried to deaden its magic...only to have it swipe at her, raking its claws across her arm.

She gritted her teeth and stabbed it through, focusing on one farther back. The press of creatures pushed her crew in tighter, everyone battling with everything they had. Tarian slashed one through with magic, another with his staff. Faelynn did the same. Gorlan whirled like a machine.

Daisy couldn't feel the creatures. It wasn't like working with that magical device—real life felt totally different.

You've practiced in real life, Faelynn said through a spark of pain. She shoved the feeling away like Daisy might've. This fae might not say a whole lot, but she was just as tough as all the others. *You've nulled me, remember? Lennox, Gorlan—you've nulled us. Even Tarian. It isn't different. You're just not targeting the source.*

Follow the magic, Tarian said, twisting at the last moment. Claws barely missed his arm. *Feel the thread of the magic and follow it. You don't need sight for this. You need to feel the threads of Faerie. They're everywhere—in everything. Someone conjured these creatures and gave them life.* That *is what you need to null—the root.*

The contraptions never said anything about threads and roots and conjuring. What sort of half-assed training did they have in this place?

She worked harder, limping, breathing heavily. Her stomach was on fire, pulsing in pain. Her legs throbbed, one barely holding her up. Still she pushed, fighting through the creatures. They weren't hard to kill, given the magical knife parted their flesh like silk, but there were just so damn many of them. They kept coming, on and on, no break in the onslaught.

The root. Feel the root.

No, wait—the threads. Feel the threads...

Images flickered through Daisy's mind, from Tarian and then from Gorlan, pictures of the magic weaving within itself. Of it shimmering and dancing and beautiful. She didn't see any of that through her dull, sad-sack human vision.

Emotions rolled through her now, Faelynn feeding her a different perspective. She *felt* the threads around her, the magic washing against her, the writhing forms of the creatures.

Okay, that made more sense.

We all connect with Faerie differently, Faelynn said, her mind like a flowing river within a vibrant green field. She was like a meditation session just by opening her mind. *Find the way you connect, and you will find the magic.*

Yelling and battle calls erupted over the din of their efforts. Weapons swung through the air, and creatures started to drop at the outer periphery. The *Fallen* had arrived.

We'll be good, Tarian told her. *Figure out your magic.*

She limped back into their protective circle, tight now

and pressed from all sides. She stood, most of her weight on her better foot, dagger in hand, and closed her eyes. They'd tell her if she was in danger.

She didn't immediately feel for the magic. No, she remembered when Lexi was trying to learn hers. It was a magic that lent best to one's ability to feel it. They'd tried to teach Lexi how, but she'd been a visual learner. They'd had to change their style of teaching.

Those early lessons, though, had stuck in Daisy's head. She'd watched from the sides, curious and wary, concerned for her caregiver and ready to help with remembering the tough stuff if Lexi needed it. Lexi hadn't, but now Daisy called up what had been said then and after, when Lexi could describe different aspects of spirit.

Spirit made up the framework of the human world. It was the support system for souls, both in the world with the living and beyond, in the afterlife. It existed everywhere and outlined everything. A body came and went, but a soul was forever, or so Lexi believed.

This magic was in everything and existed everywhere, right? Take it away, and a fae died. Mess with it, and a fae panicked and went nuts, doing everything they could to protect that part of themself. Spirit could do that to people.

The similarities ended there, but that might be enough.

She pored over the teachings, years old but still seeming so fresh. She didn't tend to lose sight of extremely dangerous magic. She had a lot of notes on

Dylan and Thane, too. Even Jerry. They'd never want to turn into her bad guys.

Eyes closed, feeling the soothing river in Faelynn's mind still streaming through hers, Daisy clued in. She felt around. She touched Tarian, with whom she was comfortable, and Gorlan, whom she knew. Then she branched out, finding the *Fallen* cutting their way closer, almost to them now. Each of them registered. Niall added to Faelynn's lovely scene, wildflowers popping up in brilliant colors and the breeze ruffling her hair. So did two more, adding details that felt like a weave of magic. Between them all, rotting magic flowed. In and around, pulsing one moment and dying away the next, most flowing back into the area surrounding it. Some of it headed back to its maker, though.

Feeling like she was floating, and not afraid of it because of all the times Lexi had described to Kieran or Bria how she moved through spirit, she followed. She drifted, feeling the push and pull of magic, the playful dance, the nightmarish, dangerous pull. It weaved within each other in some places, fought in others, separated and came together. It was a perfectly composed mess, like Eldric's library.

Like Eldric's library. Huh. He existed in his information gathering like a fae existed in Faerie.

Suddenly, everything made sense. It crystalized in her mind, like the ever-changing landscape the *Fallen* were showing her mentally. The wildflowers that wilted, died, and popped up again in the spring. The water moving through and away, always replaced with something similar but not the same. And maybe it was because she had Lexi's Demigod blood gift, could feel souls, and had a magical nudge toward spirit magic, but in the middle of all that chaos...she found balance. The light and the dark, the living and the dead. Complex but oh-so simple. Natural.

She found the root like it had a big arrow pointing at it. A mass of gross, twisted magic surged and sparked and melted the surrounding air, wrong in every way. She couldn't tell if it was a fae or a beast, an individual or eight. She applied the chalice magic like a candle snuffer cutting out the oxygen to a flame.

The rot around them spun and twisted but eventually withered away, evaporating back into the framework whence it came. Another magic waited, though. Around the corner, skulking in the shadows. A vile magic from something that didn't register as fae. Not anymore. She really got now why they referred to magic gone wrong as twisted...

It was wrong for this place. It was a sore on the healthy body that was Faerie.

She didn't snuff that one. It would be wrong to allow that creature to continue plaguing this realm. No, she stole from it. Yanked its magic away like a toddler stealing her brother's last piece of candy. She took it, and she chewed it up and swallowed it before the original holder could get it back.

They heard a cry of abject terror and then rage, followed by a strange growling. Footsteps in the distance were cut short, and something heavy hit the ground and sounded like it tumbled. One of the *Fallen* took off in that direction, followed by a couple more. She didn't have to see it to know; she could feel it. She could feel them, their magic weaving within the flow of Faerie. It was...incredible. Beautiful.

All lay still and quiet around her except for heavy breathing, everyone trying to catch their breath. She gradually opened her eyes, wanting to stay in that magical headspace a while longer but knowing this was not the place, now was not the time, and her body was crying for more healing and a bed.

Everyone was facing her, swords down, staring. Their expressions were hard but blank, giving nothing away.

She lifted her eyebrows as she put her knife away. "What?"

Tarian

Tarian stared at Daisy for much too long, dumbfounded, playing everything that had happened in his head again. Strangely, none of his *Fallen* reacted, either. Everyone stared at the human who had just rooted out and extinguished Faerie magic as though born in this place. As though born to this magic.

Are you sure she's human? Gorlan asked, his voice holding awe. *She figured that out all on her own. She accomplished it like she's been doing it all her life.*

A surge of pride gushed through Tarian, so unexpected that he staggered.

Yes, she was human. Yes, she was new to magic. To all of this. Yes, she was a genius who was good in a pinch and a valuable member of this team. She'd always shown she could be, and now she'd proven she would be. She'd help them win. If anyone could—if any human in all the realms could see them to the finish—it was this precious, beautiful little creature.

"Seriously, what?" Daisy cocked her hip in that way that said everyone was an idiot.

He was too shocked, too numb, too...full of pride, maybe, to laugh or smile.

Instead, he put away his sword before he scooped her up into his arms and held her tightly to his chest. His heart throbbed from the closeness. His body tightened with need. To feel her more thoroughly against him. He'd never wanted anyone so badly in all his life, and with each passing day, instead of that feeling waning, it grew stronger. More solid. Un-fucking-breakable.

"Nothing," he said.

How could you put all that into words? *Any* of this into words? She'd figured out a complex magical lesson... with a couple of shallow hints from his crew. That was...

He started to laugh.

Eldric was correct. She would be fit for the scribes. Mentally, anyway. She wouldn't open the gates for a rush of more humans to follow, though. There weren't many like her. She was proving to be truly exceptional.

As usual, she took his silence for some kind of

answer. Her brain kept spinning in that dizzying way it did.

His body is tense, she observed. Always observing. *His jacket is cut and slashed in a dozen places. Blood is welling up in a few of those places, but all his limbs are still attached. His wounds aren't what is troubling him.*

"But seriously, what?" she demanded again. "I did it, right? I did the job. I'm not great at it, or fast, but I did it. That's something. Right?"

He could feel the insecurity in her mind. Had to clench his jaw to stop from gushing all over her. Even now there might be eyes on them. He was already being too obvious in his partiality. Showing his intense and deepening feelings would surely result in the royals taking her and tormenting her in front of him. He couldn't bear that. He wouldn't live through it, because he'd kill as many of the palace residents as he possibly could before they brought him down. If they harmed her, he'd lay waste to this place. He'd sacrifice his duty to claim vengeance on her behalf. No hesitation. No remorse.

"Yes." He turned a corner, his jaw still tight. "That is something."

She studied his face, her arms wrapped around his neck. His knees nearly buckled at the soft look in her eyes, speaking directly to the warmth radiating in his middle.

The soft look currently warring with her annoyance, at any rate. He felt like laughing. Definitely scribe material. Above all, she wanted answers. Well...him and answers. Equally so. He wanted to comply, but not yet. Not until they were in the safety of his chambers and she was properly seen to.

"What did I do wrong?" she asked. "Should I not have killed— Oh shit, did I kill the princess? I couldn't tell what sort of creature it was. It was too far away for me to feel its soul—if it had one—so..." She grimaced, fear running amok. "Fuck, I wasn't thinking. *Fuck!* It was just that...it was so twisted and wrong. It was—"

"Daisy, steady," he said, holding her tighter. "I don't know what—or who—it was, but it wasn't any of the royals. The king wouldn't have allowed them to leave. None of the nobility would leave, either. The *Fallen* will report to us shortly."

"Okay, seriously...what, then?"

He reached his chambers and pushed open the door. Once inside, he cut straight for the bedroom. He set her on her feet and slowed, his gaze stopping on the blood crusted on her dress.

It's ruined, she thought absently, noticing his gaze. *Not that my alterations hadn't already started the transition to "unwearable."*

He smirked. She had an acute eye for fashion. He absolutely loved that about her, especially when she was hard on herself for it. Everyone else thought her alterations were fantastic. She'd only roll her eyes to hear it.

He delicately lifted the fabric over her head. She slipped off her bangles as she bent to look at her stomach. Five puncture marks were evident, all of them somewhat healed but bleeding again from her exertions a moment ago. They were as clean as if a sharp knife had pierced her. Magic, obviously.

He gritted his teeth as a wave of rage tugged him under. The princess would watch her world burn for what she'd done to Daisy. He couldn't directly harm her, but he knew enough to indirectly tear everything down that she held dear. Every fae courtier, every priceless relic, every last comfort she thought she kept private. She didn't know what pain was. He'd show her.

"Stay there." He stopped in his turn to go and put out a finger. "I mean it. Don't move."

His tone means he's serious, Daisy thought, unable to help her running commentary. *But then, isn't he always? I'm not accustomed to—*

He lifted one eyebrow.

Her mental commentary reduced to a slight buzz of internal pain. It would have to do.

He nodded and left the room, still paying attention to her mental voice. It never stopped, and it wasn't quiet.

Her mind replayed images of the fight, the magic, and how she'd used her power to snuff out the threat.

Maybe I shouldn't have killed the creature on the other end, she thought as he grabbed a bowl, water, and bandages. *It didn't make sense not to, since they were attacking, but...maybe there are...some rules I don't know...*

He shrugged out of his jacket, laid it on the back of the couch, and brought the supplies into the bedroom.

"Here."

Her eyes widened in fear and worry. Images tumbled through his mind, her projecting without meaning to. It was something she did when in a heightened state of anxiety. Blood marred various places on his ripped undershirt. The wounds lay open and bleeding. Pain throbbed from them, but they looked worse than they were. Mostly.

"Oh my—" Her hands shook as she reached for him. "Don't *here* me—Tarian, hell—get something on that!" She snatched away the washcloth he'd brought, threw it on the bed, and reached for his undershirt.

"I'm fine. I'm fine—" He pushed her hands to her sides before reaching for the washcloth. "Daisy, I am *fine*. I'll heal. I'm fae. Let's get you taken care of."

More thoughts and images jumbled in her mind.

This feels like back when I was a Chester without the Demigod magic and they babied me because I got a scrape. Images accented the thoughts. Scents. Feelings. A random song played in the back of her head that didn't pertain to anything at all. *Well, now I have magic. I'm not even* remotely *as breakable as these arrogant fucks think. I will not be babied. It's insulting.*

Her eyes narrowed as they moved around his face, violence imminent.

I don't want to punch that pretty face... came floating out. *A fat lip would ruin him for kissing.*

He chuckled. In times like this, it was impossible not to laugh or react.

He applied the cloth to her stomach. "Okay, you are not as breakable as fae might think. Yes, that Demigod magic does help. Honestly, you'd be dead now if it didn't. Yes, you will very likely give any fae competitors a run for their money. Okay? But Daisy, just—shut the fuck up and let me tend to you. Hide your thoughts."

She rolled her eyes and pushed backward, lying on the bed. *Fine. If I'm forced to be an invalid, I'll go fully into it.*

"Yes, *thank you.*" With a smile, he sat on the edge of the bed next to her, the bowl balanced near her hip. His hands trembled, too, as he saw the blood and remembered the helplessness he'd felt while watching her writhe in agony. The rage when he finally became action. The despondency, not protecting her as he had said he would. As he'd *promised.*

He applied pressure, scared to hurt her and thankful he could hear her thoughts to ensure she wasn't hiding how bad off she was. He worked quickly but gently, soft and careful, wiping away the blood and smoothing the wounds with his fingers. Guilt tore at him, but he tried not to let it show in his expression or his bearing.

Her gaze never left his face. She caught every emotion he thought he was hiding.

"Will you tell me what the problem is?" she asked softly.

He tried to keep his tone even. "I didn't protect you like I promised. That's one thing." He pulled up her knee and looked at the cuts and scrapes there. Most were nearly healed already. They'd been shallow, thank the Divine Collective. Her ankle wasn't great, though.

He bit back the wave of rage-induced misery and owned it.

"I exposed you to the court and served you up for the slaughter."

"That princess has lost a few screws where it concerns you. She was always going to walk this path," she said in total indifference. She wasn't at all concerned about how close the princess had come to killing her. How useless he'd been in shielding her.

No, maybe she wasn't human, after all. Nor fae. She was some other creature, born in the fire, used to dancing in the flames.

He smoothed her hair back from her forehead but resisted the urge to lie beside her. He had work to do still.

"We'll just need to look out for her," she continued. "This was necessary, Tarian. Everyone saw you kiss and fuck me. They'll know if they try it, you'll kill them. Right? That's common knowledge?"

He let out a breath. "Yes." He pulled the cloth away to check the wounds.

"And they are scared of you, more so now that you stood in front of them all—in front of the king—and threatened the princess."

He could hear the pleasure in her voice. The lust in her mind. She'd liked his menacing show of possession and vengeance. She was such a similar creature to him.

"She made a deal," he said. "I'm living up to my end of it. They all heard it."

"What do you mean?"

"I told her I'd kill her treasured pets if she harmed you. She did. Now I will."

"That's not a deal. That's an ultimatum."

"In this court, that is close enough."

She sighed as he got up to get a fresh cloth. He refreshed the water so it was clean.

"Right, so that's them sorted," she said, fatigue entering her voice. "We just need to watch out for that princess." She swallowed thickly. "And the king."

"The king..." His stomach pinched with what he'd learned tonight. He'd need to go over it in detail, change some plans, form others. She was in more danger than either of them could've known.

He braced a hand beside her, looking down at her. "I didn't know we'd have this problem with him. I had no idea he was so...infatuated with humans."

"It kinda makes you think he's got some ulterior motives for going into the human realm."

Tarian pushed up to sitting again, trying to hide his wince of pain. "He knows very well that if he stays in this realm, he'll be killed. There is no return for him. It might not be the Celestials—it might be other kingdoms seeking to right this wrong—but someone will handle it. He's on borrowed time. Initially, however..."

His heart beat faster with the implications as he finished cleaning her up before standing and stripping off his shirt. He didn't bother looking down at himself. Daisy noticed each and every scratch, served up in her mind. He had many rips in his flesh and messy wounds leaking down his stomach. He grabbed the bandages he'd brought in and wrapped himself up. One wound needed tending, but Faelynn would handle that when she got here.

"I fully believe he wants to rule without being

governed," he went on. "He wants a kingdom that knows no bounds and a throne no one can contest. But yes, it seems there is more to it." His lip curled as anger pooled hot within him. As their fates loomed.

"I know how to null now. For the most part. How fast is he? How hard will things be if I kill him before you're ready? Because I won't suffer the touch of him. Sorry, Tarian. I know you are counting on me, but some things... I just can't stomach."

His hands slowed. He looked at her and knew pain flashed in his eyes. In his body. "I would *never* ask you to endure something like that for me, dove. Not for anyone. You choose the path you need to choose, and I will be ready." He sat on the edge of the bed again and took her hand. "Stay alive and keep yourself from breaking however you need to. Do you understand?"

"Burn it down," she whispered.

"To the ground."

Chapter Twenty-Six

Daisy

The next morning, after a night spent in Tarian's arms, each of them resting and healing, Daisy exited Tarian's empty chambers to see Lennox and Niall sitting on the couch with a blanket spread out under them. They each had a book in hand.

"Honestly." She clucked her tongue. "You have clothes on, and he doesn't ejaculate. What are you even worried about? You don't need the blanket."

"It's gross," Niall said, not looking up. "It's the principle of the thing."

She rolled her eyes. "Where's everyone else?" She sat on the couch opposite them.

"Information gathering, errands, coming up with a plan to kill the princess's favorite toys. She covets them, and she expects Tarian to go after them. It won't be easy to get to them, but if anyone can make it happen, Tarian is that male."

"Right. And...after all she's done to him, why wait until now?"

They both looked up over the edges of their books.

Lennox answered, "Because it would've incited a retaliation, and he had a duty to find those chalices. Also because..." He stalled.

Niall looked back down at his book. "Because of you." He turned a page. "He dealt with that decay for years and shouldered the stink. He didn't want to put us or our plans in jeopardy. But he will not suffer anyone touching you. He's finally pushing back. *Hard*."

"Fucking *finally*," Lennox said under his breath. "It killed me to watch all that and see him pretend to shrug it off and get back to work. I felt responsible."

"Me too. We all did. It was fucking unbearable. The good news is that the king wants a turn with you." Niall looked at Daisy.

"Ah." She leaned back. "If it wasn't me, that would indeed be good news, yes."

Lennox went back to his book. "Told you," he muttered.

Niall used his finger to hold his place and lowered his entertainment. "How in the fuck are you blasé about that? Tarian said you were, but we didn't believe him."

"I did," Lennox cut in.

"Fine. *I* didn't believe him. Most of us didn't."

"The ones that are around her the most did," Lennox said lightly. "Except...for you."

Niall rolled his eyes before his accusatory gaze came back to her. "Are you pulling a Tarian? Are you dying inside and won't tell us because you're noble and doing a duty and whatever bullshit excuse you have? I don't know your family, but they raised you, and you're a good sort of female, so I can't imagine they'd be okay with that."

She grinned and looked at the object resting on the table. It was propped there with little stoppers to keep it from rolling off the flat surface. The smooth onyx exterior showed large cracks that a hand couldn't feel, their color a dull orange. Until it was activated, that was. Then an orange-red glow peeked out through the cracks, pulsing higher until a yellow-white point denoted that the chalice was at its maximum power.

Daisy's presence in this court had activated them all. For the first time since Tarian had brought them here, they were working. They were boosting power. Tarian had sent for Eldric late last night to discuss it.

The royal family attributed this to—what they thought was—the crystal chalice (which was actually the diamond chalice). Tarian had known they would. It was why he'd waited to bring Daisy here until he had that chalice. Well, one of the reasons.

Come to find out, several of the chalices had been taken from the library, all by the royal family. The female fae that had attacked them with shadow creatures had been holding one last night, an onyx chalice. She'd used it to garner more power and send those creatures after Daisy and her crew. The king had held the diamond chalice on the throne. Everyone now believed the princess hadn't acted with someone else, but that she'd had a chalice of her own. They were learning how to use them, and sooner rather than later, they would think they didn't need Tarian anymore.

"It's not rocket science," she told Niall.

"Rock—what?" he replied quizzically.

"It's not complicated," she tried again.

"Apparently, it is for Niall," Lennox murmured.

"Tarian should be half ignoring me so the court doesn't think I'm all that valuable to him," Daisy said. "Instead, he's doing the opposite. It's fine that he doesn't like to share, sure, but he's putting too much emotion into it. They might not fuck me, but they'll target me. They'll want to hurt me or kill me to mess with him or bring him down a peg. To hurt him. It happened in the past. It *worked* in the past. But this time, the king wants a turn. He wants me alive long enough so he can mess with me. He's made that clear. I'm now mostly off-limits until the king has had his fill. If the princess can manage to kill me accidentally before that, she will. Otherwise, the king has dibs. After that, no more rules. Everyone Tarian has wronged in the court will come for me. That seems like a lot of fae."

"No, right, yeah." Niall scratched his nose. "We know all that—"

"And *she* knows all that." Lennox turned another page. Could he possibly be reading and listening—and interacting!—all at the same time?

Yes, Lennox said.

And eavesdropping, too. Add that to the list.

Noted, he replied.

"So..." Niall leaned forward, putting the book on the couch next to him. "You're blasé about all that because you think the king will keep you alive longer?"

"Not really. The princess will be gunning for—after me in those games. An oops will be pretty easy to navigate behind the scenes. She seems cunning enough to pull that off. I'm worried about her, actually. She'll be playing in the shadows, and I need to be very careful not to reveal what I am while also not getting killed. I need to find an ally, which will be very hard to come by. But the king? He'll take me to his chambers, get super gross, make a move, and realize he has no magic. It'll be him against me. We should all really hope I can take him. And also that I can escape once I have. Tarian is asking Eldric to dig up and deliver me a map of the king's chambers. We need plans in place. Many plans in place...except we have no idea what we're planning for."

Both guys were looking at her, something strange moving behind their eyes. She couldn't quite tell what it was, though, so she just asked.

Lennox glanced at Niall before going back to his book.

Niall hadn't looked away. "You're confident about all that," he said. It wasn't a question. "The games, the king, the princess—you're confident going into all those unknowns."

"I mean...yeah." She looked at that chalice again. "I have to be, right? There's no alternative. Welcome to my life. Before Demigod Kieran, we had a certain set of problems, mostly to do with staying alive. Keeping a roof over our heads, having food to eat. I didn't know it then, but that was actually the easiest time in my whole life. I was scared a lot then, but the problems were manageable. They didn't feel like it at the time, but now I know they were. After Demigod Kieran, it was battles and extreme danger for all of us. Death would've been a better path than what had waited for Lexi had we failed. Once that was settled, it was mostly danger just for me. With occasional assassination attempts on the Demigods, obviously."

They nodded. They were fae. They got it.

She shrugged. "Now I've got a different set of problems. Being worried about it, or afraid of it, will drain my energy and deplete my resources to analyze. I need all the facts, all the angles, and then...to stay alive."

After last night, that seemed like the hardest part of all.

The next day, she wore somewhat formfitting trousers strapped with visible weapons. Her top was loose, the shirt under it tight, and more weapons were strapped to her torso. Her magical knife had a sheath, with a strap over the hilt to secure it in case someone should reach for it. She'd been practicing a quick draw so that the strap didn't waste valuable time.

"Remember our signals." Tarian walked with her in his princely attire, his shoulders back and straight, his gait relaxed and unhurried. It was time to present her into the games.

"Yup."

"If it is your life or theirs, always pick yours."

"Obviously."

"After each battle or any time you need it in the holding areas, you are allowed your healer." He glanced behind him at Faelynn. "Use her."

"Okay." They'd been over all this, last night and again this morning, but the reality of the situation was crashing down on Tarian right now, like it had crashed down on her when she'd visited Eldric. He was second-guessing the decision.

Too late now.

"Remember your training." They turned a corner. Other groups of fae ambled down the hall, the champions easy to spot. They were large, hulking things, most of them, with rounded shoulders and a certain walk that said they meant trouble. None of them looked around at the competition, staring straight ahead intimidatingly.

He slowed her as another noble veered in front of him, centering themselves in a line. At the end of the hall was an archway and various attendants checking people in. The nobles walked away. The champions continued on.

Butterflies filled Daisy's belly.

Remember your training, Tarian said again, reaching down and taking her hand. *Remember Zorn's teachings. Make him proud.*

It was what she needed to hear. The strength she

needed to keep stepping forward, one foot in front of the other, heading to a place where she'd be on her own with a bunch of magical fae who wanted her dead.

Tarian stopped her and turned, looking down into her eyes. He put his hands against her cheeks, holding her face gently. *You will never be alone, little dove. Faelynn will be on hand. She is skilled in combat, more so than any other healer in this entire kingdom. But remember, you also have this.*

He reached down and touched her knife.

Think to me, and I will hear you.

Right. She'd forgotten about that, a Faerie sort of telephone.

She nodded.

He kissed her lips softly.

You shouldn't show me so much affection, she said, falling into the feel of him. *Everyone else will clue in to what the princess already knows.*

You are human, a champion, and mine—you are already a target. I don't want to pass up the chance to feel your lips, even for a moment.

He slipped his tongue past her teeth, and she groaned, clutching him tightly. He took his time, savoring their contact, before finally stepping back.

"Okay, let's get you admitted." He squeezed her upper arms.

Admitted? That didn't sound promising.

They waited behind a couple of other nobles, and then it was her turn. Tarian gave his name and nudged her forward, and the attendant checked off "human." Why bother with details?

Protect yourself, Tarian said as she was motioned forward. *Come back to me in one piece.* He squeezed her upper arms. *I'll see you soon.*

Faelynn stepped around them, and then Daisy was walking through the arches. Almost immediately, someone grabbed her upper arm from the right.

Don't fight, Faelynn said. *You are a slave and now a prisoner. Go where you're told. They won't hurt you.*

She didn't sound sure, and Daisy didn't make any promises.

A long, low tunnel led to a large, circular room. A few dozen people sat around the stone floor in the dim light, chains attached to their ankles and bolted to the floor. Everyone faced her direction, all those eyes watching who was led into the room. Assessing. A great many scoffed or smirked upon seeing her. They looked past to see who was next.

That's a good sign, Faelynn said, following behind. *They underestimate you.*

Will we be able to see the fights that come before or after us?

No. You are held until it is your turn, and then you'll be returned after. They don't want the champions knowing what they will face until they are facing it.

That was good and bad. She wanted to catalog the strengths and weaknesses of these others. That would greatly help her plan. But she'd be routinely underestimated, and that was no small thing. It had always been her greatest asset.

Your greatest asset is now that chalice magic, Faelynn said, drifting away as the large attendant jerked her to a stop and pushed her down to sitting. He bent to attach the manacle around her ankle. *Use it.*

The chalice magic.

Daisy had pressed Tarian about that last night after everything had been seen to. She'd asked why he'd been acting so strangely when he picked her up after the scuffle in the hallway.

"You've been training for three days," he'd said, shaking his head at her.

"And?"

"And you managed to analyze and understand the magic here in a way that took me *years* to learn. That many fae still don't know how to do."

"I assume you were in my head as I figured it out, right?"

"Yes."

"Then you saw how I did it. I analyze magic, Tarian. I have since I entered the magical world. I internalize it. I stew on it. You've heard me do it. Lexi's magic has some similarities. When you connect all the dots, all you have to do is go with it. It took me years to learn, too. I just applied that knowledge here, that's all. It's no great mystery."

He'd kept shaking his head. "Your mind is a rare and amazing thing, my treasure. I think you would've been approached for the order of scribes."

"Approached, not selected?"

He'd grinned and pulled her closer. "There is no way in the depths of Sylreth's bog that you would've devoted your life to something so mundane as their order. You would've turned them down, insulted them while you did it, and never looked back."

True enough.

On the floor, she pulled up her knees and hugged her arms around them as other champions came in. She didn't notice them. Instead, she watched those who did. Watched them size up their opponents and the subtle change in their posture or body language. Felt the magic ebb and flow around the room, clinging to those with more capacity for it and drifting around those with less.

Healers sat at tables around the edges, drinking, eating, and occasionally chatting, their focus on each other and not the champions chained to the floor.

The prickle of eyes on her drew her gaze to the right. A mousy character looked at her from between long sheets of black hair. Its eyes were watchful and solemn and its bony shoulders tented the drape of the black fabric it wore. She couldn't tell if it was female or male, and it didn't matter, because she *could* tell it was sizing her up in a way no one else was. Subtle violet light flickered in the depths of its eyes, magical in a way she hadn't seen before. It didn't blink. Didn't look away. Just continued to stare as though it were a member of an audience waiting for Daisy to perform.

Soon, that was exactly what Daisy would do. They all would.

Chapter Twenty-Seven

LEXI

The various colors of spirit lit Lexi's way as her soul moved beyond the veil, stepping out of the physical world and into the metaphysical. Daisy was alive, but her tension had increased. She was in a holding area of sorts. That couldn't be good. She was separated from the fae that had gotten her there and so far kept her alive. Lexi didn't know Daisy's situation with that fae, but he hadn't harmed or mishandled her. That was something.

Now, however, she had a new challenge to face.

Panic welled up. Because of some spirits they'd met along the ever-winding and -shrinking trails, they knew how to get to the Obsidian kingdom's royal castle. They knew the landmarks to look for and a hazy set of directions. But it would still take days, and if Daisy had been thrown into a more dangerous situation, days might be too late.

Lexi coasted within spirit, learning about this new realm and how things worked. Souls lingered but stayed somewhat removed, feeling her "otherness." Her "humanness." The fabric of this place didn't support her spirit in the same way the human world did. The makeup of it was different. The structure. But it was the same idea, and so she'd quickly learned to navigate through it.

A strange reverberation contracted the space around her. Echoes of a more prominent being put pressure on Lexi's spirit. *Shit.* The maker or guardian of this place had realized she was moving through. It would most certainly check on her, and she wasn't sure how a fae would react to a human hanging out in its territory.

She yanked herself more quickly toward her body, currently guarded by Kieran and the crew. It was a dangerous thing, leaving one's body in the wilderness as she'd done, with no locks or walls or anything to keep danger away. But she'd had no choice. She just had to hope they had her covered.

The pressure increased. The spirit around her blistered into darker colors, peeling away to reveal her. A strange feeling, like a poke to her forehead, made her reel.

She put all her energy into the escape, increasing the danger of her journey, but wanting to get the hell out of there. She tumbled toward her body. Slammed back into it.

Her eyes fluttered open as a roar startled her, deep and loud and much too close. Fire crackled nearby and everyone had their weapons out, looking through the darkness between the trees.

"You let us know when she is back in her body," Bria said, crouched and ready.

"I'm here," Lexi said, feeling the creature's soul. It waited just off to the right, but she couldn't see it. It was perfectly hidden in the deep, black night.

"Where is it?" Zorn asked, his machete in his hand. "It keeps throwing its roar."

Lexi grabbed hold of the creature's soul as the Line blazed to the right. Iridescent colors wafted in the dark night, and a person-sized shape filled the space.

The creature in the darkness gave a pained roar and charged. Bria turned that way, and Zorn spun, but Lexi ripped the soul from the casing. The creature fell, and Lexi hurled the soul at the being staring out at her with furnaces for eyes. The soul and spirit blasted the being, but it didn't so much as step back. Instead, it waved the bombardment away.

"What magic is this?" it asked, its voice everywhere and nowhere. In her head but all around.

Kieran started, reaching out for her. Because of their connection, he could see the being, the veil, and ghosts, but he was lost to the finer elements of her magic. He was of no use now.

She pushed up to her knees as Zorn and Bria ran to get the creature. They'd decide if it was edible. No point in hunting when the predators came directly to them.

"I am here for my ward," she told it. "I'm human. The Celestials granted us passage."

She barely kept from holding her breath. This thing felt powerful. It felt like it could reach right into her chest with the power of Hades and take her spirit with it. It had to be a god.

Her body started to shake in the silence. "I have to move through spirit to find her," she added. "I don't stay long and I don't disrupt—"

"I know very well what you do in my domain, human!" it bellowed. "You did not ask permission to enter my space."

"I'm sorry. I didn't know I should have. That's not a requirement where I am from."

Its blazing eyes surveyed her for a long moment before it looked around the clearing. "What other of these humans can use this magic? That one is looking at me. Can it?"

"Just me. I'm a Demigod of Hades, our god of the underworld. I traverse the spirit. Only me."

"And you kill with this gift."

He called it a gift. That was good news. "Yes, when I need to. That predator was—"

"And you trap spirits with this gift." It noticed Mia and John. Frank must've taken off running.

"They are not trapped, as you must know. They—"

"They are mine for safekeeping." It ripped their souls from the lands, tucking them deeply into the veil behind it.

"No!" She stood, reaching out to them. "This isn't their home. That isn't where they belong."

"You should've thought of that when you brought them into this realm."

She breathed heavily, feeling its power. Its resolve. She didn't have the ability to go through it. She'd have to wait until it was distracted and go around, sneak in and grab Mia and John when it wasn't paying attention.

The being smiled for the first time. It took on a male vibe. "You care for them. That is good. I will look forward to this warfare you plan. Now go. Stop disturbing my domain."

"But I need—"

The veil closed, trapping Mia and John within it. Emotion welled up. Lexi was worried on their behalf, frustrated she couldn't do more. But she hadn't felt fear within that domain. She hadn't seen anything to make her think that god abused the souls it collected. They'd be okay until Lexi could get them back.

And she *would* get them back. First, she had to get the living. She had to get Daisy. And now, she couldn't use spirit to check on her. They were flying blind.

Chapter Twenty-Eight

DAISY

Murmured voices tore Daisy away from her thoughts. She had spent hours sitting on the cold floor, without food or water. Without a bathroom. Thankfully she didn't have to go, but others weren't so lucky. The healers had come and gone, most of them barely keeping an eye on their charges. Most of those chained weren't held in high esteem, and the healers didn't want to trouble themselves.

Faelynn sat quietly, not talking to anyone. Her gaze was never far from Daisy.

A door opened at the side. Wheels squealed as they rolled along the tracks. Darkness waited beyond, occasionally interrupted by a wavering voice in the distance. A singer, perhaps.

They are getting ready to bring out the first champions,

Daisy heard. Tarian, mentally speaking through the magical knife. *Each of you will compete against a prisoner. The fight is to the death.*

A stocky female walked through the wide doorway. She unrolled a scroll and looked around, spying a male at the edges and pointing. Two guards stepped forward from the walls to grab him, and a healer stood from the tables. She then chose another. They'd go first.

After that, in various increments of time, a dozen others followed. Only half of them returned. Of those, only three hadn't been gruesomely injured.

From his seat, Tarian had a great view of the fighting arena. He played for her what he saw, allowing her to get a glimpse no one else would get. It would give her an edge.

It also jangled her nerves. She'd anticipated prisoners like she'd seen in the cells: starved, weak, and frail. Instead, muscled mammoths swung huge arms as they walked onto the floor, teeth missing and gums black. Full of rage and hate and fire.

They usually bring the frail and weak prisoners out first, yes, Tarian replied to her observation. *The games have never started this viciously before. Serious contenders have been taken down. Nobles are shifting in their seats, either from anger or surprise. I'm not sure what's going on.*

The king had places to be. In the human realm, specifically. He'd been hurrying Tarian and Eldric along to get those chalices set, tested, and ready. They had all they needed. They just had to put them in the right order. The king wouldn't want this taking up Tarian's valuable time.

Very likely, Tarian murmured.

They still didn't have an exit plan. Tarian didn't have the right information to free himself from his shackles. Their time was running out, especially now, assuming the king was hurrying this along.

"You."

Daisy looked up, finding herself at the end of the guard's pointed finger. Her turn.

The butterflies in her belly turned ravenous.

I've done this before, she thought as the guards undid her manacles and Faelynn stood from her seat. *I've trained with huge guys before. Magical guys. Skilled guys. This is not new, and their magic cannot hurt me. I'm fast. I'm agile. I've got this.*

She took deep breaths as she stood. The guards' grip on her upper arms was bruising, a warning that she should not try to run. No one had. Not yet.

She siphoned off a little magic from them for no other reason than to give her something to focus on. They tensed but didn't otherwise react. It was, honestly, a perfect magic for her, rooted in thievery. As morally gray as a magic could be.

The darkness of the hallway swallowed them, almost no light with which to see by. Then they turned a corner, and a white glow surrounded a black object, the edges stained purple. A curtain.

The guards didn't slow as they reached it. An unseen hand pulled the curtain back, and the light flared brightly. She squinted as her eyes adjusted and quickly looked around. Nobles in their finery lounged in their seats, little smirks pulling at their lips when they saw her.

"The human," someone whispered as she passed.

"She won't last a moment."

The king sat on his dais, leaning against the arm of his throne. His eyes shone with interest. The princess's eyes hardened, hate fueling her gaze.

Daisy tucked away her thoughts so they couldn't eavesdrop.

Splatters and splotches of blood marred the pristine floor along her path, slick when stepped on. At the center of the room, where the nobles usually spun and twirled to the music, pools of crimson shone in the brightly lit space.

Tarian watched her approach with somber eyes. He leaned his elbow against the arm of his couch, his fingers lightly touching his jaw.

The guards shoved her forward. Her foot hit the slick edge of the puddle and slipped, throwing off her weight.

She could've stabilized herself. She could've bent her legs, centered her balance, and slid into the center. But that would've hinted at her skill.

Instead, she let her weight keep going, gravity dragging her down. Her arm hit the floor and her hand *thunked*, jostling her. She cried out in alarm, in disgust, her face a horrified mask of fear as she flailed within the evidence of death. Blood coated her clothes and covered some of her weapons. It matted her hair and wet the side of her face.

Shaking and distraught, she climbed to her feet amid uproarious laughter. Fae slapped their thighs and bent over in their mirth.

She looked sheepish as she caught movement from the side. A tall male stepped into view, wearing furred briefs. A leather strap across his torso held a serrated blade, and a ponytail with wavy hair fell down his back. Corded muscle rippled as he moved. Each step held power...but lacked balance. He was a warrior, but not a good one. Not of the caliber she was used to.

Magic curled around him. It swirled through the room and dusted the floor at his feet. She established a connection with it as his gaze raked over her. He sneered, not bothering to reach for his knife.

She quickly, and with shaking hands, grabbed for hers. Not her magical knife, though. No. A throwing knife, which she held as though it were a dagger. She bent her knees and braced, slipping and sliding as she tried to back away from his advance.

And the Oscar goes to...

She could feel Tarian's confusion. She was even fooling him. *Well done, Daisy.*

The hard part would be winning while making it seem like an accident. She'd never done that before.

Do not take any chances, Tarian warned.

Yeah, yeah.

"Do not kill the human," the king said as the other champion stopped at the edge of the bloody puddle. She noticed his feet had extra tread for traction. Her shoes were smooth soled, the ones Tarian had chosen switched

304

out before being led out here. They'd given her lot a disadvantage from the start. "But you may break her into pieces if you wish."

Tarian rubbed his fingers across his lips. He didn't comment, but his eyes burned. He was not amused.

She had no idea why not.

Her lip trembled. She edged around the puddle until she was opposite her attacker. Her magic started siphoning his slowly. She then had to release it from her body, because her vessel was full. This was just practice and to see if taking from him would weaken him. It should, but how quickly? She hadn't tested that while fighting yet.

"Commence," a voice boomed.

The male didn't hurry. He walked across the pool of blood like he had all the time in the world.

She looked around her like a frightened rabbit and thought of all the ways this could go. The male nearly reached her—she hurried out of the way. He followed her without a change in expression. It was almost like he was trudging after a petulant child who, when caught, was going to get dragged to the naughty corner.

She avoided him one more time, licked her lips as she looked back at Tarian furtively, then darted forward with her throwing knife. The male stopped, waiting for her, and she "tripped" when she drew close. She fell, slid, and crashed into his legs.

He reached down for her, not as fast as she'd expected or maybe not really trying. She slapped at his hands with one hand, screamed, and struck upward with her knife in the melee. The blade lodged home...right into his ballsack.

Tee-hee!

He jerked violently, and she increased the suction of her magic, pulling more from him. He didn't notice, bellowing in pain and reaching between his legs where it hurt the most, bending, his knees wobbling.

She surged up, "off-kilter" and with a flurry of "panicked" movement. Her magical dagger was in her hand in a flash, and her shoulder bashed into his solar plexus. The force knocked his weight backward. She "slipped," kicked out his foot with hers, and forced him to do the splits before he could get his knife. His scream increased in pitch, and she had to work very hard not to grin. *Fuck* she loved fighting dirty. It was so much fun.

His weight was still going backward. She clutched the strap across his chest to "keep from falling" and "accidentally" shoved her knife through his middle. It elongated on its own, really the best knife a gal could have, and she ripped him to the side as she "fell."

He landed with a half-strangled cry, cut short by her landing on the knife, driving it in the rest of the way. She scrambled off him, rolled and fell and sobbed, taking her knife with her. Before she was completely off, she yanked her throwing knife out of his balls and gave a legitimate *ugh* as she did so. Fuck that was gross. Dirty play was fun...until the cleanup.

She sat in a little ball, shaking and willing tears to trail down her blood-splattered face. It wasn't easy. That had been a fucking good time. Though...she didn't know if siphoning magic had made her enemy incrementally weaker.

Thank all the gods you are such a vicious little weasel, Tarian said affectionately. *I have said it before—the fates chose perfectly. That was masterful. I have never seen anything like it. You pulled it off seamlessly.*

Silence descended as the reality of what had happened worked through the nobles. Slowly, voices started to murmur. Then a slow clap issued from the dais. The king's blood-red eyes were alight with humor. He grinned as he spoke.

"As I said, humans are so much fun to play with. You never know how it will go. Take her away."

Daisy hastily put away her weapons before the guards hoisted her up and set her to walking. She chanced a glance back at Tarian. He sat with a drink and a bemused expression.

Well done, Faelynn said when she rejoined Daisy and the manacles were being refastened. She crouched in front, putting her hands on Daisy's head. *Except for a few very fluid knife strikes and draws, to a casual observer, it looked like dumb luck.*

Good. That was the goal.

She nodded, lifting Daisy's chin to examine her eyes and pulling up her hand to check it over. *As soon as the rest of the champions have gone, you'll get to rest.*

Here?

No. You'll be taken somewhere more comfortable. That is where you can meet the others and gain as much information as you can.

307

But there was no information to be had. Not for her, at any rate.

The holding area was a large room with rows of cots, one for each champion that had entered the games. Half would be empty, apparently more than any other game in the history of the court. Or so one of the guards said absently, complaining that they'd had to make them all up when they wouldn't all be used. The toilets were a line of tubs along the far wall, and the wash station was an enclosed, outdoor area with a few washbasins and a bunch of dirt. Male, female, it didn't matter. Everyone for themselves.

She tried not to show her embarrassment as she used one of the tubs, or her wary revulsion as one of the males watched with interest. In the wash area, she made sure to face the others, male and female alike. She didn't want to catch a surprise knife or dick in the body. Thankfully, no one ventured near. No one so much as touched her. Where a stray hand might find another of the champions, everyone actively stayed away from her. They knew what Tarian would be forced to do if they got intimate, and they weren't taking any chances.

She'd never been so damn glad for a claim in all her life. Thank the gods she hadn't been able to control herself, or that they'd had to prove themselves in the court. The others weren't allowed to force each other or fight, but there were no rules where it came to humans. The king had made that perfectly clear.

Food materialized at a table against the wall by the door. Haunches of meat, cheese, bread, and fruits. The pitchers were filled with water, and while some of the champions groused that there was no wine, she was thankful she wouldn't be confronted with going thirsty or trying the equivalent of Faerie alcohol. Faelynn had said Daisy could trust these meals—they wanted all deaths to be in front of an audience—so she was free to quench her thirst and sate her hunger.

After she'd eaten and drunk only enough to keep her going and not enough that she'd have to use the tub very much, she sat on her cot with her magical knife in her lap.

I'll need clothes for tomorrow. All they offered was a drape, she thought, hoping Tarian was paying attention.

I am, was his reply, and she could hear the fatigue in his mental voice. *The healers are allowed to supply their champions with whatever they need tomorrow, including the weapons Faelynn stored for safekeeping tonight.*

Every champion only had one weapon left to them in here, just in case. She'd obviously chosen the magical knife.

What have you been doing? she asked, missing him. Feeling homesick for him in a way that she'd only ever felt for her family.

It felt like lips pressed against hers, his phantom, magical touch. *Fulfilling my promises.*

Images of a hallway, a door, and a room beyond filled her mind. Of a beautiful man screaming. Of revenge. The princess had mishandled his toy, and he was now breaking all of hers...and breaking them in specular fashion. His vicious brutality would make even Zorn blink rapidly.

Shivers washed over her body.

I never claimed to be a nice boy, remember? Tarian told her. *I am a nightmare forged in fire. I am not dark by nature. I am dark by necessity. I wield their shadows like a weapon.*

She knew that. She loved that about him. Still, his refined brutality made her belly dance, a confusing blend of nervousness and excitement.

Get some sleep, little dove, he murmured. *Tomorrow, your opponent will likely be harder. Stay alive. It won't be long now.*

She wanted to ask for more details. To ask if he'd gotten enough information to find their way out. He was the one working out the end game in the shadows. She was the distraction, the reason Tarian couldn't miss visiting the court and now something for the king to focus on, but she wished she was more of a participant.

She didn't ask, though. She trusted him. They'd made a pact to work together, and so far, he'd followed her lead blindly. If he wasn't giving her more information, there had to be a reason.

She just hoped they were close. She didn't think she had much time before the shit hit the fan.

Chapter Twenty-Nine

D<small>AISY</small>

She startled awake right before a hand closed over her nose and mouth. She struck upward with her knife, her fingers curled around it in sleep. The blade sliced through the covers. The body she was aiming for barely twisted out of the way.

A crushing blow slammed into her side, the force so extreme that bone cracked. Pain flared, eclipsing her thoughts for a moment. The large hand cut off her air.

As always, Zorn's voice shoved its way to the forefront of her mind.

Panicking will slow down logical thought and might mean the difference between life and death.

She tried to cut out the pain as the shadow of an arm cocked back, readying to throw another punch. She angled her knife and sliced, the movement sending waves of agony through her torso. The attacker didn't twist enough this time to get out of the way. The blade cut through skin, earning a deep grunt.

Her lungs burned, needing air. Trying to force his hand off would cost her valuable time, though.

She braced against the pain and thrust her dagger, but the blow had already started to descend. If he hit her again, the broken rib might splinter, piercing a vital organ. She healed fast, but not fast enough for a wound like that.

The male was ripped to the side unexpectedly, allowing her much-needed breath. His fist went low. It thudded off the wood frame of the cot. She finished her strike, agony nearly drowning her. Her blade hit home, but given he'd moved, not where she'd aimed. It wouldn't kill him.

He grunted again as she gritted her teeth and prepared for another strike, yanking out her knife and aiming. She turned it so it would find purchase and nearly blacked out from the pain of her broken ribs. The male fell, though—no, he was forced down, shoved by someone behind.

A creature hiding in shadow lifted a knife and brought the hilt down hard. It hit the attacker's head as the body finished the fall, splaying across the ground. Dead or knocked out, she wasn't sure.

Tears rolled down from the corners of her eyes as she tried to see who held the knife, wondering why they hadn't used it.

The shadow drifted away as the creature stepped

forward. Lank black hair hung beside a pinched face with full lips. It was the fae that had been looking at her earlier when everyone else ignored her.

I didn't save your life, said a beautiful voice, high and light and like a spring morning breeze through meadows of blooming flowers. The sound felt so distinctly fae that Daisy would've wept if she hadn't already been crying from the throbbing pain.

(And she was a mindgazer. What in the fuck was she doing in here?)

Okay, Daisy replied (no idea if that was true or why she'd say it).

The female nodded and looked down at the male at her feet, then at Daisy putting a hand over her ribs.

Okay, the female murmured before bending and grabbing the male's arm. She dragged him through the cots, her lack of effort not at all matching the size difference. Like Daisy, she had more strength than what was apparent. She dragged him out to the wash area. If anyone was awake to notice, they didn't stir or move to look. When she came back in, so light and graceful in her step that she practically danced, it was without the male.

Without another word, the skinny female climbed into the cot beside Daisy. It hadn't been occupied when Daisy had fallen asleep, just like the other nearby cots, still empty.

Thank you, Daisy thought at her. Whether the female had saved her life or not, she'd definitely helped a great fucking deal. Another blow like the first one would've crippled her until Faelynn could get here. Maybe even beyond.

She just barely saw the female nod before turning her back on Daisy and settling.

With each breath, pain stabbed into Daisy's side. It hurt to move. It hurt to *exist*. When she did move, the bones sounded like they were grating against each other. The break was bad.

Faelynn is trying to get in, but they won't let her, Tarian thought, his tone flat and colorless. He was trying to control his rage. *Can you hang on until morning?*

I'm going to have to. How long have you been listening? Did you notice the female with mindgazer magic?

I woke up when your surprise registered. I did notice, yes. That talent is not listed on any official documents, but then, most talents aren't. It is unusual to sacrifice a bloodline with mindgazer magic to games such as this, though, and more unusual to sacrifice that kind of power. She seemed...lost when she fought, though. Unfocused. She won, but barely.

She'd been called directly after Daisy, and Daisy had been busy getting locked in. She'd missed that battle.

Tarian replayed what he remembered of it, a hazy memory within his concern for Daisy and the frustration that they had to do this at all. The frustration of an unsure future. The memory was enough. Plenty, actually.

Daisy would've chuckled, but the excruciating pain prevented her.

The female did seem lost, unsure where to stand or

which foot to lean on. Her movements were clunky, and her blocks were usually clumsy. The sword strikes she missed emphasized her scrawny arms and lack of muscle tone. But the strikes that landed...

Daisy couldn't have landed them better herself.

She didn't barely win, just like I didn't accidentally win. She's not a sacrifice at all. She doesn't look like much—

Neither do you.

I beg your fucking pardon, Mr. Adonis, she thought, faux-scandalized. *I look like a little dove, weak and fragile and sometimes pretty in flight. I look like the sort of creature a predator snaps up, and so does she. She cultivated her image, just like I did.*

Is that what you think I am calling you? He paused. *Of course you do. You wouldn't know any different. Well. Yes, I agree, she is not as she seems, just like you. Be careful there. She has an ulterior motive in helping you, and that is likely to get close to you. And that is deadly in your situation.*

Yes, Mother, thank you. I had no idea how the world works. What sort of dove are you talking about?

I'll find out who put her forward as a champion. In the meantime, get some sleep. Faelynn will be in as soon as she can. I'll see you tomorrow.

With that, his mind slipped away.

The pain controlled her world, a dull throb of intensity she couldn't filter into the background. There would be no sleep for her tonight. She might as well replay everything she knew, from the battles to the male who'd accosted her in her sleep with no real desire to kill her, to the female who'd helped her.

It was the female she kept coming back to. What was her game here? She could see helping Daisy so as to get closer and get information, as Tarian had said. But why reveal the mindgazer magic? That was huge. It hinted at her power level, the status she should have, and the strangeness of ending up here. Something definitely didn't add up.

Daisy was missing something, and as Tarian had said, that could prove deadly.

The next afternoon, Daisy winced as she shifted. The blood covering the marble floor was slick on her smooth-soled boots. The nobles lounged in their places, eating and chatting as the next opponent came out.

The male from last night. Surprise, surprise. He'd tried to get an edge by roughing her up. His benefactor had known who his opponent would be.

If only Faelynn's healing and Daisy's blood magic had worked faster. She wasn't in tiptop shape. It hurt to twist, and extreme movement might buckle her knees. Luckily, this lump of muscle had a big welt on his clean-shaven head from where the female had hit him last night and a healing line of puffy skin where Daisy had stabbed him. He wasn't in tiptop shape either.

"As before," the king said, on his dais with those unnatural, gleaming eyes, "do not kill her. Break her, only. I wish to use her before long."

These fights were to the death. Except hers, obviously. She was special, with a future much worse. *Goodie.*

"Commence," the voice sounded, and this time, Daisy didn't wait.

She snatched all five throwing knives. She tossed up the first, grabbed it by the blade, and threw. The next she plucked out of her other hand and threw. The next, the next. All five were in the air in quick succession. Just like last night, this fucker was slow to react.

He twisted jerkily, obviously in pain. He didn't get far enough out of the way. The first knife lodged in the lower part of his neck, just off center. The second farther down. The next three in his chest. Those wouldn't go deep enough to kill him, but they'd slow him further.

His body jerked with each strike.

A slash of stinging magic made her falter. She called on the chalice magic and cut it out. If he realized it, he didn't show it.

Her next steps landed with purpose. There was no slipping and sliding today. No falling and flailing. That shit hurt too much. There was just ending this fight as quickly as fucking possible.

She whipped out her magical knife as he recovered, plucking the knives from his body. Blood gushed from his neck. It spread out over his mostly bare chest, save for the crisscrossing straps to house his knives. He grabbed one of them and stepped forward to meet her.

But he didn't have a magical knife like she did.

Cluing in to her thoughts, the knife grew longer and longer. It stretched out into a spear.

Daisy took a deep breath, held it, stepped, and thrust. Pain flowered in her chest and shocked her system. Her knees went wobbly, and she cried in pain as her spear lodged into his side. Fuck. That wasn't the right place.

She staggered as she yanked it back. He staggered as he helped pull it out of his flesh, knife in hand.

Look down at it, you dumb fucker. Look down at it! Give me a second to adjust.

But he didn't look down, knowing what would happen. He advanced, shaky on his feet, losing a lot of blood but not falling. Great, she'd gotten a highly motivated one.

She backpedaled. Her foot slipped, and she went down, catching herself on a knee. Her breath turned ragged from the searing pain in her side. It had been a full break. A bad one, as she'd thought. The bone hadn't totally stitched back together.

"Fuck," she said through gritted teeth.

The male slashed with his knife. She ducked away but couldn't stomach rolling under him to the other side. She was worried she wouldn't get back up.

To give in to one's pain is to give in to death, Zorn's voice echoed in her mind.

The pain wouldn't kill her.

The wound would not kill her.

Failing to act because of either would *certainly* kill her.

Fucking Zorn was always fucking right.

She ground her teeth as the knife slashed down, and then she rolled out of the way. The agony welled up, flashing like lightning through her middle. She didn't stop. Couldn't if she wanted to survive in one piece. She completed the roll, forced herself to kneel, and struck with everything she had.

Her scream punctuated her shortened spear sticking through the side of his ribcage. Magically sharpened, it sliced through bone and lung and kept going, elongating on its own until it hit the heart. She wondered if it had bent inside his body to get it. The sword wasn't relying on her; it was acting on its own, doing what was required to get the kill.

The male screamed with her, the hand that held the knife spasming. He released it and grabbed for the spear, but it was too late. The damage was done.

He collapsed as she did, withering to the ground. The difference was, he wouldn't get back up. She would. Eventually. Some day.

The guards grabbed her upper arms, and she screamed again as they lifted her.

"I got it." She tried to struggle away, straightening her legs. "I got it—"

"Bring her here."

The king's voice stopped her heart. She clutched one of the guard's arms, looking back for her sword. Faelynn crouched beside it, her face slack. She'd been collecting Daisy's items and frozen. That wasn't good.

Daisy couldn't go with the king. Not like this. Not without the ability to fight back properly. Not without a weapon!

Her body started to shake with very real fear. The

kind of fear that spoke of the soul and not the body. That spoke of wounds worse than mortal wounds.

Help me, she wanted to shout. Please, Tarian, *help me*!

But she wouldn't. He'd already said when it came to the king—when it came to the royal chambers—he could do nothing. Some battles she'd have to fight alone. Which had been fine...when it didn't feel like a spiked hammer hit her in the ribs every time she fucking moved.

The royals sat to the sides, one of the males interested, the other picking at his nail. The queen swished her gown, not looking at Daisy. The king choosing a sex toy right in front of her had to be so demoralizing, though not as demoralizing as being that toy. The princess had a smug grin. She knew what the king planned to do—how he longed to break the human.

A teardrop of blood dripped out of the king's left eye. His lids were hooded, lust burning brightly within.

Everything in her recoiled as she walked closer, then was dragged, not wanting to go. Not able to stomach this. Not able to save herself.

"No, please," she begged. "Please."

Chapter Thirty

Daisy

The guards stopped in front of the dais, and the king stood. His robes swirled around his slippered feet. An item glittered in his hand.

The diamond chalice.

The river of diamonds within sparkled and shone, throwing the blood-red lights on the dais. The smooth surface had not one smudge, as though the king's touch would never leave a lasting impression. It pulsed within her, sensing her. The white-hot light in her middle flared, pounding, spreading. It filled up her body and smoothed over her ribs, dulling the pain, reducing it to a fine point, and then washing it away entirely. Her fatigue from the sleepless night, her aching muscles from the battle—they washed away as well, leaving a pleasant smell of lavender in its wake.

A hand with unnatural, leathery skin reached for her, and she jerked her head away. Even that violent movement didn't bring back the ache in her ribs. She nearly cried in relief, which would've joined the tears of pain from a moment ago. The tears of fear.

The fingers were cold and revolting when they grabbed her chin. Twisted magic crawled across her face and tried to seep into her flesh. He angled her face up toward him.

"You are such a beautiful little creature." His breath smelled like mold and decay. Her stomach churned.

The chalice throbbed, so close to her. Power and strength pulsed in her middle, peeling back the effects of his magic. The feel of it.

The chalice had never reacted like this in the human world. It hadn't called to her before being trapped in this kingdom. It sensed the danger she was in. Or maybe it sensed the danger Faerie was in from the twisted magic. One and the same.

His gaze stopped on her lips, and his fingertips slid from her chin to her neck, leaving a slimy trail in its wake. She shivered and couldn't stop her eyes from filling with the hate she felt.

"I don't think I have looked upon a daintier, prettier human that was also so deliciously fierce," he said. "I can see now why Tarian protects you so viciously. He wants you all for himself." The smile froze her heart. "Too bad he has no say in the matter."

The fingers of one hand closed around her neck, squeezing. She wasn't sure if he was collaring her or if he wanted to watch the life ebb out of her. His thumb pushed at her chin, forcing it to stay high and her to keep eye contact. His gaze was malicious and still sparkled brightly with lust.

She held her breath, not from the pressure, but because she wasn't sure what he would do. Wasn't sure if he might kill her.

In a moment, his fingers slackened. The touch drifted away.

"I am torn, however," he said. His tongue glided along his unnaturally wrinkly lip. "I enjoy watching you fight. It is delightfully erotic, given the thoughts and desires it evokes. Maybe a private display..." He wavered in indecision. She could see it. Her future lay in the balance, teetering with him. Her knife was somewhere behind her, but she had others tucked about her person. They weren't magical, but they were iron. Given she could move now, they would work.

They would have to.

His gaze flicked up and focused. The malicious look twinkled in his eyes.

"Hmm," he said, then stepped back. A glance said he was looking at Tarian, who still sat in his seat. His expression had closed down, stoic and unimpressed. He was giving nothing away.

"Take her back." The king motioned her away. Before he returned to sit, however, he angled his head. His attendants waited on the sides of the dais, and to those on the right, he said quietly, "Prepare my quarters for a human. You know how I like it. The manacles should be small to suit her. Keep him away from her. No exceptions."

The guards grabbed her by the upper arms and tugged her toward the holding quarters. Faelynn moved to follow, weapons in hand, but another guard stepped in her way. The guard took the weapons and barked at her to stay put. He followed behind.

Her thoughts raced as doom lodged in her gut. It was like not knowing how to swim while being dragged down a pier. The end was in sight. Her mettle was about to be tested. Maybe not today, maybe not even tomorrow, but soon.

She looked over her shoulder, wanting to plead with Tarian without knowing what to say. Wanting to yell at him to hurry but knowing he knew what was at stake.

Tarian had his elbow on the arm of the couch, a couple fingers resting over his lips, the picture of indifference. His other hand, though, the one resting on his thigh, had tightened into a fist. The knuckles blanched as he watched her go, still no emotion playing across his face. If he wanted to grab her later, he'd have to fight his way in, and he knew it.

They didn't go the way they'd come, and Daisy had a moment of panic that they were headed to the king's chambers right then. Thankfully, it was another holding place for prisoners, this one much smaller than the other. Cots of the correct number existed in rows. Some had already been taken out of formation and spread into the eating area by the other champions who'd already fought and won. They didn't want to be too close to their enemy.

The wash area was still outside, but now there was a grassy area beside it.

No fence closed them in. The land curved, and she glimpsed the top of a jutting cliff. Far below, water sparkled in the moonlight.

The guard handed over her weapons and left, turning his back on Daisy without any tension. He wasn't worried about her.

Taking advantage of the lack of people, Daisy quickly rinsed off the blood and the grime. She scrubbed where the king had touched her, the feeling of his clammy fingers still present across her flesh. Dressed in a nondescript drape that everyone would wear, she helped herself to food and bubbly water.

"I wouldn't, if I were you." One of the largest champions stood at the other end of the table, holding the square wooden platter that served as a plate. He glanced over with a lifted eyebrow, his gaze touching off her freshly poured drink. His light brown hair was cropped short, and his pleasing face and strong jaw were devoid of any scars or hints of violence. He'd done well so far. "We're on a cliff for a reason."

She hesitated, eyeing the clear liquid. It was the only drink offered.

He shrugged. "It's up to you." He picked up the cooked leg of a large bird, bigger than an average human realm's turkey.

Still she hesitated, watching him scoop up the various dishes and dropping them onto his platter. He could be joking, or he might be trying to keep her dehydrated, but after he finished piling up his platter, he didn't take any of it, either. Instead, he grabbed a cup and headed for the washroom. There, he filled his cup and went out to the grass to sit down.

Following his lead, she did the same and headed out to an area close to him. She settled on the grass, not being obvious about looking over. He picked up his cup and drained half its contents.

They ate in silence for a while. A champion that had recently won their fight drenched themselves in water behind them.

"This is my third time in the court games." The large champion drained the rest of his drink. "The first year, I drank the elixir. I nearly tried to fly off that cliff. It takes a lot of elixir to fully take over my mind, though, and I was able to resist. Flying, that is. Not pleasuring the guards."

She swallowed what was in her mouth, just picking at her food. She didn't have nearly the appetite he did.

"Pleasuring the guards?" she asked.

"The guards, the other champions—we had three times as many champions by this point last year and the year before. This year, the king is killing people off early. Anyway, yeah..." He reduced his volume. "The elixir cuts out inhibitions. It reduces logic. The inside became an orgy, and the outside had people jumping off the cliff and laughing all the way down. There was no violence. None at all. Then the next day...the headache crushed me. I nearly lost my fight because of my throbbing head. I was paired against someone who hadn't partaken. Healers won't be allowed tomorrow. Just wait and see."

She sat back and finally took a drink of water.

"Why did you tell me?" she asked. More champions must've been filing into the holding area, but none came out to sit on the grass. She'd noticed him on his own the day before—no one wanted to get too close. To either of them.

He didn't look over at her. "Your benefactor will kill anyone you get intimate with, right?"

"Yes. He's compelled to. Except the royals."

"Right. Well, I don't need you crawling into my lap later. I might have a moment of weakness and not see the dawn."

She looked out over the drop. "So you won the last couple years? For..."

"Lady Lavinya. You're Tarianthiel's toy. I am hers."

Lavinya...Daisy didn't recall the name. But then, she didn't know many of the names, just faces.

"She likes to watch me battle," he continued. "A lot of the nobles do. It's why we wear so few layers. I was surprised you were so covered up. Though...I guess yours is a lot more possessive than most. Lady Lavinya loans me out if it will bring her favor."

Her eyebrows lifted as she drew up her knees and looped her arms around her shins. "You don't sound beat up about that fact."

He huffed out a laugh, looking at her with a smirk. "I came from nothing. Less than nothing. My mother was killed in the wylds, and my dad didn't bother sticking around. We were left to fend for ourselves. I would've died if not for Lady Lavinya. I tried to steal food from her manor, and her guards caught me. She gave me a choice: be her pet, or receive my punishment." He finished the last morsel on his plate. "I eat like a king. I spend my days training and fucking. Only twice has she loaned me to a male, and for that I suck it up, but otherwise, I pleasure and am pleasured by the nobility in this kingdom. I've never had it so good."

Couldn't argue with that. He clearly wasn't put out by his situation.

"So you've won the last two years?" she repeated.

"No. I might've. Last year I was the strongest and best champion, but when the competition gets too fierce, the lady pulls me out. She wants me alive. How about you? Tarianthiel seems to want to keep you alive, too."

"It sounds like the king is going to pull me out before Tarian can. He has taken...an interest."

The male jerked, his face whipping toward Daisy. He didn't say anything for a long moment. His expression was neutral, but she didn't miss the pity in his eyes. He nodded, though she wasn't sure why, before looking out over the cliffs again.

"Maybe you should drink the elixir after all," he said softly. "Flying would be a nicer way to go."

Chapter Thirty-One

Daisy

Three people flew. They took a running leap, stretched out their arms, and said *weeeee* all the way down.

The rest didn't get much sleep. All but three reveled in each other's bodies, and the three sober ones tried to stay out of the way—Daisy, the big champion...and the female who'd helped Daisy the night before.

After telling the female about the elixir, Daisy had said, "I am not saving your life." It was probably even true.

She'd earned a small smile and a slight nod. They were even.

But now that female walked out of the dark hallway and into the glow of the Court Hall. Her lank hair fell beside her thin face, her eyes darting this way and that.

K.F. Breene

She already held a knife, clutched tightly in her small hand. Her knuckles were white.

Daisy let out a slow breath as her stomach twisted. She replayed all the fights she'd seen with this female, as seen through Tarian's eyes. She reassessed the movements, the strikes, and the feints. Then she tucked her thoughts down deep where they couldn't be found. Not that it would matter—cutting out magic would take care of that naturally.

The floor was slick with blood at Daisy's feet. The nobles were all in their places, having watched all the fights for the day, save hers. She and this female were last.

The king waited on his dais, his blood-red eyes gleaming. The diamond chalice sat beside him on the chair, his long, spindly fingers wrapped around it.

The female stopped on the other side of the pool of blood. Her gaze flicked down to it, over to the king, then finally to Daisy. Her expression was unreadable. Her free hand flexed and then curled into a fist. The female had helped Daisy, Daisy had helped the female, and now one would kill the other. Welcome to life with the fae.

"Do not kill the human," the king called out. "Break her, only. If you can."

He leaned back on his throne, his smile predatory. He'd pitted Daisy against arguably the weakest of the champions, save Daisy herself. Both of them were hiding their true skills. Neither could hide any longer.

"Commence," the voice boomed.

The female's eyes took in the blood at their feet again.

She stepped forward once, christening the soul of her boot.

Daisy withered the female's magic as she ripped out one of her throwing knives. She took it by the blade, balanced, and threw. It somersaulted in the air, end over end.

The female barely looked up. She didn't even sight in on the throwing knife. She leaned to the side, and the knife went right on by, slicing a strand of hair as it did so.

Daisy expected the female to attack, but she didn't. She paused, actually, her gaze going down and to the right, like she was listening. A couple people yelled, someone screamed, and chairs and couches scraped against the floor. The knife flowered blood in a noble's shoulder.

The female's eyes lifted, a violet sheen glowing within them. Mirth twinkled in their depths. If she was worried about Daisy taking her magic, she didn't show it. She must have known it, though, because she could no longer read Daisy's mind. She simply wasn't concerned.

Uneasy with the enigma, Daisy took out two more knives, stepped one foot over the other, and threw in quick succession. Her technique was perfect, the throws on target, and the knives left with speed. Daisy didn't expect them to land, not when the female had been looking right at her, but she did expect the female to jerk out of the way. To give a pronounced twist or feint.

Instead, the female took an unhurried, graceful step to the right.

She shouldn't have been able to get out of the way

with the slowness of that step. She barely moved a shoulder, and both knives flew past.

Daisy couldn't have gotten out of the way like that. On her best and fastest day, she wasn't that good.

Unease jiggled her stomach. She didn't bother looking to see if any nobles got hit. She took out her magical knife and thought about taking out a dagger too.

The female stepped farther into the pool of blood. Her eyes tracked Daisy as she, too, stepped. Another foot, the knife loosening a bit in her hand. She didn't look frightened—she had to know that Daisy wasn't fooled.

To rush or not to rush...

Daisy stood her ground as the female took another step. Then another. The female's knees bent just a little. Her body was completely loose. Ready.

Fuck, this was going to go badly. Daisy could feel it in her gut.

She grabbed the dagger and started forward. There was no point in delaying. Time to see what this female could really do.

When she'd cut the distance in half, her steps confident, the female stepped forward. Daisy slashed with her dagger, expected the easy dodge, and thrust forward with her elongating magical knife. The female stepped and slashed, the strike coming so fast and with such precision that Daisy barely got her hand up to block in time.

Their forearms clashed. Daisy dragged her knife, point down, and her arm away. The blade just caught flesh.

The female didn't so much as flutter her eyes. It was like she hadn't felt it at all.

Daisy struck with the other knife as she stepped. Pulled back and struck again, rotating them. The female stepped with her in perfect synergy. Her knife flashed out, raking across the air right in front of Daisy's chest. Daisy replied with a strike of her own, equally missing.

On they went, stepping and thrusting, dodging and attacking. The female might've been Daisy's mirror, the steps perfectly timed, the strikes all a fraction too short or too wide. It was as if she wasn't trying to hit Daisy, but rather was toying with her.

Unexpectedly, the female launched at Daisy.

Daisy spun and kicked. She made contact with a shin. The female faltered, and Daisy was there, batting the knife out of her hand and to the ground. She kicked it away before stabbing forward.

The female ducked and turned. Her leg came out of absolutely nowhere and swept Daisy's ankles. Her weight shifted, and she went down.

"Sweep the leg, Johnny," Daisy muttered as she rolled, barely avoiding a downward thrust of a knife that hadn't been in that female's hand a moment before. "Sweep the leg!"

"What?" the female said, slipping as she tried to stab down at Daisy.

"A movie. Lexi has odd taste." Daisy hopped up and changed tactics. She didn't have enough skill to go at it with just a knife. Time to try mindfuckery.

Her magical sword changed into a staff, and Daisy

attacked, moving and swirling it to throw the female off track. She stabbed, parried, and launched herself at the female. The female tried to backpedal, but Daisy was on her, grabbing her shoulders while swinging herself around. She went for the eyes, missed, then hooked her fingers into the female's cheeks and tried to rip and tear. It was hostile and weird and off-putting all at the same time. Often those with superior fighting skills didn't do well with these rough-and-tumble tactics.

The female flailed, as though overcome. Daisy didn't miss that her knife was perfectly positioned, though. She just couldn't get out of the fucking way!

The blade sliced across Daisy's forearm. She sucked in a pained breath and reached for the wrist. Another knife materialized in the female's other hand and she slashed.

"Are you...a fucking...magician, or what?" Daisy twisted, grabbed around the female's middle with her legs, and used her leverage. She spun around and down, ripping the female to the ground with force. Daisy landed first and rolled, reaching for her knife as she scrambled up. The female flipped, kicked her feet, and suddenly tackled Daisy to the ground.

How the fuck...?

"Release my magic," the female whispered as she wrestled Daisy through the blood. "I need to speak with you."

So she *did* know Daisy had cut out her magic, but she wasn't confused or concerned. She didn't ask how. Did she know what Daisy was?

No, that was impossible. She couldn't.

Wary, unsettled, Daisy tried to cut the female's side. Once again, she got air as the female rolled away.

"I need to speak with you," she hissed as she grabbed Daisy's hair and yanked her head back. She stuck the knife in Daisy's thigh. "Please."

Daisy cried out in pain, and for reasons she didn't know and would never understand, she did as the female said. She released her magic, still continuing to grapple and half wanting to give up. This female was better than her, faster. She was a fucking wizard.

Never say die, Zorn's voice echoed in her head. *There is always a chance you may live.*

In this case, there was a chance she'd be broken into a thousand little pieces.

When the time comes, you must not be greedy for the kill, the female said through Daisy's mind. If she had any other magic, she didn't use it. *One must never let down one's guard, even when the enemy is on the brink of death.*

She slashed another part of Daisy's body, not taking any damage of her own.

Wait... This female was saying Zorn's words. His teachings. Did she shoplift those out of Daisy's mind at another time? Why?

Tarian cannot help you, she said. *Not will not...* cannot. *You must do this. Remember your resolve. You are the only one who can save him. Who can save them all.*

They rolled around, slashing at each other. The female grabbed Daisy and forced her onto her back, laying her on the ground. The female's eyes were right over hers, urgent.

You are the key. The only one who can do it.

Daisy's dagger filled her hand, though she hadn't grabbed for it. Her magical knife suddenly rested against her skin, magically strapped to her side under her garments. This female was arming her.

What the fuck was going on?

The female's fingers wrapped around Daisy's wrist, and she yanked. The dagger pierced her stomach. The female elicited a bloodcurdling scream before convulsing on top of Daisy. Not usually what a stomach wound would do.

Violence will set you free.

With that, the female died. She draped down over Daisy and lay still.

Daisy breathed heavily for a long moment as hot liquid spilled over her, trying to make sense of it all. Trying to understand why the female would urgently feed Zorn's teachings back to her and then kill herself for the trouble.

Clapping pulled her focus away, and then rough hands were grabbing her. Pulling her. The dagger was ripped out of her palm as she was set on her feet. Large, clumsy hands pulled weapons out of the sheaths wrapped around her body and haphazardly patted her down to find any others. A palm touched the magical knife under her clothes but didn't stop, continuing to search.

That done, the guard roughly grabbed her arm and

yanked her toward the dais. She limped badly, the knife wound in her thigh screaming.

The king leaned against the arm of the throne. The other royals lounged, ready to be through with the evening.

"Well done," the king said, stroking the diamond chalice. "I thought she had you there."

Laughter and chatter went on behind her, the nobles having a wonderful time with each other now that the entertainment had finished.

The king's gaze roamed over Daisy's body, stopping on the areas the female had cut or slashed.

"And not too banged up. Fantastic." He put up his hand. "Take her to my chambers. Strap her in." His gaze lifted, and given the direction, Daisy knew he was looking at Tarian. "You need fewer distractions. If you finish quickly, however, I will let you have one last night with her."

After all... His red eyes rooted Daisy to the spot. The royal black around his irises started to move, increasing in size and speed, flowing around his pupils. *You'll still be useable even with a broken mind.*

He jerked his head. The two guards yanked her to walking. This was it. It was happening. She was on her own with a magically diseased creature hellbent on destroying her. Not just pain, either, but torture. He'd try to break her spirit little by little until there was nothing left.

But she had her knife. And she had her resolve. She

might be human, but she was not as easily breakable as they all thought.

The female still lay in the center of the marble floor, surrounded by a sea of red. She didn't move. She'd given her life to help Daisy and, through Daisy, Tarian. Yet Daisy didn't have any idea how she fit into all this. Why she was helping? What did she know?

Tarian hadn't stood. He hadn't moved since the last time she'd spied him. But now he lowered his hand from his lips, his expression hard, his eyes concerned.

Into her mind, he said, *Some toys come alive in the middle of the night...*

He let the sentence linger. Her sentence, spoken to him when in the human world.

She finished it. *And kill you in your sleep.*

His smile was slight.

Come back to me, he whispered, and then she was being walked through a side door into a lavish hall made for royalty.

Pain ripped through her heart at having to leave him, especially like this. At the uncertainty in his voice and the terror she'd heard beneath the words.

She wanted to curl into herself and shut off. To reflect on what had gotten her here, what had gone on in that room —that battle—and how the fuck this had all become her journey. She realized she'd gotten used to Tarian being around to protect her in this place. Used to the *Fallen* watching her back and dogging her heels. Even in the prison they'd been watching. She had no such luxuries now.

She pushed down her confusion, her fear, and the complete ickiness of her predicament and started paying attention. She noticed each turn and the face of each servant. When they entered through a grand set of double doors, she noticed the furniture, the sharp objects, and the items that could crush a skull, just like Kayla had first advised her.

Servants scurried around and out, giving the guards privacy. They'd likely do the same thing for the king, knowing he'd want to play with his new toy in peace. That was great fucking news.

Not great news was the straps the guards were leading her toward. They existed in an obvious bedchamber and looked like kinky torture devices popular among people with safe words. She doubted she'd get to choose one of those.

They took her along the side of the main bedchamber to a washroom. Without ceremony, the guards stopped. One of them yanked her around to face him before reaching for the buttons on her clothing.

"Whoa there, bud." She slapped his hands away. "I'm going to need dinner and dancing first."

The guard scowled and lifted his arm. She braced for the impact of his palm. When the blow came, she purposely stepped onto her bad leg and fell into the other guard.

"Do as you're told," the first guard gritted out.

She didn't point out that he hadn't actually told her to do anything.

She slipped the knife she'd just stolen from Guard Number Two into her pants pocket.

"Let me do it," she said, taking a step back. She lifted her hands to show she was unarmed.

The first guard narrowed his eyes but grunted assent.

She undid the buttons and sacrificed a little dignity to give them a booby show as she figured out the knife situation. It was magically glued to her side, after all, and she needed to shed it in a way that these fools didn't notice.

Thankfully, the moment her fingers brushed the sheath, the whole thing slid down to the tucked-in portion of her shirt. She bunched it all, waved her boobs around for good measure, and then put shirt and sheath in a ball in the corner. Her pants went next. She turned and bent to shimmy them down her thighs. The guards got a peek of certain areas that needed shaving, and she kept the stolen knife. Distracting males did not take a lot of brain power.

Knowing guards would not be interested in doing cleanup, she kicked her balled-up clothes more toward a corner and covered herself in mock embarrassment. There they wouldn't be so obvious to the actual cleaning crew.

"Wash," the first guard said.

She stared at the tub and the water contraption. Hesitantly, she reached for the chain. They stepped back to give her space. The king obviously wanted a clean toy.

After the most awkward bath she'd ever taken—which still wasn't as awkward as that guy in the apartment in San Francisco, where she busted in, tied him up, and left Zorn to torture him—she wrapped herself in a towel and waited for instructions.

"Come on." The guard reached for her, but Daisy backed away again. She turned and quickly bent for her clothes. "You don't need those," he said.

Well, no shit, but she had an ulterior motive, and these guards were thankfully too dumb to see that.

"They're mine." She bundled them up in a ball and hugged them into her chest as though they were her teddy bear.

"You don't—"

"Leave it," Guard Two said impatiently. He motioned her on, not bothering to secure her arm.

The first guard grabbed her upper arm and pulled her with them, walking back to the bedchamber where the outer doors had been closed. She ignored the huge four-poster bed and the golden cuffs that hung from two pegs in the headboard. Against the far wall, where there was space to swing a whip or just stand back and watch, leather covered the stone with manacles hanging at the sides. More pegs had been drilled in and a few splotches of blood hadn't been cleaned off the floor from the last unwilling participant.

The cold from earlier was back, lodging in her stomach. Shivers ran through her length.

She had weapons and was being escorted by two dead guys. It would be fine. This would be fine. She was not in over her head here. Not yet.

Guard Two veered toward a chest. He opened it and pulled out a black, lacy garment with red ribbons. He flung it at Daisy, who dropped her bundle in "surprise," "missed" catching the garment, and "accidentally" dropped her towel in the process.

It wasn't hard to call up tears as she bent to pick up everything, her lip quivering and her hair lank from the bath. She looked pitiful and she knew it. Counted on it, actually. She needed a second to think. To gauge the situation.

She sniffled as she straightened with the garment, limping and shuffling to get her balance. Her feet hit the edge of her bundle as Guard Two said, "Put it on."

She cried harder as she bent to do as instructed, creating a tent with her towel as she tried to put on the item. Her knife was right there, at her fingertips. She could grab it and launch herself forward, getting one in surprise and the second right after. Then what? If those two were needed elsewhere, their absence would be noticed. Someone would come in looking for them, and before she knew it, she'd either have a pile of bodies or be outnumbered. If the former, it wouldn't be long before they sent enough people that a sneak attack would no longer work.

Both of those scenarios ended with her getting caught and used. Broken, maybe not of mind but of body, and no use to Tarian. She couldn't have that.

She stepped into the garment and looked back at the contraption on the wall. The chains looped through metal rings at the top corners and ended in metal mana-cles with heavily worn leather around the insides. The king liked to play, first with pain, then probably with pleasure. Little hooks stuck into the stone in various places were used to keep the chains at certain lengths, and that length changed based on the captive's various positions, so she assumed.

Would the king mess with that himself? Would he be the one altering the positioning?

She guessed not. He'd have attendants for that.

When it came time to move the captive to the gold cuffs on the bed, he'd have attendants for that, too.

She pulled the garment up her body, looking again at the guards. Were they the attendants?

She didn't think so. They'd been far too interested in nakedness thus far. If they were used to seeing all this, they'd be bored with skin at this point. Anyone in a sex club dungeon in San Francisco could tell you that. She'd had enough dealings with information exchange to glean that much.

She looked at the manacles as memories tumbled into her mind. Snippets of conversations she'd overhead. Dots connecting. A picture emerging.

It's no secret that simpering clown wants to kill the royalty and take their place but can't because of the magic locking him in his station.

The king has a tighter hold on me, actually. Once outside of court, his leash loosens.

Tarian cannot help you. Not will not...cannot. You are the only one who can save him. Who can save them all.

The answer slammed into her. The reality of her situation. The reason Tarian had kept her in the dark.

You are the key. The only one who can do it.

It was she who needed to kill the king, since Tarian couldn't. Obviously, the *Fallen* couldn't either. It was up to her. She was his freedom. His salvation. She always had been. To rescue him, she had to kill his jailor. That was why he'd allowed her to be in harm's way. He trusted her, believed in her, to get this done.

She didn't know if it was because she was the crystal chalice or because she was the only one who would get the opportunity and who would want to, but the way forward was suddenly clear. Horribly, accurately clear.

Her whole body started to shake.

Fuck. This was a risk. A big fucking risk.

But she was making a choice, and that mattered. Come what may, she would get this done. If she had to take a break from reality to distance herself from her body, so be it. Her family was worth it, and she realized with a start...so was Tarian. He was worth all of this. Because she loved him.

She fucking loved him.

She loved his mind and his humor, his brutality and the softness he showed only her and his *Fallen*. She loved being with him, touching him, and the gentle caresses he trailed across her skin when they were spent and snuggling in bed. He'd weaseled his way into her heart and taken root. She would do this, do anything, to free him. To save him...and save her family and his.

Taking a deep breath, she finished putting on the mostly see-through garment and bent for her clothes. Needing a distraction, she shuffled everything around, stood up, and "accidentally" dropped the stolen knife.

Then, in mock terror, she whimpered and backed up quickly, shoving the magical knife into the strap at the back of the garment.

But the garment wasn't tight enough to hold it.

She juggled it as the guards looked in confusion at their knife. They startled. The owner quickly bent to fetch it, and the other looked at his sheaths to make sure his weren't missing. She tried to twist her knife in the straps, then tried to find another strap with which to hold it. Her towel, blocking the view of all this, slid from around her bust as she maneuvered.

She gritted her teeth, fumbled the knife, and prepared to attack. Her options were limited.

Instead of falling, though, the knife stopped in its slide. It caught on the middle of her back, within the satin and lace, and magically stuck to her skin. It hadn't wanted to stay put when only half was tucked into the strap, but now that it was covered, it was happy. That female had given her knife a new trick.

Who the fuck *was* that female?

By the time the guards looked up, she'd lifted her hands, backed to the wall, and let the towel fall down around her ankles.

"You d-dropped it so I grabbed it, just in c-case," she stammered.

Guard Two's face closed down in wary uncertainty. He wasn't sure when he could've dropped it. Guard One, however, looked over with a *you're an idiot* expression before advancing on her. He didn't seem worried about her in the least. Her performances in the court battles must've been convincing. The last certainly had been, with how that other slight champion had handled her.

He grabbed her hand while smirking down at the loose garment, too roomy in the bust and not fitting properly around her hips. If she hadn't been human, the king wouldn't have bothered with her at all. She didn't fit the mold he was looking for.

She tried to slither away, pushing at the guard, begging and pleading with him to let her go. The other guard hastened over. He grabbed her free wrist while the other was clasped into the metal manacle. Then the second hand. The leather kept the chill of the metal away. Its well-worn nature brought in the waking nightmares.

They didn't mess with the chains. They didn't worry about her reaching forward and grabbing them or her discarded items at her feet, even though one of their knives had come out of it. With her dealt with, they hurried out of the bedchambers like their asses were on fire. They clearly didn't want to be here any more than she did.

She'd been right, though. They would've been missed.

But now she had willingly allowed herself to be caught. She was at the king's mercy.

Chapter Thirty-Two

Daisy

The door opened, and a masked and robed figure walked in with their head bowed. Another entered behind, their faces not visible within their hoods. They peeled off to the sides, making way for the king to follow on their heels. From his neck to his ankles, he wore a strange black bodysuit with a light sheen. A deep red robe was draped over it, dusting the ground as he walked. In one hand he held an obsidian scepter, and balanced on his other palm was the diamond chalice.

He didn't say a word as he covered the space between them. His magic flowed over her, its vileness seeping into her pores. Her heart quickened as he stopped in front of her. He held out the items he carried, and his minions glided forward to take each.

"Hmm." The sound sent disgust shivering across Daisy's skin. His gaze took in every inch of her. "I have always detested humans." He held out a hand. One of the minions supplied him with a whip. Her breathing grew shallower, but she didn't show her growing trepidation. "Detested, but desired."

He slung the instrument. Steel-tipped leather sliced across her skin. She sucked in a breath and trapped it behind her teeth. The garment the guards had supplied tore. The pain flared as blood welled up.

"So beautiful." He swung it again. "So breakable."

Fuck this guy was the worst. He was so concerned about *breakable*. She wanted to turn those words against him.

She fell into the pain as it rippled across her body. Fell into the feeling of him slicing her flesh.

She wasn't like most humans. Lexi had given her the gift of the gods. Now, she wasn't any more breakable than fae. Than him. She'd proven it in those games. She would prove it still.

"You do not deserve life, most of you," he said, and she gritted her teeth against the pain. "You are good for only amusement."

He hit her harder, high and low, her arms and face. Her legs. Her feet. Blood flowed down her skin, covering every square inch. Pain made her woozy, but she held on to it like a lifeline. If she felt pain, it meant she was alive. It meant she could still fight. And she would. She was a captive at this moment, but they would eventually release her. They would move her. She would be ready for it.

"Your kind needs a ruler." He was breathing heavily when he finally stopped. "*I* will be that ruler. But by then...you will be dead. Turn her."

Fear punched a hole through her middle, but she didn't react. They might find that knife, but she could still kill with her bare hands. Zorn had made sure of that. When this king didn't have his magic, they would be equals.

Only worry about that which you can control. For the rest, wait...and be ready to move.

The chains pulled at her wrists, stretching her, and she let them. The excess was hooked on a peg so she'd stay put, and she waited for them to find the knife.

Steel sliced across her back. Liquid dribbled from the cuts. Again. Again. The cool air touched each slash, elevating the sting to something worse. Like salt being poured into the wound. It kept her grounded. Kept her tethered to reality. To this world.

She could hear the king's excited breathing, heavy even over the sharp sound of the whip. Lacy bits of fabric stuck to her wounds, soon numbed from the harsh treatment. Any moment they would find that knife, still stuck to her skin. Hiding behind material that was slowly but surely being cut away.

The bottom of the garment waved as it fell from her body. The instrument continued to work. The top followed shortly thereafter. No clothing covered her now.

The knife stayed put.

It should've been on full display. Yet there was no mention. The lashes kept coming.

She reveled in the pain. Bathed in it. Her mind wanted to sink away to save her consciousness, but she wouldn't let it. Instead, she clung to the thoughts of those she loved to keep her strong. To the fact she would be a hero, come hell or high water, and Mordecai would be so mad at her for sacrificing herself to achieve it. Pettiness for the win.

When he was done, sagging with the effort, Daisy was covered in blood. It ran freely down her skin in a wash of crimson.

"Yes," the king said, surveying his work. "Good. Take her to the bed. I'll have her there."

Her wailing barely made a sound now, having been forced out of her somewhere along the way. Her fatigue silenced her voice. That was just her body, though. That wasn't her mind. And when the mind was strong, the body didn't matter.

It wasn't as eloquent as Zorn might've said it, but whatever. It worked.

The minions released first one manacle, then the other. Her knees gave out, and she collapsed onto the floor in a puddle of her own blood. Her body quivered.

Okay, maybe the body mattered a *little* bit...

They bent and reached for her, their hands stained with strands of black. The king lay on the bed, nude and prone, waiting for her. It would become his deathbed. Somehow.

She closed her eyes, feeling the magic of the room. Feeling the eddies and flows, twisting and bending from a few areas but tranquil and smooth in another.

The diamond chalice.

It had come alive because of her. It had called to her in the Court Hall. It stood by now, ready.

It had damned well better be. It had ultimately gotten her into this mess.

The hands grabbed her, but she focused on the diamond chalice. Felt it. Reached for it with the magic it had gifted her. Had cursed her with.

Its bright, hot pulse in her middle made her sob. The heat expanded, filling her up...and then overflowed. It pushed out onto her skin and coated her. Blanketed her. But it didn't heal her. Blood still cascaded down her torn flesh, dripping in places, oozing in others. If she used it to heal that, the king would know she was more than he suspected. More than a mere fragile human.

The pain dulled, though. Numbed. Her energy sparked as the hands picked her up from the floor. The minions tried to steady her on wobbling limbs. She let them, breathing deeply, feeling the life flow down from her middle and into her aching limbs. The pulse grew. Blossomed. With it, so did her strength.

She took a step forward, using the minions to steady herself. Mumbling nonsense. Her head lolled; she was acting now. Her sobs made her hiccup.

"Please," she whispered, balancing her body. "*Please.*"

"Yes," the king cooed. "Beg. That's right, human, *beg for your life.* I will grant you your wish...if you pleasure me."

He was lying. She could hear it in his voice. Taunting

her, as the royals liked to do. As Tarian had warned her about. Trained her for, though she didn't need a lesson to know this king was full of shit. Growing up had taught her not to trust people like him. He wasn't even a fae anymore. He was something that needed to be exterminated.

"Do you want me to let you go, human?" the king taunted her.

"Not at all..." she said, ripping an arm away from the minion on the right. "I'll do it myself"—she snatched her knife from its sheath—"you miserable fuck."

She spun on newly strengthened legs and dragged her blade through the air. It opened a red line across the minion's chest.

He started as the knife turned into a dagger, her favorite weapon. She withered both of their magics, then turned and stabbed Minion Two through the heart. Back again and she evaded a punch. These things didn't have any weapons.

Slipping behind him, she grabbed his hood and tugged it lower, over more of his face. Her knife sliced across his throat.

Magic, the king's, ballooned in the chamber. She latched on and sucked it in as hard as she could. He didn't get to stay in control. He didn't get to fight like he normally might. He would learn what it was like to be at a human's mercy.

The diamond chalice pulsed power into her. More strength. Speed.

Where had this been when she was crossing the fringe?

The king snarled as he bounced up from the bed. His leathery body was like a badly tanned animal hide covering bone and sinew.

"Fucking hell, you're gross," she said, pulling more magic, forcing him into a frenzied state. "No wonder the queen doesn't object to your finding different bed partners. She probably encourages it. She doesn't want to touch you."

The king ran at her, jerky and halting, his hands out like claws. Drool dripped from the corner of his mouth.

He was fast, though. Very fucking fast.

She stepped forward to meet him and slipped on the blood around her feet. Thankfully, because of the last few days, she was used to fighting in such conditions. She righted herself as his body barreled toward her.

She stepped at an angle and caught him with one hand. The other peppered him with knife strikes. Stab, stab, slice—she got in as many as she could before he bellowed and turned for her. His arms caught her skin but slid off, the surface slick with blood. He'd been trying to create lube with the blood, but instead had made it harder for him to combat her. *Suck on that, donkey fucker.*

His nails clawed down her arms, leaving fire in their wake.

She gritted her teeth and didn't bother acting this time. She would never act for him again. She'd kill him or he'd kill her. There was no other outcome of this fight, not since she'd yanked at his magic.

A loud thump hit the chamber doors. The doorknob jiggled as someone tried to get in. Another thump, someone ramming it with their body. She had to get this done before they got in to help the king.

"You...will...fuck-ing...die," she grunted as she yanked back his hair and stabbed at his throat.

He spun at the last moment, *so* fucking fast. Thank the miserable gods he was out of his mind with frenzied panic. He wasn't relying on skill or training, just animalistic brute strength and manic clawing.

She yanked more on his magic, as hard as she could. She stabbed at his side. His nails raked down the side of her face, and she took the pain as she lined up another strike. A normal person would've gone down, even a fae. This creature wouldn't succumb to the destruction.

She grappled one-handed to ensure the other held on to the knife. He grabbed her throat. Another slam hit the doors. Wood cracked. They were forcing their way in.

His hands squeezed with incredible strength, cutting off her air supply. She didn't stop. Couldn't. She pummeled him, holding his shoulder for leverage. Black spots danced in her vision. Still she stabbed, ruining his chest. She hit his heart and still the fucking creature would not go down.

Why isn't he dying?

Her lungs burned. Blackness crept closer. Blood drenched them both.

She went after his neck with more force, trying to sever his head. Her knife turned into a saw.

He ripped her down, and they fell, but neither of them quit. She sawed into his neck. The diamond chalice fed her strength. It was the only reason she was still conscious.

The door burst open. Time was up.

Chapter Thirty-Three

D<small>AISY</small>

Violence will set you free.

The king should've been dead. Punctured heart, half a neck—this creature should've been dead.

When the time comes, you must not be greedy for the kill. One must never let down one's guard, even when the enemy is on the brink of death.

You are the key. The only one who can do it.

Because she was the crystal chalice. It wasn't a weapon that would kill this rotting, twisted, sour-magic *thing*. It was depleting his magic. It was taking the root of Faerie out of his body.

Shouting filled the bedchamber, but she couldn't make sense of it. All she knew was her knife and the now motorized movements of sawing, every spare ounce of energy spent siphoning his magic. Her body had gone numb. Her vision had blurred and blackened to the point of uselessness, and so she closed her eyes.

Please, she said. She wasn't pleading to the gods, though, neither old nor new. She was pleading with the king. Begging. *Please, fucking die. Just fucking die, you saggy-balled prick.*

She sawed for all she was worth. Pulled that magic. Continued to swear at him in her mind.

Hands grabbed her. Tried to pull her away.

No. No sound came out, not without breath to use. *No,* she mouthed, eyes closed, darkness sucking at her, trying to pull her away.

It was time to die. Past time. Lord Death was waiting.

But she would not give in. She would not leave Tarian to his fate. Besides, she hadn't gotten this far in her shitty life, done so much to be the Big Chester Hero of the human magical world, to give in before the twisted fae king. She'd walk into the afterlife with no reservations...but not before this piece of shit went before her. She'd die on her terms, not his.

She yanked at the diamond chalice.

Power gushed into her. Stuffed her to bursting. Light flared behind her eyes. Strength fueled her increasingly limp body for one more push.

She redoubled her efforts. Renewed her sawing. Siphoned the last of his magic.

The fingers around her throat loosened. Then released.

A sweet blast of air filled her lungs. She coughed and gasped but kept going. Kept sawing.

"Be at ease, *dewdrop*." His voice was like a gift from the heavens. His touch made sobs bubble up in her throat. Tarian. "Gods, help me. What did he do to you?"

He pulled her closer, but she resisted, hand still gripping that disgusting, bony shoulder. Knife still working at the end of an arm she could hardly feel—fingers that had long since gone numb.

"Almost..." Her voice was barely audible. She coughed, refusing to let go. "Has to...die."

"Faelynn!" Tarian yelled. "*Hurry!*"

Tarian slapped the king's hands away from her throat. The hands didn't reach back for her. Trying to siphon magic came up dry. Her knife finally broke through, and the head rolled away. Twisted, churning magic clawed at her. Scraped against her. But that, too, released. Dissipated back into the fold, washed away by the pure, vibrant magic coursing within the room. She hadn't known the twisted magic had been lashing at her. The hands strangling her had been more pressing.

She sucked in another sweet though ragged breath, clutching Tarian and trying to crawl farther into his arms.

"It's over." He rocked her gently, cradling her to him. "It's all over."

Faelynn knelt by Daisy's side, pushing Tarian to give her room.

"No," Daisy whispered, refusing to let Tarian go. She buried her face in the fabric of his shirt.

"Let her help you, little dove," he murmured, his lips against her hair. "Let her heal you. You're still bleeding. We need to stop the bleeding."

The bleeding was nothing. Now that she could breathe again, the blood loss alone wouldn't pull her under. The scars on her face, however...

Tarian chuckled softly, helping her turn within his arms so her front faced Faelynn.

"No, it's okay. The chalice can help," Daisy rasped, pulling on the diamond chalice once again. The king hadn't been able to use it, not when it was across the room. He had to touch it. She had no such barriers. It was only now that she could fully appreciate the distinction. She wondered if Eldric knew.

"Get her something to wear!" Tarian barked.

This time, when Daisy pulled the white-hot power into herself, it smoothed over her body and took the slices with it. The scrapes.

"Why are you here?" she asked as the bleeding slowed. As the wounds began to stitch together. "I thought you couldn't get in here?"

"In coming here, I might've destroyed my chances of getting free, but I couldn't help it. I couldn't—"

"Tarian." Lennox's voice had an odd ring to it.

Daisy realized all the *Fallen* stood around Tarian, their souls registering now, whereas before she couldn't focus on anything besides staying alive and breathing.

Tarian stiffened. His fingertips dug into Daisy, almost bruising.

She opened her eyes, her breathing leveling out. Faelynn's widened eyes were just moving from Daisy's quickly healing skin to the nearby body. Steam rose and curled from the king's shriveling remains, the skin crackling like burned paper. His head, too, quickly deteriorated, his leathery flesh turning flaky and dusting off his strangely weathered bones.

"The magic that killed him...was also keeping him alive," Faelynn said with a slow release of breath. She recoiled from the shivering remains as they dried and wrinkled and flaked. "That was how he kept going, even after Daisy had destroyed his heart and mostly severed his head. The magic was animating him. I've never heard of anything like it."

"Like a zombie," Daisy whispered, her throat hurting from all the screaming. Faelynn helped her into loose garments. "A magical zombie."

Tarian's beautiful green gaze moved to Daisy's. His eyebrows pinched as he looked at her. Then he smiled.

"You'll like that change," he said, and she was too tired to ask what the fuck he was talking about. He shook his head, letting it go. "He died because you withered his magic."

"Siphoned it. Took it away."

His gaze turned focused. "No one else could have killed him. We heard accounts over the years of people trying. Not often, but occasionally, a rumor would circulate about it. I never believed them. Poisoning, assassins, his daughter trying to take the throne—I figured they were either tall tales or the king's guard had stopped the attempts. His guard is one of the more robust of the realm. But seeing him still living after all that damage, struggling when his fucking neck was half cut off..."

"The twisted magic must regenerate the flesh,"

Faelynn murmured, looking over the still-shriveling body, half the size of its natural counterpart. It was as if it were decomposing before their eyes. "I didn't know twisted magic could actually kill. I didn't know it would...do this —keep its host alive so it could infect others."

"No one has ever let it go on this long." Tarian's gaze washed across the room, lingering on the bodies of the minions and sticking to the blood against the wall. Daisy's blood. Fire kindled in his eyes. "Do you think the Celestials could've handled this?"

"Not with the deal they struck," Lennox said, standing over them. "Maybe with a combined effort from the other kingdoms, but many of them seemed more interested in going over the fringe and conquering new lands."

Tarian looked down at her again, his eyes deep. So vivid and beautiful. He stroked her cheek with his thumb. Then his eyes went distant. Lost focus. His brow pinched, and he looked to the side, as if searching for something.

Lennox stepped back, sucking in a breath. Daisy could feel other souls giving her and Tarian space as well.

"What is it?" she asked, pushing out of Tarian's arms. Her body ached dully. Her skin stung, the magic taking its toll from how much she'd used. That, or just healing pains from regenerating skin so quickly. She could fight, though. She had enough strength to keep going.

It didn't seem like Tarian had heard her. He braced a hand against the ground, leaning heavily on it. With his other, he hesitantly reached across his chest and to the back of his shoulder. He touched gingerly before glancing at Lennox.

"What?" Daisy asked again.

Tarian rose, his play of muscle delicious and graceful. He grabbed his shirt and pulled it over his head before throwing it to the ground.

"You did this," he said, his voice tinged with awe and gratitude. Reverence. He turned his back to Daisy, but he wasn't looking at the *Fallen*. He was speaking to her. "This is because of you."

Blood welled up around the five discs of obsidian in his back. Red ran down the black ink. Then, one by one, each disc popped off. They slid down his skin and fell to the ground, leaving a bloody gash in their wake.

"I..." Daisy pushed to standing, still wobbly. Faelynn stood with her, bracing her.

He shivered, and a sheen of gold glistened across his skin. Starting from the top and working its way down, the black ink in the swirling designs on his back changed. Transitioned. Little by little and then all at once, gold ate the black...and then diamond dust ate away the gold until it had overtaken the entirety of the tattoo.

"Oh fuck," she said on a release of breath. "What the fuck? I thought you said your kingdom's ink was gold? Fuck that! I only get a tiny one and you get all that?"

He looked back with a confused expression as faces went slack around him. As eyes widened. The design on his chest caught and threw the light, pulling his focus. That design had changed from black to diamond dust, too, so breathtakingly beautiful. Like him.

His gaze snapped to her, staring hard. His eyes... didn't have gold anymore. The black was long gone. Now they had a ring of diamond dust. Not silver, as they'd talked about, but what actually looked like granules of diamond in a circle around his pupil.

"Oh my..." She shouldn't have been this angry. She really shouldn't have been. "What in the fuck, though! I did all this, and *you* get all the diamond shit? Fuck you! Take me home. I quit."

Tarian laughed despite the situation. An image solidified in her mind.

Her—disheveled and looking helpless but alive—and with a circle around her pupil...in the same diamond dust as him.

"Mine should be gold," he said softly. "I have no idea why it changed. I can only guess it has something to do with you. You've used your chalice magic for the good of the kingdom, and it has marked you as something special within this realm. And maybe you've...marked me. The ink matches the royal color ring in a fae's eye. You only have a small bit of ink right now, but it does match. I just have a whole lot more."

She released a breath. A smile spread as her heart bloomed. Daisy had no idea why it was happening and did not really care. She just wanted him. She loved that she matched him. That they shared this remarkable transition.

"Forgiven," was all she thought to say, her feelings too big for words. But not needing words with him.

Something moved behind his eyes that she couldn't

read, and his entire bearing shut down unexpectedly. His expression went neutral.

She sighed. "Now what? Let me guess. I need to find the princess and the other royals and try to kill them too. Or some other horrible thing? I wouldn't be surprised."

A blast of magic so potent it made Daisy's eyes water pulsed through the room. A delicious, earthy scent tickled her senses.

Tarian shook his head. "You've done the heavy lifting. You've killed the guardian of my cage. You've freed me."

She'd been right. That made it all worth it.

Well...killing the king was its own reward, but enduring the steel-tipped whip was now justified.

Tarian's power manifested as a physical entity, a sexual pulse that ached gloriously through every inch of her body. Invisible hands burned across her sensitive skin. "Rest now, my little dove. I'll take it from here."

His heat saturated the space around her. His magic ballooned, so immense that it filled the room, a pressure unlike anything she'd ever felt. A power that seemed endless. It shook the very foundation of the castle.

The Celestial in the human world hadn't felt like this. Neither had the Celestials guarding the fringe. This was a level unto itself. Royalty, probably, but also...

"The Ancestral Magic of Sevens," he murmured. He pulled her into his arms. "A gift from my mother. The curse of the kingdom. My bane to bear."

"Your weapon to wield." She pulled his neck down so she could capture his lips. "The wicked never rest,

Tarian. Don't you know that? Let's go kill those fucking royals."

He laughed and squeezed her tightly. "Yes, *dewdrop*. Let's. But first..."

Wings flowed out from the back of his shoulders, delicate like a dragonfly's. They were colored like the sky at dusk, with peach and pink tones leading down to indigo and navy, covered in a glittering sheen of gold. Not dawn after the night, but dusk leading into the darkness. Just like him. They were stunning. Her breath caught to behold them.

They flared to the sides, snapping taut. Light flowed through the webbing, showing the glimmer, like the failing light dancing across the surface of a lake. She reached out and slid her fingers along the velvety, soft edge. He shivered, goosebumps rolling across his flesh.

Later, dove. I want to feel you stroke my wings—and other things—later. Right now, we have some wrongs to right.

She expected him to lead her out of the chamber, but instead, he took her hand and walked beside her. His wings fluttered, and his tattoos glittered, a fucking specimen to witness. She didn't much care about the enormity of his magic, but he was so fucking hot, so ethereal—godlike—that she was surely going to get a complex. She wasn't nearly attractive enough for someone like him. Not nearly close enough in pedigree. Maybe it was a good thing she had a noble death awaiting her. She wouldn't have to suffer the heartbreak of watching him lose interest before finding an incredible beauty with titles and gold and all the things handsome princes were sure to want.

"Question," she said to distract herself as they entered the outer chamber. Bodies lay prone and bloodied. Tarian had fought his way through to get to her. "Before I do the magnanimous thing and sacrifice myself for the good of the realm, can I get a bigger tattoo? Assuming it'll be diamond dust. Even in death, I'd rock that thing. I was made for it."

He tugged her closer. "Yes. We'll get one to match. How's that?"

"I mean, sure, if you want to be cutesy about it."

He chuckled darkly as they left the king's wing and entered the corridor.

"Question," she said again. His magic stuffed the space full of blistering, potent magic. It wasn't billowing black shadows this time, though. Pale gold, coral, lavender, and cerulean sparkled in a magnificent display of dusk-like colors, coating the walls and swirling through the air. The magic was clean and pure and playful while still deadly and menacing. Fae. It lifted her soul and made her want to burn down the world all at the same time.

"Yes?" he asked, jostling her out of her stupor with the beauty of his magic. One being should not be allowed to be this overwhelmingly gorgeous. It simply wasn't fair for the rest of the worlds at large—both the fae world and the human. And any other world out there that she didn't know about.

"Why did you come for me? You never said. I thought you couldn't."

They turned the corner. "I'll explain it all later. Right now..."

Guards waited in the hall, weapons in hand and bodies tense. They sighted Tarian and pivoted to face him. They must've known he was coming.

"Not known," he said as he walked toward them with a purposeful stride. His wings fluttered behind him, proving to everyone what he was. "Feared. And now their fears will come true."

He didn't raise his hand. Didn't give the signal for his *Fallen* to cut down the fae in his way. He simply...*flexed*.

His magic tumbled down the corridor, a wall of might that stole her breath. It ripped and tore a path ahead of him, laying waste to the opposition and a couple of passing nobles. Only the servants, hunkering down with their hands over their heads and shaking in fear, were spared. He not only had power, but incredible dexterity with his magic.

"Demigod Kieran would give his left nut to have you in his arsenal," Daisy murmured as they stepped through the bodies and reached the doors. "Any of the Demigods would."

"Except for your Lexi." He didn't try the lock but blasted the double doors open. "She wouldn't care what I was—she'd only care what threat I posed to you. Isn't that right?"

"I see someone has a lot more strength in his mindgazer magic."

"A lot, yes. I want to experience you, but that will come later, too."

Now the *Fallen* did run in front of them, weapons out, teeth bared. Tarian let them, holding out his hand and having it filled with Daisy's magical knife as Faelynn passed.

He handed it to Daisy. "Per our deal, when you don't have this knife in your possession, you are allowed to kill my *Fallen*. Let's keep them safe, shall we?"

"I still have a green light to kill you."

"Yes, you do. And the magic to render me vulnerable."

She didn't know about that. She was good, but she wasn't indestructible. The court battle with the fae female had proven that. Daisy didn't think she had the same training hours as he did. Not even close.

"That doesn't matter." His voice was subdued and reverent. He looked at her as his warriors laid ruin to those around them. "I would never lift a hand against you. If you decided to kill me, I wouldn't stop you."

She opened her mouth to call bullshit but didn't get the chance. The princess appeared in a doorway at the back of the chambers. Her dress billowed. Two objects filled her hands, both of them glowing. A blast of shadowy power rose up and rushed toward them.

Chapter Thirty-Four

DAISY

Daisy didn't get time to think. She reached out with her magic, the same magic that could stop someone using her if she so chose, and sapped the strength from those obsidian chalices. Just as she'd brought them to life, now she deadened them. Eldric had said it was within her power to do so. It was why the crystal chalice was always meant to be a thinking, logical being.

Her knife elongated into a sword, ready for battle.

"No." Tarian put out his hand to stop her. "This is my fight."

His magic didn't well up like with the guards. Instead, he pulled his own magical knife from its sheath. It glowed in the dim light as the princess's face crumpled into a mask of rage. Her vile magic swirled around her. It didn't get the boost from the chalices she was looking for.

Still, she had plenty, and she attempted to use it.

"Do you want me to wither her magic?" Daisy asked as Tarian's sword elongated into a staff.

He chuckled darkly. "Her magic is nothing to me now. An annoyance. I'll keep it at bay."

The *Fallen* continued to fight with vigor. Tarian walked right through the center of them, his staff whirling, the light spinning. The princess flung out her hands. Shadowy magic curdled the air between them and met his gorgeous resistance of dawn. The new day would bleed away all the night's power.

He was on her, thrusting with his staff. She snatched a blade from a sheath at her hip and countered. He twirled and struck, cutting off a necklace, then a beaded, decorative broach. She parried, blocked, stepped back. He was everywhere at once, striking at her, putting her on the defense. Always advancing. It wasn't until they were in her bedchambers, Daisy running to stay close, that Tarian's sword work intensified.

"You always wanted me in here," he told the princess, too fast for her. Stripping away her layers of wealth one strike at a time. He was like a vengeful god, mighty and masterful, beautiful to watch. "You always wanted me bared and at your disposal. I told you that someday I would have my vengeance. Well, you can thank a human female for allowing my claims to come true."

He slashed, opening a streak of red across her stomach. Again, down the middle. Insides fell outside and streamed down. She screamed, trying to protect herself. Trying to gain the upper hand. But he showed how he'd gotten those ten rings on each arm. He proved why he was the best, not just in magic, but in all things.

A limb hit the ground. Another. Then her head followed.

She didn't die, though. She didn't stop flailing. The mind was dead—well, detached, really—but the magic forced the body to live on. The reality of that would give Daisy nightmares. Zombies weren't supposed to be real.

Tarian drove his staff through the princess's chest and into the floor, skewering her and keeping the body put. Without arms, she'd be hard-pressed to get free.

"Drain her, dove," he said, watching her with cold, heartless eyes. "End her."

It would've been better if Daisy had some fire starters and a little time, but they'd have to settle for figuratively burning this shit-box to the ground.

She siphoned away the magic, and as she did, the body convulsed wildly. The feet kicked and braced, trying to help the body up. Even now—*with no head!*—the creature was trying to get at Daisy to save the life Faerie gave it.

In the silence that followed, Tarian breathed heavily, looking down at the corpse. He didn't say a word, but he didn't have to. Daisy could read the thoughts racing across his face, understand the pain, remembering how he'd suffered by the princess's hand.

Daisy scooted closer and slipped her arm around him. He pulled her in quickly, hugging her close, not looking away from what used to be the princess.

"It doesn't erase the..." He didn't finish. Daisy

nodded against his shoulder. "But it does close the book on that chapter of my life. It is the ending I sought." He kissed her forehead. "I needed you for this. I've always needed you for this. The gods must've known."

He tilted up her head and kissed her lips softly.

"Now," he said, "let's go get the others. And this time, we'll bring a match. How's that?"

It didn't take them long. None of the nobles stood in their way, not wanting to sacrifice themselves for the good of the kingdom. Or maybe they knew *this* was for the good of the kingdom, and they didn't want to stand in a Celestial's way of chopping down the rotten royalty. The innocent servants and slaves who'd had no choice in this life weren't harmed. They were freed and sent on their way, allowed to take any gold or jewels they could for a fresh start. Apartments and bedchambers were burned. Flames contained to the royal chambers danced in glory.

Strangely, people recognized Tarian for who he used to be—a Celestial prince—but not for the position he'd recently had. It seemed as if getting his old identity back had erased the temporary persona. They bowed or knelt, looking up at him with reverence or fear or both. It was a stark contrast to the mocking snarls the nobility had borne, or the avoidance the servants had employed.

If any of the nobles thought they'd get to go over the fringe, now they knew otherwise. Given other kingdoms were interested, the spies fled upon learning what was happening, evading anyone trying to stop them. It meant the corruption would continue to spread, and the human world was still not safe. Tarian had known that would happen, and if Daisy had had any doubts, they had been laid to rest.

By the time they got back to Tarian's quarters, they were both exhausted from the carnage.

"Secure the worst of the nobles," Tarian told Kayla. "What's left of them, anyway. Tell Eldric to finish the setup tonight. We'll use it tomorrow morning. Make sure no one stands in our way."

"Yes, sire." Kayla offered him a bow, and her eyes sparkled with joy and relief. She'd gotten her identity back as well.

"What about her wings?" Daisy asked when he had shut and warded the outer doors. "They're Celestials, right?"

"They agreed to have their wings stripped when they stood forward on my behalf. They don't expect it, but my aim is to rectify their sacrifice and return their wings."

"How?"

He took a deep breath. "I have to travel across the Sea of Stars and up the Forgotten Mountain. The Oracle of Aethras, a being integrated into Faerie while still being removed, is there. That Oracle is not indebted to the gods and does not follow their will or their rule. The scripts say it is older than time. Older than the stars and the fabric they hang from. The Oracle can restore their wings, though I'll need to trade something dear to grant the boon."

"And that will be?"

He looked down at her with a heaviness in his gaze. "My life, though it won't mean much to me at that point. Balance will have been restored, and so the last thing I will need to do is wipe myself from this land and allow my family to resume their lives in peace. That's where I'll trade myself for the good of the realm."

Her heart filled with such pain that she nearly couldn't bear it. Couldn't think of a world that didn't include him. Didn't want the separation that death would bring.

"But I thought...you'd be appealing to the gods?"

"No. Something older and more powerful than the gods. Their creator."

She had questions, but she didn't have the ability to ingest any more information right now. Fatigue consumed her. She needed to relax. She wanted quality time with Tarian, the last she'd have. This was it. Her time was done. They had this one night left, and she intended to make the most of it.

First they took a bath, washing and soaking and making love. Then Tarian brought in a royal inker, as they were called, to apply the tattoo that had better fucking glitter.

They'd decided on a design together, something to integrate his royal Celestial chest design so that the finished product would encompass the part of him he'd lost, regained, and would trade himself for. The part of him that would soon be lost forever. And something she thought was really pretty.

The finished result was breathtaking, dainty and

intricate at her bust and dipping between her breasts. It was, indeed, diamond dusted. Once finished, the royal inker stared at them both with a pale face and shaking limbs. At one point, he'd picked up a knife, looking at Tarian like he wanted to kill the Celestial. A burst of magic had made him reconsider, and his tense posture over leaving had indicated he wasn't comfortable with what he'd done.

"It's that diamond-dusted myth or whatever, right?" Daisy asked as she looked at her tattoo in the mirror. "He's afraid we'll ruin the kingdom?"

"Something like that."

"Well..." She turned to him, running her hand across his matching design. It didn't bleed like a human tattoo. It didn't hurt. It was almost like he'd simply painted it on. "We will, right? We've already started."

"Yes. And they've brought it on themselves." He bent to kiss her. "Anything left on your trucker list?"

She furrowed her brow. "My trucker list? What's that?"

He cocked his head. "Isn't that what humans call the, like, last things they want to do with their time?"

She laughed. "Bucket list. The things you want to do before you die. Trucker list? Where did you get that? Do you even know what a trucker is?"

He smiled, his hands drifting over her hips. "Your mind just told me. I have no idea where I heard it. I picked it up wrong."

"Clearly." She reached for the buttons on his pants, backing him out of the room. "Yes, there is one thing left on my trucker list. I want to fuck you on all the seating areas the *Fallen* think is safe and not tell them until after they've used them."

A river of diamonds ran around Tarian's pupils. She watched in fascination. With each new reveal, this Celestial became more handsome, more interesting to look at.

"Before we do that, it's time to set some things straight." He led her to the couch and settled in. "I owe you answers."

She took a deep breath and nodded. She didn't need to voice the questions again. She knew he remembered.

"I always could've stormed the king's chambers," he admitted, and her middle tightened. She wondered if she wanted to ruin her last night with the truth. "I always could've come for you—tried to save you—but it wouldn't have done any good. Because of his hold over me, I couldn't hurt him. With those obsidian discs in my back, I couldn't hurt any of the royal family. If I could've killed them, believe me, they would've been dead a long time ago. The *Fallen* couldn't either. Nor could any of us tell someone else how to free me—and them through me."

She nodded. She'd figured some of that out. And now she knew the reason he hadn't said anything. He hadn't given her the plan. He couldn't. It had to be her, but she had to do it on her own. Very tricky of the gods.

It was his turn to nod, having heard her thoughts. "We couldn't hire someone, or outright ask someone, to kill him on our behalf. We had to wait for someone to do it on their own." He sighed. "Well, we waited. And waited. But the unrest here, especially in the beginning when the magic was starting to twist, never yielded any results. Sure, there were rumors, but nothing happened. The king never missed a court gathering. Never missed a day sitting on his throne. Never looked wounded or hurt. Clearly, that was the magic, but we didn't know that. I began to lose hope."

He brought his hand up to trace his thumb along her chin.

"Then I found the crystal chalice, someone with incredible training and the right amount of viciousness—hard to find among humans, especially non-magical ones. I should know, I've looked. Your trainer's upbringing must've helped—and his fae blood. His own viciousness, honed by his past. He then passed all that on to you, a human he knew could handle it. He knew you were special without knowing about the chalice. Or much about fae. But I wasn't sure you could do it. Without telling you what was needed, I had no idea how I'd get you in front of the king. Or if you'd accomplish the goal when I did. If you could."

"You didn't even know I could null magic or siphon it."

"No. The odds were that you would die, and it would add *years* to my search while a new crystal chalice was formed. I was prepared to wait. To learn from your failings and help train another to be better prepared."

"You were taking me to slaughter."

"Yes." His eyes held deep remorse. "In the beginning, when in the human lands, I didn't care. Not totally. You'd be sacrificed for the greater good. I was attracted to you—

attraction doesn't even describe it—but I thought it was because of the chalice magic. Even before you had it, I assumed it must be that. It made it easier."

"Made what easier? Dragging me to my doom?"

He didn't even hesitate. "Yes."

She sat back, her heart aching, but didn't let him know that.

His eyes were so deep, so full of regret. "In the beginning, I didn't care if I lost you." He said it without flinching. "I had a job to do. One human wouldn't stand in my way of doing it. I was attracted, as I said. I thought of you all the time, dreamt of you, couldn't wait to see you again —that kiss nearly undid me—but despite that, I knew what must be done. Had to be, for my *Fallen,* for my family, and for this realm. I would sacrifice you...and myself. I had no hesitation."

Heat pricked the backs of her eyes. Her heart ached to hear all of this, even though at that time, she'd known it. She'd known his intentions, his ruthlessness, and she hadn't balked at his cruelty. Now...it broke her in a way that the king never could've.

"But somewhere along the way..." His voice reduced to a whisper. "No, not somewhere. I know exactly when. The moment you decided to trust me in crossing the fringe, things changed. Everything changed. I started to slip in my motivations." He licked his lips. "To fall. We had attraction in the beginning, but it wasn't the gods. It was what any two strangers might have. It was mutual interest. It was a feeling. It was surface level."

It was what Lexi and Kieran had had, despite their

situation and his actions. Despite the danger. Daisy remembered looking on in confused wariness that Lexi would be so stupid as to be interested in a guy like him. As far as she was concerned, Lexi had been out of her mind. Completely illogical.

She got it now.

"The moment we stepped over the threshold as a team," Tarian continued, "what was surface level grew roots. Depth. Deeper and deeper as we battled together. As we made choices to help the other—I didn't save you from those poisoned thorns because you were the chalice. At that moment, I wasn't thinking at all. I just knew I couldn't bear to lose you. I couldn't continue to exist if I had to witness seeing the vicious light dim in those beautiful eyes." He swallowed. "I did it to protect you. The more I've gotten to know you, listened to your thoughts, reveled in your fire, the more I've fallen. Until the other morning, when you learned about my trials in this court and vowed to burn it all to the ground on my behalf... That was the instant I knew."

She barely dared to breathe. "Knew what?"

"I knew I was irrevocably, undeniably in love with you. That I wanted to mark you, not as my property, but as my mate. And that I wanted to be marked by you."

Her breath caught as she flattened her hand against her chest. "This means I'm your mate?"

He didn't answer for a moment. Didn't break eye contact. "That design doesn't, no. That's merely a promise. A promise that I will not be long in following you into the afterlife. Because when you go, I will be a hollowed-out creature. You will have taken my soul with you. My heart. I will merely finish my duty, and then I will find you again. If you are reborn, I will return, only so I can meet you anew. So that we can fall in love naturally, without all this shit around us, and have a chance at the forever that is currently denied to us."

She let out a slow, quivering breath. A tear overflowed from her eye.

He reached for her with a shaking hand. "I thought I loved Sansa, and maybe I did, but it didn't feel like this. It wasn't this strong. This powerful. It'll kill me how this ends, but I'm glad the chalice turned out to be you. I'm glad I was able to know you, to feel you, to spend even this short amount of time with you. We've lived through hell and have yet to meet the gods in the afterlife, but each touch from you has been like living among the stars. A blessed life. And so, when the king took you, even with your new magic, I couldn't stand by and allow it to happen. Each fight in that court took every ounce of willpower I possessed to leave you to it, but once the king had you, I couldn't... I couldn't risk things going wrong and losing you like that. Subjecting you to that."

"You certainly took your sweet time."

His smile at her quip didn't linger. "The king anticipated me. He had three times the number of guards barring my way. It was why the other royals intensified their defenses as well. They all knew I'd go for you and, despite the magic trapping me, would find a way to kill him. And I did...through you. You didn't need me at all."

"I mean, if we're being honest, I could've used you *before* he sliced me up and wrestled me to the ground..."

Now the smile did linger, a teasing tone riding each word. "Ah, but...you wouldn't have figured out the new facet of your ever-expanding magic. You really should be thanking me."

Fat fucking chance.

He laughed and kissed her deeply. "I was about to pull him away from you when you called me off. You did it. In the end, you did what I always needed you to do, and it turns out, it had to be you. The gods are surely entertained."

"The gods can get fucked." She rested her forehead against his, closing her eyes. "I think you were right—what you said in that hotel room what seems like a lifetime ago. When I had my knife pressed against you, and you said I wouldn't be able to kill you? You were right. At this point, even if my life depended on it, I wouldn't be able to."

"Nonsense." He slipped his hands under the hem of her shirt. "For your family, you'd slit my throat and be pissed at me for breaking your heart in the process."

"Breaking my heart?"

"Yes." He ran his hands over her breasts. "Because you feel this every bit as much as I do. You just don't want to admit it. That's okay. I have all night to get a screaming confession out of you."

(She had admitted it—to herself, at least—but now... Well, she liked his extra motivations...)

He pulled away with a quirked eyebrow, knowing she'd thought something away from his prying mind.

"I still can't read those thoughts," he murmured with a smirk.

"Good. It would be annoying if, in addition to everything else, you were also all-knowing."

He pulled off her shirt and bent, flicking her nipple with his hot tongue. She groaned, scooting back so she could hurriedly work at his pants.

"We've already made love on the couch," she said as she freed his hard length.

He waved his hand. A burst of power stopped her breath. Their clothes vanished completely. She didn't stop to marvel. She didn't even check into the currents of magic. There was no point. She didn't have much time with him. She didn't want to waste it on analysis.

Instead, she rose, her heart hammering, needing him. Needing this. Wishing she'd known about the mates thing when they were getting marked. She wanted that now. Fearing intimacy and commitment was for another life. Another person. Daisy wasn't that person anymore. Now, she wished she had more time.

She wished she had forever.

At least they had tonight. They had *right now*. She'd make it last for as long as she could.

She sat down onto him, both of them groaning, their breathing labored, their hands frenzied. She jerked her hips over him, feeling the delicious friction. He used his fingers on her apex and his magic to spiral her higher.

"I assume you don't mind if I cheat in this, either," he

murmured, speaking about when she said he could cheat in pleasuring her by reading her mind. Now he was using his magic.

"Not even...a little," she breathed, winding up to incredible heights and barely able to take the impossibly good sensations.

She clutched his broad shoulders. Ran her fingers over his perfect chest, his perfection heightened with the diamond dust. He kissed down her neck as she moved, loving the delicious slide of his body in hers. Loving how incredibly right this felt.

"Our fate is fucked, but I wouldn't trade knowing you for all the safety in the world," she said, holding him tightly, feeling her body bracing at the edge. "From our very first meeting, your memory stayed with me. Your eyes, the feel of your proximity. It just got stronger and stronger. Until now." She grabbed his hair in two fists. Rode him hard. Then, instead of waiting, just let the truth spill out. "I love you. I think I always have. I know I always will."

His hands gripped her. He swung up, burying himself deep inside her, over and over. "Of course you do," he whispered, rolling with her and laying her on her back. He strove harder. Held her tighter. "I'm easy to love."

"If you...were easy...to love"—she groaned as his magic rolled through her—"I'd get...bored."

He laughed darkly, then hooked his arm under her knee and lifted, giving himself more room to strive. He slammed into her with bruising strokes. She swung up to meet him, calling his name. Holding on for dear life.

"I love you too," he said, and she exploded. She shuddered against him, and he shook as he climaxed. Her name was ripped from his lips as though in devotion to the divine.

The pieces of her flew apart, and she broke in the most glorious of ways. She wrapped herself around him and let him gather up her pieces, remaking her, fitting sections of his heart into hers, and keeping some of hers for himself. They were entwined in a way she'd never experienced. Never heard of. They had to be in order for her magic to work. In order for them to create greatness. They had to be...in order to trust each other as they did. With more than their lives, with their souls. With everything they were.

His breath was heavy as they came down. An image ran through her mind as he shared his thoughts with her.

A stunning, magical scene came into focus. He walked around a bush in the wylds and caught a sight that made him hitch in his step. A bird perched delicately on a branch. He held his breath, as if breathing might scare the creature away. The little body glowed with vibrant, iridescent colors. Golden-orange hues glimmered along its tail and wings, with a teal and emerald body. The wings shimmered with a trail of light made of soft, glowing particles. Surrounding the bird, delicate white blossoms and green leaves danced and swayed in the breeze.

He stared in wonder, in astonishment, because the

sighting of such a bird was so incredibly rare. They were almost a myth, these creatures, existing so deep in the wylds and being so elusive that seeing one was a once-in-a-lifetime event. A privileged, rare occurrence.

As he watched, it cocked its head. It launched off its perch and dove in a stream of light. Nearly at the ground, it spread its wings for a fast stop before raking its claws across the eyes of its prey. It pecked and gouged, waiting for the creature to shriek and roll before digging in for the heart. They were predators, these beautiful little birds, but one would never know it by their appearance. They drank honey and blood and sang so sweetly that it would make a minstrel weep.

"That is a dove in Faerie," he whispered. "That is what you reminded me of the moment I met you. A rare sighting that I would remember for the rest of my days."

"Yet you marked your kills with a human dove."

"I couldn't very well try to track down a Faerie dove. It would kill me for stealing one of its feathers. They're small, but they're fierce."

"It's not the size of the ocean. It's the motion of the waves."

"What?" He paused, digging through her memories for what she meant. He laughed. "In my case, dove, it's both. Come on. Let's switch to Niall's favorite chair and I'll prove it."

Prove it he did, over and over. They fought the dawn, relishing in the night. In each other. All too soon, though, the fates came calling. The power that had given her magic was a power that expected its due.

Chapter Thirty-Five

D A I S Y

They walked down the corridor hand in hand. A Celestial and a human. A joke in the making.

A Celestial and a human walk into a bar...

He wore princely attire, clothes he'd had made years ago, using them as a carrot to keep him motivated. His hair was straight and flat as befitted a Celestial, the effect applied with magic and saving *so much time*.

She wore something he'd recently had made for her, taking his favorite designs from the human world and having the fae tailors bring his vision to life. He couldn't have known at the time how perfect the result would be.

The straps at the shoulders looped down to the bodice, mostly open at the chest, revealing the gorgeous diamond-dust tattoo, sparkling and shimmering in the hall lighting. A wide belt of fabric circled her waist before the silk cascaded down her legs and flowed around her feet. A cape-like addition was attached at her shoulder straps and trailed out behind her, giving her presence a majestic feel. A queenly feel.

It was a real pity he hadn't had a tiara handy.

Nobles pushed back against the wall, hands often at their chests, looks of reverence or fright covering their faces. Those with tainted magic often tried to slip away, and Tarian let them. He would not play judge and jury. He'd let the cleansed Faerie magic do that. He'd let Daisy initiate that.

Servants didn't run like their noteworthy counter-parts. Instead, they faced the pair and bowed, their hands not on their chests in fear, but on their hearts in respect. Help had come. The fear of turning twisted like their employers was at an end.

They continued on, his measured pace befitting someone of his rank. She couldn't help thinking of it as a death march, though. Butterflies filled her stomach, but she did not balk. She did not allow the tension to stiffen her shoulders.

Instead, she thought about her family. She thought about their good times, recalling a memory with each one.

Play them for me, Tarian said, and he slowed a little more. *Play each memory for me so that I can bear witness.*

She walked closer to him, their arms touching. Her eyes filled with tears as she looked over at him, then nodded in thanks. He'd carry their memories on for however long he remained here.

Even though Lexi had saved her, she played memories of Mordecai first. Of that morning in the hospital when he'd been cured. Of the hope in his eyes. The subsequent spring in his step. His miracle.

Lexi was, of course, next, Daisy thinking of all the times Lexi had worried about her "kids'" wellbeing. All the stress she'd endured on their behalf. Then of the day she'd realized her kids were taken care of and their money troubles were over. Daisy would never forget the look of supreme relief on her face and the love in her eyes.

She thought of the rest, of their banter and laughter, their fierce expressions when telling Daisy to stay out of trouble. She had so many uncles and aunts now. So many people who cared about her.

She wondered what they'd think of her, with this crazy though exhilarating magic. With the ability to shrivel a person's magic or take it away entirely. The latter likely wouldn't kill a human, since the magic worked differently there, but it would certainly surprise the hell out of them. And in that time...she'd dance a little closer and slit their throats. Easy-peasy.

Tarian huffed a laugh. "What a joy that would be to see. Despite my level of discomfort, it was a damn good time seeing you fight in the court games. Your ability to manipulate your opponent was exceptional."

"Not as good as that other small-statured female. Who the hell was that? She could've killed me. Instead, she helped me—helped *you*—and killed herself."

He shook his head as they reached a wing of the castle she'd never been to. His grip on her hand tightened. They must be close. "I don't know. She was listed as Xanon's champion. But, of course, Xanon was dead. It was assumed another noble did it, but no one knows who. His champion should've been forfeited but...she went ahead. The guards put her into the rotation."

"Unless she wasn't Xanon's champion."

"Or maybe she was the one to kill him. Another thing —her body has vanished."

Daisy looked over at him. "What? Are you sure?"

"Yes. She was dragged into the room with the other dead, but there is no record of her body being buried or incinerated. After the games, there is no record of her at all."

"She did seem to die too quickly from that wound."

"I confess...I hadn't been paying attention to her." He stopped in front of a nondescript door, but instead of opening it, he yanked her to him. His eyes were urgent. "We don't have to do this, Daisy. We can find another way. I'm free now. The king is dead. We can appeal to the Celestials for help. I'm a prince again. I have status and clout. I have a way to help these people—help Faerie —without sacrificing you."

"Your brother nearly killed you, Tarian. Everyone who matters in the court distrusted you. You were a threat, and surviving an assassination attempt makes you more of one. Then you walk into that same court, a court in distress, with all your magic and the crystal chalice on your arm? Are you kidding?"

"They don't have to know what you are. We could resume calling you a toy. I know it's not ideal, but—"

"I have a diamond-dust tattoo and rings around my

pupils, Tarian. I'm not a complete fucking idiot. I know that has to do with the crystal chalice in some way. With the magic. I don't know why you have it, but whatever the reason, you'll stand out more than you did in the past. You'll be a bigger target than ever. It'll require alliances and political maneuvering to get help. I know how these things work, as do you. The Guardians are split, and the royalty is at each other's throats for the throne. You could try to get your dad on track, but recovering from a death that he helped cause would take a second. All of that—*all* of it—would take time. Time Faerie doesn't have. And sure, why would I care? Except the Diamond Throne is directly responsible for the protection of the fringe, and that puts my family on the line. No matter how you look at this, there is no other way. We don't have the resources to hunt down the twisted magic without the Diamond Court, and they've got problems. Problems you've indirectly created. Those are facts. This is the solution. You know that."

She laid her palm on his cheek. His eyes glistened with unshed tears.

"So hard, so ruthless...and he comes apart so easily," she whispered.

"What can I say, you've broken me." He hugged her tightly. "I can't do this. I won't."

"You will," she said. She backed off enough to kiss him. "You're going to have to kill me, babe. Sorry, I don't have a cute term of endearment like 'dewdrop.' You'll have to take what you get until I get more creative." He smiled sadly. "You need to go through with this. I need you to. Okay? I need you to give it all you have. My family needs you. I need to play hero and you need to help with that."

His sigh spoke of a breaking heart. "Okay."

"Okay. Let's get this done."

The room beyond was empty in that all the furniture and wall decorations had been removed. There was just a large, rectangular area with a dull wooden floor. Upon that floor, though, was an elaborate setup of objects, each working with the others to create a twisting, circular design around the center. Within that center, which had enough space for two large people, waited one object. The diamond chalice.

It wouldn't be the diamond chalice alone that created the godly power and killed her. Nor just it and Tarian. They'd need *all* these chalices working together to create the heights Tarian needed. Pretty hardcore.

Upon her entering the room, the items lit up, one by one at first and then all together, like a greeting. The diamond chalice sent out a peal of thunder. It rolled across the floor and soaked into the walls.

Eldric, at the far side with a pile of scrolls, startled and looked around. He saw Daisy and Tarian before turning and walking their way.

"Please, Daisy," Tarian whispered, not allowing her to step any farther into the room. "Give me a day to think this through. With Eldric's help—"

She let go of his hand and stepped without him. She didn't fault him for his waffling decision-making. It was easy to have courage when she was the one calling the shots. When she was the one playing hero and wouldn't have to suffer the agony of losing the one she loved. Of being responsible for the death of her beloved.

"You are, you know," he said, hearing her. She wasn't hiding anything from him. "You are my beloved." He turned to her again. Eldric paused near the edge of the configuration. "You won't be long ahead of me, okay? It'll seem like no time at all. Wait for me. I will find you in the afterlife. Wait for me and we can be together."

She wrapped her arms around his neck. "I'll be just beyond the veil, okay? I'm not waiting around in real life because the veil might close or something, and then I'd just be hanging around, seeing people who can't see me back. Apparently, it's a real shit existence. My uncle knows from experience."

"I don't know...what the veil is, but I'll find you."

"Okay, well...just go toward the death beacon—you'll know what it is, apparently—and *I'll* find *you*, okay? I know way more about all this stuff than I ever wanted to, but it'll help. Hopefully."

He kissed her fiercely and faced Eldric. "Let's go," he said in a rough voice.

"Yes, fantastic." Eldric glanced up from one of his scrolls. "Look at that beautiful ink, Daisy. The crystal chalice was always meant to shine, placing it above all others of its kind. This is why the Diamond Throne was reduced to gold ink—the chalice should have no competition, since there is always only one. Simply gorgeous."

Tarian lifted his eyebrows at that, and Daisy laughed.

He'd been out of the loop. If the High Sovereign had known they were reduced to gold, "second best," they hadn't told him. For all their arrogance, they likely tried to ignore it.

"I see you've finally gotten the rings around your pupils," Eldric continued, ignoring the exchange. "I wondered about that. Some of the texts mention that sometimes the markings will hide to keep the chalice safe. Since you've killed the king, it is safe to reveal what you really are, I think. Now, you might want to remove your clothing. There are some records that mention flames licking up from the power. I can only imagine this means the chalice being set on fire, and clothes will make it burn hotter. Fuel, you know. That does not sound like a pleasurable experience."

"Will any of this be a pleasurable experience?" She shrugged out of her dress, leaving just her underwear.

"No, but there is also no reason to make things worse. Don't you agree?" He glanced at Tarian. "You as well, sire. Welcome back, by the way. I was privy to the situation, of course. My kind are known for the information they are able to obtain—"

He cut off as Tarian unbuttoned his shirt. His eyes widened, and he waited for Tarian to finish revealing his torso.

"What..." Eldric looked back and forth between them. "What happened? How..." His eyebrows pinched together, and he stepped forward quickly, looking into Tarian's eyes. "Why do you have diamond dust and not gold? What..." He looked back and forth again. "I must've missed something. I don't recall reading anything about this."

Tarian took off his pants. "Given my ignorance about the crystal chalice magic, that doesn't surprise me."

"*Your* ignorance doesn't mean anything. You're supposed to be ignorant. As one of the order, *I* am not. Is it...a mutation caused by fornicating with the human?"

Now Daisy's eyebrows lifted. She gave Tarian a crooked smile. "There could be worse side effects of fornication..."

Tarian chuckled, running his hand across her shoulder before pulling her closer. "Very beautiful side effect you have there, human."

She spared him a kiss, then copped a feel before walking to the edge of the configuration. The objects all hummed and glowed. The diamond chalice gleamed, a solitary item amidst its kind.

"Okay, enough stalling. Let's get this done," she said.

The smile fell from Tarian's face. His expression cleared and hardened.

"Yes, fine." Eldric frowned at her. "I would've liked more time to look into the ink situation, but fine. I suppose the sooner we deal with the rot that has been allowed to escape this court, the better. Head into the middle there. Tarian, you with her."

She did as instructed, careful not to disturb the setup. Tarian followed, his hand on her shoulder before sliding down to capture her hand.

"I hate this," he murmured as she stopped beside the diamond chalice. Its magic sizzled within her middle, white hot and ready to expand. Tarian stared down at it for a long moment, then at everything around it. His breath was heavy, but he didn't say anything further.

What was there *to* say, really?

Except, "I love you."

"You've been my blessing in an otherwise cursed existence. You are the first rays of the sun that peek over the horizon at dawn. The beautiful colors washed across the sky at dusk. You've made me the best version of myself, my little treasure, and I will cherish you for it, always. This is merely a parting. I'll see you soon, remember? We won't be apart for long."

"Well, just so no one is caught off guard..." Eldric paused in looking at his scroll. "She won't survive this. Not unless she stops the progression. Which...given how painful it is said to be, she might. But if she—"

"We're aware, thank you," Daisy said dryly. "For all the shit you give humans, it's as if you never hear yourself." She looked deep into Tarian's eyes. "If there is a way you can avoid trading yourself, I want you to promise me that you will take it. Do not die unnecessarily. Live for as long as you can. Become king and make sure Faerie stays balanced. Take a surly queen that scowls at everyone so you might remember me. Live your life to the fullest, Tarian. I'll wait. Hell, I'll be dead. All I'll have to do is wait. Time won't matter to me. Lexi has said that often enough about other spirits that I know it is true. Live. That's all I ask."

"There will be no living without you."

She took a shaky breath, her heart breaking, but she

was determined. Wanted the best for him. "There will. Give yourself time to heal, and you'll forget. Plus, bonus —you and your dad will have something in common. If that isn't an *in*, I don't know what is."

Tarian kept shaking his head, but Daisy ignored it. She motioned for Eldric to get going.

Eldric's lips pursed. "Yes, let's begin. It seems you've already ignited the chalices, so bend and pick up the diamond chalice."

"Hold on to me," she told Tarian. "The last couple times, this thing knocked me flat on my ass. I'd hate to mess up Eldric's hard work."

"That did not sound genuine," Eldric mumbled.

Tarian turned her to face him and took her cheeks in his hands. They bent together. She reached for the diamond chalice.

"I am so sorry, Daisy. I am so sorry that I dragged you here. That I forced you into this."

"You gave me a way to repay my family for everything they have done for me. This is the best way to go." She closed her hands over the diamond chalice and expected the kick. Instead, the white-hot power in her middle intensified. Strength filled her. The magical currents in the room flowed perfectly naturally.

"Understanding the magic has changed the way you interact with it," Eldric said, watching her. "You welcome it now, whereas before you surely opposed it. The chalice has the power to negatively react."

That part of things had always been unconscious.

She stood, and Tarian with her, his thumbs stroking the bottom of her chin.

"Okay, Tarianthiel." Eldric's finger traced a line across his scroll. "You know what to do. Enact the chalice. Goodbye, human. It has been as pleasurable as I'm sure one of your kind can be."

"I love you," Tarian said, and a tear slipped down his cheek as magic gushed into her.

It was unlike anything she'd ever experienced. There were no words. No way she could've prepared. No way she could see her way out of it. If she'd thought she might survive, she knew now why the scrolls said she wouldn't.

The magic was like a tidal wave. It swept her up and ripped her along, turning her end over end, spinning her around. The might of it submerged her, stole her breath, and pressed on her lungs. It blistered across her skin and ate down through her, acid on her bones, poison to her blood. If she was screaming, she couldn't hear it. Standing? She couldn't feel it. In this bubble, this vacuum of unimaginable pain, all she knew was the mountain of magic she was buried beneath. Its weight grew and grew, tearing her apart. And still her middle throbbed. The diamond chalice was there, always there, feeding more magic into her. Crushing her bones into dust. Giving her an out. All she had to do was reach for it and she could end this. She could stop this tumult. The agony. Her death.

If she could just reach it...

Chapter Thirty-Six

Lexi

Kieran's air magic tore down the door within the large archway in one of the castle entrances. Souls surrounded her, but not the one she wanted. Not her kid.

"Hey, you!" She stopped at the first spirit she saw. Lightning crawled the walls around them. Rocks rolled down the hallway, ready for action. Kieran stopped beside her, looking at the slight man with a plethora of jewels adorning a strangely styled jacket. "Have you seen the human they brought here?"

The man looked behind him.

"Yes, I can see you. Have you seen the human they brought here? To the castle. Where might I find the human?"

"Oh. Yes," the spirit said, still incredibly surprised.

"The human. I remember seeing that human. Very little—"

"*Where?*" Lexi yelled.

His face closed down into a mask of pompous indifference. Before he could respond, Kieran stepped into his face.

"You will tell me where you saw that human," he demanded, and the spirit's face went slack.

In a moment they were running, following the spirit, who was suddenly feeling very helpful. Kieran did have a way with unvoiced threats.

The halls seemed empty for a castle and kingdom of its size. What must've been servants up the way stopped in their tracks when they saw the rocks and people running. Their eyes widened at the lightning, and then they scattered out of the way.

Farther in and another ghost joined them, this one higher in status and laden with so many jewels that they would've torn off his jacket in life. He kept pace with the first until he learned what was going on, and then he turned and put up his hands as though he were about to do magic.

"Nope." Lexi grabbed him up and kept hold. If they happened across a body, she'd have a powerful spirit to fill it with.

"Unhand me!" the spirit yelled as the first slowed.

"What is it?" Lexi asked their leader.

"Well..." He pointed at an archway.

The doors stood open, and Boman and Donovan rushed forward to check it out.

"Looks like a hall of some sort—" Boman started.

"It's the Court Hall—" said the spirit.

"Do you feel that?" Mordecai asked, looking right. He put up his finger as though he were testing the direction of the breeze.

"You do not belong here, you vile humans!" the spirit she held yelled.

"After this, I do not know where she might be," their spirit leader said apologetically.

A fae male spirit popped out through the doors of the hall, his expression curious. "More humans?"

"There." Lexi flung her finger at the fae. "Kieran, he knows about Daisy."

"I smell her." Mordecai ripped at his clothes. "I smell her!"

Mordecai shifted into his wolf form as a female servant edged around the corner. She had dark, lank hair draping either side of a pinched face and a dainty frame. Her movements were much too graceful compared to the other servants scurrying around, and the way she held herself, as though playing up her stature, reminded Lexi of Daisy. This female was probably just as devastating in a fight.

The petite woman put up her hand, pointing down the hall. Mordecai was already running.

"Go, go, go!" Lexi dragged the one spirit behind her, making him bob on the ground as he went. It wouldn't hurt him, but manhandling was incredibly degrading and annoying to his kind. It was the little things.

That same female was up the way, at the corner,

pointing. The soul was the same. Did they have Apporter magic in this place?

Then again, another corner farther along. That female was creepy as fuck.

"Did you see her eyes?" Zorn asked from somewhere behind.

"No, why—"

Bria cut off as a strange throb changed the pressure in the air. The walls seemed to bow. A great heaviness filled the corridor and pressed on Lexi from all sides.

"What is that?" Henry shouted from behind.

A breeze Lexi couldn't feel externally swirled her insides. The lighting flickered. The walls waved, pushing out and leaning back in. The floor looked like the wood had turned into waves.

"Magic," someone said, out of breath.

It did feel like magic. Like something present but unidentifiable. It felt like the wylds after one of those magical, tropical rains. It felt like a lightning storm, but without the bolts of lightning. It felt like death and rebirth all rolled into one.

Mordecai whimpered and ran faster. He'd always had a sixth sense when it came to Daisy. Since the moment she'd entered their world all those years ago, Mordecai had always kept track of her. Been there for her. Supported her.

Right now, he was worried about her, and that meant, despite the odds, she had something to do with this.

Lexi put on a burst of speed. She gave everything she had, following Mordecai. He wasn't even sniffing anymore, just running with all his heart. Running blindly toward his sister.

The ground shook, but it wasn't the magic from earlier. She could feel the tides, this place surrounded by water and Kieran having control. He was bringing up the currents in case he needed them. Filling the air. Fae thought they were so far above humans, but they didn't know dick about Demigods. They were about to get an education, just like all the fae before them.

Mordecai turned a corner and skidded to the side. Lexi saw why. A cluster of well-organized individuals guarded a plain door in the plain, somewhat small hallway. Hair wild, they all had buns or knots on top of their heads, braids every which way, and flowing hair down their backs and some over their shoulders. They wore plain servants' attire but stood with weapons like they'd been born to them. The guard.

"Get out of the way and we won't kill you," Lexi said in a loud, clear voice. She wasn't sure if she was lying. That seemed like the fastest approach.

Her crew came up behind, breathing hard as they caught up. They filed in around her as Mordecai whimpered. They didn't have much time.

"What are you?" a female asked, stepping to the front of the others.

Lexi continued forward. "Your ticket to the underworld if you don't move out of my way. I've come for the human. I will be taking her with me. Fight or move. Choose now."

A male stepped up with the female. He put his large

hand on the female's shoulder. He had wheat-blond hair and a bunch of shit tying his beard tightly to his chin. He almost looked like a Viking who'd lost a bet with a hairstylist.

"What are you to her?" the male asked.

"They're human," someone else said.

"She chose this." Another female stepped up, redheaded, tall, and very fierce. "Daisy chose this. She is helping save Faerie."

"She doesn't give two fucks about Faerie," Amber said from the back, and it was surprising that she would speak up. Or maybe not, since she'd always had a soft spot for Daisy. "She'd burn this place to the ground if she could. Get out of the fucking way or I will gut you."

The female put up her hands, palms out. She had a big smile for some reason. "You know her well. You must be this family she speaks of. I shouldn't be surprised that you survived the fringe and the wylds and have come to her rescue. I am...but I shouldn't be. She has already burned several royal chambers, with our help. And you're right, she mostly doesn't care about us. But she does care about her family. You. She is helping you and your kind. She is balancing the magic of Faerie and strengthening the fringe. She alone has the power to do this. She *chose* this."

The Viking said, "She's playing hero." Then he sang in a monotone voice, "Na-na-na-na-na."

Mordecai bristled. Lexi looked over at Kieran with wide eyes. That was definitely Daisy, and it sounded like they knew her well enough to know who her family was and the type of things she said.

"Chose *what*?" Lexi demanded, walking closer. She reached out and grabbed hold of a few spirit boxes, ready to rattle them if needed and easily kill them if necessary.

"Chose to sacrifice herself," the female said, losing her smile. "For you."

Emotion welled up unexpectedly. "No," Lexi said. "She doesn't have magic. She only has a Demigod's gift. My gift. That's it—"

"She has Faerie magic," the Viking said. "Or...the magic Faerie gods gift one human at a time. Your magic was the final piece."

"What?"

"A non-magical human, enhanced by man—"

The female pointed at their group. "Her trainer. Zorb."

"Zorn," another male said. "She was always repeating his teachings."

"Right, yes. Zorn." The Viking nodded. "Ah. And that is...you, then?"

Zorn stepped up beside Lexi, his machete clutched in a tight fist. The pressure in the hallway increased. A strange sound reverberated through the door.

"A non-magical human enhanced by man—Zorn's training—and blessed by the gods." The Viking pointed at Lexi. "Your blood gift. You were the final piece to create the chalice. That thing she touched and made her fall over? The items that lit up in her presence? Those are chalices. And through your...help, she is saving our realm, and indirectly your realm as well."

"No," Lexi said, her knees feeling weak. She remembered that diamond thing. The other items lighting up. "But—"

A familiar scream tore through her thoughts. She lost all sense of reason.

She was running for the door. Everyone in her way wilted, hitting the ground with screams of their own. She didn't kill them. They knew Daisy and held no animosity toward her. That meant Daisy must've liked them, or she would've made their lives a living hell.

She reached the door, but a big man was blocking the way, grabbing his chest and rolling from side to side.

"Move!" she shouted, shoving at the door over his wilted form.

The scream cut off. Kieran bent on one side for the male and Zorn was on the other. Lexi had to push back to give them room, and then they were clear, opening the way. Zorn got in first, Lexi right behind.

"No, Daisy—" A guy knelt on the ground. His face was buried in Daisy's neck, his arms wrapped around her tightly. "Wait for me. I won't stay here long without you. Please."

Daisy lay still, her eyes closed, her face relaxed.

"Oh no, Daisy." Lexi called up the veil. It blazed to the right, more iridescent than in the human realm but doing the same thing. Within it, that male from before— that god—stood with his hands crossed over his chest and a smug smile below gleaming violet eyes. Behind him,

K.F. Breene

dimming, was Daisy's back as she walked through. She had succumbed to the siren call of the afterlife. Or, more likely, the god had sent her on her way, erasing any hesitancy to cross. "No! Daisy! Come back. I can fix this. Don't leave your body. We can fix this!"

"She's mine now," the god said.

She fixed him with a hard glare, kicking the chalices out of her way as she went to the fae holding Daisy's body.

"She's not yours," she told the god. "She might be in your house, but she is not *yours*. If I have to walk in there with you, I will fight her back out, you miserable sonuvabitch. Now fuck off and let me work."

She used a gush of her power to shove the veil away. He could've forced the issue, but he didn't. Maybe he wasn't all that invested when she wasn't messing with spirit. Good.

The fae male hadn't looked up. He clutched Daisy's body so damn tightly, breathing so heavily into her that it looked like he was on the verge of breaking. His emotion was genuine. And suddenly, Daisy's willingness to help made a lot more sense. Love made a person do a lot of stupid shit.

But he was in the way.

Lexi grabbed him by his hair and yanked him back.

His blast of magic nearly made her black out. She reacted, as did Kieran, two streams of magic fighting his. It almost wasn't enough. This fucker was *powerful*.

Zorn didn't care. He muscled his way in, grabbed the fae, and ripped him away. Bloody gashes tore lumps of

406

skin from Zorn's arms and chest, but he didn't so much as flinch.

"If you value Daisy's life, you will let Alexis work," Zorn growled.

The fae stilled, confused, reddened eyes blinking. His hair was mussed, and his face was the picture of agony. Worse, his gaze was hollow. He'd just watched— maybe helped—someone he loved die.

She would not be gone forever.

No time for sobbing, Lexi pushed up her sleeves and bent beside her kid.

"What did she die of?" she barked, feeling the spirit box with her magic. All the prongs that were needed to hold the soul in place had been shattered. Daisy never did do anything by halves.

Her body wasn't cold yet, though. It wasn't beyond use. If they could heal her body and fix some of the prongs, using spirit to patch everything together, they could keep Daisy alive.

They needed that soul, though. She couldn't cling to life without her soul.

"What did she—" Lexi cut off as a plethora of thoughts and images rolled through her head, so fast she almost didn't grasp them. Then she *saw*, through the fae's mind, his thoughts, his feelings. She saw the whole thing —the pain, the magic, the amount of sheer power that had gone through her kid's body. It had fried Daisy and evac- uated the soul. But the magic hadn't lingered. It hadn't stayed. It had blasted through, like electricity looking for ground. She needed to be jump-started. Her heart, it needed to be—

"Faelynn!" the fae yelled, command in his voice.

A female ran in on shaky limbs and with a deathly pale face. She hadn't gotten over the fright from Lexi's magic. That was pretty common the first couple times.

"She's a healer," the fae said. "She can help."

Kieran took Lexi by the shoulders. "You focus on those prongs and the soul. You need to pull her back and get her soul in this body. If she's gone too long, the body won't be able to repair. I'll work on her heart."

Tears dripping from her eyes, she moved to Daisy's feet and bowed her head. She worked those prongs, rebuilding, and got ready to call Daisy back over the line. She got ready to fight her way through that guy standing in the way. She could do this. She *had* to do this.

Chapter Thirty-Seven

Daisy

The colors around her were so calm and tranquil. Comforting. She felt...at peace in a way she never could remember before.

She moved through the space, like walking in a meadow at dawn.

Dawn...

Why did that ring a bell?

She couldn't really remember. Wasn't exactly troubled to think about it. This felt right, this place. She belonged here. She felt that.

She closed her eyes, kind of a weird idea, since she didn't actually have a body, and prepared to drift away. To roll with the winds of time and the fluctuations of forever. To exist but not. The afterlife really wasn't so bad.

"Hey."

A man leaned against a doorframe in a place where doors weren't present. For some reason, that didn't seem odd. He looked vaguely familiar but also like he didn't belong here. His magic was all wrong for this place. Foreign.

"Wow, when you give in to something, you really go all in, huh?" he said, wearing a smirk. His eyes narrowed as he looked closer. "Ah. Yeah, gods are tricky. We can help a spirit find peace, whether they like it or not. But you took it and ran. There are no halvsies with you. Now I get why you all but threw your panties at that fae. Don't get me wrong, he is hot as fuck, isn't he? A wet dream walking. But I expected you to give him more guff at the start." He shrugged. "Why resist when they are that bangable? I get it. I've been known to make a bad decision now and again when it comes to pretty partners. They wrote a whole fucking myth about it. I can't seem to live it down."

Strange feelings vied for attention. Strange memories, pulling at a heart she'd left behind. Pulling at her very core and squishing out sadness. Loss.

A moment of panic snapped her out of her peaceful state, grasping at a memory that wouldn't quite form. A need not realized. This place seemed *off*. Not right. She shouldn't be here. She couldn't—

"*Shh, shh,*" the man said, putting out a hand. A wave of peacefulness again enveloped her, washing away the panic. "You'll never remember things like that. Not here. Let's get you in the right headspace. How's this?"

The strange plane turned into her bedroom near the dual-society zone line. Her computer was aglow with squares of imagery, cameras picking up the beautiful day and cultivated yard. She sat on her bed with the man in a chair near the window, lounging like he'd been there all his life. His ankle was crossed over his knee, and he wore jeans and a button-up.

The familiar setting eased her, and she took in his appearance. Late twenties and with clear blue eyes, he was a looker. He had slight bags under his eyes and tousled hair. He almost looked like James Dean, an appearance he could choose.

"Hades," she said, bouncing on the bed. It felt normal. The temperature, the dust motes floating through the air—it all felt normal. Comfortable. She breathed a sigh of relief. "Why are you bothering me?"

She'd first seen him at the Demigod convention when everything went to hell. Since then, he'd hung around occasionally, working with Lexi and her magic. He liked to listen to the guys poking fun at Daisy and each other, but usually he didn't engage with Daisy directly. He was usually too enamored by Bria.

"Because you're a favorite of my favorite, why else?" He leaned back and stretched, yawning as he did. "I got an invitation here, did you know? These fae have their own god of the afterlife. It's a different sort of place than what I run, but it's okay. Too pretty for my tastes. With beings that are too...fucking arrogant, if I'm being honest. It's like hanging out with an entire race of Zeus wannabes. What. A. *Nightmare*."

She struggled to make sense of what he was talking about. She felt so...tired. So ready to rest eternally.

"Why'd you get an invitation?" she asked.

"Because you lot are very entertaining. Lexi is, as we all know, and now you? The gods here are placing bets and undermining each other. It's great sport. But"—he leaned forward—"I have a little skin in the game myself. I couldn't help myself. If I lose, I have to be a toy. They didn't specify what that meant." He gave her a deadpan look. "It's a fuck-toy, isn't it." It was a statement more than a question. "They essentially want to make me a fuck-toy for a while." He lifted his eyebrows but leaned back. "So we obviously can't have that. I like to call the shots, not the other way around. If I win, I get to abduct the god of my choosing and keep her for a while. That is also code for a fuck-toy, just so we're on the same page. I already got her all picked out."

Daisy's eyebrows settled low. "You guys have problems."

"I'm well aware. But eternity gets boring, so you need to live on the edge. Anyway, where are you going?"

She looked around in confusion. Nowhere. This was home.

Wasn't it?

It no longer felt like home. It felt like a memory.

The snap drew her focus. Hades waited for her to look at him before speaking. "Lexi came for you, did you know?"

Confusion bled into her again.

He nodded. "She isn't the type of woman to let a

different realm stop her from protecting her own. I hear she got you into this mess. Well, magic comes at a price, kid. Now you know. She didn't have it easy either. Know what I mean? But if you listen real hard, you might find that taking an eternal nap might not be the right choice."

A voice echoed in the sudden darkness. Her room had cleared away into a strange violet field. Hades was back to leaning on a doorframe that wasn't there. That voice reverberated all around her. Called her name. Offered her comfort.

Lexi.

"She...came for me?" The shroud of confusion started to lift. Memories of her life filtered in. Panic threatened, pulling at her. Turning her in circles. She knew where she was. Feared the unknown of it.

Daisy...

That voice was so familiar. So comforting. More so than the call of eternity. Than peaceful sleep. That voice was home. It was love. It was life.

She was rising without knowing where she was going. Without knowing how she was doing it. Hades rose with her.

"She's being cock-blocked," Hades told her. "The god of this place had a big bet that once you crossed into his domain, he'd keep you put. He knows what magic she has, see, and he's swinging his dick around. She's fighting him about it, hence her voice getting through, but he's got more power. You've got to do your part. Help her, help you. Go back to that dreamboat of a fae. Come on, kid. I am not interested in being a bored god's fuck-toy." He jerked his head right and tensed. "I gotta go. I'm cheating pretty badly right now, and soon I'll get found out. Do me proud, kid. You've got some of my magic, after all. You've been initiated into the troublemaker clan. Make your own rules."

With that he was gone, and she was left floating in nothingness.

Daisy...

~

Lexi

"I feel her." Sweat ran down the sides of Lexi's face. She didn't dare look at Kieran and the healer fae's efforts. She didn't dare look at Daisy's deathly pale skin, cooling to the touch. "That fucking bastard keeps blocking my attempt to grab her, though. I need more power."

"Here." The male fae picked up one of the items at his feet.

"No, no!" Another fae, much older and with jewels or something in his gray hair, hurried forward. "No, those are the wrong chalices for her. She's spirit, right? Here." He held out two items with a glowing amethyst hue within their depths. "These are the most powerful of the spirit chalices. They'll give you more power—until the little human's magic completely fades away..."

She took the objects and ignored his words. She didn't know about the magic, but Daisy would not fade away. Lexi would break through in time. She *would*. The prongs were nearly rebuilt. A little bit more and they would hold. The body just needed a soul.

"Push your power through it and pull it back into you before using it how you normally would," the younger male said.

That sounded confusing, but when she tried it, the magic ballooned. "Awesome," she muttered, pushing hard into the chalices and blasting into that spirit realm.

Daisy, she called through spirit, reaching out. The pull deadened, but she tried again, and again, shoving back at that god. *Daisy!*

The feeling of her kid intensified. Pulsed. Lexi squeezed her eyes tight, drew as much power as she could, and pushed harder. Gave it everything she had.

DAISY!

The feeling of Daisy was like an inferno barreling through the spirit. Once it had a direction, it incinerated everything in its way. The god turned, startled. Lexi used the opportunity to work around him, slink past him, and then she was reaching into spirit, grabbing up her kid, and pulling her home.

"Hang on," she said through gritted teeth as that god tried to sever the bond. "Hang on to me, Daisy. Don't let go."

"She won't," the male said, his voice confident, his tone infused with hope. "She won't let go. If she wants to come back, no one will stop her, not a god of the afterlife or the creator herself."

Lexi resisted the god's attempt. She kept power

pumping through those items and gasped when they got stronger. Hummed harder. It was as if Daisy's soul getting closer gave them more power.

Something pulsed. Magic, it felt like. A surge of magic.

Lexi peeled her eyes open, sighting in on the pretty item that had knocked Daisy down in the human world. The fae male followed her gaze, his hands clutching Daisy's. He released one and grabbed the item, pulling it closer and putting it to Daisy's palm.

The pulse sounded again. And again. Lexi got the illusion of heat and light pulsing through spirit, following the line connecting Lexi and Daisy.

Magic flowed over that connection. Traveled along it. Strengthened it and then slammed into Daisy. The god bellowed, frustrated, and Lexi could just barely feel Hades behind him, sporting a shit-eating grin.

What the hell was *Hades* doing in this realm?

Didn't matter.

Lexi reeled Daisy in, grunting from the effort. The pretty item pulsed. The feeling of light and heat intensified, and then Daisy stepped out of the veil. She wore a flowing satin dress, the same material that was pooled on the floor near the door. A cape billowed behind her in the spirit wind, and her gaze found Lexi. Her eyes shone with determination and pride.

"No one cock-blocks my mom-type," Daisy said.

"Mom-type?" Lexi replied with a wry grin.

"You're too young to be my actual mom. There'd be all sorts of questions. I've told you that." Daisy stopped beside her body, but she wasn't looking down at herself. She was looking at the handsome fae who knelt beside her, holding the pretty item to her palm. He looked at Lexi urgently, wondering what was going on.

"I hear your thoughts. I know what is going on," he said. "Come back to me, Daisy. Please. Let her fix you. Let them all fix you. I'll find a way to stay in this life if you'll come back to me."

"I apologize to you, Lexi," Daisy said, kneeling. She didn't reach out to touch the fae. She'd heard Lexi telling ghosts not to touch the living often enough.

"What for?" Lexi asked through tears. She tried to close the veil, but the god was not having it. He looked out with a glower.

"For giving you a bunch of shit about Kieran in the beginning. I get it now. I chose this fae despite everything." She held out a finger. "I'm swearing because you can't physically punch me in the face. Besides, I've earned it at this point."

"Daisy, get in your fucking body," Kieran barked, and thunder boomed around the castle. "You'll have time enough to eat crow when you're back in the world of the living."

Startled, Daisy grinned and shook her head, at a loss. "What do I do, just...like...lie down in it? Fuck, this is the worst. I'm a ghost. I *hate* ghosts."

Lexi didn't waste any time. She stuffed Daisy in and started working those prongs.

"She needs her body to live now," she said. "I can manage the soul, especially since she is holding on tightly, but I need that body to keep going or it'll just evacuate her again."

"Oh yeah?" the god said. "Maybe you need a distraction."

"Shit, Lexi," Hades called from somewhere behind the god. "Shouldn't have said that. These fae hardcore cheat. He's—yup, he's getting an army of undead brewing. You better hurry the fuck up."

Chapter Thirty-Eight

LEXI

"We got company!" Lexi yelled, not moving. Not even looking away from Daisy. Instead, she started using her increased power to pull her spirit people to her. They were in that mishmash of fae spirit, with the strange magic and odd storms, but she had figured out enough to learn the lay of the land. She used that now, since the god blocking her way was currently busy.

"Lexi, are you animating these cadavers?" Bria called in. "I really hope so, because their power feels intense."

"Fuck," Lexi muttered, working on those prongs. She would not leave her kid. They were so close. "Bria, get active. Get those spirits out of those cadavers!" she yelled. "What's the story with Daisy's body?" she asked Faelynn and Kieran.

"She's close," the female fae said, sweat beading her

brow. She held one of the items—a chalice. It glowed in her hand. "The body suffered extensive magical trauma and has been shut down for a long time, but she's coming along. She's coming back."

"I'm trying to will myself, for what good that'll do," Daisy's spirit said, holding on.

The prongs of her soul kept breaking, the body trying to give up and get her out. Lexi fixed first one, then the other, docking her tightly and putting as much spirit into the prongs as she could.

"Jack!" Kieran yelled, pumping Daisy's chest to get her heart working. They were moving toward the red line. Healing her needed to happen now.

Jack jogged in, his eyes tight. "Yes, sir?"

"Take over." Kieran jerked his head to bring Jack over. "I'm needed out there."

"Of course." Jack kicked the other chalices out of the way and slid in beside Daisy. His hand moved in as Kieran's moved away. "Come on, Gremlin," he murmured through clenched teeth. "Come on. You don't die, remember? You don't get saved. You save yourself. *Save yourself.*"

"Can you tell him that that is very unhelpful right now?" Daisy drawled. "I don't have hands with which to pump my own heart."

Lexi repeated it, and the handsome fae at Daisy's side looked at Lexi hard. "You can actually hear spirits?"

"Don't you start," she muttered as Jack pumped and Faelynn did...whatever it was she was doing.

"It is not uncommon to hear spirits," the old fae in the

room said, looking on. "But repairing the body to accept the soul...that *is* uncommon. How very interesting. I have so many questions."

"He's like a smart version of Frank," Lexi mumbled. "Equally as annoying."

"I heard that!" Frank said from just outside the door. He'd definitely run away from that god the first time and was now keeping his distance.

"Come on, Gremlin," Jack pushed, bending to blow air into Daisy's mouth. "Come on. Don't stay a spirit. It is not fun. You'll hate it."

"Also not fucking helpful," Daisy said, which Lexi repeated, minus the swear. Daisy chuckled.

A grin worked up Jack's face. "She's got fight. She can do this. Just hang on, Daisy. That was my problem. I didn't hang on long enough. Lexi will fix you. Just hang in there."

"It's Faelynn we need," Lexi said as yells rang through the halls. "Fuck." She was needed out there. An army of undead required a Spirit Walker. "What the fuck is up with that god? Usually they are happy to have their people live. Mine is ecstatic I can save people as well as kill."

"These gods aren't like yours, and fae aren't like people," the handsome male said. "The gods here are using me for sport in their mundane existence. And now...they are using you as well."

"As the gods will it," the older male said.

"You should go, Tarian," Faelynn told the handsome male. "You're needed there more than here."

He leaned down and put his forehead to Daisy's. His eyes closed tightly, his words whispered but impassioned. Urgent. "C'mon, little dove. Fight your way back to me. Back to your family."

"This isn't the time, and I know that, but we've got a score to settle regarding her," Jack told the fae—Tarian.

"She won't let you settle that score," Tarian told Jack without moving away from Daisy. "We'll just have to ask forgiveness rather than permission."

"I can fucking hear you," Daisy groused. Lexi didn't bother repeating that.

"Hack up those bodies!" Bria yelled. "Hack them all up. Now is not the time for a weak stomach, *Jerry*. Get in there!"

Mia popped out from behind the veil, followed by John.

"Go!" Lexi shouted. "Help with the spirits coming our way."

They didn't need to be told twice. Mia disappeared, and John ran for the door.

Daisy's body gasped. She started coughing, and Tarian cupped her cheeks, nearly knocking Faelynn out of the way.

"*Wait*, Tarian," Faelynn scolded him. "She's not out of danger yet. Back off."

To his credit, Tarian did, giving her space, though his eyes didn't leave Daisy's. He cared about her very much. Very, very much. Lexi's heart softened.

Daisy coughed and clutched the pretty item held

against her palm. She pulled it tightly to her chest before reaching back for Tarian's hand.

"That's it," Jack said, backing off now. "There you go."

Magic pumped—Lexi could feel it. She wasn't sure if it was spirit or in the air around them, but she could feel it building higher. The items all around them started to pulse. They hummed in waves, a throbbing sound.

"No, what are you doing?" Tarian sounded panicked. "You didn't survive it the first time."

"Trust me," Daisy wheezed, and they stared at each other for a long moment.

He nodded, as if she'd said something else. Reading her mind. She seemed to be okay with that.

She closed her eyes, and that strange current moved around them. It was so like the feeling of spirit that Lexi wondered why she couldn't see it.

"We've got it," Faelynn said with a smile. "She learns fast. Thank the gods she learns fast."

"Yes, she is very astute for their kind—" Eldric intoned.

"Fuck your gods," Daisy interrupted, laboring through a scratchy throat.

Tarian laughed and brought her hand up before turning it over and kissing her pulse point. He breathed an immense sigh of relief against her skin. It must've been an inside joke, though Lexi didn't see the humor in it. She wholeheartedly agreed. Tarian laughed harder.

〜

Tarian

I feel like I've been chewed up by a darkrend and spat out again, Daisy thought. *Fuck.*

She cataloged her issues, from her body and head aching to her limbs feeling like they were numb and tingly.

But she was alive. She was fucking *alive*! Tarian couldn't believe it. He couldn't be more grateful. Somehow, Daisy's human guardian had worked spirit in a way he'd never heard of. She'd even ripped her out of Nvram's clutches.

I'm not in any shape for what fuckery is going on out there, she thought, and he couldn't help chuckling despite the situation. She'd just returned from the dead, and she was still as surly as ever. She was still his little dove, delicate and beautiful and a vicious killer. Perfection.

Her family and Tarian's *Fallen* yelled directions and warnings at each other out in the hall. They weren't working together. Tarian needed to unite them, or Daisy's rescue would be in vain.

"Okay, let's go." She struggled to sit up.

"Not yet. You aren't healed enough yet—" Faelynn started.

"Her soul will hold." Daisy's guardian—the angel of the stars—sat back and wiped sweat from her forehead. Lexi, they called her. Alexis, maybe for him, given he was a stranger. Her gaze was watery, but she appeared relieved.

"Why did you come for me?" Daisy demanded. "It's dangerous here. You shouldn't have done that!"

That was supposed to come out angry. Her mind pinged with anger, anyway. She'd thought she was the weakest link in their family. She hated to think they'd put themselves in danger for her. Instead, her tone was heavy with emotion. Love that filled her whole body.

I'll forever be grateful, she thought, looking upon Alexis. *Grateful for my family's extreme power that helped them survive getting here, and for giving me my second miracle. For reuniting me with Tarian. For giving us a chance to stay together.*

Now it was Tarian's heart that filled his whole body. He held her hand tightly, barely stopping himself from pulling her into his arms. She needed to speak to her guardian angel right now.

"Don't be a fucking idiot," Alexis told her as a tear overflowed. He barked out an unexpected laugh. Yes, they were family. "Of course we were going to come for you. We will always come for you."

"I owe you a punch in the face for swearing," Daisy rasped, laughing.

"Do as I say, not as I do." Alexis reached forward to grab Daisy's hands, and Tarian let her. She helped her up. "Jack, can you carry her—"

"I've got it." Tarian scooped her up and stood, hugging her close. He looked down at Alexis, ignoring... Jack, his name was, looming close. Thoughts of vicious actions filtered through Jack's mind. They were justified, so Tarian didn't pay them any attention.

"Thank you," he told Alexis. "For saving her. I know you didn't do it for me, but thank you all the same."

Daisy tapped him. "I'm fine. Kieran needs your help—"

"Thane, go active!" Kieran yelled from the hall.

Daisy startled, and Alexis jumped up.

"Thane is..." Daisy let the pure, absolute destruction that was Thane play through her head. He seemed like a darkrend in human form but without the direction. Without a shred of control.

Tarian started to jog toward the hall, but Alexis grabbed his shoulder and turned him. She put her finger in his face, and her eyes flashed. "You keep her alive, do you hear me? As a gift to her, I am not killing you, but if I suspect your ill intentions for one moment, I'll rip out your soul, stuff it back in, and make you dance."

It's her favorite threat, Daisy told him. *Also, she will do that.*

He didn't need to be told. Various examples of her doing just that flashed through her mind.

She's scary as hell, Faelynn thought. Tarian had to agree. Daisy had always been in good company. This crew of magical humans seemed more feral than the rest. More unhinged, and a lot closer and more trusting with each other.

He liked them immediately. He could tell Faelynn did, as well.

"Keep...her...*alive,*" Alexis told Tarian.

"With pleasure, ma'am." He jogged toward the hall, not putting Daisy down. His *Fallen* had their weapons and were hacking at the dead bodies one of their crew had brought in. A woman named...Bria was on the ground, with smoking items and bells, trying to control any spirits left in the bodies. He was fascinated, but he didn't have time to dally.

"Good to see you, Daisy," a fierce-eyed woman said. Amber. Concentration and relief flowed over her face. Her gaze slid to Tarian. "Fuck you, fae."

Fair.

"You won't be a favorite for a while," Daisy told him, trying to get out of his arms.

"You're not well enough to fight." He firmed up his hold. "How much can I trust your people to lead and look after my *Fallen*?"

"Tell them to follow Kieran's lead to the letter. He won't forsake them. He has his people well in hand when it comes to danger."

Tarian didn't need to be told twice. He trusted her, and if she trusted him, so be it. He walked forward, and his *Fallen* fell in behind him.

"Good to have you back," Lennox told her.

Kayla winked.

"We're fighting our way out of here," Kieran called back as the Berserker transformed up in front of them. His body grew and bulged with muscle. In a moment, he gave a mighty roar before his feet thumped against the wooden floor, and he was off. Tarian stalled, never having seen anything like it.

It was then he could see the hallway stuffed with dead bodies animated with spirits. The magic Daisy had helped balance had killed those too far gone to recover. Nvram had used them for his army of the dead.

Cheating piece of shit, Daisy thought softly.

"We can get through this," Tarian said, pushing past...Boman, Donovan, and Jack.

Knives flew through the air, many bouncing off the Berserker. They didn't seem to stick. Bad throws? He bowled into the cadavers, knocking their lines askew and tearing limbs from bodies.

Holy shit, Lennox murmured. Tarian had to agree. He'd heard of those types of magical humans, but he'd never seen any in action. They were...something else. Fun to watch.

Alexis ran that way, her hands up. Bodies fell to the ground in front of her. Daisy had made mention of her ripping souls from bodies. It was more effective than Tarian had ever seen.

Fucking hell, Niall muttered, and Tarian had to agree with that as well.

Demigod Kieran lifted his hands, and a blast of air filled the hallway. Any bodies still standing were shoved backward, giving everyone more time.

That wasn't all, though.

The ground shook. The walls trembled. Water burst in through the windows, flowed out through doors, and took on a life of its own. It gathered and tumbled, a growing wave controlled by Kieran. He was a Demigod of the sea, but...this was beyond what a human should be capable of. Wasn't it?

"That...is not possible," Tarian said softly.

"Ha!" Daisy pointed at his face. "Shoe is on the other foot now!"

Tarian squeezed her, glancing back at his *Fallen* with wide eyes. Their surprise showed on their faces. He faced forward again and started jogging to keep up with those in front. Zorn was there, ready with a machete, but the Berserker, Alexis, and Kieran were handling it, beating the bodies back. Spirits didn't have the power of the living, even here. Kieran and Alexis showed they were plenty strong enough to deal with what the god of the afterlife had thrown at them.

"What's the plan?" Kayla called up.

Tarian shook his head as they turned a corner up ahead. "Follow their lead to get out of here, regroup in the wylds, and choose our next steps."

Daisy tightened her hold around his neck. "Your next steps better include me. I'm not leaving you."

He looked at her. Love and adoration shone in her eyes. In his eyes, he knew. "Your mom-type gave you the gift of rebirth. I will not ruin that for you. I will do what needs to be done, and you will go safely back to the human world. It's been fortified. You'll be safe there. The rest of Faerie is up to me—"

He cut off as everything changed. As the yells and shouts of the Berserker, the rush of the water, and the clang of weapons all died away. The castle halls disintegrated into a world of white marble. Grand architecture reminiscent of an ancient temple rose up in columns and elegant details around them. Statues and reliefs were visible throughout.

They stood on a large marble floor in the middle. Daisy's family and Tarian's *Fallen* stood behind them, looking around warily. The Berserker—Thane—had been returned to his normal state. In front of them, a wide set of stairs led up to a raised platform framed by columns and domes. Three large marble thrones each existed in their own alcove. Then two more thrones each, on the right and left, seven in all.

The breath left Tarian slowly, and he hugged Daisy to his chest.

"Where are we?" someone asked behind them.

"The white walls of the Divine Collective," someone answered in hushed tones. "The meeting place of the gods."

"Oh for fuck's sake," Daisy grumbled.

Chapter Thirty-Nine

DAISY

As one, the gods populated their thrones and chairs, noble beings with purple velvet robes and large crowns of glowing starshine. Each was larger than life, twenty feet tall or more, towering over the marble space with an omniscient presence.

"That one in the middle," Zorn whispered, pushing up closer to Daisy. He ignored Tarian's presence entirely. "I saw her as we crossed the Faegate. She was kind of translucent, huge, like she is there, and leaning over the wall, looking at us. Laughing."

"Yeah. They're a bunch of absolute fuckers," Daisy told him. "I'll explain everything later—if we're not gruesomely killed first."

He grunted and stepped away. That was good enough for him.

Tarian turned to glance over his shoulder at Zorn. *How likely is he to attempt to kill me in my sleep?*

Daisy snickered. *If you wrong me, very. Unless he can find a way around your power and torture you when you're awake. If you're nice to me, he'll forgive you. Eventually.*

That...I doubt.

The female on the throne in the very middle raised her hand in salute, and suddenly, the raised platform was right in front of them. The gods had reduced to normal fae size, if a bit on the tall and robust side, except for one. The female on the throne to the right of the middle stared at Daisy between strands of somewhat lank black hair. Her face was familiar, her posture and poise more so.

She was the female from the games. The one who had helped Daisy and killed herself in the process.

Daisy also recognized one of the two males. He was the god of the afterlife, his eyes shining with a violet hue and the flames gone. In fact, all of their eyes burned violet in their depths, marking what they were.

The god of the afterlife was looking past the others, appearing intrigued as he noticed Lexi.

"The crystal chalice, in the flesh," the middle god said, her voice everywhere and nowhere, in Daisy's head but out loud for everyone to hear. "Daisy, that is your name, correct?"

Daisy inclined her head. "Yes."

"Put her down, Tarianthiel. She is strong enough now." The female waved her hand.

In a blink, Daisy appeared beside him. She felt

refreshed, as though she hadn't just come back from the dead.

Tarian reached out his hand to her. She took it and scooted closer, glancing behind to make sure her family and his were all intact.

"Well, I am impressed." The female smiled at Daisy. "Call me Equilas, child. As I was saying, I am impressed. We have known all the crystal chalices, of course. Even if they were never discovered, and most were not. Hardly any ever learned their magic. They didn't have a guide, like you did. So few ever realized their true potential. Their inherent power. None, not one, has ever survived the magic they were able to boost. Until now."

Elbow braced on the arm of her throne, she leaned, bringing up her hand to partially cover her simpering smile.

"And this is the most power we have ever seen come out of a crystal chalice," she continued. "Isn't it?"

She turned to the others. All of them reacted in some way, to maybe lean, or sit back, or narrow their eyes in thought, but none answered the question.

"And that is because of the Ancestral Magic of Sevens." Her shining eyes switched to Tarian, and the violet within them glowed. "So much power. So much potential. So young and inexperienced. Your power should've protected you, but instead, it was the key to your downfall. It has been so interesting, watching jealousy and wariness and loss destabilize a kingdom that had never been so solid. It was about time someone shook it all up."

"Forgive me," Tarian said respectfully, "but how could you let things get so bad? The magic so twisted? The whole of the realm was suffering, leaking into the human realm. Scrolls said that, in ages past, that was enough for a war of the gods."

She turned to the female on her right. "I think he wants an explanation."

"*I* would want an explanation," another female said, looking around. "It has been an amusing distraction, but it certainly did go to extremes."

"Yes." Equilas looked at Tarian for some time before her gaze roamed to Daisy. "Are you not curious why your ink turned from the gold of your birth to that which you now wear?"

"I did wonder, yes. Eldric didn't know."

"I'm back here, Your Mightiness. I do admit, that was a glaring hole in my knowledge base. I—"

She waved her hand, silencing Eldric magically. Her gaze never left Tarian.

"Your birth was of great interest to the more romantic of us," Equilas said, and the god of the afterlife rolled his eyes and hunched in annoyance. Clearly, he wasn't one of them. "The moment you came into the world, Elysara *Saw* your fated match." Her gaze switched to Daisy, who froze. "Elysara is the Divine Seer, the youngest of the sisters."

The female to Equilas's left, her white-blond hair glowing as though made of stars, inclined her head. "It has been an age since a *Sight* has been so riveting. So wrapped in love and loss, feast and famine. A tale of torture and pleasure. And without an outcome! I *Saw* events as they *could* be, as they *might* be, but not as they *would* be."

"As you know, my task in this collective is to keep balance," Equilas said. "Your death would've been a natural return to that balance. You had too much power, Tarianthiel. You pulled too much at the tapestry of Faerie for the position you held. Taking the throne and mitigating your power in intervals would've worked. Your family knew that even though you did not. They knew the choice was your death...or your elevation to the Diamond Throne. For you, there were no other options. Even now. I think you know that."

He pulled Daisy closer still. He knew, and it was why he'd resigned to trade himself. Not for the gods' entertainment, but to protect his family. To protect his father.

She let go of his hand and wrapped her arms around his middle, her thoughts whirling. He covered her shoulders with his arm.

"So yes, your death would've relieved the pressure on the fabric of Faerie," the god continued. "But..."

"Your fated mate was to become the crystal chalice!" Elysara exclaimed, and Daisy's stomach filled with butterflies.

She looked up at Tarian in disbelief. He met her gaze and sudden understanding lit his eyes. His smile was just for her.

It wasn't the gods at all, he thought. *It was destiny.*

"Yes, that," the god went on. "And...well, you were always my favorite, Tarianthiel." Equilas smiled behind her fingers at him. "So dashing. So handsome. I'd thought to take you for myself..."

"Definitely not." Elysara glowered at her.

"He should've been mine," the god of the afterlife said. "He would've died fairly. He would've been a great favorite in my domain."

Elysara extended her hand toward Daisy. "And deny him that? And her that?"

"Anyway." Equilas dropped her hand. "It was thought you needed another chance to fulfill the *Sight*."

"And while they waited, they thought it would be fun to take bets on the outcome," the female with black hair said in obvious disdain.

"Would it kill you to have a little fun?" Elysara rolled her eyes.

"Half the Obsidian Court is dead," the other said. "The magic was so twisted by the end that it had taken on a life of its own."

"They would've been killed anyway." Equilas waved it away. "Plus, your obsidian prince still lives. He can take over. You liked him best anyway. I know you've dabbled with him." She lifted her eyebrows at her sister, who didn't respond.

Equilas smirked, returning her attention to Daisy and Tarian.

"But...what if I had failed?" Tarian asked.

"We would've handled it. We were monitoring you every step of the way—"

"And taking bets," Black Hair murmured.

"I have to admit..." The god of the afterlife scratched

his chin, back to looking at Lexi. "It was interesting there toward the end."

"So you see—" Equilas tried to continue.

"Long story *long*," the other male muttered.

Equilas sighed in annoyance. "*So you see*," she went on pointedly, "her markings are divine crystalline, as befits her station and her magic. Crystal holds energy. It boosts power. As her fated mate, Tarian, she gifts this great marking to you, the noblest in the realm."

"Her station?" Tarian asked guardedly.

"But of course. She is the prize of Faerie, child, chosen by the stars. Her magic grants her eternal life and the potential for godly power."

"A power that'll kill me," Daisy said.

The simpering smile was back. "Yes, that is the drawback. Eternal life doesn't go very far when the highest form of power ultimately kills. It keeps things fresh. But look, you have a resource to keep you alive. The very same creature who granted you the power in the first place. This whole journey has been so very interesting."

"Fascinating, definitely," the other male said.

"*That* is why your gold ink has turned to crystal," Elysara said with a beaming smile. "To correspond with your fated match. To proclaim yourselves to the world!"

Daisy's heart soared. It felt like it filled her whole person to bursting. She was glad it had turned out the way it had. Because of Tarian's dire situation, that in turn had affected her, they'd fallen in love the hard way. They'd had to deny their attraction as much as possible until they'd earned it. Until they'd learned to trust each other and depend on each other.

She'd go through it all again to end up at his side—and hate his gods just as much.

Tarian's thumb stroked Daisy's shoulder. It was a reminder that the gods weren't done with them yet. She could fall into this new information later. First they had to secure a future.

"You kept me alive so I could find my fated mate... only to kill her?" The tremor this time was in anger.

The other male chuckled. "With great love...comes great tragedy."

Elysara sighed dramatically. She leveled Tarian with a flat look. "It was the only way *some of us* would agree to see this out—"

"At the peril of Faerie," the god of the afterlife said.

"But if you proved yourself true," Elysara went on, "and used the power to do your duty as a prince, *future king*, and Guardian, then it was decided that she'd be returned to you."

"Yet that fucker tried to cock-block me to do just that," Lexi said angrily.

"Okay, okay." Hades materialized off to the side, his hands out. He glanced over his shoulder at the Faerie god of the afterlife. "Let's not piss him off and get me into a fight, okay?"

Daisy felt Tarian tense in confusion. She was damn surprised to see Hades, as well. And now she was damn glad for him. They hadn't needed these horrible gods to save her. They'd needed Lexi...with a little help from the god who had granted her the power.

"No, no. I enjoy her spunk." The god of the afterlife sat forward. "My children should be able to employ magic similarly to what she does, but none of them have figured it out. I'm intrigued."

Hades put out his hands. "I mean, I helped, hello? What am I going to do, leave all the tricks up to the humans to figure out? Half of the magic would go unused."

"The problem here is, he didn't think of it," Elysara said with a smirk. "It's not the *children* at all, is it, Nvran?"

He ignored her. "I would've returned her...after the prince had given up hope. That would've won me the bet. As it was, I think helping the humans counts as cheating."

"Oh ha! *Who* was cheating?" Elysara asked, outraged.

"Umm..." Nvran pointed at Black Hair. "Did she think we'd miss her in the games?"

"I didn't care if you did or you didn't," Black Hair spat. "All of you were cheating in one way or another. The chalice showed more promise than most of the fae. She didn't deserve any of this. Neither did the prince. I swear, if you'd spend more time amongst the star children, you wouldn't find such a need to torment them."

"Amongst them?" Equilas lifted her eyebrows. "Is that what you're calling it?"

A few of them snickered.

"Anyway." Equilas lowered her hand to the throne arm. "Tarian, you have a choice. You've always had a choice, and if the issue with your mother hadn't come to pass, I think you would've been given it. Will you be king of the Diamond Throne, or will you let Nvran take you to the afterlife? You have one chance. Choose wisely." She paused. "Choose to be king. You'd hate to waste all of this. All you've been through. You'd hate to lose her again."

Tarian looked down into Daisy's eyes. "She's human. What would become of her if I were king?"

"Weren't you listening? She is the crystal chalice, boy. Human or not, the crystal chalice is of high status in Faerie. We have made it so. She would be at your side as queen. You would use her magic in tandem with yours to be mightier still."

And when his back was turned, she'd forever be a target. Forever in danger. People would seek to use her or cut her down so his magic wasn't so indestructible. Besides, chalice or not, to fae, she'd always be just a human and would never fit in this world, just like a Chester didn't fit in magical San Francisco. If she were also in a position of authority, even as a figurehead, the grievance would be more insulting still. She'd never find a moment of peace. She felt that in her core.

If the gods heard any of that, they ignored it.

"You two can live happily ever after," Equilas went on, "or the chalice will watch her mate die. We wouldn't allow that clever human to bring him back."

"If I were to take the throne, what of my father?" Tarian asked. "My family?"

"Tarian," Equilas said in irritation, "your heart is bleeding all over your shoes. It's embarrassing. You know how a fae takes the throne."

Death, Tarian thought. *Treachery. I have already killed my mother. I'd now have to kill my father and any family that rise up to oppose me. I have many siblings. They will form alliances against me...and with me. We'd be a throne divided, as it is now. In turmoil. To end it would require bloodshed.*

That was always what he'd hoped to avoid. He'd just wanted to earn his place as prince and make his mother's sacrifice worth it. He didn't want to spit on her grave by causing more harm. Daisy knew all of that, knew him, without having to ask.

But the alternative was death...

"No." She tore her eyes away from him. Fuck that. Fuck these clowns. "I fulfilled my duty as the crystal chalice...and I lived. My family tore me from your clutches. We would've gotten out of that castle, and we would've gotten through the fringe. I don't owe you shit, and neither does he. We've danced to your tune, and we're done. Besides, the crystal chalice was always meant to be a thinking, rational, logical being—or as close as a human can get." She was quoting Eldric now. "The chalice was meant to be a being *not* of Faerie, without the pitfalls of life here." She paused to let that sink in. "*You* created those rules. I *have* to go back to the human lands...and he's coming with me. Here, he'd choose death anyway."

"Daisy..." Tarian said.

She held up her finger to him. "You abducted me against my will. Welcome to payback." She stared at Nvran. "The person—entity, whatever—that would lose out on this is you. He'd be a favorite in the afterlife, I realize that. I also realize your contrarian personality." She glanced to the side. "Hades, are you going to go along with this, or am I going to get Dylan to tell Zeus all the stuff you did on this side of the divide?"

Hades smirked. "Blackmail. Nice. I knew you were worthy of my magic."

She looked at Nvran but realized she would have to appeal to them all. "I want to make a deal."

Chapter Forty

Daisy

The equivalent of three human days later...

In the end, it wasn't Daisy who made the deal. It was mostly Kieran, with insightful input from Amber, two people who had studied under Valens and had to make deals with Demigods and powerful people all the time. He was ruthless in his strategizing and wouldn't give the gods an inch, demanding what was best for Daisy and Tarian and the human world as a whole, and accepting only what he absolutely had to in order to get it done. The whole time, Hades had stood by with a grin, occasionally commenting on the tight nature of Poseidon and all his children.

The result was something they could all live with,

with grievances and wins on both sides. The bottom line was, Tarian would get to live in the human world, but not strictly as a human. He'd have rounded ears to stay under the radar and subtler magic that wouldn't grow roots and go wild, but his blood would be steeped in Faerie. He would keep his princely title, and his family would know he had left so they could live in peace. They could even visit him, and he them, but he would have no shot at the throne. The last was a declaration from the gods, obviously in spite.

"Tell me truly, how do you feel about it all?" Daisy said after they'd all appeared on the grasses somewhat removed from the Obsidian kingdom's castle.

His *Fallen* waited off to the side with grins but sorrow in their eyes. They'd gotten back their wings, something the gods had planned to do anyway. They'd also been given a choice: go with Tarian and get the same treatment to ears and magic...or regain their positions in the court.

Daisy had thought it would be a no-brainer. They could rejoin their kind, use their training, and go back to their lives. Tarian could visit them as often as he liked. And three of them did decide just that. The other seven, though, chose to keep their allegiance and go with Tarian, where Kieran had a new job in store for them. They'd be Guardians...on the human side. They'd monitor the portals and keep unlawful fae from sneaking into the human lands.

Tarian ran his hands up her shoulders and gently cupped her jaw. His eyes were vivid and deep, and the ring of crystal around each pupil was incredibly beautiful, though she planned to tell the humans it was actually diamond. That sounded more posh.

"I think you are an idiot," he said with a grin. "A while ago, before I used you as a chalice, you thought about how far above you I was. My title, my appearance—for thinking any of that, you are an idiot. I wanted to tell you at the time, but I was marching you to your death. I'm glad I can tell you now."

She frowned at him. "Super. Great. Not what I was asking."

He laughed and kissed her. "I'm relieved. I've never wanted the throne. As the last and youngest child, it wasn't something I thought I'd be a contender for anyway. I never wanted to be that locked down or to answer to my kingdom."

"But now you won't even live in Faerie. Tell me truly, how much are you going to resent that, and how much will you resent me for not caring in the least?"

He laughed again. "I love the human world. I've spent a lot of time there over the last few years. I'm excited to learn more about it. To discover all the beautiful places there like I was able to do in Faerie. It's freeing. This way, I can still visit the parts of Faerie I love, and I can take my mate with me..." The "diamond" turned into a river as his gaze roamed her face. "How do you feel knowing your fated mate is a fae?"

"Really depressed, actually," she lied, tilting her smiling face up to him. She put her hand on his chest. Given no one in the human world knew what a mate design was, they'd decided to keep their mutually created design as a symbol of what they were. But the gods had other plans. They'd noticed the Demigod's mark that Lexi and Kieran had applied to each other and decided Faerie should have something like that, too. Their first trial subjects were Daisy and Tarian.

Kieran had shaken his head. Demigods had used that mark as ownership at first, often applied without consent. As a society, they'd had to create strict rules around it enforced by their top tier of government. Without those systems in place, Faerie would likely travel the same path.

Which he'd told the gods.

Which they'd ignored, mostly with smirks. This would be the next bit of entertainment they'd create and watch play out. They really were a bunch of fuckers.

"There is only one fae in all of Faerie with a human fated mate," Tarian said. "And it's me. That is...pretty fucking amazing."

The fated mate of the crystal chalice was always a fae. Given no one was a crystal chalice at birth, that meant she'd essentially been "assigned" her fated mate on the day she'd ascended to the magic. Which meant, whatever fated mate *he'd* had at birth...was no longer. Or maybe he had two. Who knew?

Well, the gods knew, but they weren't bothered about answering. They were too worried about Nvran getting to go to the human underworld with Hades and learn a few tricks. Gods weren't really supposed to cross the borders. Hades had gotten an invite and didn't give a shit

446

about rules, and Nvran didn't either. Kieran had made sure his time in the human world would be short-lived, and no one else was welcome.

"I'm the only human shackled with a fae," Daisy said. "Everyone *will* think I'm an idiot."

"I mean..." Donovan passed by with his hands out and eyebrows raised. "If the shoe fits..."

She narrowed her eyes, and he grinned.

Bria walked over with dark circles under her eyes but a bubbly disposition. Instead of resting as Kieran had worked out the details, like everyone else, catching up on sleep and getting to know each other, Bria had explored the marble city. She'd been admitted everywhere she wanted to go, allowed to look in cupboards and go through closets. She'd come back empty-handed but with stories of servants and mounds of gold and strangely hollow areas that felt like there was no matter to it at all. Like the creators of the universe hadn't gotten there yet.

She had a very odd sense of enjoyment.

"Well." She braced her hands on her hips. "I never thought I'd see the day."

"What day?" Jack asked as he and Dylan wandered closer. Then Jerry and Boman. The others were checking the packs and figuring out travel plans.

"When you gave away your heart," she responded.

"Oh, come *on*." Jack rolled his eyes.

"That was pretty sappy," Jerry said, crossing his arms over his chest.

"It was just an observation, *Jerry*," Bria said. "The

Gremlin usually doesn't like people enough to fall in love. I never thought she would."

"She didn't have a choice." Jerry pointed at Tarian. "Those dickhead gods basically shoved this guy at her."

Bria put her hand out to Tarian. "Can we call you a guy now? Or is that triggering? I mean, let's be real. It won't matter either way, but it'll be nice to know what to pick on until we get to know you better."

Boman huffed out a laugh as Jerry nodded solemnly.

Clouds gathered quickly in the darkening sky to the west. Lightning flared in the gray depths. Dylan turned to look that way, the sudden winds ruffling his hair.

"Dylan won't be the hottest guy around anymore," Boman mused.

"Nah, he will," Bria said.

Jack turned. "When the fuck did you become the pageant director for the guys?"

"What?" Boman looked between Dylan and Tarian. "I know when someone is attractive, and these two are very attractive. I'm just noticing."

"It's not that," Jerry drawled. "Jack is just ugly in comparison."

Jack's jaw dropped, scandalized. "Speak for yourself, *Jerry*."

Bria and Boman laughed delightedly.

"It's not ugliness," someone said from over the way. Niall, standing with the rest of the *Fallen* and listening in. "Daisy calls it having a good personality. I have a *great* one, apparently. Isn't that right, Daisy?"

A smile spread across Bria's face. Her eyes sparkled.

"Oh, I like him. Are they all like that? They've been awfully quiet so far."

"They speak in their minds," Daisy told her. "We're going to get contraptions to help you all learn to shield your thoughts."

"Yes, please," Tarian murmured. "It's disconcerting hearing how viciously everyone wanted to kill me and now how little wiggle room I have. 'One wrong step' seems to be on everyone's mind..."

Bria lifted her hand. "Guilty."

Jack lifted his as well. "Guilty."

Jerry followed.

"Yup." Boman nodded.

"That isn't a natural storm," Dylan said, watching the clouds. He looked over at Kieran, who glanced up.

"Trouble?" Kieran asked with a growl.

"No." Tarian lifted his hand, turning to show he was talking to Kieran. "It's natural for Faerie, which you know isn't saying much. It's not trouble, though. It's a herd of stormbacks. They're our rides."

Lightning forked across the sky and plummeted to the ground as the large herd of creatures circled in their descent. Dylan directed the lightning far away from where they stood, the humans all watching curiously and the fae planning who would ride with whom.

"What's your magic again?" Henry asked Daisy

"I cannot *believe* the Gremlin has magic!" Bria said, shaking her head. "There'll be no stopping her. You guys are fucked, Jack. You'll pick on her and she'll end you."

"She could've always ended us," Jack said. "I sleep much too soundly to keep her from killing me."

"I'll show you when we get home," Daisy said. "It might be better with a demo." Certainly more surprising when she used the magic as she was attacking them.

Tarian smirked, hearing that thought.

Bria pointed at Tarian's face, looking back and forth between him and Daisy. "She just thought something, didn't she? Pay attention, boys. We got some facial expressions that snitch when the Gremlin is getting sneaky."

Tarian's expression almost cleared, but he couldn't wrestle the smile completely away.

They are a treat, he told Daisy privately. *What is a gremlin?*

You'll need to watch the movie for that one to make sense.

Ah. More movie references. I should've guessed.

He really should have.

The stormbacks landed nearby, but only Stratow approached. He looked at Daisy as Tarian explained how riding them would work.

So, little human. You triumphed and lived to tell the tale, he said to her.

I lived, yes, but the gods forbade me to tell large parts of the tale. I can't say why. They didn't want all their trickery to get around. As if people didn't know how horrible they were.

That's for the best, Stratow said. *You would inevitably tell it too many times and annoy your friends.*

There was that, she supposed.

Faerie is as pure as I've ever felt it, he went on. *You have done a great service to this land. You are a friend to us, little human. If you need us, we will come.*

She touched her heart. *That means a lot.* Though she had no idea how she'd ever call in that favor. *How did you know to come?*

Tarianthiel had a need, he replied. *The need flowed on the winds.*

She nodded, making a mental note to ask Tarian about it. *Thank you. My family has had a long journey.*

His focus was stolen by Tarian and Kieran, with Kieran explaining how he could alter the winds to help the creatures take flight. That Demigod was widening a few eyes in this realm, just as Lexi had with her soul grabbing.

While everyone was getting sorted, Mordecai approached her. He'd been quiet the last few days, mulling things over.

Now he stopped in front of her and wrapped her in a tight hug.

"You scared me," he said. "What were you thinking, trying to sacrifice yourself?"

"You would've done the same thing."

"You would've been just as pissed at me for it."

Too true.

"Thank you," she told him, hugging him back. "For coming. You shouldn't have."

"You would've done the same thing."

"You would've been just as pissed at me for it."

He laughed, stepping back. He wiped the corner of his eye where it glistened. "I'm glad you're coming home, but you could've been queen. You could've been the highest queen in the land!"

"Of *this* land, yeah." She made a disgusted face and shook her head. "I'm sure it's really pretty and it has some amazing qualities—or so Tarian says—but the gods are shit and the creatures are way overboard. You should see what the twisted magic does. It's not pretty. Leathery zombies. Seriously. Nah, this is better. Going home—bringing him home—is better."

His gaze was deep. "You really do love him."

"I do, yes. I really do."

"He's it."

"Yes. Fated mate aside, yes, he's it. He and his people will fit in perfectly, you'll see."

He nodded. "How scared am I going to be on those huge, winged creatures?"

She laughed and shoved him. "Hopefully not as scared as I was. I didn't look down."

He blew out a breath and looked that way, spying Tarian coming over and monitoring his progress. Once close, Mordecai stuck out his hand. They'd been introduced in the marble city, but they'd been busy working on the deal and not much had been said.

Tarian took his hand, their grips tight.

"Take care of her," Mordecai said.

"You're not going to give me an *or else?*" Tarian asked.

Mordecai smirked. "I don't need to. She *is* your *or else.*"

He let Lexi drag him to the creature he would be riding.

Tarian turned to her, but stiffened. He glanced to the right, where Zorn was finally approaching. He'd been sitting in on the deal-making, too, hardly sparing her a glance. She hadn't pushed. He'd say what he needed to say when he needed to say it.

Tarian went to step away, but paused. He nodded. Zorn had said something mentally. He knew what Celestials could do.

"Gremlin," he said in his gravelly voice, stopping in front of her. He didn't say anything else for a moment. His eyebrow quirked.

She grinned and rolled her eyes, reading his subtle cues and really having missed him. "He tried to talk me out of it, in the end. He's really not so bad."

"Remains to be seen."

"Sure, sure. How was the trip here? Any close calls?"

He cocked his head. There was certainly a story or two in there, and they didn't have the time.

She nodded. When they got home to safety, they'd have all the time in the world to catch each other and everyone else up. She couldn't wait.

"I'm glad it worked out like this," Zorn said. "Even though..." His eyes flicked Tarian's way.

K.F. Breene

"Yeah, the start wasn't great. But hey, I have magic now, and a *very* cool tattoo. I don't have to walk in the shadows anymore, either, so I can show this baby off at galas and events. Wait until the magazines get a hold of me!"

"I wouldn't reveal that you have magic," he said.

"Why not?"

A ghost of a smile flowed over his lips. "Because then how would you fuck with them?"

She outright laughed this time. "Good point."

Before heading over to crowd around with the others, he turned to Tarian and stuck out his hand. Tarian took it.

"She is my work of art," Zorn told Tarian. "But the student has not outstripped the teacher. Yet. If you hurt her, I will make you feel pain in ways you never thought possible."

Tarian's face was somber, but his eyes belied his mirth. "I don't doubt it, sir. She is, indeed, a work of art. Your efforts made her unstoppable."

Zorn inclined his head. "Be good to her. She deserves better."

"I don't doubt that."

Zorn nodded, didn't bother glancing back at her, and walked away.

"Well," Tarian said softly, draping an arm around her shoulders, "that was fucking terrifying."

"Why?"

"Because he let run through his head all the gruesome things he was thinking about. He definitely has fae in his blood, and it shows."

She laughed, feeling so light. So great. So loved. Given Tarian enjoyed Zorn's ruthlessness, she knew they'd get along. They'd all get along. The fae would have a learning curve in their new homes, but at least they'd be stepping into a larger family that would accept them, unlike how they'd spent the last four years.

"Are you ready?" Tarian asked, taking her hand.

Her happiness died as she looked at Stratow. She let go of a breath. "I guess. Maybe this time I'll look down."

"No, this time you aren't going with him." Tarian's wings flowed down his body, so beautiful. He scooped her into his arms. "This time, you're going with me."

She nestled against his chest as he shot into the sky, so high and fast and powerful. She looped her arms around his neck and felt secure within his hold. She kissed his neck, then his cheek. His lips.

"We're going to fly low," he murmured, holding her tightly. "I want you to see a little bit of Faerie before we go. I want you to want to come back and explore more."

And so they did, soaring over the green vegetation and sparkling creeks. She saw creatures scurry into brush and beautiful meadows filled with iridescent flowers. He was right. The wylds were lovely. The living things were interesting, if deadly, and she wondered how her magic would work on them—if it would at all.

Mostly, though, she relished in the flight. The climbs and dips, the feeling of his strong arms wrapped around her as he reacquainted himself with the sky. She was excited for her return home and to have him in her life.

Epilogue

"I do not smell like a million dollars right now," Jack said, walking into the kitchen where Donovan was unloading groceries.

"Not unless that million dollars was stuffed into a sweaty ass crack, no," Bria replied.

Daisy sat at the island with Bria, both of them with chopping boards in front of them, a knife each, and no desire to help out. The guys did always try, though.

Jack put his hands on his hips, pausing to look at Bria. Mordecai came into the kitchen as he tugged off his wet shirt. Sweat glistened against his dark skin, the workout with Jack having been incredibly taxing.

"I need a shower," Mordecai said, passing behind Daisy and giving her a shove.

"Keep it up," Daisy warned him. "I'll turn off your ability to heal quickly and give you a pounding."

"Promises, promises," Mordecai said, laughing.

She'd given them all a demonstration of her magic

once they'd made it home. It turned out that stealing a human's magic didn't result in the same craziness as stealing a fae's. Taking all of it didn't kill them, either—something she'd tried on a guy sent to assassinate Demigod Kieran. She could deaden the magic just the same, though. And she could boost it.

Kieran and Lexi were keeping that information close to their chests. No one would know that Daisy was anything other than a Chester—something they'd cleared with her first. She had a shining opportunity to fit in, they'd thought, and they didn't want to take that away from her. But they were wrong.

Tarian and the *Fallen* had been living in the human world for six months now, learning the customs and language. Kieran had introduced them as half-fae, with similarities to fae but with magic suitable for the human world. He'd gotten a lot of pushback. Because of that, Daisy knew that if she went public with a rare and unheard-of fae power that could strip magic, she would very likely be viewed with more hostility than a simple Chester.

No, keeping her Chester title and simply fucking with people was so much more palatable.

Jack turned to Donovan. "Where are we?"

"*I* am clean, smell good, and am getting things organized," Donovan said, scooting away from Jack's big frame. "*You* are headed to take a shower before you infect this whole place with your stench."

Bria smirked as cars pulled up in front of the house. Daisy's heart beat faster as she recognized the Aston Martin

Superleggera that Tarian had picked out and insisted on having. He was as much a hound for fashionable things as Daisy, and had impeccable taste. He'd cashed in all the riches he'd acquired and stored in Faerie, plus the treasure troves he'd collected and hidden in the human world, and had been sent the substantial wealth due to him as a prince of the Diamond Throne. The guy was loaded, and he didn't hold back on extravagance when it came to the finer things in life.

People were wary of him, but he'd still hit the magical San Francisco scene by fucking storm. Paparazzi followed him everywhere, publishing write-ups on his various looks, commenting on his handsomeness or evil-fae-ness, and snapping pictures of his flying overhead. He'd taken some heat off Lexi, for which she was grateful, especially because Tarian didn't care in the slightest. He'd endured far worse in the Obsidian Court. This didn't even register.

Kieran was working with Demigods and non-magical territory leaders to set up the guardianship of the portals and borderlands. It was Kieran's goal that Tarian become the director and overseer, Tarian's duty by birth and his desire.

The others thought that gave Kieran too much power. The negotiations raged on. There was a reason Kieran had been so good at making a deal with the gods.

"Where were they?" Bria asked, watching Donovan place a carrot on the chopping board in front of her. She didn't reach for the knife.

"Shopping," Daisy replied. "Tarian wanted to see if

he could outfit Lexi any better than I could. Fat fucking chance."

Bria started to laugh. She knew the trials with Lexi's lack of fashion sense.

Donovan pointed a bundle of celery at Daisy. "Don't fuck up that relationship. He's cool. The Fallen are cool. They're also *damn* good fighters. Gorlan keeps kicking my ass. It's starting to give me a complex."

"I like Kayla," Bria said. "She's—"

"She's what?" Kayla entered the kitchen, wearing jeans and a hoodie and carrying a single department store bag.

Bria pivoted seamlessly. "A real pain in my ass. Hard to tolerate. Terrible jokes."

Kayla spat out a laugh. "Hard to tell a joke that people will laugh at harder than your whole personality." She put her bag down on the counter.

"Burn!" Donovan clapped. "No! Get that thing off there. Put it somewhere else."

Kayla picked it up again and put it out of the way on the ground. She stopped by the island, waiting for a comeback.

Bria narrowed her eyes in thought.

"No?" Kayla asked. "Nothing?"

"It'll come to me..." Bria bit her lip.

Donovan chuckled as Kayla relieved Bria of the cutting board. "I assume this is waiting for a home."

"Yup." Bria inclined her head.

Kayla enjoyed chopping, cutting, slicing—anything

involving a knife. She said it gave her practice. Which...it probably did. Daisy still hated cooking.

Tarian entered the kitchen with a smile, holding a couple bags. As usual, his gaze hit Daisy before anyone else, lingering on her and sending butterflies throughout her middle.

"Hey, *dewdrop*," he said softly, stopping behind her.

She leaned back into his warmth. "Hey. How'd it go?"

He snorted. "I hate it when you're right."

"Told you! Did you get anything for her?"

"We did." The bags crinkled. "I just need...to figure out...what..."

Bria and Daisy both erupted in guffaws.

"She has good height," Daisy said, "a good bust, average hips—clothes off the rack should fit her. Yet...somehow..."

"She always looks like a clown," Bria finished. "It *should* fit her, but stuff always ends up looking like Bobo's painting frock and you have no idea how or why the transformation happened."

"Oh my god, are you serious?" Lexi asked, walking in with a couple bags. "Are you talking about me? Listen, he has good taste, I've said that. We all know that. And yes, the stuff he picked out was nice, but it just... I wasn't..."

"It was Bobo's painting frock," Bria helped. "We get it."

"We'll find more," Tarian said, not leaning away from Daisy. "We'll get it. Some tailors, maybe..."

Bria and Daisy started laughing again.

More of the *Fallen* filed in, Lennox with a very impressive suit, trimmed hair, and still all that shit in his beard.

"I really wish you'd shield more of your thoughts," he groused as he passed through the kitchen. He lifted a bag-laden hand and pointed at Donovan. "I'll be back in a minute to help out. I need to change."

"He's hot," Bria said when he was out of earshot.

"You always say that." Kayla grabbed a peeler. "Why don't you do something about it?"

Bria shrugged, pushing off the stool and going to the fridge. "I'm just noticing, is all. I'm...seeing someone. Kinda."

"Wait, what?" Daisy turned to her. "Who?"

Bria put up her hand, grabbed an invisible chain, and tugged. "Toot, toot."

She'd boarded the train of bad decisions. The person she was seeing was bad news. Obviously, that wasn't stopping her.

Zorn and Boman entered, freshly showered and in casual clothes. They'd all be staying in tonight for a big family dinner. They couldn't all fit at the table anymore, so they did buffet style and roamed around the house, eating and talking and having a good time.

"*He's* the hot one," Kayla murmured, glancing up at Zorn.

Zorn pretended not to notice. His dating life was kept very private, and he didn't seem open for business. He nodded to Tarian and took a seat at the table.

Daisy grabbed the cutting board and knife and got ready to hand it back to Zorn.

"Nope," Zorn said.

Daisy smirked and put it down.

"How'd it go, Lexi?" Boman asked with a cockeyed smile. He had been training instead of shopping, and now he was poking the bear.

"I just do not understand why I can't use a professional." She pushed the hair out of her face, dropped her stuff in the corner with Kayla's, and sat at the table. "No offense, Tarian. I know you are very knowledgeable about human fashion...despite your only living here for six months and hopping in and out before that—"

"She is talking so much shit right now, you don't even know," Donovan murmured gleefully under his breath as Jerry and Dylan came in with Niall and his brother, Darryn. Both of them had gotten stylish haircuts and stylish clothes, and taken on a posh demeanor. Despite their humble appearance, they were a hit with the ladies.

"She's not the only one," Niall said, his brow furrowed as he spied Daisy.

Whoops. She should've thought that one in the darkness.

"No, no, it's fine." Niall flicked a speck off his very cute jacket. "I can take it. Because yes, I am a favorite. Thank you for noticing."

Bria rolled her eyes. They'd all been studiously practicing with the devices to keep their thoughts to themselves, and everyone but Daisy employed the training.

She was just too used to thinking out loud at this point and didn't much care if people "heard" anymore.

"I wish you would," Darryn muttered.

"It's just—" Lexi started.

"Show them what you got," Tarian pushed, putting his bags down. "Just show them and see what they say."

Lexi made a disgruntled sound and went to get her bag. Kieran, Gorlan, and the rest of the crew came in as Lexi was pulling out the first dress. They were also freshly showered and dressed. These houses had turned into community property, always available for showers and food and gatherings, and no longer just a home that Daisy and Mordecai often stayed at. For one, Daisy and Tarian had gotten their own place farther into the city. They could walk downtown hand in hand, freaking people out or disgusting them and laughing about it. Mordecai had gotten a place fairly close to Daisy and spent a lot of time over at Daisy's. So did the *Fallen*, who had also all gotten places close by and came and went as any family might.

If they wanted a bigger space to hang out in, they visited Lexi and Kieran near the water, or they all gathered here. Just as Daisy had thought, they all fit in. They all got along. The integration had been seamless. Her circle of trust had grown, and it was the center of her whole life.

Kieran snaked his arm around Lexi's waist, kissing her temple and then looking over her shoulder at the dress.

"That's really pretty, baby," he said offhandedly.

Lexi huffed at him, making Bria laugh. "I mean, yes, it is. But...it just hangs weird."

"Did you tell her to stop doom-hunching?" Daisy asked Tarian. "You have to tell her to straighten up or else she *makes* the item not fit right."

Lexi glared at her.

Jack returned with a smile. He clapped his hands before rubbing them. "Okay, let's get this show on the road. Who's helping? Just kidding, that was rhetorical. Daisy, the celery won't chop itself."

"Here, I got it." Tarian gently moved her out of the way. He took her seat and pulled her to his side so she leaned against him.

"Good man." Jack handed off the celery. "Who is making the salad? Bria?"

"Make the salad, *Jerry*," she said.

"Yeah, *Jerry*," Niall intoned, quick to pick up all the banter and always giddy when participating. The guys loved him for it. "You can't just sit there and play with your rocks all day."

Several people laughed as Jerry took a seat at the corner of the table and ignored them like usual. Somehow, that always made it funnier.

People roamed, many heading out of the packed kitchen to the living room. Those who stayed helped with the food prep. Kieran opened a bottle of wine and passed around glasses.

Do you still think you made the right decision? Daisy asked Tarian as she drank in his proximity.

Yes, though next time, I'm going to have a better plan

of attack.

She laughed, running her hand along the back of his neck. His hair was still long, though not straightened. He wore it a little wild, and it looked just as handsome as always. *No, not taking Lexi shopping. I mean...the human world. With us. Are the* Fallen *still okay?*

He stopped cutting and reached around, wrapping his arm around her upper legs and pulling her in tighter. *They are absolutely loving it. There is a freedom here that we don't have in Faerie. A looseness to the people. They are still brutal and vicious, but more secretive and refined about it. I like that. I love it here.*

If only for the plumbing, am I right?

He laughed. *If only for the plumbing. And for you.* He pulled her around for a kiss, light at first and then quickly turning passionate.

"Ew," Bria said with a grin.

Someone shouted. Loud thumps echoed into the kitchen. Everyone paused. Kieran's crew all turned and looked at her. Lexi glowered.

"What was that?" Niall asked, half standing.

"Daisy!" Lexi said. "What did you do?"

"Nothing." Daisy waved it away. "I rigged a trap for Mordecai. He really should pay better attention. The stairs are his nemesis. He'll be fine."

"*Daisy!*" Mordecai yelled.

Home sweet home.

The End.

About the Author

K.F. Breene is a *Wall Street Journal, USA Today, Washington Post, Amazon Most Sold,* and #1 Kindle Store bestselling author of paranormal romance, urban fantasy and fantasy novels. With millions of books sold, when she's not penning stories about magic and what goes bump in the night, she's sipping wine and planning shenanigans. She lives in Northern California with her husband, two children, weird dog, and out of work treadmill.

Contact info:
www.kfbreene.com

Made in United States
Cleveland, OH
03 January 2026

30659628R00277